Available in June 2010
from Mills & Boon® Blaze®

BLAZE 2-IN-1

Hot-Wired
by Jennifer LaBrecque

&

Coming on Strong
by Tawny Weber

Letters from Home
by Rhonda Nelson

Every Breath You Take...
by Hope Tarr

HOT-WIRED

"You clean up nice, Ms Bridges."

He leaned down and for one heart-stopping, pulse-pounding moment she was certain he was going to kiss her. There was a lambent sensuality in his eyes, in the way he bent his head. Her whole body tingled in anticipation. The air between them seemed to crackle.

He canted his head to the left, his dark hair teasing against her cheek, and sniffed delicately. She could almost feel the faint scrape of his five-o'clock shadow against her neck. She was on the verge of spontaneous combustion.

COMING ON STRONG

"I wasn't the one who ran out on the wedding," Mitch argued.

Belle frowned. "That's your own damn fault," she declared. "If you hadn't put such an insane price on your body, we'd never have ended up in that mess."

He was speechless. "My body?"

"I wanted sex," Belle stated. "Simple, uncomplicated sex. But no, you had to turn it into something else. You ruined it."

He clenched his jaw, struggling to find a response. In Belle, he thought he'd found the perfect woman. And she'd walked out on him. Well, he'd blown his chance once. He wasn't stupid enough to blow it twice.

"You want sex?" he rasped, anger and lust deepening his voice. "Don't worry, Belle. I'll give you enough sex to last a lifetime..."

First published in Great Britain 2010
Harlequin Mills & Boon Limited,
Eton House, 18-24 Paradise Road, Richmond, Surrey TW9 1SR

Hot-Wired © Jennifer LaBrecque 2009
Coming on Strong © Tawny Weber 2009

ISBN: 978 0 263 88133 2

14-0610

Harlequin Mills & Boon policy is to use papers that are natural, renewable
and recyclable products and made from wood grown in sustainable forests.
The logging and manufacturing processes conform to the legal environmental
regulations of the country of origin.

Printed and bound in Spain
by Litografia Rosés S.A., Barcelona

HOT-WIRED
BY
JENNIFER LaBRECQUE

COMING ON STRONG
BY
TAWNY WEBER

MILLS & BOON

HOT-WIRED

BY
JENNIFER LaBRECQUE

After a varied career path that included barbecue-joint waitress, corporate numbers cruncher and bug-business maven, **Jennifer LaBrecque** has found her true calling writing contemporary romance. Named 2001 Notable New Author of the Year and 2002 winner of the prestigious Maggie Award for Excellence, she is also a two-time RITA® Award finalist. Jennifer lives in suburban Atlanta with one husband, one active daughter, one really bad cat, two precocious greyhounds and a chihuahua who runs the whole show.

Thanks to Brenda Chin and Margaret Learn
for helping me make this a better book.

And to Alison Kent, Julie Miller and Lori Borrill,
all top-notch writers. It was great fun creating
the world of Dahlia, Tennessee. Wish we
could go for a visit.

And last but not least, to all the drag racers and
their crews who devote endless hours to putting
on a great show, especially the ORSCA folks.

1

BEAU STILLWELL could kiss her ass. If she could ever find him, that was.

Her temper beginning to fray at the edges, Natalie Bridges silently huffed and carefully picked her way through yet another row of big pickup trucks, trailers, motor homes and some of the loudest, gaudiest souped-up cars she'd ever had the misfortune to see. Welcome to Dahlia Speedway, where big boys and their toys hurtled down a quarter-mile track to see who could go the fastest. Quite frankly, she didn't get it.

What, or rather who, she needed to get, however, was Beauregard Stillwell. She'd called and left messages every day for two weeks with the secretary of Stillwell Construction. He'd summarily ignored them. She'd doggedly left messages on his cell and home phone. No call back.

She jumped as a car cranked next to her with a near deafening roar. Was there another wedding planner in Nashville, Tennessee, who'd go to these lengths to get the job done? Maybe, maybe not, but she was bound and determined that Caitlyn Stillwell and Cash Vickers would have the wedding of their dreams—if she could ever get Caitlyn's brother, Beau, to cooperate.

Caitlyn and Cash had the *most* romantic story. Call it fate or destiny or karma, but fresh out of college with a degree in film and video, Caitlyn had lucked into shooting a music video for rising country music star Cash Vickers at an antebellum plantation outside Nashville. In a nutshell, they'd fallen in love with each other and the place during the filming. In a wildly romantic gesture, Cash had bought the plantation, Belle Terre, for him and Caitlyn. They both had their hearts set on getting married there. However, while a faintly neglected air worked for a video for "Homesick," a song about finding where you belong and who you belonged there with, it didn't work for a wedding. Caitlyn didn't trust anyone with the renovations except her big brother, Beau.

Which was all good and fine, if Natalie could just get him to talk to her about the renovation schedule. In the two-week span of being ignored, Natalie could've lined up another builder to handle the remodel, except this was a sticking point with Caitlyn. No Beau Stillwell, no remodel. No remodel, no wedding.

And come hell or high water, in which hell might very well take the form of Beau Stillwell, Natalie was planning and executing this wedding. Cash was being touted as country music's next big thing, and being in charge of his and Caitlyn's wedding would set Natalie apart as Nashville's premier wedding planner…but only if everything went off without a hitch. She'd either be ruined or all the rage. Ruined wasn't a viable option.

Hence, she'd finished up the rehearsal dinner for tomorrow's wedding between Gina Morris and Tommy Pitchford, settled them and their families at the private banquet room at the upscale Giancarlo's Ristorante, and left her assistant, Cynthia, to deal with any residual problems. Natalie had driven the thirty miles out of Nashville and parted with twenty dollars at the gate to gain entry to the one place she knew for sure she could find Mr. Stillwell on a Friday evening—the Dahlia drag strip.

Dodging a low-slung orange car with skulls air-brushed on the front and side as it pulled down the "street" in the congested pit area, she thought better a drag strip than a strip joint. Although she had thought it was pretty interesting the one time she'd tracked down a recalcitrant groom and dragged him out of a strip club. Her seldom-seen, inner wild girl had thought she wouldn't mind doing a pole dance for someone special in a private setting.

Even though she was about five unreturned phone calls beyond annoyed, she had to admit the drag strip was an interesting place. Apparently drag racing pit areas were wherever the car's trailer was parked. She tried to ignore the stares and titters that followed her. Maybe three-inch heels and a suit weren't the dress code at the drag strip, but changing would have meant driving all the way back across Nashville when she'd had the girl genius idea of coming here to track down Beau the Bastard, as she and Cynthia had dubbed him earlier today when he'd blown off her call yet again.

She clutched her purse tighter against her side. There was almost a carnival atmosphere. An announcer "called" the race, giving statistics and tidbits about each driver over a loudspeaker. The cars themselves were beyond loud, spectators whooped and hollered, people zoomed around on four-wheelers and golf carts, and there was plenty of tailgating going on at the race trailers. It sort of reminded her of holidays at her parents' house—chaos. Although, unlike at her folks', there was at least some structure and method behind the madness here.

She passed a concession stand located behind the packed spectator bleachers and the smell of hamburgers and French fries wafting out set her mouth watering and her stomach growling, reminding her she hadn't eaten since breakfast. God, she'd kill for a greasy fry dredged in catsup right now—the ultimate comfort food. However, she was probably packing on another five pounds just from smelling them.

She walked away from the people lined up at the burger window. Directly across from the food concession, she noticed a T-shirt vendor displayed his, or her, wares. Natalie nearly laughed aloud at the one that proclaimed "Real Men Do It With 10.5 Inches."

She didn't get the inside joke and it was rude and crude, but still kind of funny. And she had to smile at the "Damn Right It's Fast, Stupid Ass" next to it.

She was so busy laughing at the T-shirts that catching her heel in a crack caught her totally unawares. Arms flailing, she pitched into a guy…carrying a hot dog and a plastic cup of beer.

"Damn, lady," he yelled, "watch where you're going." He shot her a nasty look. "And that cost me my last eight bucks."

Natalie righted herself, dug into her purse, pulled out a ten and shoved it in the man's hand. "Sorry."

Mollified by his two-dollar gain, he changed his tune. "No problem." He looked down her chest and grimaced. "Napkins are over there." He turned on his heel and returned to the concession counter.

She glanced down. Her favorite cream silk blouse with the lovely ruffle down the center clung to her in a beer bath. Bright yellow mustard and red catsup obscured the flowers on the left breast of her jacket. She wasn't sure that blouse and jacket weren't both ruined. She quelled the urge to laugh hysterically. Napkins. She needed napkins.

She started toward the round, bar-height table that held the napkins, along with the hamburger and hot dog fixings, and realized she'd wrenched the heel off her right pump when she'd stepped in the asphalt crack. She limped over to the table and grabbed a napkin.

A blonde with dark roots in jeans and a halter top

gave her a sympathetic look. "The bathroom's right around the corner."

"Thanks."

Five minutes later, she'd managed to work some of the mustard and catsup stain out of her jacket and she'd blotted at her beer-soaked blouse. She'd toyed with, and promptly dismissed, the notion that she'd be better off trading them for one of the graphic tees. No, that would make her look even more bedraggled than her stained clothing.

For the thousandth time, she silently cursed Beau Stillwell. This was all his fault. Maybe he wasn't personally responsible for the asphalt crack she'd caught her heel in, but if he'd had the common courtesy to return just one of her phone calls or, at the very least, left a message for her with his secretary, Natalie wouldn't have been reduced to chasing him all over Dahlia, Tennessee, and her heel wouldn't have gotten stuck in the damn crack in the damn first place because she wouldn't have been here.

She smiled grimly at herself in the chipped mirror and tucked her hair back into what was left of her chignon as best she could. She reapplied a coat of pale pink lipstick and rubbed her lips together. She didn't care what they said on the Style Network— doing that funky top-lip-against-the-bottom-one smear smoothed out the color. Dropping the lipstick tube back in her purse, she stood up straight, squared her shoulders, and gave herself a pep talk.

Granted she fell a little short of the mark—she always aimed to project an elegant professionalism—but she didn't *really* resemble the walking wounded, she reassured herself. And killing Beau Stillwell when she found him, or at least braining him with what was left of her right pump, was not in her best interest. Dead, or even slightly brained, would preclude her nailing him down as to the remodel schedule on Belle Terre, which was why she was standing in the shabby, smelly bathroom of the Dahlia drag strip reeking of beer, mustard and catsup rather than attending Nashville's latest art gallery opening, where she was sure Shadwell Jackson III, the guy who had Prince Charming written all over him, was supposed to be.

Heck yeah, she believed in Prince Charmings and wanted one for herself. How could she be a wedding planner and not believe in happy-ever-after? She was detail-oriented and a devotee of true love—it was a career tailor-made for her.

She came from a long line of happy-ever-afters. She figured it was a genetic thing. No one in either her mother's or her father's families had ever gotten a divorce. And none of them were living in misery. Sure they had problems to work through, but all of them had sound marriages. Her parents were still absolutely in love after thirty-two years, raising Natalie and taking in foster kids on a regular basis.

She'd known for years what her Prince Charming

would be like when he swept her off her feet. She'd always envisioned her Mr. Right as an urbane professional who donned a suit and tie every morning, refined, gallant. And instead of meeting Shad, an imminent candidate for that position, she was here, tracking down pain-in-her-ass Beau Stillwell.

She sucked in a deep, calming breath, which proved a mistake in a public toilet. Blech. She limped back outside where the scent of fast food underpinned the acrid smell of burning rubber. Beau Stillwell, did not know the measure of the woman he was dealing with. She could handle this. She *would* handle this.

Smoothing her hand over her skirt and tweaking her stained jacket into place over her stained blouse, she fixed her best smile on her face rather than a scowl and gimped forward on her broken heel toward the pit area for Stillwell Motors Racing.

She'd employ charm and tact and whip the elusive brother of the bride right into shape.

THE FOUR-WHEELER towed Beau and his '69 Camaro into their pit area beneath the two green pop-up tents next to the trailer. Before he'd even climbed out of the car, his motor guy Darnell and general crew member Tim were pulling the hood pins, eager to read the spark plugs and tweak the setup.

Beau tugged off his helmet and stripped off his neck brace and fireproof gloves. A grin split Scooter Lewis's face as he walked over, waving Beau's run results in his hand. "That was a helluva run. Even with your tires spinning a little off the line, you beat him off the tree and at the sixty-foot. He didn't have a prayer of catching you."

"It was sweet, wasn't it?" Beau said, the adrenalin rush that came with rocketing down a quarter-mile track in less than four and a half seconds was beginning to subside. It was like a five-second orgasm with an unpredictable woman. From the instant the light went green, signaling him to go, he was never sure what would happen on the run, but it was guaranteed to be a rush. "If we run that again tomorrow, we should qualify first."

"I'll ramp it down some and that'll take care of the spin," Darnell said, glancing up and handing off the socket wrench to Tim.

Beau nodded. As crew chief, Scooter oversaw all the adjustments based on track and weather conditions, but Darnell was damn near a genius when it came to motor setups. "Who've we got to beat tomorrow? Mitchell or Taylor?"

"Mitchell. They dropped in a new motor but you're still the better driver."

And without arrogance, Beau knew it was true. Driving a race car was in his blood. He'd been born with a need for speed. It's what the Stillwell men did. His father had raced, his grandfather had raced, and stories of his great-grandfather Theodore Stillwell outrunning prohibitionists in a Model T in his day was local legend around Dahlia, Tennessee. Before that, the Stillwell men were hell at the helm of a buggy. In fact, family rumor had it that Stillwells drove a mean chariot in the day. That, however, was totally unsubstantiated Stillwell family lore.

A couple of fans stopped by to check out the car. Beau recognized the guys as motorheads who showed up at every race. They were still looking over the engine and bending Darnell's ear when a blonde and a brunette in matching jeans and what he'd guess to be double D's in tube tops strolled into the pit area.

"Hi, I'm Sherree," the blonde said, "and this is Tara. Would you take a picture with us?"

"Certainly, ladies." He offered them his most charming smile.

Sherree shoved a camera at Scooter, and within seconds Beau was sandwiched between heavily perfumed feminine flesh, those matching double D's pressing against his arms on each side of him.

"Say nitrous oxide," Scooter instructed.

"I thought it was cheese—isn't it cheese?" Tara asked.

On the other side of the camera, Scooter, ever the prankster, grinned.

"Cheese is fine," Beau assured her. He wasn't particularly surprised when one of them grabbed his ass a second later.

Scooter snapped the photo and returned the camera. Sherree murmured a thank-you and turned her attention back to Beau. "Want to party with us later?" she asked.

The invitation didn't surprise him any more than her copping a feel. Women liked him. They always had. And he liked them, too. And no doubt Tara and Sherree had a good time in mind and it was sort of crazy because it'd been a while since he'd *partied* and they were hot, but he just wasn't feeling it.

He shook his head. "Unfortunately, I've got a busy evening, ladies. No partying for me."

Sherree offered a moue of disappointment and another rub of her bodacious silicone tatas against his bicep. "Then you'll just have to call us for your celebration party when you win." She tucked a piece of paper into his jeans pocket, sliding her fingers suggestively along the edge of his pants.

"I'll keep that in mind."

They left, mouthing in unison "Call me" over their shoulders.

"Lucky bastard," Scooter muttered. They both knew he was just talking. Scooter had lost his wife, Emma Jean, two years ago and had never mentioned another woman. Scooter didn't say much, but Beau knew he missed her. Hell, they'd been married longer than the thirty-two years Beau had been alive.

A father and his young son, both wearing Stillwell Motors Racing T-shirts, came by for an autograph. They left and Beau and the crew spent a few minutes discussing setup adjustments for 10.5 qualifying the following day.

"You staying here tonight?" Scooter asked.

"Might as well." His major sponsor had shelled out the money for a sweet setup at the end of last year's winning season. They'd outfitted Stillwell Motors Racing with a toter home and race trailer that were both nicer than what he was living in now. But soon…

If he walked away with the 10.5 championship again this year, he'd have his money in place to build his house. Just as he'd promised his father before he died sixteen years ago, Beau had taken care of his mother and his sister. But it had been more than a deathbed promise.

Before he drank himself to death, Monroe Stillwell had bankrupted them and they'd lost everything— their home, cars, even their furniture. They'd been left with the clothes on their back, tattered pride and precious little else. As a teenager, Beau had vowed he'd never owe a red penny to anyone again. If he didn't owe, no one could come in and take what he considered his.

Between racing and his construction business, he'd made enough money to build his mother a house and set her up with a dress shop in downtown Dahlia. He was damn proud that his mother had turned Beverly's Closet into a thriving enterprise. He'd put Caitlyn through college and helped her find a job. Now it was his turn.

His cell phone buzzed at his side and he glanced at the caller ID—speaking of the devil. He let it go to voice mail. Scooter raised an eyebrow in inquiry.

"Caitlyn," Beau said. "Between her and that wedding planner, they're driving me bat-shit crazy."

"Why don't you just talk to the woman and get it over with?"

"She wants to know when I can start the remodel on Belle Terre. I haven't had time to get out there." Which suited him just fine. Everyone looked at Caitlyn's fiancé, Cash Vickers, and saw Nashville's newest rising star. Beau looked at Vickers and saw heartbreak for his sister.

He didn't like Vickers. He didn't think for a second the guy was good enough for his baby sister. To begin with, women were all over the guy, and he seemed to like them in return. Second, Beau had been most unimpressed when Cash had bought Belle Terre. It seemed like a extravagant, fiscally irresponsible move to him. Caitlyn had already been the victim of one financially irresponsible man— their father. She sure as hell didn't need a husband who spent money like water. And forbidding Caitlyn to marry Vickers would simply push her in his direction all the harder. Not to mention that his sister was old enough to do whatever she wanted to do. But Beau figured if he dragged his feet long enough, time would prove his rope and Vickers would hang himself.

"And that wedding planner needs to get a life. She's called me twice a day every day for two weeks."

He'd been legitimately busy the first week, but her nagging calls had irritated him to the point that this past week it had become a game to try and drive her as bat-shit crazy by avoiding her calls as she was driving him.

Scooter shook his head. "You might as well surrender now. Women and weddings. You ain't gonna know a minute's peace until they trade I-do's." He should know. His daughter, Carlotta, had gotten married the year before Emma Jean died.

"You never surrender until you've put up the good fight."

"I'm telling you, Beau, you might win a skirmish or two, but they'll win the war."

Beau grinned when he remembered the voice mail Ms. Natalie Bridges had left him earlier today. She'd been polite but he didn't miss the terse impatience underlying her message. She was frustrated. That was good. Maybe she'd quit and Caitlyn would have to start all over with another wedding planner. All of which meant more time for Vickers to screw up and show Caitlyn his true colors.

"I've got a couple of good battles left in me. Let Nightmare Natalie bring it on."

THERE IT WAS. Black toter home and trailer with Stillwell Motors Racing emblazoned on the side in purple and silver. Finally. Now that she'd rubbed a blister on her heel from hobbling along in a broken shoe.

Three men in uniforms that matched the black, silver and purple color scheme were under what should've been the hood of the car. Except the hood was sitting on a rack to the side. Whatever. She cleared her throat, interrupting.

"Excuse me. I'm looking for Beau Stillwell." She glanced expectantly from one man to the other. A short guy with thinning red hair had the name Scooter embroidered on his shirt. Next to him stood a lanky fellow with a crew cut, whose shirt designated him as Tim. On the left side of the car was an African-American named Darnell.

The short man exchanged a quick, almost imperceptible glance with the other two and stepped forward. "Scooter Lewis," he introduced himself. He grimaced and shook his head with a grin. "You'd probably rather not shake my hand right now."

"No problem. I'm Natalie Bridges and I'm—"

Scooter—she was so sure his mother hadn't given him that name at birth—interrupted with a nod and a quick grin. "You're that wedding planner out of Nashville."

Lanky Tim couldn't contain a snicker, which earned him an elbow in the side from Darnell. "Hey, man, watch it." Tim groused.

"Yes. I'm the wedding planner. It's so nice to meet you, Mr. Lewis." She tilted her chin up a notch while keeping her smile firmly in place. She didn't have to be the sharpest tool in the shed to figure out that if these three had heard of her it wasn't because their boss had been singing her praises.

"Just call me Scooter. Everybody does. And this here's Tim and Darnell."

"Gentlemen." She nodded and smiled a greeting while Tim shuffled his feet and blushed and Darnell bobbed his head in a quick acknowledgment. "I can see you're busy and I apologize for interrupting. If someone could just tell me where I might find Mr. Stillwell…" If they told her he'd just left the track, she wasn't so sure she wouldn't just pitch a hissy fit right here, right now.

Scooter jerked his thumb over his shoulder. "Beau's in the toter. I'd go get him for you, but…" He held up greasy hands. "Just let yourself in." Melt-down averted.

She skirted the car and gave a wide berth to a jack. She didn't know squat about cars, but even she recognized that was one big motor, which probably accounted for why Beau was the points leader. The overloud announcer had mentioned it exhaustively during her trek.

She stood on the lower step of the door Scooter had indicated and raised her hand to knock. "Just go on in," Scooter yelled, waving her on. "Don't worry about knocking. Folks come and go at the track all the time."

Okay. Far be it for her to screw up the way things

were done at the track. She grabbed the silver latch on the door that reminded her of her grandparents' camper and stepped into the motor home, clicking the door in place behind her. The similarities ended there. This certainly wasn't her grandparents' camper.

Instead of orange shag carpeting and yellowed Formica countertops, she was standing on hardwood flooring, looking at granite counter tops and a tiled backsplash. A baseball game, the sound muted, flickered on a flat-screen TV mounted over the opening to the cab's cockpit to her right. Dark, blackout curtains were drawn over the windows in the front, affording privacy inside.

And still no Beau Stillwell. "Hello?" she called out.

The panel door to her left slid open. Oh. My. All the spit in her mouth evaporated. A whoosh of heat roared through her as she stood rooted to the spot.

Tall. Big. Heavily muscled arms, chest, and legs. Dark hair on his head…and his chest…and his legs. Wet and naked, save for the white towel held precariously low on his hips. But it was the mocking blue eyes fringed with sooty lashes in a rugged, square-jawed face that did her in.

"Can I help you?"

"Are you Beau Stillwell?"

He bowed at the waist, overwhelmingly masculine, overwhelmingly arrogant, overwhelmingly almost naked. "At your service."

What she meant to say, what she fully planned to

say fell in the category of offering her name by way of introduction. But, honest to Bob, she couldn't even remember her name because just breathing the same air seemed to have annihilated all of her brain cells. Obviously. Because what came out of her mouth instead of a calm professional introduction was, "You can kiss my ass."

2

"THAT'S THE MOST interesting proposition I've heard all night," Beau said in a deliberate drawl despite the adrenaline rush that slammed him. He felt as if he'd been turned upside down just looking into her light brown eyes, which had widened with surprise and then narrowed with temper. He hung on to his cool…by a thread…because this woman shook him up…and he was never shaken up. "But maybe you could hop in the shower first to lose the beer smell." He moved the hand holding his towel in place, as if he were about to pass it to her. "You can borrow my towel."

She whipped around, presenting him with her back, before he got the last word out of his mouth. "Keep the towel," she snapped, staring straight ahead. Her rear view did nothing to settle him down. Beau liked his track straight and his women curvy, and she had nice curves from head to toe.

She drew a deep breath. "Look, I'm sorry. We got off on the wrong foot and I apologize for barging in. Mr. Lewis told me to just come on in without knocking."

"His idea of funny."

And she was his idea of hot.

Was that a snort?

"I'll step back out until you're decent," she said.

He itched to reach out and pull the pins from her hair and watch it tumble down around her shoulders. "No need to step outside. It'll take me no time to dress, but there's no guarantee I'll be decent. Clothes don't make the man."

She wanted to tell him to kiss her ass again. It was there in the rigid set of her shoulders. Instead she said, "Fine. I'll wait."

"I'll just be a minute," he paused for effect, "sweet thing." Beau slid the bathroom door closed and took two steps into the bedroom to "get decent." He was pretty sure the *sweet thing* business had been over the top. He'd sounded like a bona fide asshole. But that was the point—to goad her into quitting to delay the whole wedding thing. He'd told her to wait in the toter home because she was obviously uncomfortable with him being undressed, and the more uncomfortable she was the better. It didn't have a thing to do with some crazy-ass notion that now that he'd seen her he didn't want her to leave.

He pulled on fresh underwear and a pair of worn jeans. Natalie Bridges, he recognized her voice, was a wreck. He'd seen guys barrel-roll cars and climb out afterwards in better shape. But insanely he found her hot and sexy in a way he hadn't found the tube-top twins earlier.

Maybe it was the flash of anger in her brown eyes or the lush fullness of her pink lips or the semitumble of her hair. It was her mouth. There was something so damn sexy about the fact that with the rest of her obviously a mess—he was almost certain that was mustard on her left breast—her lipstick had been perfect. In fact, he was pretty damn sure she had the most perfect mouth he'd ever seen.

He tugged a black T-shirt over his head and tucked it into his jeans. She wasn't at all what he'd expected. He realized he'd sketched her in his head as thin, angular, rigid—a paragon of cool efficiency. But this woman was all curves, and she'd just blown a gasket with him.

If he pushed just a little harder, he'd have her right where he wanted her, so frustrated she'd toss in the towel and Caitlyn would be forced to start all over.

He hung his own wet towel on the hook outside the shower and slid open the door. She was still standing with her back to the bathroom.

"I'm as decent as I'm going to get. Now, what can I do for you, sweet thing?" Damn, he sounded obnoxious.

She pivoted to face him. Even with her mouth tightened like that, her lips were lush and full. "I'm Natalie Bridges," she said, extending her hand.

"Ah, Nightmare Natalie." He'd never been rude to a woman before, but he was doing a damn good job now. He took her hand to shake it, and it was as if a sparkplug had fired inside him. Her brown eyes widened but he wasn't sure whether it was because she felt the same surge or a reaction to the name he'd hung on her, or perhaps both.

She reclaimed her hand and totally threw him off track when she laughed, a husky, rich sound. "That's flattering...coming from Beau the Bastard."

He chuckled, thoroughly enjoying himself. "I've been called worse."

"No doubt." She smiled sweetly, and it had the same effect as when he hit the nitrous switch on his car and three G's slammed him back against the seat.

A brief knock sounded and then the door opened. Scooter, wearing an unrepentant grin, stuck his head in. "We're outta here." He nodded toward Nightmare Natalie. "Nice to meet you, Ms. Bridges."

"It was a pleasure, Mr. Lewis."

Ha. All three knew Scooter had set her up to walk in on him in the shower.

Scooter laughed. "Yes, ma'am. See ya in the morning, boss."

Scooter closed the door, once again shutting out the track noise and leaving them alone. She shifted awkwardly from one foot to the other, and he realized it was all the more awkward because she was missing the heel on one shoe.

"Have a seat, Miss Bridges. Or is it Mrs. Bridges?"

"Thank you," she said, perching primly on the edge of the couch. "And it's Miss. I'm not married."

"Here, let me help you out." He squatted in front of her and grasped the back of her left calf in his hand. She gasped and her muscle flexed against his palm. Her skin was warm and soft and he quelled the urge to stroke his hand along that tantalizing expanse from knee to ankle. Instead, lifting her leg in one hand, he plucked her shoe, the one with the heel still attached, off her foot. Her toenails were painted a similar shade of pink as her lips. Sexy.

"What are you doing?"

He stood. He placed the long, narrow heel on the counter with the rest of the shoe facing down. Beau slammed his hand down on the back, rendering her former stiletto a ballet slipper. He handed it back to her. "Now they match."

She quickly leaned forward and slipped the shoe back on, as if to preclude him from doing it. "Thank you…I think."

"You're welcome…I'm sure." He dropped to the sofa, more the size of a love seat, beside her, angling toward her and stretching out his legs. Deliberately invading her space and crowding her should definitely up his asshole quota.

"So, you're a wedding planner who's never been married? It seems it might limit your qualifications." He stretched his arm out along the back of the love seat. He was invading her space and conversely she was invading his. He was intensely aware those luscious lips of hers were ever so close, and all he had to do to release those hair pins was lean a bit to the right, raise his hand and pluck them out.

"Some professions don't require firsthand experience, Mr. Stillwell." He gave her points for standing her ground and not squirming closer to the kitchen counter. "Morticians. Brain surgeons. You know, that kind of thing. They manage just fine and so do I." She pulled a day planner out of her purse and opened it. It was a schedule and a neat script had pretty much every space filled in. She was a busy woman. "Now if we can just nail down some dates, I'll be more than happy to get out of your hair, Mr. Stillwell."

She obviously wanted to be anywhere other than in his company. That she wanted to leave, in and of itself, was something of a novel experience, except he had gone out of his way to be a jerk. Most of the time women were eager for his company. And while he'd been looking forward to watching some test and tune runs of the other drivers, he was actually having a damn good time needling the unorthodox and intriguingly unpredictable Ms. Bridges.

"Why don't we discuss it over dinner?"

"As appealing as that may be—" yet another kiss my ass "—I'm not particularly dressed for the occasion and as you so gallantly pointed out, I need a shower."

"The offer still stands to use my towel."

"Ever the gentleman, but I'll wait until I get home."

He'd been turned down. By Nightmare Natalie, no less.

"I JUST NEED a date when you'll have the remodel complete."

For God's sake, just give me a date so I can get the hell out of here. She was desperate, or maybe all the stress was getting to her and Beau Stillwell had just pushed her over the edge because he was arrogant and infuriating and the reason that a several-hundred-dollar outfit, shoes included, was now ruined, but some crazy, totally irrational part of her had wanted to accept his dinner invitation.

She had the oddest sense he was deliberately goading her. It was possible he was just an obnoxious jerk who went around calling women "sweet thing" and then insulting them in the next breath. There were plenty of sexist men who operated that way, but there'd been a flash of something in his blue eyes… And Natalie's foster-sister Shelby and Caitlyn Stillwell had roomed together in college. In all the time Natalie had known Caitlyn, which had been casually for almost five years, the younger woman might've been occasionally exasperated with her big brother, but there'd never been any doubt she respected him. It was difficult to imagine strong-minded Caitlyn respecting a jerk.

"How about a guesstimate," she prompted.

He shrugged those impossibly broad shoulders. "I can't give you a finish date until I get out to Belle Terre and see what has to be done."

"That makes sense." She nodded in agreement, trying to get along. "When are you available to do that?"

His eyes captured hers. Natalie found herself drowning in those blue depths. "When do *you* want to *do it?*"

A lazy, sensual spark in his eyes issued an invitation to wicked pleasure. A single, singeing look that tightened her nipples and dampened her panties.

She wet her lips with the tip of her tongue. Every thump of her heart seemed to echo *do it, do it, do it.* "Do it?"

"Yeah. When are you available?" His dark lashes formed a spiky frame for his eyes. She couldn't look away, couldn't think, could barely breathe.

"Available for what?"

Mocking amusement replaced sensual promise. "Try to keep up here, honey. When do you want to go out to Belle Terre with me to go over the remodel?"

Embarrassment flooded her. She'd prefer a hot poker in her eye. Actually, she'd prefer a hot poker up his ass. "I don't want to go out to Belle Terre with you. I don't need to be there. I just need to know a date you'll have it done."

"It'll go much faster if I have you there to explain exactly what Caitlyn wants done. And you can take notes for me."

"I know you have a secretary, Mr. Stillwell. I've spoken to her so often she's now on my Christmas-card list."

"Ah, but I need her in the office…to answer the phone."

Did he have any idea how busy she was? It was spring—high wedding season. Actually, the real question was did he care? And that answer was obviously *no*. "Fine. I'll make myself available to accommodate your busy schedule." Hopefully he wasn't impervious to sarcasm.

"How about Sunday, after the race?"

"No problem. As it happens, I don't have a wedding on schedule for Sunday. What time?"

"Probably around four. Just show up here and we'll go when I get through."

She managed not to gape at his total arrogance and disregard for her schedule. As if she had time to stand around cooling her heels at a racetrack while he indulged his testosterone-laden hobby. "I'll give you my cell number and you can just call me and I'll meet you out there."

"I'll try not to forget."

"I'll phone you to remind you."

"Sure. You've got my number." He all but smirked. They both knew how successful she'd been with him and the phone.

She gritted her teeth and mustered up a smile. If he was on some power trip and she had to kowtow to his schedule, then so be it. "I'll just come here. That way you won't forget."

"It's a date, then."

She tried to steadfastly ignore the way his voice seemed to caress the word *date,* but she couldn't stop her heart from beating faster.

"Yes. Four o'clock here on Sunday." Good. She had what she'd come for. An image of him still shower-damp and clad only in a towel flashed through her mind. Okay, she'd gotten more than she came for.

She jotted the time and notation in her day planner and stood. She hated to admit it, but it was much more comfortable with both the heels ripped off her poor shoes. "I'll see you then."

He stood, as well, dwarfing her in the close confines of the motor home. "Where'd you park?"

"The lot on the other side of the three-story building."

"Spectator parking. I'm heading up to the tower—" she assumed that was the three-story building "—to check on tomorrow's ladder. You can ride with me. It's a hike from here to spectator parking."

She wanted to turn him down but she was well aware of just how damn far it was. "Thank you. That'd be nice."

They both moved toward the door. "I'm a nice guy."

And she was Mary Poppins. "I'll take your word for it."

He reached past her to open the door, his shoulder brushing hers, his clean scent enveloping her. Her legs weren't quite steady as she walked down the two steps. Night had descended, but the racing continued. Cars were still being towed behind four-wheelers and golf carts. Across the pit "street," a crew was frantically working on a car under the glare of big floodlights mounted on stands.

He cupped his hand beneath her elbow and his touch sizzled right through her. "Okay, on you go. You might want to ride sidesaddle."

She looked from him to the four-wheeler he'd stopped beside and back to him. "You're going to take me on this?"

"Yeah. It's the best way to get around the track. Do you have an issue with four-wheelers?"

"No issue, I've just never been on one before." There'd never been money in her family for anything like a four-wheeler. And she'd never dated a guy with a four-wheeler—they weren't her type.

She caught a flash of his teeth. No doubt a mocking smile. "Ah. Your first time. I'll make sure you like it."

Did he have to make it sound like a seductive promise? Did her body, even knowing he was arrogant and manipulative and toying with her, have to respond with instant heat?

Make that a *yes* on both counts.

She stepped onto an open-grid platform and slid her butt to the back of the seat, keeping both her legs on one side and her knees pressed together. It wasn't so bad.

He climbed on in front of her, straddling the seat, presenting her with a solid wall of masculinity. He spoke over his shoulder, "You comfortable?"

Comfortable? With his absolute maleness crowding

her space? With his hip and leg pressed against hers? With her entire body humming at the proximity?

"Absolutely. Never more comfortable."

He cranked it. Not only was the engine loud, but she felt its vibration through her seat, which was strange, inappropriately erotic under the circumstances.

"You'll want to hold on," he said as he rolled to the edge of the pit road and looked both ways to see if the coast was clear. She lightly put one hand at his waist. The less body contact, the better.

One minute they were sitting there idling, the next they were off like a bat out of hell. She instantly, automatically wrapped both arms around him, hanging on for dear life.

"Woo!"

She heard his yell above the din and the rush of blood in her ears. Once she realized they weren't going to die, she had to admit she rather liked it—the rush of wind past them, the thrill of going fast. And, heaven help her, the feel of *him*.

Her right cheek and breast pressed against his back. She felt the play of muscles beneath the cotton T-shirt as he drove. Likewise, there was no mistaking the six-pack ripple of his belly beneath her clasped hands. He felt even better than he'd looked wearing that towel—and that was saying something.

She had the craziest, hormone-fueled desire to nuzzle the muscled expanse of his back, to slide her hands beneath the edge of his T-shirt and explore the hard ridges of his belly…and lower. Natalie's bad-girl side had the urge to experience skin on skin with Beau the Bastard.

He made a quick left, ground to a stop and killed the engine. He climbed off. He'd parked in the area chock-full of other four-wheelers and golf carts between the bleacher entrance and the tower. The starting line was right ahead of them, on the other side of the fence.

He reached for her and his hand engulfed hers as he helped her off. Much as she'd have liked to shrug off his assistance, her legs felt like rubber.

"Do you always drive like a maniac?" She tugged her hand free of his, determined to regain her equilibrium, which had seemed to fly out the window during the ride. It had to be his driving and not the fact that she'd been reduced to jelly legs from being wrapped around him. From wanting to stay wrapped around him. Dangerous ground, that.

He laughed. "A maniac?" He shook his head in pretend consternation, his blue eyes glittering. "Now that's disappointing. Since it was your first time, I gave you the slow ride. I'll try harder next time to make it better for you. By the way…" He reached out and casually brushed a hank of hair out of her eyes— her chignon was seriously destroyed at this point— as if he were a lover with every right to do so. His fingers barely grazed her skin but his touch echoed through her. "Two suggestions for Sunday. You might want to dress down a bit and you might want to lay off the beer."

He pivoted on his heel and strolled away, leaving her standing there.

She hated Beau Stillwell.

3

On Sunday afternoon, once she left Nashville behind on her way out to Dahlia, Natalie powered down her windows and let the wind blow through the van as she drove the twisting, turning back roads through the Tennessee hills. She could've taken the expressway route she'd opted for on Friday night but this was so much nicer. It reminded her of the drive out to her parents' farm. How could anyone be alive and not love springtime here?

She cranked the CD player, singing along with Seal to "Kiss from a Rose," when her cell phone rang. She didn't recognize the number but she turned down the volume and answered. Being available came with the job.

"Natalie Bridges."

"Are you coming?"

No salutation, no identification, no nothing, just that husky-voiced question in her ear. Beau Stillwell. She didn't even have to close her eyes—which was a good thing, considering she was driving—to imagine that voice in her ear asking that very question in very intimate circumstances. It was that kind of voice and he was that kind of man.

"I'm almost there." Dear God, what was wrong with her? She'd answered him on a matching husky note that implied intimacy when she'd meant to use her normal, efficient, brisk tone.

There was a long pause and her skin felt too warm even with the breeze blowing through the windows. He finally spoke. "Good. We're about to go to the finals. I'll send Scooter to pick you up on the four-wheeler. What are you driving?"

She cringed. She didn't want to tell him. Most of the time she didn't care. Sure, she'd like a sexy little European sportscar—she practically drooled every time she saw an Audi roadster—but that wasn't practical in her business. Practical had been buying the family vehicle from her folks at a deep discount. It was nice enough, but this was a man who was all about fast cars, and hers was anything but. She patted the steering wheel by way of silent apology to her mobile workhorse.

"It's a silver minivan."

He laughed—the son of a bitch actually laughed—in her ear.

"You try hauling a wedding dress or a wedding cake in anything smaller."

"I guess that's true enough. I'll tell Scooter to look for a silver minivan."

He disconnected the call before she had time to

respond. She returned her cell phone to the center console. "Bite me," she muttered as she turned the volume on he CD player back up.

She would not let him get to her today the way he had Friday night. She cringed inside every time she remembered telling him to kiss her ass. She'd suffered a severe case of temporary insanity due to extenuating circumstances but she'd make sure it wasn't repeated.

Friday night had been weird all the way around. She'd seen men in bathing suits, underwear—she'd even seen a couple of them naked. So what was the big deal about Mr. Stillwell draped in a towel?

Maybe because he was ripped and gorgeous…if a woman found that combination of muscle, black hair, intense blue eyes, a slightly wicked grin and a faint scar across the perfection of his left cheek appealing. Her assistant, Cynthia, would do backflips over him. Because he was Cynthia's type. He was not, however, Natalie's type. Natalie preferred her men more polished and urbane. Therefore she put it down to the total weirdness of the night and that from the instant she'd laid eyes on Beau Stillwell's near nakedness a minivolcano had sprung to life inside her. She'd felt hot, flushed, unsettled.

She turned left at a sign with an arrow indicating Dahlia Speedway. Even a shower and a small glass of chardonnay hadn't settled her down on Friday night. Despite the fact that she'd gone to bed mentally reviewing her checklist for the Morris-Pitchford wedding the following day, the same as she always did the night before an event, he had plagued her in her dreams. Crazy dreams.

She was directing a rehearsal and then the dinner and somehow it became the wedding itself, and just when things were going smoothly, Beau Stillwell would appear with his mocking grin and Natalie would look down and discover she was only wearing a towel. She'd hurry and find her clothes and put herself back together, only to have Beelzebub Stillwell reappear, and once again she was appalled to find her clothes gone and a towel about her sarongwise.

She'd woken up tired and out of sorts, and she'd nearly left the last-minute sewing kit behind on her way out the door to the pre-wedding photo shoot. All *his* fault.

And this morning? She'd tried on at least five different outfits until she'd finally settled on a fitted cotton-spandex apricot T-shirt layered beneath a short green jacket with wide-legged jeans and wedge heels. Casual but still professional. This was, after all, work and not a social engagement. And then she'd dithered—might as well call it the way it was—over whether to pull her hair up in a ponytail, or her work chignon, or leave it down. The chignon seemed too fussy, the ponytail too girlish. In the end she'd left it hanging loose over her shoulders and down her back.

Natalie had no delusions about what she looked

like. She wasn't traffic-stopping beautiful and she needed to lose ten…okay, fifteen, maybe twenty… pounds. She was average. Average height. Average overweight. Run-of-the-mill brown eyes. But her one point of vanity was her hair. She'd been blessed with good hair. It was long and thick with just enough curl to give it body.

All told, it had taken her far too long to get ready but it was absolutely *not* because she was concerned about what Beau Stillwell thought of her appearance. No. She couldn't give a fig whether he found her attractive or not. She was not trying to compensate for having given a general first impression of a walking, talking disaster.

She stopped at the gate and flashed the ticket she'd bought Friday evening. Before she'd put the minivan in Park in the far corner of the crowded lot—there were lots of people here today—Scooter pulled up in front of her van.

"Nice to see you again, Ms. Bridges. Climb on the back." He grinned. "You're just in time to see Beau open a can of whup-ass."

"I can hardly wait." Despite her sarcasm, she returned his grin.

He handed her a blue wrist band. "Put this on."

Natalie complied but asked all the same, "What is it?"

"It shows you're a pit crew member. C'mon, let's go race."

Whatever. She'd only shown up to make sure Mr. Stillwell didn't conveniently "forget" their appointment. However, if being a pit crew member was what it took to drag his butt out to Belle Terre, then she was pit-crewing.

She shrugged and climbed up on the four-wheeler behind Scooter. Today she wasn't riding sidesaddle, and instead of wrapping her arms around his waist, she merely held on to the rack that fanned out over the rear fenders. Hmm. In retrospect she could've held on to that rack on Friday night, too. Oh, well.

"You settled?" Scooter asked over his shoulder.

"Yes, sir." Even though he'd sent her in the toter home the other night knowing good and well she'd probably find Beau in some state of undress, she liked Scooter Lewis. With his freckled face and dancing eyes, he reminded her of a mischievous elf.

They took off with a roar, but instead of going to the left in the direction of the pits, Scooter drove into an eight-lane asphalted area where cars, some still attached to tow ropes, were lined up one behind the other and drivers milled about. At the front, the cars converged into two openings and then rolled forward for their turn down the track.

"Staging lanes," he yelled over his shoulder.

She nodded in return. Staging lanes. Okay. Whatever that exactly was, she wasn't sure, but it was loud and noisy…and kind of exciting. Above the din of car engines and male voices, the announcer sounded like a circus barker. "Get ready for some driving, folks. It's the event you've been waiting for—the bad boys of outlaw racing, 10.5's Beau Stillwell and Jason Mitchell taking it head-to-head down the track. Nitrous versus turbo in the final round."

Scooter pulled up next to the black and purple Camaro and she climbed off the four-wheeler. Every inch of her was aware of Beau Stillwell, but she deliberately looked at and spoke to his crew members, Darnell and Tim, first. A whoosh of red ran up Tim's face at her hello. He was obviously one of those guys more at ease around a fan belt than a female.

Finally, she turned to face Beau Stillwell. He wore a half-cocked smile but it was the lazy sweep of those bright blue eyes framed in dark lashes down and back up her that sucked the breath from her and sent her mind skittering to naughty places. "You clean up nice, Ms. Bridges." He leaned down and for one heart-stopping, pulse-pounding moment she was certain he was going to kiss her. There was a lambent sensuality in his eyes, in the way he bent his head. Her whole body tingled in anticipation. The air between them seemed to crackle.

He canted his head to the left, his dark hair teasing against her cheek, and sniffed delicately. She could almost feel the faint scrape of his five-o'clock shadow against her neck. She was on the verge of spontaneous combustion. He straightened. "You smell a whole lot better, too."

He smirked and she wanted to do something aw-
ful to him. Instead she smiled sweetly. "You smell
terrible."

Okay. Not the wittiest comeback in the world, but
good lord, he'd paralyzed over half her brain cells
when he'd leaned in close that way. Her heart was still
tap-dancing against her ribs. It was the best she could
do on short notice and short-circuit.

"You're not into eau de oil and sweat?"

"Afraid not."

Tim, she could've kissed him, chose that moment
to interrupt. "I brought the tires down to ten and
quarter and heated the bottles to nine-hundred." He
handed Beau a jacket, which he shrugged into.

Beau zipped up the jacket. "Good deal." He
reached into the open door of the car and took out a
black neck brace and snapped it into place. He pulled
on a helmet, buckling the chinstrap, leaving the visor
up. Unfairly, he was even more gorgeous in a helmet.
Last was a pair of black, heavy gloves.

Natalie had never been much of a uniform woman.
Cynthia, her assistant, got all hot and bothered by
firefighters, cops and soldiers. She said the uniform
did it for her. Icing on top of a male cupcake. Natalie
had always favored a man in a suit and tie, but Beau
was all suited up in racing gear and looked sexy and
hot, and it was even more galling that he was the one
who was flipping her switch.

He folded himself into the car, sliding between

foam-covered bars that formed a cage inside. "Wish me luck," he said with a flash of a smile.

While she'd wanted to do him bodily harm two minutes ago when he'd left her feeling like a fool, she quite suddenly realized that all that safety gear was in place for a reason. Even though he was annoying and infuriating and generally rubbed her the wrong way, she wanted the arrogant bastard to win safely. She *was* wearing his pit crew band, after all.

"Good luck."

"When it's a pretty woman doing the send-off, it's customary to offer the driver a good-luck kiss."

His gaze lingered on her mouth. That look in his eyes and the very thought of kissing him weakened her knees and sent a bolt of heat through her. "I'll pass."

"Too bad." He winked at her and clicked his visor down into place.

Tim leaned in, fastened a heavy-gauged "net" over the window opening and slammed the driver door shut.

Darnell handed her what looked like an old-fashioned headset. "Put these on. They're ear protection. It's about to get loud."

She put the headset on and she could still hear, but everything was muffled. The car roared to life and she was glad to have the protection, because even with it, the sound was loud enough to vibrate through her body.

Inside the car, Beau sat with his hands gripping the wheel, staring straight ahead.

."He's going through the run in his head, visualizing it," Darnell said, next to her.

She nodded to let him know she'd heard.

The rest happened fast. She and Darnell rode the four-wheeler up to an area closer to the starting line, on the other side of the low wall that separated the track from the stands. Spectators packed the stands. The crowd's excitement was a nearly palpable thing. She knew how they felt. From the moment Tim had slammed the door and Beau had started the car, she'd been revved up inside.

Tim was out between the two cars with a video camera but Darnell stayed with her on the four-wheeler and explained what was happening as Beau "smoked" the tires in the burnout box, which was essentially standing on the brake and the gas at the same time. This created a cloud of choking tire dust but heated up the slick tires so they'd stick to the asphalt track. Scooter then stood in front of the car, giving hand signals, directing Beau left or right, lining the car up "in the groove," where the tires would have the best chance of gripping.

A final tap on the hood by Scooter, a sharp nod of acknowledgment from Beau and he rolled the car forward until the yellow bulb on "the tree"—the staging sequence of red, yellow, green bulbs in the middle of the starting line between the two cars—lit up. Then the roar really became deafening as both drivers revved their engines. The lights changed and they were off. Fast. Furious. For a second it looked as if the driver racing in the other lane was going to swerve into Beau's lane and Natalie thought her heart might very well stop.

And then it was over. Darnell pumped his hand in the air and yelled, pointing at the signs flanking the end of the track. The sign on Beau's side had a lit bulb over the top, designating him the winner, and below it a display of 4.192, 184.92.

Even she could figure it out. 185 miles per hour in 4.40 seconds.

Damn right that was fast, stupid ass.

BEAU TOSSED the wet towel onto the bathroom floor. Tim would clean the toter home up when Scooter got it back to his place. Such was the lot of the gofer on a crew. Such had been Beau's lot when he'd first started out in racing many moons ago, when he was the gofer and his dad was the one climbing behind the wheel of a race car.

He retreated to the bedroom and took his own sweet time dressing. He pushed aside a twinge of remorse. He'd been wasting Natalie's time for a full hour and a half now. After the tow back to the pits, the Horsepower TV reporter had conducted a quick interview and then fellow racers and fans alike had swarmed them. The racers offered congratulations. Most of the fans wanted autographs and a picture with Beau and the car.

Natalie had stood by quietly, out of the way, but those big brown eyes of hers hadn't missed a thing. The tube-top duo from Friday night, Sherree and Tara, had shown up again with a celebration offer. Ms. Bridges had merely quirked an amused eyebrow in his direction and a faint look of disdain, as if they were all somewhat distasteful.

And the whole time he'd been thinking about the way she'd smelled when he'd leaned into her neck before the race. The tickle of her hair against his cheek. The curve of her sexy, sexy mouth. And the crazy, out-of-control feeling she stirred in him.

He squashed any guilt at wasting her time. Given a choice between wasting her time or sitting by while his sister made a mistake marrying Cash Vickers… Well, there was really no question which was more important.

All told, he thought his plan was working okay. He just needed to watch himself, because in the staging lanes, for a second, when he was teasing her, deliberately letting her think he was about to kiss her, he damn near had. She had the most luscious, inviting mouth, with a full lower lip and a cute bow for the top one.

He sauntered back outside and found the enemy consorting with his troops in the small lounge in the front of the race trailer. She was laughing at something Scooter had said, some crazy bullshit no doubt, and his body tightened as the musical notes seemed to dance through the air. Her smile stiffened when she noticed him in the doorway. Good. That was what he wanted, wasn't it?

"Ready?"

She nodded, her chestnut-brown hair moving over her shoulders in a gut-clenching sensual slide. "I just need a ride back to my car."

"Leave your car and we'll pick it up on the way back. We've got to come this way anyway."

Tim spoke up. "You can ride up front with Scooter, if'n you want to," he offered, a flush of red whooshing from his neck to the top of his crew cut before he even finished the sentence. Scooter always drove the rig and the passenger seat was a place of honor, sort of a gimme, for Tim, who mostly handled the grunt work. And now the grunt was willingly giving up that honor. Tim seemed to have developed a crush.

A small frown furrowed her brow as she glanced from Tim to Beau, obviously confused, and equally reluctant to hurt Tim's feelings by turning down his offer. "Ride with Scooter? We're all going to Belle Terre?"

"No, ma'am," Darnell said. "We're all going to Headlights."

"Headlights? What is Headlights and what happened to Belle Terre?"

"Headlights is the ice house and local watering hole between here and Dahlia." Darnell shot Beau a chastising look. "We usually stop off for dinner at the end of a race weekend."

Another chastising look—this one from *her.* "You didn't mention dinner."

All part of his plan. Beau shrugged. "I forgot. We'll head on out to Belle Terre after we eat."

Scooter snorted. "C'mon and ride with me. And dinner's on us."

She deliberately turned her back to Beau, presenting him with a view of her well-rounded bottom, and beamed a smile at the other three. "Charming companions and a free meal. How can I turn down that offer?"

A quarter hour later, they were seated at the number nine picnic table, the number painted on each end in fluorescent orange, after much backslapping and high fives as they made their way across the peanut-hull-littered concrete floor in the noisy din that was Headlights after a race. No matter how crowded it was, however, Jeb Worth always held the number nine for the Stillwell crew. It was a long-standing tradition. Beau wound up sitting next to the Nightmare.

"What do you think of Headlights?" he asked. She didn't strike him as an ice house kind of gal.

"So far, so good. The music's loud." She said it as if it were a bonus. "If the beer's cold and the fries are greasy, we're in business."

Sandy Larabie, her tongue as acid as her heart was big, showed up to take their order, a doe-eyed girl in tow. "This is Gina. She's in training, so you behave." Sandy shot Scooter a steely-eyed glare. Scooter lived to aggravate Sandy. Actually, Scooter lived for mischief in general. "A root beer for Junior," Sandy told Gina, jerking her head in Tim's direction. Sandy referred to anyone under legal drinking age as Junior. "And a pitcher of what for the rest of you?"

"Bud Light. We won." Scooter smirked.

"Three or four mugs?" She eyed Natalie in question.

"Four." Natalie didn't hesitate.

"I would've pegged you for a white wine drinker," Beau said.

"I would've pegged you for a mullet." Ha. He'd never gone in for the longer-in-the-back hairstyle. "I guess we were both wrong."

"What exactly happened to you the other night?" Scooter asked.

She laughed, shaking her head, and it struck Beau as ball-tightening sexy. He had no problem imagining her on top of him, shaking her head just that way. "I got distracted by the T-shirt display about the same time my heel wedged in a crack in the asphalt, which led to an accident with a guy and his beer and hot dog."

Scooter made a sympathetic clicking sound. "Did it ruin everything?"

"Pretty much. The skirt made it through."

"You know Caitlyn and Beau's ma, Beverly, has a right nice shop there in the square in Dahlia. Drop in sometime and let her fix you up. We'll cover the bill."

Had Scooter lost his mind? "The hell you say," Beau said.

Scooter fixed him with an unyielding eye. "She

wouldn't have been at the track if she hadn't been looking for you."

The Nightmare couldn't contain a little smirk in Beau's direction.

"It's not my fault she's clumsy," he said, deliberately goading her. There was a tantalizing sway to her hips when she walked, but it damn sure couldn't be classified as clumsy.

She narrowed her brown eyes. "I am not clumsy."

The trainee delivered the beer and Tim's root beer. Darnell poured and they all hoisted their mugs in a toast. "To another win…and many more to come," Scooter said.

The wash of beer was bust-your-kneecaps cold going down. Beau settled his mug on the table. He'd nurse the rest of it through dinner. He knew he wasn't the man his father had been, but Beau always held himself to a one-drink limit.

Tim unfolded his lanky length from the picnic table, muttered an excuse-me and headed to the jukebox. Scooter groaned and Darnell rolled his eyes. The Nightmare looked at Beau, a question in her brown eyes. "Prepare yourself for a Kenny Chesney miniconcert."

She laughed, her mouth curving in an easy smile and for a second he felt damn near light-headed. He shook his head slightly. Maybe he'd just skip the rest of his beer.

"I like Kenny Chesney."

"So did we…the first hundred times we heard him," Darnell said in a mournful drawl.

"Could be worse," Scooter said. "Could be Cash Vickers we was listening to. Ain't that right, Beau?"

Beau shrugged and he felt the woman next to him eyeing him in inquiry. He deliberately didn't look her way. Not that it was a state secret, but damn it'd be nice if Scooter could just hold his tongue and not stir shit up.

"You're not a Cash Vickers fan?"

Caitlyn hadn't known Cash nearly long enough. And Beau wasn't certain that Cash was good enough for his baby sister.

"Not particularly, no," Beau said. Let her make what she wanted to of that.

Sandy and Gina showed up bearing five red, paper-lined baskets loaded with burgers and fries. "Y'all need anything else?"

"We're good."

Beau tucked into his burger. Lunch had been a long time ago.

"Would you pass the catsup, Mr. Stillwell?"

"Sure thing, Ms. Bridges."

Scooter shook his head. "You can't sit down and have burgers and beers and still be Mr. Stillwell and Ms. Bridges. Nat'lie, meet Beau. Beau, this here's Nat'lie."

Beau passed the tomato-emblazoned bottle. "There you are, Natalie."

"Thank you, Beau."

Damn, that sent a little shiver through him.

"That wasn't so hard, was it?" Scooter said.

"Almost painless," the little smart-ass shot back, upending half the bottle in a corner of her basket.

Alex Morgan and "Black Jack" Riley stopped at the edge of their table, Jack's arm slung around Alex's shoulder, staking his claim.

"Nice finish today," Alex said, with a quick nod of her blond head, "You must've changed your setup."

"Yeah, we changed the heads this week," Darnell said. "It's the best sixty-foot we've had."

Darnell was talking but there was no disguising Alex's frank curiosity about Natalie. And Beau had been deliberately obnoxious but he couldn't totally abandon the manners his mother had drilled into him.

"Natalie, meet Alex Morgan and Jack Riley. Alex is one of the best mechanics in Dahlia. She owns the garage out at the track and another one in town with her dad. They're partners. Jack's from your neck of the woods. He's a DEA agent out of Nashville." He looked at the couple. "Natalie's a wedding planner. She's working with Caitlyn on the big event."

The pleased-to-meet-you's went around, and from Alex's look she clearly speculated why his baby sister's wedding planner was kicking back post-race with him and his crew. In fact, she rather pointedly glanced from Natalie to Beau and back again, silently asking if they were an item.

Sharp-eyed Natalie didn't miss the unspoken question. She wrinkled her elegant little nose, almost as if she'd caught a whiff of a bad smell. "Uh, no. Certainly not that." Hmph. That she'd be so damn lucky. He could name half a dozen women, round that up to an even dozen, who'd like to be sitting right where she was parked now. She didn't need to look as if he were something scraped from the bottom of the barrel. "Mr. Stillwell...I mean, Beau, is a hard man to get in touch with. My job title is wedding planner but sometimes that involves being a tracker—"

"Stalker," he interjected under his breath, garnering a laugh from everyone except the accused, who slanted him the evil eye.

"—and a babysitter."

"Warden," he corrected. "We're heading out to Belle Terre after this to figure out the remodel schedule for the wedding."

Jack squeezed Alex's shoulders. "You might want to hook up with her," he said to the petite blonde, and then looked at Natalie. "I'm trying to talk her into getting married before the end of the year, but she says she doesn't have time to get it together. I'm thinking you could help make this happen."

"Absolutely." Quicker than the staging lights rundown she had two business cards in her hand and was passing them across the table, one to Jack and one to Alex. "I can handle as much or as little as you want me to. Give me a call or send me an e-mail and we'll talk about what you want."

"We'll let y'all get back to your supper, and I don't want to hold you up from getting out to Belle Terre. Just wanted to say congrats on the win." Alex tucked the card into the top pocket of her denim overalls. "I'll give you a call next week."

Natalie beamed a megawatt smile at her potential client. "I'll be looking forward to it."

Alex and Black Jack were barely out of earshot when Scooter started filling Natalie in on Jack posing as a driver to uncover a drug ring and the whole mess that followed. Even Darnell chimed in with the skinny on Alex growing up a motherless tomboy. Beau knew it was all over when Tim screwed up his courage to relate how Jack and Alex had fallen in love.

What was wrong with this damn picture? He'd dragged her out to the track and along to dinner to tie up her time and frustrate her. He'd figured she'd hate the raucousness of Headlights. The whole plan was to push her buttons until she tossed in the wedding planner towel and quit on Caitlyn. Instead, she was swilling beer and chowing down on burgers, holding court with his guys and charming her way into picking up new clients.

This was just damn wrong on so many levels. It was definitely time to step things up a notch.

4

Natalie walked out of Headlights into the relative quiet of the crowded parking lot, surrounded by her new friends, Scooter, Darnell and Tim. They were all sweetie pies. The thorn in her side had stopped to talk to the restaurant owner—she thought he'd introduced him as Jeb—on the way out.

"Looks like y'all are gonna run out of daylight," Scooter said.

True enough, the day had begun to soften around the edges, making way for a Tennessee spring evening. Already, a sliver of a moon was showing itself in the sky. That was okay. Afternoon, evening or night, it didn't matter. She was determined they'd get this done.

"It'll be fine." She patted her purse, "I brought my flashlight."

"Smart thinking," Darnell said in his quiet, reflective way as they crossed the gravel lot to where the big outfit took up several parking spots. Of course, Stillwell Motors Racing wasn't alone. Half a dozen race trailers commandeered spots.

Natalie checked her watch. Nearly seven o'clock. "We'll definitely need a flashlight at this rate. Does he have any concept of time?" Was it her imagination or did Scooter and Darnell exchange a look? "What?"

"I didn't say anything," Darnell said.

"I didn't say nuthin', neither," Scooter seconded.

While Darnell and Scooter looked guilty, Tim appeared confused. "Beau's always on time, for everything."

"Really?"

"Yes, ma'am. He's amazing. I keep the log book on all of our runs but I don't really need to. He can tell you what the track temperature was and our setup from three races ago. Beats anything I've ever seen."

"Wow. That is pretty amazing." Uh-huh. And he didn't like Cash Vickers. This was getting more and more interesting. "Sounds like he has a heck of a memory, too."

Tim nodded, reminding her of one of those bobble-head dolls. "I keep telling him he oughta go on one of those game shows. He'd win, for sure."

"Tim, whyn't you go check the tire pressure on the trailer tires?" Scooter suggested. "It'd be bad to have a blowout on the way home."

"Yes, sir." He ambled off to the rear of the trailer.

Scooter lowered his voice. "You can't pay Tim no never mind. His daddy went to county jail last year and since then Beau's really taken him under his wing. Tim sorta idolizes him."

She refused to feel all warm and gooey inside because Beau had mentored a kid. She absolutely was not going to add a gold star to the top of the heap of attraction that was simmering inside her. Sitting next to him at dinner… "That's sad."

"Which part?" Darnell asked. As far as she could tell, Darnell didn't miss much.

"Both."

Beau, the man of many faces, crossed the parking lot, his long legs eating up the distance. Her pulse began to race as he closed the gap. "I'm ready if you are. We're burning daylight."

He made it sound as if he'd been standing around waiting on *her*. She ground her teeth and resisted the urge to thwack him upside his too-handsome head with her purse. "I've been ready." Generally speaking, for the last two weeks. Specific to today, since four o'clock.

She bid the other guys goodbye and this time headed toward Beau's truck. Funny, but she thought he'd hesitated for a second before walking around to his side, as if he was going to open her door for her and reconsidered at the last minute. She was finding herself more and more intrigued with exactly who and what Beau Stillwell was.

She climbed into the truck, settled against the tweed upholstered seat and buckled up. The floorboard was a utilitarian, uncarpeted vinyl. A worn aluminum clipboard sat in the center of the bench seat along with an orange measuring tape. While it was neat and clean, the truck obviously had both miles and years on it. "I'd have put you in a Corvette, Camaro or Mustang," she said.

"Have you ever tried hauling two-by-fours in one of those?" He turned the key and started the truck.

"Guess that wouldn't work out too well," she said. "Why does your engine sound funny?"

He hung a left out of the parking lot onto the highway. "It's a diesel." He patted the dashboard, "She's a workhorse."

They rolled along and silence filled the space between them. She noted his hands on the steering wheel. He had broad, square hands with a smattering of dark hair on them. His nails were short and clean. They were the capable, masculine hands of a working man and they suited the hard-muscled rest of him that she'd seen. A warm flush spread through her. She could almost guarantee they'd be callused and rasp against a woman's skin—more specifically, her skin.

Natalie was abruptly achingly aware that only about a foot separated them. How was it that he always seemed to invade her space when she was around him?

And what in the heck was wrong with her? She'd spent two weeks tracking him down to sit idly by and contemplate his hands? Not hardly.

She opened her day planner and flipped to her notes detailing the particulars of the Stillwell-Vickers wedding. "Caitlyn's discussed with you what she wants done at Belle Terre?"

"As my granddaddy used to say, is the backside of a pig pork?" He slanted a sideways glance her direction. "If you know my baby sister at all, you'll know she has no problem telling someone what she wants and when she wants it." Evident affection underscored his wry exasperation.

Natalie chuckled. The few times Natalie had been around the pretty little blonde, when her sister, Shelby, had roomed with her at the Watkins College of Art and Design, Caitlyn had always been forthcoming and occasionally demanding. However, she didn't strike Natalie as spoiled so much as indulged—a subtle, yet important difference. "Yeah. I guess that's true."

"Right. You've worked with her on the wedding."

"And I met her a couple of times when she and Shelby were roomies. Have you ever met Shelby?" Her baby sister had mentioned Caitlyn's older brother occasionally. She mostly just groused that he was more of a father than a brother and complained about him being overprotective.

"No. I've heard plenty about her from Caitlyn but I've never met her. I keep a busy schedule." A flick of his blue eyes in her direction set her heart beating a little faster. "Is she as pretty as you are?"

All her breath lodged in her chest. He thought she was pretty? She'd always been the practical one, the smart one, the organized one, but out of a long-running list of foster sisters, she'd never been described as the pretty one. She curled her fingers into her palm.

And this wasn't about her. He'd asked about Shelby, even if it had been in context with Natalie. Shelby and Beau Stillwell? Over her dead body. Beau Stillwell had heartbreaker written all over him. "She's too young for you."

"How old do you think I am?"

She'd guess early thirties. Chronologically he wasn't so far out of bounds. Experiencewise, however… And it wasn't simply because Natalie felt as if she'd been caught in a deep current of desire and was being swept along that every part of her rebelled at the thought of her foster sister dating him.

She was her parents' only biological child, but she maintained the role of oldest child rather than only child because her parents had started fostering children when Natalie was five. Even as a child she'd been the one to try to bring some semblance of organization to their household. Her hippies-at-heart parents had never figured out that having structure was liberating rather than confining.

All her big sister instincts rose to the surface. She didn't think Beau was actually interested in Shelby but just in case… "Too old for my little sister."

He offered a challenging smile that sizzled through her nonetheless. "You don't like me, do you, Natalie?"

No. *Like* wasn't a word she associated with him.

It was as if he bypassed every reasonable, rational, functional aspect of her and tapped into her elemental core. When she was around him, she felt everything with a new intensity. It was as if she were supercharged. She'd never been so aware of herself as a woman and him as a man. But did she like him? Did she particularly like feeling this way? No. But then again, it was a rhetorical question. "That's really immaterial, isn't it?"

"I don't see it that way. We're going to be working closely together on the remodel."

Working closely with him on anything struck her as a lousy idea. He turned everything in her world topsy-turvy and Natalie didn't like topsy-turvy. "Once we get the dates down, it really doesn't have anything to do with me."

"That's not the way Caitlyn sees it." He looked altogether too smug. "She said that's what she was paying you for." His voice dropped and slid over her like the play of velvet against naked flesh. "She assured me you'd be at my beck and call."

Her. Him.

Naked. Needy.

Wet. Hot.

Beck and call.

The very idea sent a shiver down her spine and a rush of slick heat between her thighs.

"Within reason," she managed to say.

"Reason's not part of the deal."

WHAT THE HELL? He liked women. He liked spending time with women, but he *never* got caught up in them. But that's exactly how he felt about Natalie Bridges. Caught up. Tangled. Intrigued.

Interested…aroused, even…was fine, but that wasn't what all of this was about, he reminded himself. Caitlyn was going to make a big mistake and it was up to him to make sure she didn't, by whatever means possible.

Beau rounded the last curve beneath the arch of overhanging oaks and Belle Terre spread before him. Son of a bitch. Cash Vickers would have to show up with a harem and light a crack pipe to get his baby sister to walk away from this.

Set on prime rolling Tennessee hills, even with its vague air of neglect reflected in sagging and missing shutters, Belle Terre was spectacular. The house itself boasted an imposing front of soaring columns and two stories of floor-to-ceiling windows with a second-story balcony overlooking the front door.

"That's a helluva tax write-off, wouldn't you say?" he said.

Natalie pushed her hair back over her shoulder. Thick and shiny, it was the kind of hair that left a man itching to run his fingers through it—or hungry to feel it teasing against his bare chest, his belly and finally his thighs as it followed the trail blazed by her lush mouth over his body. She quirked an eyebrow in inquiry. "You haven't seen Belle Terre before? Not even the video?"

He pushed aside a ripple of guilt. Videographer was Caityln's professional calling, but it wasn't his deal. "Nope. I don't spend a lot of time watching music videos." Apparently the video—Caitlyn's project and her intro to Cash Vickers—that went with his hit song "Homesick" had been shot at Belle Terre. According to Caitlyn, Vickers had bought the place because she'd fallen in love with it. "First I heard of it was when he gave her Belle Terre and a ring. I've been meaning to get out here but I've been busy."

He glanced over at her. The dying sunlight slanting in through her window picked out red threads in her hair.

"You know, Caitlyn has her heart set on having the wedding here," she said.

He had the oddest feeling that they could have been discussing their own child, years from now. It was the first time he'd ever felt someone really understood the level of responsibility he felt for Caitlyn. "I caught that."

"Then it's a good thing we're sequencing out the remodel today. It's a bit of a tight timeline."

Yeah, if they were actually looking at an August wedding. And he caught on right away that she was taking him to task. He was quick that way.

He parked in the circular driveway that fronted the stately columned home. "My sister is obsessed with

Gone with the Wind." He didn't need a psychology degree to figure out that she'd identified with Scarlett O'Hara losing everything. He'd figured her latching on to an iconoclastic heroine was better than developing a drug addiction or identifying with some goth singer who looked like the Grim Reaper and wore makeup. His sister, however, was amazingly well-adjusted considering her childhood. "It's a wonder she hasn't tried to change the name of the place to Tara."

A spontaneous smile—as opposed to her usual I-have-to-be-nice-to-this-asshole smile—curved her lips and lit her eyes. "She did." It left Beau with the oddest feeling that he and Natalie shared a bond. "Cash put his foot down on that. He said they had to respect the history of the place."

He nodded. Much as he didn't want to, he felt a measure of grudging respect for Vickers on that. Beau knew from experience that telling Caitlyn *no* wasn't easy. He also gave Vickers points on standing behind Belle Terre's history.

"Beautiful Land is certainly a fitting name." The house sat on a knoll with gently rolling green hills beyond it. The Miscanauga Creek lay at the foot of the slope to the right rear of the house.

"It is, isn't it?" She pressed the button to release her seat belt. "Shall we start with the outside since we seem to be losing daylight?"

"Sure, sugar pie." That ought to grit her teeth and kill the camaraderie he felt squeezing in with the sexual tension that was thick enough to cut. Sexual tension he could deal with—revel in, in fact. Camaraderie was outside his realm of experience. "You've got something to take notes on?"

Her smile tightened around the edges but she kept it in place. She held up a notebook. "Right here, sugar pie." Touché. "Just let me know when you're ready." She tugged at her seat belt, a frown blooming between her delicately arched brows. "It's stuck."

He very seldom had passengers but he recalled that belt had wanted to stick the last time Scooter rode with him to the parts store. "Come to think of it, it's been kind of temperamental lately."

"Temperamental?"

"Yeah. You know, a little stubborn. Difficult. Let me see what I can do." He grinned. "It just needs the right touch."

"Oh, and you have it?" Something hot and sexual and exciting danced between them.

"It's worth a try since you're not doing such a hot job releasing yourself." His voice came out all warm and gravelly because he'd just painted a picture in his mind of her stretched out on his bed, her head thrown back, that mane of thick hair hanging over the side of his mattress as her fingers delved between her spread thighs, stroking, her brown eyes hot and sultry, her breath coming in short, quick pants as she sought gratification.

He reached across the expanse separating them

and his fingers encountered hers. She jerked her hand away, as if she felt the same rush he did. "There's a button…" he said, the backs of his fingers pressing against the curve of her hip. "You have to touch it just right—not too hard." She turned her head and her delectable mouth was right there. His jeans seemed to shrink, growing tighter across his crotch.

He pressed the button. Nothing happened. He pressed again. He shifted. "Got to find the sweet spot." The tip of her tongue peeked between her lips and left a moist glistening trail between the plump pinkness of her lips. Did she know she was slowly killing him? He was pretty sure she didn't. Still stuck. "C'mon, baby, let go," he coaxed.

The seat belt, if anything, pulled tighter against her chest, throwing her breasts into distracting relief.

"Can you, uh, see what you're doing?" She sounded breathless.

He was damn glad to hear it. Breathing was an increasing challenge on his end.

"I don't have to see. It's all in the touch."

"Well, obviously you don't have it any more than I do."

"Let me try from another angle." He got out and walked around to the passenger side. He opened the door and leaned in, across her. Her breath gusted warm against his neck even as her scent slipped around him. His arm brushed against her right breast as he leaned in. Totally an accident, but the result was the same. Her indrawn breath seemed to echo the tightening and clenching low in his belly.

He pressed the button and tugged, but it didn't budge. "I can't get it out."

A breeze blew through the open truck doors and a few strands of her hair danced along his jaw.

"Maybe you should try lubricating it."

"I've got just the thing." He stepped to the toolbox in the back and quickly returned. She was still sitting there strapped in. There was no way he could've deliberately jammed the seat belt but this was perfect. Well, kind of perfect because she didn't look nearly as pissed off as some women would've been. Actually, she didn't look pissed off at all as she tried to release the jammed mechanism.

Why hadn't he ever noticed before how sexy a woman could look with a seat belt bisecting her chest? He'd have to be a dead man to not see the way it showcased her breasts, tugging her shirt tight over them, her nipples outlined in taut ball-tightening relief. He wasn't anywhere close to dead.

"WD-40," he said.

He reached between her and the seat belt to spread a clean work rag over her thigh and hip. "Scooter's already got me paying for one outfit. I don't want to buy another. By the way, are you always getting into jams?"

She sputtered…actually sputtered, but her brown eyes sparkled with laughter and desire. "You… I… Ohhh."

"Hmm. Should I take that as a yes or a no?"

"You should take that as a *you* are a bad luck omen. I never had these kinds of problems before." But there was no real ire in her voice, and her eyes had darkened.

"You're debunking all kinds of myths for me. I expected a wedding planner to be more even-tempered."

"You seem to bring out the best in me."

"Ah, am I tapping into your inner bad girl?"

She shook her head, sending her thick fall of hair on that sinuous slide over her shoulders that he found so hot. "I don't have an inner bad girl."

He didn't believe it for a minute. "How disappointing." The flash of heat in her eyes told a different story. "I think you've got plenty of bad girl just waiting to be released."

"You are so wrong."

"Am I?" He abandoned the seat belt and reached up to wrap a thick curl around his finger. "Are you sure? There aren't any wicked bad-girl thoughts running through your head right now?"

"Maybe one…or two."

She parted her luscious lips and tilted her chin in a classic invitation to a kiss.

"Ah, Natalie has a naughty side…"

HEAVEN HELP HER but she wanted to kiss Beau Stillwell. Ever since she'd walked in and seen him nearly naked, she'd wanted this. It was as if he were some dark angel sent to torture her. And if she hadn't wanted him before, his gravel-filled "Naughty Natalie" did the trick.

Beau released her hair to trace the line of her jaw with one finger. He angled his head and her breath quickened in anticipation. She slid her hand around the back of his neck, her fingers testing his corded muscles.

He brushed his mouth over hers. Sampling. Coaxing. Teasing. Nice. She kissed him back. A civil exchange.

Totally unexpected, he swept his tongue against her lower lip and then dragged it into his mouth between his own lips—a delicious faint scrape of teeth and then a sucking.

"You have the most delectable, decadent mouth," he murmured and then proceeded to make delectable, decadent love to her mouth. She strained into him. Restricted by the seat belt, she pulled him closer.

They nipped, licked and then segued into hot, hungry, openmouthed kisses. She moaned in the back of her throat, a wordless entreaty. His big hands found her breasts, and nothing had ever felt as good as his mouth on hers and his hands cupping her through her clothing, his palms rubbing against her erect points. She arched her back, pushing her nipples harder into his hands. Hungry. So hungry.

He released her mouth and unleashed a tormenting torrent of kisses down her neck, his tongue dipping and delving along her collarbone. It wasn't enough. Not nearly enough. She tugged his head further down and then his mouth was on her breast, mouthing her through her cotton spandex T-shirt and her bra. He caught her tip in his teeth, and the light abrasion sent her into the stratosphere. Her eyes fluttered closed when he drew her into his wet mouth, suckling her through the cloth.

Where or when it would've ended she'd never know, because in the very dim recesses of her still-functioning mind, she registered the sound of an approaching vehicle.

She pushed against his shoulders, her breathing frantic gasps. "Someone's coming."

A little more time and it could've been her. What, what, what had she been thinking?

His blue eyes glittered when he raised his head and looked beyond her shoulder through the back window. He shook his head slightly, as if clearing it. "Tilson Dobbs. He's a retired Marine who's handling security for the place. I'll go check in with him." She was still trapped by the seat belt. He glanced down her chest to the wet, puckered material. "You might want to button your jacket."

5

HE MIGHT JUST HAVE TO kick Tilson's ass. They'd spent an hour and a half now going over the exterior and the downstairs, listing the necessary repairs and remodel required for the wedding and reception. Natalie actually had a good eye and an equally good grasp of what Caitlyn wanted done. But for the last hour and a friggin' half, Tilson had stuck to them like glue.

When Tilson had driven up, Beau had explained he was checking out the house and Tilson had been all set to ride his Mule, the all-terrain vehicle he drove over the property, off into the sunset to "secure the perimeter." And then Natalie had emerged from the cab of the truck. She'd resourcefully loosened the seat belt straps by pulling them and then climbed out.

Tilson had taken one look at her tousled hair and kiss-swollen lips and decided the perimeter didn't need securing nearly as much as he needed to check out the new female on the Dahlia horizon. Beau was pretty damn tired of Tilson trotting along with them and he didn't care for the way he kept eyeing Natalie. Sort of like a dog circling a juicy bone.

The guy was a persistent son of a bitch, Beau thought as Tilson followed them out of the house, into the now-dark night. They were finished making their list so Tilson could vamoose. Beau flicked on his flashlight and Natalie pulled out a pink one.

"Y'all want to grab some dinner now that you've wrapped things up out here?" Tilson asked as they covered the distance to the truck.

Beau cut him off at the pass. "We ate at Headlights on the way out here."

"How about grabbing a cup of coffee and a piece of pie at the Waffle House, then?" Tilson didn't even pretend to include Beau in that invite. "I can give you a ride to your car afterwards."

Once again, Beau didn't give Natalie a chance to answer. He opened the truck door for her, light from the dome spilling out into the dark, and said to Tilson, "We've got to discuss scheduling on the way back to her car. Got to use that time wisely."

Hell no, he wasn't feeling proprietary at the thought of Tilson nibbling at the fullness of her lower lip or mouthing her tightly budded nipple through her T-shirt the way he himself had earlier. Not a whit, because Beau didn't do proprietary with women. They were fun, a good time was had by all, and he moved on. Nope. It was simply that Natalie taking off with Tilson didn't fit in with his plan. That was all. Nothing more.

Natalie shot Beau a look that promised more to say

on the matter later. However, she said to Tilson as she slid into the cab, "Thanks, but we do need to wrap up the business."

Beau closed her door. "See ya, Tilson," he said as he rounded the truck to his side. Tilson looked decidedly unhappy but that wasn't Beau's problem, now was it?

Natalie sat buckled in the middle. She gestured to the mess next to her. "That seat belt is done for. I can't get the buckle loose and the belts won't retract."

He grinned and slid in next to her. "I'm not complaining." He buckled up and they headed back to the drag strip.

They weren't touching but he felt her body heat with mere inches separating her hips, thighs and shoulder from his. He caught an occasional whiff of her perfume, or maybe it was just her shampoo and the smell of her skin, but he liked it. He was more than ready to take up where they'd left off when Tilson had arrived.

"Just to set the record straight. I'm a big girl and fully capable of answering for myself."

What? Like he was just going to sit back while Tilson moved in and screwed up his plans? Not likely. Plus, she didn't have any business getting involved with the former Marine.

"Tilson's wife left him while he was on his last tour of duty in Iraq. He has issues." There. *Issues* was one of those girly buzzwords he heard his mother and sister and their friends use. He'd give her something to relate to and reveal his softer, feminine side.

"So, that's why you acted like such a jerk."

Obviously his softer, feminine side hadn't come through. "Don't you think *jerk's* a little harsh?"

"Harsh? I gave you the benefit of the doubt."

"I was being thoughtful. Gallant, even. I only had your best interest at heart."

She snorted. "And there I was thinking you were simply being manipulative and high-handed. Regardless, I'm fully capable of making my own decisions. And just for the record, Tilson's not my cup of tea."

He knew a moment of smug satisfaction. He nodded. "What is your type?"

"Suit and tie. Professional."

That was no real surprise. "Ah, a sissy boy with soft hands. Someone who doesn't break a sweat to do his job."

"I prefer to think of it as brains rather than brawn."

Maybe. And she could go on about brains and a suit and tie all day long, but he'd bet his racecar her panties had been wet earlier. "I'd say someone easily managed, who asks how high when you say jump. I think you have control issues."

She sputtered, actually, honest to God sputtered. "I…you…you…" And then she laughed, more with incredulity than amusement. "*You* think *I* have control issues? Okay."

He could tell there was so much more she wanted to say, except she was working for his sister. He bit back a chuckle. He'd like to hear what she *wasn't* saying.

"So, do you have one of those sissy boys on a string back in Nashville? I'm just asking because I'm not so sure he'd approve of the way you kissed me earlier."

"Wait a minute! You're seriously confused if you think I kissed you. You kissed me."

He hazarded a glance her way in the dashboard glow. Was that a flash of devilment in her brown eyes?

"No confusion here. And I can tell you now, sugar, if you were mine, I wouldn't want you kissing someone else that way."

He sensed—no, felt—the shift in her before she ever took action or opened her mouth. He'd pushed her to her limit. "Really? And if I were yours, be still my beating heart, how would you want me to kiss someone else?"

She released her seat belt. and before he could draw a breath she had twisted and curled one leg beneath her, levering herself up and bracing one hand on his shoulder, her warm breath teasing against his neck. "Like this?" She nuzzled beneath his ear and then nipped the tip of his lobe.

Holy hell. The sensation shot straight to his dick. She caught the recently nipped spot between her lips and sucked. His balls tightened as surely as if she'd cupped them in her hot little hands and gently squeezed.

He acknowledged the contest of wills. "No, baby, definitely not like that."

"Then what about this? Would this be acceptable?" She trailed hot, open mouthed kisses down the column of his neck and he was damn glad to see the drag strip entrance to his left because at this point he was DUI—driving under the influence of her distracting mouth.

He pulled into the spot next to her minivan in the nearly deserted lot and threw his truck into Park. "Definitely not acceptable."

He released his seat belt, turned and reached for her. She intercepted him, pushing him until his back was against the door, and leaned up on her knees. "Then maybe this?" Her mouth skated over his and she delivered light, flirty kisses that had his heart thumping out of control. Her hair tickled against his neck and he spanned her waist with his hands.

"Or this," she murmured against his mouth and then moved on to deep, soulful kisses. She captured his tongue and sucked and stroked it with hers. Stroke, suck, stroke, suck. It was a mind-numbing, cock-hardening, ball-tightening rhythm. If she could do that to his tongue he'd love to have her work that magic on his cock. He groaned into her mouth.

She pulled back and started to slide across the seat. "Did you find that acceptable?"

FIRE. She was playing with fire. She was *on* fire. While it was true that Beau had provoked her, she'd *wanted* to kiss him again. She needed to get out of here while she could still think about something other than how good he felt and tasted and the achy, hot need coiling tighter and tighter inside her.

Before she could move any further, he reached out, wrapped his big hands around her arms and hauled her back to the solid hardness of his body. "I'm still trying to decide if that's acceptable. I think I need a replay."

Her heart hammered against her ribs and a rush of wet heat surged between her thighs. If she had an ounce of sense, she'd skedaddle. He'd sort of man-handled her into his lap but she didn't feel threatened. If she insisted, he'd let her go. Deep inside, she knew he was one of the good guys. But apparently her last ounce of sense had abandoned her because she didn't want to leave. Instead, she wanted to flirt and tease and kiss him some more.

"You should pay closer attention the first time around," she said. She ended on a tiny gasp as he bent his head and nuzzled at her neck, and then she felt the faint scrape of his teeth followed by the velvet stroke of his tongue. That felt so *good*. She moaned and closed her eyes.

"Maybe I just wanted seconds…" he said in a husky murmur as he worked his way up her neck, "…or thirds."

She laughed softly and wound her arms around him. She'd only *thought* she was on fire before. His mouth found hers and she was drowning in the magic of his kiss. She molded the ridges of his muscular shoulders. He slid his hands beneath the edge of her T-shirt and spanned her waist. He stroked upward until his big hands cupped her breasts. She pushed harder against his fingers and he dipped them into her bra, finding the hardened tip. His fingers… his mouth…she pulled away and drew a ragged, gasping breath.

Severe tactical error on her part. She was about one kiss away from being in way over her head.

She tugged her shirt back down and slid across the seat to the passenger side. He let her go, but there was no mistaking the glint in his eyes.

"If you were mine," he said, "I'd have to vote for you not kissing anyone else at all, in any way at all."

She snatched up her purse and opened the passenger door. "Then I guess it's a good thing I'm not yours."

She slammed the door behind her.

MONDAY MORNING, Natalie looked up from her day planner on her Queen Anne desk in the back corner of the bridal shop as the bell jangled over the front door.

"It's just me," Cynthia called out.

Natalie was doubly glad to see her assistant. Not only did she genuinely like Cynthia, she was more than ready for a distraction. She desperately needed to think about something, someone other than Beau Stillwell. Living above her shop was convenient on several fronts. She didn't have a commute. She saved on rent.

The downside was she'd never really had a space all her own. Growing up, from as early as she could remember, she'd shared her room, and clothes and toys with foster siblings. And now she shared her home space with her business. One day, she wanted a house of her own. But, for now, she'd take advantage of no commute and always being in the office, ready for the day, by seven-thirty. This morning, however, Natalie had hit the office at six-thirty, ready to lose herself in work, details, planning—anything but thinking about Beau.

Although she was tired last night, nothing had satisfied her. She'd run a bubble bath when she got home, dumping a generous portion of lavender bath salts in. Between the warm water and aromatherapy she should've been out like a light. Nope. She'd tried reading a book. Not interested. Nothing on television. She'd popped in *Pride and Prejudice*—A&E's Colin Firth as Mr. Darcy, thank you very much—but not even *P&P* struck a chord for her.

She'd finally admitted to herself that she was sexually keyed up and taken matters into her own hands. It was a rather sad fact, but the truth of the matter was that not all orgasms were created equal. She'd had her orgasm but she'd still felt all empty and achy and needy inside.

Masturbation simply didn't mimic the nuzzle of Beau's mouth on her neck or the delicious pressure of his hand and mouth on her breast. And the very thought of his mouth between her wet thighs… Yeah, that had been the fantasy that sent her right on over the edge to hollow satisfaction. Kissing him had been analogous to playing with fire. She hadn't gotten burned, but she was definitely singed. How could a man so wrong, so different from what she wanted in a man, turn her on so thoroughly, so completely?

And it didn't matter. This, too, would pass. She'd finally gotten him out to Belle Terre. Now all she needed was the schedule from him, which she could most likely go through his secretary for, and she was done with Beau Stillwell until she had to see him again at the rehearsal dinner. Months. Woohoo.

"How was your Sunday?" Natalie asked as Cynthia put away her purse and beelined for the hot water in the back. Natalie wandered into the stockroom behind her and leaned against the doorjamb.

"I spent most of the day parked on the sofa reading a romance novel, just to remind myself there are decent men out there, and eating popcorn. But I didn't cry. Not even once." Cynthia measured out loose English breakfast tea leaves into the stainless steel ball.

Natalie would've hugged her, except Cynthia wasn't the hugging type. The last couple of months had been tough for her assistant. Cynthia had been expecting a proposal from her live-in boyfriend, Josh, after two years together. Instead, she'd gotten the news that Josh was going to be a daddy—the sticking point being that Cynthia wasn't the mommy. And he'd even robbed her of the pleasure of kicking him to the curb. He'd moved out and sent her a text message breaking both pieces of news while Natalie and Cynthia had been in the middle of directing a rehearsal. Bastard.

"Good," Natalie said. "That's real progress. Double good because he's so not worth it."

Tears shimmered in Cynthia's eyes but she squared her shoulders and raised her chin. "But enough about me. Did you get the remodel schedule down? What was the race like?" She cocked her head to one side and assessed Natalie, her lips pursed. "And what's different about you this morning? You definitely look different."

"We got the remodel list made. We didn't get as far as the schedule. The race was, believe it or not, kind of exciting. And I suppose this is what I look like when I'm losing my mind."

Cynthia dropped the tea ball into the hot water. "Why do I get the feeling we're not talking about your standard garden-variety lose-your-mind?"

Natalie brought her up to speed on most of the day while Cynthia opened a Pop-Tart and dropped it into the toaster. "His pieces aren't quite fitting together. His crew member tells me the guy can remember stats from two races ago but I have to schlep along behind him like a hired hand, taking notes. That doesn't add up."

"So what are you saying?"

"I don't know. See, that's the problem. I can't think

straight." There. She'd admitted it. He was messing with her head.

"So, call Shelby up and grill her about this guy. That girl loves to talk."

It was true. Her younger foster sister was a motor-mouth, which was great considering the quiet, with-drawn kid she'd been when she'd shown up as a thirteen-year old. Natalie was adaptable and she got along well with almost all the kids her parents took in, but she and Shelby had really bonded. "She's never met him."

"It doesn't matter," Cynthia said, stirring a spoon-ful of sugar into her tea. "There's no way Caitlyn didn't talk about her home life, about him. Find out what Shelby knows."

Shelby had had plenty to say about how overpro-tective Caitlyn's big brother could be, but that was simply from overhearing conversations and Caitlyn's complaints.

"I don't want her to think I'm…" Natalie hesitated.

"You're what?"

Natalie crossed her arms over her chest. "You know…interested." She gave a one-shoulder shrug. "Personally or anything."

Cynthia's spoon clanged against the side of the cup and her mouth dropped open. "Oh my God, you are, aren't you?"

"Definitely not. So not my type. And he's obnoxious. And he wastes my time. And I made out with him." She buried her face in her hand.

"Sheep shit on a stick. You made out with him? Define *'made out.'*"

"You know, he kissed me. Then later I kissed him." She left out the part about masturbating to the thought of him going down on her. Some things were just better left unsaid.

"I'm totally confused. I thought you said he's obnoxious."

"He is."

They left the stockroom.

"And you were kissing him, why?"

"To prove a point…and he is obnoxious…in a hot way. I mean, not hot according to my standards but hot according to a lot of other standards." Natalie dropped back into the chair at her desk and Cynthia perched on one of the two chairs on the other side.

"Right. That just clears everything up…not. Exactly what point were you proving by making out with him?"

It had made sense at the time. "It's complicated."

"Apparently. I can't wait to meet him. He's the first man I've ever seen get you all discombobulated."

"I am not discombobulated. Okay, well, maybe a little." And she didn't want to think about him anymore. She'd already thought about him half the night. Make that three-quarters of the night. She was now desperately trying to adhere to out of sight, out of mind before she got to just plain old out of her mind. "Sara Gastoneau is coming in this morning—"

Natalie's cell phone interrupted with the instantly recognizable Mendelssohn's "Wedding March" from *A Midsummer Night's Dream.* Her clients loved that ring tone and so did she. The traditional recessional signaled yet another wedding completed and the start of a new life together as husband and wife. Caller ID flashed Caitlyn Stillwell's name.

"Natalie! You are such a doll."

"Hi, Caitlyn," Natalie said with a smile. Caitlyn Stillwell possessed an infectious enthusiasm. "How's life on the road and why am I a doll?"

Caitlyn offered a dreamy sigh at the other end. "Life on the road is wonderful…mostly because I'm with Cash. But we're getting some great video footage." That had been a biggie among many challenges in planning their wedding. Not only was it on short notice, but the bride-to-be was touring the country by bus with her fiancé and shooting video footage for what they hoped would be a reality show or documentary. Natalie had never planned a wedding before with the bride out of town. "And you're a doll because I just got off of the phone with Beau. You are the best."

Why did that have an ominous ring? "I'm glad you think so but I'm not sure I'm following you here."

"He told me about you helping him out at Belle Terre."

"No problem." Sometimes her business called for a little white lie. "I was more than happy to help." He'd wasted several hours of her time. And sometimes it was a whopping white lie.

"I bet no other wedding planner would do what you're doing. Even Cash is impressed."

Yay! This was exactly the response she wanted, exactly what she wanted Caitlyn to put out to the public. Once Caitlyn and Cash were married, Caitlyn would be Nashville royalty.

"That's why I'm here. I don't want you stressing about the wedding. I just want you to have fun and look forward to it."

Caitlyn laughed on the other end. "I'll admit I was stressing a little over the renovations, but now that you're personally assisting Beau with the remodel and building…"

What the hell? She wasn't personally assisting him with anything now that they'd made that list. "He swears he'd never be able to get the project done in time for the wedding if you weren't willing to come out and help him with the project," Caitlyn steamed on. "Cash and I think you're the best."

She'd already said that once. Natalie forced a smile into her voice, "Well, I'm not sure how much—"

Caitlyn interrupted. "Don't be modest. Beau said not many professionals would be willing to go that extra mile of meeting him at Belle Terre at six-thirty in the morning and then again in the evenings to work around your other projects. He was impressed with your flexibility."

"Coming from him that means a lot." She couldn't help her dark sarcasm. And it was better than screaming. What was he up to? Because he was definitely up to something. They'd no more discussed her squeezing renovation help into her already packed schedule than she had monkeys flying out her tush. Hel-lo. It was high wedding season. She was *busy*. But she couldn't say that to Caitlyn. He'd pretty much manipulated Natalie into a tight spot.

"Hey, can you hold on a minute, Natalie?" On the other end, someone was talking to Caitlyn. "Yeah… Okay… Right… I'm just wrapping up here. Hey, I'm back but I've gotta go. Call me if anything else comes up. Otherwise, I'll talk to you later."

The phone clicked in Natalie's ear. She turned to Cynthia, who'd eavesdropped unabashedly. Not that she blamed her for that.

"I guess it would be counterproductive," Natalie said, "to kill him *before* the renovation is done and he's walked her down the aisle, huh?"

It was sheer annoyance at his blatant manipulation that had Natalie's heart pounding and not the thought of being in close proximity to his wickedly distracting mouth and hands and his big, hard body.

No, *that* particular thought was responsible for her now-damp panties.

6

BEAU WHISTLED UNDER his breath as he made his way back to his truck, satisfied his roofing crew was set on the new subdivision job he'd contracted between Nashville and Dahlia. Urban sprawl was both a bane and a blessing, but right now it was a damn fine morning in Dahlia. The sun was shining, he had jobs lined up in a less-than-stellar economy and he had Natalie Bridges right where he wanted her.

He leaned against the cab of his truck and checked his wristwatch. He'd finished up the conversation with his sister about forty-five minutes ago. He figured he'd get a call anytime now. Actually, depending on how long Caitlyn kept Natalie on the phone, it could be another couple of minutes.

Natalie. Her sweet, hot mouth…her velvet tongue… Classy. Sexy. Fiery. True enough, he'd started out with the intent to shut this wedding down and that remained his primary goal, but he'd discovered two things in the last day. One, he realized he'd never had to chase a woman before. From the earliest time he could remember women just seemed to like him. But

Natalie brought out the hunter in him. Two, he wanted her. She'd told him yesterday in no uncertain terms he wasn't her type. Bullshit. She wouldn't… couldn't…kiss him that way if she didn't want him.

He scrolled through his cell-phone options. Natalie deserved her own ringtone and he deserved to be forewarned when she called. He downloaded and waited.

He didn't have to wait long. His phone trilled the opening chords of AC/DC's "Highway to Hell."

"I just spoke to Caitlyn," she said without preamble.

A fly buzzed past him and the sounds of the guys hauling up shingle bundles and recounting weekend exploits filled the background. "Great. I'm sure it's important to stay in close contact when you're planning her wedding."

He climbed in the cab of the truck, cutting off the background noise. He could've sworn on the drive from his office to the work site that he'd caught the occasional whiff of her scent from last night.

"You know, press-ganged servitude is out of vogue these days. Of course, I have only myself to blame." She paused and sighed heavily on the other end. "I should've never kissed you."

What angle was she working? Women never regretted kissing him. Quite the opposite, in fact.

"I'll have to say you've lost me there, sweet thing." He picked up the take-out coffee cup from the dash cup holder. Empty.

"Obviously I drove you beyond the point of desperate when I kissed you," she announced on a smug note. "It goes without saying I'd never go out with you, so you've resorted to manipulating me into indentured servitude."

She'd never go out with him, as if he were some substandard species? The hell, she said. The hunt was definitely on. He chuckled.

"Indentured servitude?" Well, hell, that just brought a whole bunch of things to mind. Her on her knees in front of him, her mouth on his…a little light bondage with silken cords… "Does that mean you want me to tie you up?"

"You wouldn't dare." Well, well, well. She sounded far more breathless than outraged. Just what was going on in her pretty little head? "And can you say sexual harassment?"

No. And neither could she. "Am I writing your paycheck, baby? Do I have the authority to fire or promote you? Think again. If you find yourself all tied up, it's strictly because that's what you want."

"I think you have a pretty accurate idea of what I want right now and it's not that." No man with a brain would trust that sweet note.

"I'm certain I know *what* you want, you just need to decide *how* you want it."

"Since you seem to be calling all the shots at this point, you tell me. When do you want to start?"

"I'm sitting on ready. You're the one with the rushed time schedule. Let's start this evening."

"What time?"

"Six." That ought to have her sitting through Nashville rush hour. The idea, after all, was to push her to her limits.

"Perfect."

Perfect? Ha. She was probably ready to gnaw on wood. And just to thoroughly piss her off... "And don't be late. I'd hate for us to get behind schedule because you're not punctual."

He could all but feel her kiss-my-ass radiating over the phone line. Perversely, he was looking forward to 6:00 p.m.

AT PRECISELY four-thirty, Natalie pulled into a parking spot on Dahlia's picturesque town square. There was no way she was going to sit through rush-hour traffic heading out of the city. Plus, she'd seen Beau's face when Scooter told her to replace her outfit at Stillwell Motors Racing's expense. Two could play his game, and she was more than willing to hit below the belt...at least, that's where she assumed he kept his wallet.

She slung her purse over her shoulder and locked the minivan. Was it her imagination or did the air smell sweeter, fresher here? With its refurbished store fronts around a parklike square anchored by a Confederate soldier monument, Dahlia was a refreshing step back in time—especially after the urban sprawl that had become Nashville.

She'd driven through with Caitlyn once before on their way out to Belle Terre and Caitlyn had pointed out the green and white striped awning that marked Beverly's Closet, but they hadn't stopped. Now Natalie strolled along the sidewalk, enchanted.

Early on, she and Caitlyn had discussed whether to use local businesses in the wedding or Natalie's tried-and-true Nashville contacts. Now that Caitlyn had made up her mind, Natalie needed to set up appointments to meet with the business owners. True, she could just drop in, but that seemed disrespectful of their time—and thank you, Beau Stillwell, she knew all about how it felt to have someone disregard your time.

Plus, she wouldn't mind an opportunity to "window-shop" anonymously. One of her concerns was whether the small hometown businesses in Dahlia could deliver and pull off an event like Caitlyn and Cash's wedding. Not that she didn't want every wedding to be perfect, but the way this one would be covered by the media, Natalie's already narrow margin of error had narrowed even further. This, the career catalyst that had been handed to her like a gift, had to be as close to perfect as possible.

She'd noted the bakery's location on the outskirts of town, a pink cinder block building with white lace curtains gracing the display windows of Pammy's Petals. She paused now in front of Christa's Florals and breathed a small sigh of relief. Several elegant floral arrangements on a velvet runner filled the front window. Whew! It was always a bad sign when a florist presented funeral wreaths and cemetery flowers as their primary offering.

She passed a small gallery showing several stained-glass pieces, lace and beadwork and a lovely wedding-knot quilt in shades of lavender, yellow and pink that sent a wave of nostalgia washing over her. She could almost smell the signature scent of gardenia her grandmother had favored and feel her warmth as they'd shared a similar quilt on Memaw's front porch swing when Natalie had been a young girl. She blinked. It would be beyond crazy to burst into tears on the Dahlia sidewalk because some exquisitely crafted artwork had pulled an emotional rug out from under her feet.

She walked on. Dahlia Hair and Nails. Hmm. Hard to tell, but selling Caitlyn on another stylist would be a real challenge. Apparently the owner, Lila, was Caitlyn's mother's best friend.

She paused on the sidewalk outside Beverly's Closet, ostensibly admiring the ivy topiaries and spring-mix flowers in oversized planters flanking the glass door. She realized she was nervous. As the mother of the bride, Beverly had been part of the preplanning with Natalie and Caitlyn, and Natalie liked the older woman, but she was suddenly self-consciously aware that Beverly was also the mother of Natalie's new object of full-blown lust.

And like it or not, Beau hadn't just slipped into that spot, he'd commandeered it. Dear god, even when he was being manipulative and arrogant and every other unpleasant adjective she could throw his way, damn him to hell, he tripped her trigger.

And that was highly, impossibly problematic. He was everything she didn't want in a man, wasn't he? Relationships weren't supposed to shake you up and make you feel unsettled and as if you were too much for your own skin. And that was an equally crazy thought. What she and Beau had wasn't even close to a relationship. It was a…she didn't even know what it was. Wanting to strip a man naked and work her way up, or down, his body didn't qualify as a relationship.

As if that wasn't the craziest thing. She shrugged away the silly thought and stepped into Beverly's Closet.

At the tinkle of the bell, Beverly looked up from where she was plumping a cushion in an armchair upholstered in apple-green velvet. "Can I help you…" Recognition kicked in. "Natalie, it's so good to see you again. Come on in, sugar." Beverly's genuine smile encompassed her. Somewhere in her midfifties, with porcelain skin, moss-green eyes and shoulder-length hair dyed a soft, flattering shade of blond, Caitlyn's mother struck Natalie as the quintessential middle-aged Southern beauty.

Beverly hugged her, engulfing her in a cloud of perfume. "What a nice surprise. Well, not a total surprise because Milton called and explained the ruined outfit." A delicate blush tinged Beverly's porcelain cheeks.

"Milton?" Natalie didn't know anyone named Milton.

"Milton Lewis."

Lewis? That sounded familiar but it wouldn't click into place. And obviously she still looked perplexed.

"Beau's crew chief."

Right. "Oh. *That* Mr. Lewis." Natalie laughed. She'd really liked Scooter, née Milton, Lewis. "I didn't think his mother named him Scooter."

Beverly rolled her eyes in exasperation. "Isn't that the most ridiculous thing you ever heard to call a grown man? He picked up that name in high school when he and my late husband started tinkering with cars. Since Milton was the shortest, he'd scoot underneath the car to work on it."

Natalie personally preferred Scooter to Milton, but she kept her own counsel. She'd quickly learned in this business when to hold her tongue. Well, most of the time. When she was around Beau, however, she didn't manage nearly as well. "Hmm." She, however, found Beverly's blush sweet. "So, Mr. Lewis called you?"

Color rose in the older woman's cheeks again. "To tell me you might come by."

"Uh-huh," Natalie responded with a knowing smile. Beverly was a beautiful woman and, well, bottom line, Scooter or Milton or whatever they called him was a man.

Another delicate stain of pink blossomed. "We talked for a while. I think he's lonely since Emma Jean died."

"And I think you're a beautiful woman."

"Well…why…thank you. That's what he said, too," Beverly told her in a sudden rush. She buried her hands in her face momentarily and then looked up, equal measures of excitement and mortification in her green eyes. "Oh, Lord, he asked me to go to dinner."

Natalie had the distinct impression she'd just wandered into something intensely personal but was enough of a stranger to qualify as a confidante. And for whatever reason, people seemed to confide in her. "What did you say?"

"I said I'd let him know."

Absence of a flat-out *no* meant *yes*. "Do you want to go?"

Beverly fluttered her hand nervously along her hairline. "I don't know…it's been so long… What if he tries to kiss me when he brings me home?"

Natalie pushed aside the memory of Beau's mouth on her lips and breast that seemed seared into her brain. This wasn't about her and this woman's son. Regardless, her entire body went on red alert and her nipples stood at attention. She was pretty damn sure she was wearing her own blush now. "Do you want him to?"

Straightening a row of hangers that didn't need straightening, Beverly avoided eye contact. "It's not that. I haven't… It's been… Monroe, Beau and Caitlyn's daddy, died sixteen years ago and I haven't *seen*—" she glanced up meaningfully "—anyone since then."

Seen? Natalie's curiosity and confusion must have shone in her face.

"My children needed me and I was all torn up inside, and then when Caitlyn was older, I thought it was still best not to date and it's just gotten to be a habit. What if I don't remember how to kiss? And what will my children think? What would you think if *your* mother was about to start dating?"

She'd never thought about it. She took a second to consider, unwilling to throw out a glib response to something that was obviously so important to Beverly. "I think if my dad died I wouldn't want my mother to be lonely. I think your kids will feel the same. Maybe not at first…but they'll come around. Well, I think Caitlyn's so wrapped up in the engagement and wedding and love in general that she'll be right onboard."

Beverly nodded. "I think you're right. I'm more worried about Beau. He stepped right in as man of the family when Monroe passed." The tension in the set of Beverly's shoulders eased. Apparently she was more comfortable discussing her son and the past, even if it was a difficult time, than a future date and potential kiss with Scooter. "Lord, he was only sixteen but he finished school and worked in the evenings and on the weekends and we made ends meet. I cleaned houses to keep our heads above water but Beau's the reason I have this business and the house I'm in now." There was no denying the admiration and mother's pride shining in her eyes. "That boy has worked his tail off to provide a home and this business for me and he's made sure Caitlyn never wanted for anything she truly needed. He became a man at sixteen."

Something warm and dangerous flip-flopped inside Natalie. In retrospect, she supposed she'd heard bits and pieces of this story from her sister, Shelby, but had not really paid much attention. She didn't want to think of Beau as a man who mentored Tim, his now-fatherless pit-crew member, or busted his young butt to keep a roof over his mother's and sister's heads. That all ran counter to dismissing him as just another hot, albeit arrogant, guy. She realized, rather lamely, that a somewhat expectant silence had stretched between them.

"I can see why you're proud of him. Hopefully he'll be okay with you going out with Scoot— I mean, Milton."

Beverly beamed, as if a tremendous weight had been lifted from her shoulders. "He'll just have to be, won't he?"

"And don't worry that you won't remember how to kiss. It's probably been a while for him, as well. Y'all can remember together."

Another blush, but somehow this looked more like a blush of expectation than embarrassment. She nodded, her eyes sparkling. "So, we need to outfit you because that son of mine was hard to track down." She clicked her tongue against the roof of her mouth. "I know he's busy but I taught him better manners than that. Exactly what got ruined?"

"Just a blouse and a jacket. That should cover it."

"Did the jacket go with a suit?" Beverly quirked a salon-arched brow.

"Well, yes."

She shook her head, clearly annoyed with the son she'd just venerated. "He knows better." Her eyes gleamed as she nodded. "An entire suit and blouse. I raised him better than that."

Natalie almost felt sorry for Beau Stillwell. And then she thought about him dragging her out to Belle Terre as if she didn't have anything better to do than his bidding on a construction project and offered Beverly her brightest smile.

7

NATALIE PULLED INTO the circular drive fronting Belle Terre and parked her minivan next to Beau's truck. She drew a deep, steadying breath. She was being ridiculous. It was just his lousy truck—granted, she'd had a heck of a good time in that front seat as recently as last night—and her heart was galloping in her chest. She couldn't seem to stop herself from a quick glimpse in the rearview mirror to check hair and makeup. No mascara smears, no oily spots on her face—blotting papers were a beautiful thing—and her lip gloss was fine. She smoothed down a spot where her hair was sticking up. Good to go.

She climbed out of the car and approached the house. It was imposing and, if she was totally honest, a little scary. While beautiful, there was an air of melancholy about it, but then again, how many generations had loved, lived, cried and died here? How could a place that had once held people in captivity as slaves to a master know anything but melancholy, despite the laughter that must have spilled from the shuttered windows that opened to the soaring, columned porch?

Beau opened the front door—apparently waiting on her to show up, she noted—and all philosophical and esoteric thought fled in light of her purely physical response to six foot plus of dark-haired, blue-eyed, well-muscled man in jeans, T-shirt and work boots. What had happened to her penchant for suits and ties? Gone. System bypassed in favor of hot and rugged standing with splayed legs in the doorway. Sweet, hot, immediate desire flooded her.

"You're here," he said, his dark-lashed eyes sweeping her, touching her in a way that left her breathless.

She marched past him into the foyer. "I am." She strove to bring some semblance of detachment to the situation. She turned to face him, opting for the direct approach. "Now why don't you tell me why I'm really here? You could have a high-school kid help you and they'd be more adept at this than me."

Those eyes flickered over her again and it was a replay of the scene in *The Libertine* when just one look from Johnny Depp and she was ready to crawl naked across the floor for him. "But you're the one with the insight into what Caitlyn wants done," he went on. "And after you—how was it exactly—oh, right, drove me beyond the point of desperate with those kisses…you really didn't leave me any choice, did you?"

She knew the moment that came out of her mouth she'd regret saying it. And she could only blame her lack of self-control on him. He was the culprit. There was something about him. He got under her skin. Wanting to crawl naked across a floor for him was a perfect case in point. She was good with crawling naked across the floor but not for *him*. She scrambled for some measure of sanity.

"I shouldn't have said that. Occasionally, my mouth runs away with me. And about the other, I've been thinking—"

He interrupted. "The other?"

She was altogether too, too aware that it was her and him alone in an empty house and to stand about throwing the word *kiss* or *kissing* around seemed dangerous territory. Couldn't they address the issue in a nice civilized roundabout manner? "You know what I mean."

He closed the front door with a final, resounding click. He approached her with a measured, intent tread, and her pulse hammered. "You've got to speak clearly and slowly for us he-man types who are more brawn than brains, sugar." He held out broad, masculine hands, palms up, as if for her inspection, approval. "These hands have calluses."

In less than a second, she was imagining the erotic scrape of those calluses against her sensitive nipples, down her body, between her legs. Pathetically, that sent a shiver through her and a rush of liquid warmth between her thighs.

"Kissing." Brief and to the point, and still the mere mention with him right in front of her left her tingling and aroused because her mind had taken her far, far beyond a mere merging of lips and tongues.

"Oh. That other." He grinned, an evil, wicked, I'd-like-to-seduce-you-right-out-of-your-panties grin that set her heart knocking against her ribs. He dropped his gaze to her mouth. "I'm all for it."

Good lord, she'd like to back him up against that door and eat him alive—especially when he looked at her like that. She grasped at the last few threads of sanity, reminding herself she was here to move this wedding forward and not to make out with Caitlyn's big sexy brother. "Well, I'm not."

His slow smile slid devastatingly up and down her spine. "Now you're making me feel inadequate as a man." Uh-huh. And there really was a Santa Claus. "I could've sworn you liked it."

If ever a man needed taking down a peg or two, she was looking at his wicked sexy self. "It was…" She tilted her head to one side and pretended to search for a description. She deliberately brightened, as if suddenly enlightened. "Adequate." She was dancing close to the flames again but she couldn't seem to help it.

"Oh, hell no." He shook his head. "I have standards and adequate isn't one of them." He took a step toward her and his slow, sexy smile spread a sweet heat of anticipation through her. "We're gonna have to work on this until we've passed adequate."

No, no and no. Kissing him had been like setting

a blowtorch to a marshmallow inside her. She'd never been one to hop in bed with a guy, but Beau seemed to knock every aspect of her off course. She had a sinking feeling that a little more kissing, she'd be hard-pressed to keep her legs together and her panties on. And that was an understatement. She was about two seconds from she wasn't exactly sure what, but it was dangerous.

She stepped back.

"You'll have to practice with someone else. I'm sure you won't have any problem locating a partner—" or two or ten, she thought, recalling the two women who'd stopped by post-race "—but it's not me. No more kissing."

He frowned in mock consternation, a wicked gleam in his bedroom-blue eyes. "Now that puts me in a downright awkward position, baby girl."

God, she was certifiably losing her mind because she found his *baby girl* incredibly sexy. "How is that awkward? Awkward is carrying on when we're supposed to be working."

He reached out and tilted her chin up with his fingertip. One touch—just his fingertip against her skin rendered her breathless. "I suppose I need clarification… Surprised you with that fancy word, didn't I? Do I go with this or do I kiss you when you ask me to?"

She pushed his hand away. "That's easy to answer… because I won't be asking."

"Right. You do like to take matters into your own hands." For one moment she was mortified that he knew he'd inspired her to fire up her vibrator last night. Then she realized he was referring to her showing up at the racetrack on Friday evening. "Then, for clarity's sake, just so I don't get into trouble—*when* you kiss me again, is it okay to kiss you back?"

She didn't miss his *when* rather than *if*. She crossed her arms over her chest. "Let me spell it out for you. No kissing. None. You're not kissing me. I'm not kissing you. I'm not asking. I'm not doing. Nada." Good. She'd sounded resolute. Strong. No hint there that she desperately wanted to taste him, touch him, and likewise feel his hands and his mouth on various and sundry parts of her.

Another one of those looks that tightened every cell in her body into acute, aching awareness that she was a woman. "That's too bad. Just kissed is a good look on you."

"I'll keep that in mind." Breathe. She needed to remember to breathe…and not kiss him…or take her clothes off. Work. Renovation. The matter at hand. "Now, to borrow one of your phrases, we're burning daylight. What do you need for me to do?"

"Since you just told me it's off-limits—" his glance zeroed in and lingered on her mouth, and the wanton fire inside her flamed a little hotter, higher, brighter "—I guess we'll skip to the second item on the list." A tsunami of turn-on assaulted her. One look. One moment of innuendo and she was wet, her nipples were hard and her clit ached.

"I need you to get on your knees…" He paused deliberately, and it was a small wonder she didn't spontaneously combust at the implication of her on her knees, his fly undone, his dick in her mouth. At this point he could probably talk her through an orgasm… which had never happened before but seemed totally one hundred percent plausible right here and now.

"…to scrape paint off the baseboards."

So much for her orgasm.

HE WAS HOISTED on his own petard, as his Grandpa Stillwell had been fond of saying. Beau had deliberately saddled Natalie with the most menial, uncomfortable task at hand. However, he hadn't counted on the effect of her on her knees, bending over, her tight, round ass thrust in the air.

"You know, if you make your stroke a little longer and smoother, it'll be better for you. Slow it down a little, baby girl, or you're going to wear yourself out before you even get started."

She looked back over her shoulder at him and he'd asked for it, he'd taken it there, but it was such a sexual look it slammed him in the gut.

Her cell phone went off in her purse, shattering the moment. She scrambled to get up off the floor, and he automatically scooped up her purse and handed it to her.

"Thanks," she said, her fingers glancing against his ever so briefly, but still rousing.

"You're welcome." Dammit to hell, every time they touched it was as if someone had yanked a rug out from under his feet.

She pulled out the phone and answered. "Hi, Mom… No, it's fine… I'm just working… I know… Right… Maybe sometime next week… No, I don't want Miguel to think I don't love him… No, I know it's important that he knows he's important to me."

Who in the hell was Miguel? And why'd her mother have to remind her that he needed to know he was important and that she loved him? He'd assumed, based on their conversation and the way she'd kissed him, there was no boyfriend in the picture.

"I'm just busy," she said.

Ignoring Beau, Natalie knelt down again and started scraping, propping the phone between her ear and her shoulder. Beau heard her mother's voice faintly over the line. He couldn't hear her words but he picked up on the gently remonstrative tone. He had no difficulty in discerning a Southern mama guilt trip, having been on the receiving end several times, most of the time for good reason.

"Look, Mom, I hate to cut this short but I see my appointment parking their car up front and I don't want to be on the phone when they walk in." The next part came out in a rush. "I'll see you next week. Love you."

She ended the call and shot Beau a look where he

stood propped against the staircase. "Don't say anything," she dared. "I know it was a lie, but you don't know my mother. Once she starts…"

Beau grinned. "You've met my mother? I totally understand." For a moment they both shared a laugh, her expression unguarded. The laughter died and he found himself looking into her motor oil-brown eyes and wanting…more. More than a kiss, more than her naked beneath him—although that would be damn nice. He had a hankering to *know* Natalie Bridges. What did she do when she wasn't busy aiding and abetting the attachment of ball and chain? And who the hell was Miguel?

"Who's Miguel?"

She went back to scraping, following his directive with a slow, smooth rhythm that put him in mind of her hand on his… Hell, who was he kidding? Her simply breathing seemed to put him in mind of her hand—or some equally stimulating body part—on his cock.

"My newest 'brother.' My parents foster kids. Miguel arrived last week and I haven't gotten out to meet him yet. I know. My parents are great, but they're…different."

Yeah, he'd be in much better shape to think about her parents than the slide of her smooth, soft hand against his hard… "Where do they live?"

"West of Nashville. They've got a farm with a big garden, chickens, ponies, a rambling farm house, and it's just crazy there." She shook her head, a sweet smile lifting the corners of her delicious mouth. "Always crazy. I can't tell you how many times I'd go to bed at night only to wake up and find a new sister in my room the next morning."

"It sounds—"

She rocked back on her heels, scraper in hand. "Chaotic. Total chaos. I lived for the times I could go to my grandparents' house. Memaw and I would sit on the porch swing at night and she'd tell me stories." She radiated a sweetly vulnerable nostalgia that tugged at him. He had an instant image of her as a pigtailed little girl curled up beside her grandmother. "The other kids would go over in twos or threes, but Memaw always insisted that when it was my turn, I was the only one allowed over. She knew I needed that alone time. And it made me feel special."

He nodded, sharing an understanding from his own childhood. "Nana, my dad's mother, and my mother got along about like oil and water, but Nana always made banana pudding when I came over. It's my favorite. She'd make a separate dish just for me and add extra bananas and vanilla wafers to it." He hadn't thought about Nana's pudding in years. He shook his head. "So is Shelby your biological sister or your foster sister?"

She set about scraping again, her hair falling forward in a wavy curtain of brown and red. "Foster."

She pushed her hair aside and slanted a glance his way. "And the answer to the next question that inevitably comes is, I don't have any biological siblings but I have twenty, well, twenty-one now with Miguel, siblings. And, no, they didn't all live there at once. The house is usually at full capacity with ten. But most of us come back for holidays and special occasions." She looked back down. "And they are all great, and I do feel guilty that I haven't met Miguel yet. You can't imagine Thanksgiving and Christmas. You'd have to see it to believe it." Both tenderness and exasperation marked her tone.

Paint flecks peppered her hair. "Are you trying to take me home to meet your mother already?"

Teasing her was too much fun. He couldn't pass up the opportunity.

She made a noise that sounded suspiciously like a snort. "My mother would like you." Beau preened. "She likes anyone and everyone…regardless of how annoying they are."

Beau guffawed, his laughter coming from deep in his belly. "Smart-ass."

She grinned and he felt the same knock-you-on-your-ass sensation he did when he kicked it off the starting line in a race. "I was just saying…"

He wanted her with an intensity that was foreign to him, given he was always the one in control. The mood between them shifted, intensified, thickened. Her eyes widened.

Beau moved toward her, slowly, deliberately. "Do you always mean what you say?"

Had she really meant no more kissing? They both knew what he was asking.

She steadied herself with one hand on the floor and ran the tip of her tongue along the bow of her upper lip. There was no mistaking the flicker of heat in her eyes. "Not…always."

Green light. He reached down and dragged her up his body and into his arms. Her scent, the feel of her soft curves against his hard angles, the almost imperceptible hitch of her breath… Yes, he'd wanted this all last night, all day today. "Speak now, baby girl, or forever hold your peace if you meant what you said earlier."

The scraper clattered to the floor and she placed her open palms against his chest, tilting her head back to gaze up at him. "What if Tilson shows up? He did last night."

He slid his hand up her arm to trace the fine line of her jaw. Her skin felt like velvet against his fingertips. "Tilson won't show up. Trust me."

Her eyes darkened and her fingers curled against his chest, sending his inner temperature spiking off the charts. "How do you know?"

The fall of her hair teased against the back of his hand. "Tilson won't show up because I told him you were off-limits."

She went rigid. "You what?"

"Off-limits. I told him you were mine." He plied his thumb along the fullness of her lower lip and pulled her closer still with his other arm. "Natalie, baby girl, consider my claim staked."

8

_____

I TOLD HIM you were mine. Natalie, baby girl, consider my claim staked.

He'd told Tilson she was *his?*

That was so…arrogant.

So heavy-handed.

So *hot.*

"Staking claims goes both ways." She looped her arms around his neck, bringing them into intimate full-body contact. God, this was such a very, very bad idea, but he felt so very, very good against her. "We have something in common because I don't like to share, either." She'd seen the women at the racetrack swarm him.

"Done." One step forward and he pinned her to the wall. He bent his head. His cheek nearly touched hers, his hair tickled against her skin as he commanded softly in her ear, his breath warm against her skin, "Now, say it."

She could barely think with the hard wall behind her and the hard wall of man in front of her. "Say what?"

Beau sifted one hand through her hair. "I told you

you'd ask me to kiss you." He traced the line from her ear to her jaw with the bridge of his nose, his breath deliciously hot against her neck. He was slowly, well, maybe not so slowly, driving her out of her mind. "So, ask for it."

She thought not. "If you want it, take it," she challenged him, "but I'm not *asking* for anything."

An almost imperceptible shift of his hips against hers brought his erection in direct contact between her thighs. "Do you always make things so hard?" he said.

"I'm flattered." She rubbed against him.

"You make me crazy." He groaned, resting his forehead against hers. "You have from the first moment I saw you."

It was gratifying to know she wasn't in this emotional-physical morass of self-destruction alone. "Yet another thing in common."

With a tenderness that melted her from the inside out and made her grateful for the support of the wall and his body, he brushed butterfly kisses over her eyelids, down her nose, his mouth finally coming to claim hers. Hot, strong, his lips did exactly what he'd promised— staked his claim. From the sweet, fleeting press of that well-shaped mouth against her eyelids to the devouring of her lips, every kiss proclaimed *his, his, his.*

She'd been kissed and she'd kissed, but never, not even with him last night, anything like this. She ached. She resonated with need. Every inch of her craved every inch of him.

She didn't want to want him. Wrong man. Wrong situation. But it simply didn't matter.

He kissed and felt like homemade sin. She moaned into his mouth and he answered her with a groan as their tongues mated. She slid her hands over his shoulders—she'd never seen or felt such broad shoulders—and was further turned on by the bunching play of muscle and sinew beneath her fingertips and palms. She tugged his shirt loose from his jeans at the same time he delved beneath her shirt hem.

The faint scrape of those calluses he'd pointed out earlier, along with the totally masculine feel of skin over taut muscle, nearly sent her over the top. He insinuated one leg between her thighs as if he intuitively knew her knees weren't quite capable of doing their job. In a moment of instant decision, she grabbed his shirt by the hem and tugged it up.

Beau laughed low and husky, breaking their kiss to finish taking it off. "Baby girl, I like it when Naughty Natalie comes out to play."

She leaned her head against the wall and devoured him with her eyes and her hands. She felt punch-drunk on lust. Pride, circumspection, any scrap of inhibition or reason, all became meaningless. "You have no idea."

She leaned into him and kissed the hair-roughed wall of his chest. His shudder reverberated against her, through her. She found and lapped at his flat male nipple, teasing her tongue against the eraser-tip point, inhaling the scent of his skin, of him. His heart hammered beneath her splayed hand, and his breath came in a ragged draw, much like her own.

"Natalie…baby…"

In a haze of touching and kissing, they moved, stumbling into the front room, which boasted a couch. Lit only by the hall light, she vaguely registered the room and furniture as those in Cash's video. In one swift move, Beau tugged and tossed the dust cover aside. He sank to the couch and she went down after him, straddling him, seating his erection right against her most needy part. Even through denim and under-wear, it felt so good she moaned aloud.

He swooped in and captured the moan with his mouth. Long seconds later, cool air kissed her skin as he worked her shirt up.

"You are definitely, one hundred percent over-dressed," Beau said with a toe-curling smile. "Let me take care of that for you." He tugged her shirt over her head.

"Because you're helpful that way?" she asked.

He tossed the shirt aside. Even in the shadowy light she saw appreciation glittering in his eyes. "I like to do my part."

She ought to be nervous. He was gorgeous and women flocked around him, and God knows, while she was okay in the face and body department, her boobs were real, there was a sag factor and she was carrying some extra pounds around the middle. Instead, excitement and pure sexual arousal doused any sparks of self-consciousness. And the room's semi-darkness didn't hurt, either.

She was on the verge of spontaneous combustion. "A regular Boy Scout."

He slid his hands up her sides, seemingly unperturbed by the curves, and she closed her eyes, savoring his touch. "I was never a Boy Scout," he said, his voice low and husky.

She still had on most of her clothes. They should stop. She should stop. She should crawl right off his lap, put her shirt back on and go about her business of scraping paint and planning weddings. Except *should* didn't go far when his arousal was nestled against her mound, her skin was absorbing his scent and he'd just unhooked her bra.

She opened her eyes and teased him with a moue of feigned disappointment. "Hmm. Too bad. I always had a thing for Boy Scouts."

He slid her bra off, and his swift intake of breath and the surge of his cock against her as he looked at her bare breasts stoked her own fire. He circled one pouting nipple with his fingertip. "Screw the Boy Scouts."

"Well, I actually never—" His finger grazed her hardened tip and the sensation shot straight to her womb.

"Baby girl, you are about to forget all about Boy Scouts." Before she could blink, she went from on his lap to on her back. He was good.

And then he was on her like a starving man presented with a five-course meal and she was totally, absolutely, officially rendered mindless.

The scrape of his five-o'clock shadow against her neck.

The rasp of his hands on her breasts.

Oh. My. God.

His hot, wet mouth feasting on her nipples.

His nimble fingers delving past her unzipped jeans—when did her jeans get unzipped—into her panties and then, "Oh, yes!" Her cry reverberated off the walls as he dipped his finger into her drenched folds.

"Ba-by girl…you are…so hot…so wet…."

Please… His finger felt so good but it wasn't enough…not nearly enough. A desperate yearning swept through her. She toed off her shoes and shifted her hips up, shucking jeans and panties in record time. He was equally efficient at losing his clothes, but she still beat him to the draw—work boots were apparently a bitch to take off.

She'd seen him wearing nothing more than a towel, but not even *that* had prepared her for *this*. His cock, long, thick and heavy, sprang proudly from a thatch of dark hair. She'd thought it wasn't possible to get any wetter than she already was. She was wrong.

"You've got something for me?" she said.

When had she ever been so bold, so demanding? But when had she ever felt like this? She'd known desire but never this uncontrolled need to have a man, *this* man, inside her. Her vibrator had been a poor, poor substitute last night for what she really wanted. She opened her legs and dragged a finger along her drenched channel in blatant invitation.

His hands were gratifyingly unsteady as he rolled on a condom. His fingers splayed against her thighs, he spread her further and the head of his cock nudged against her nether lips. "Natalie—"

She was somewhere past waiting. She thrust up, taking him into her body. Yes, yes, yes. More.

A low keening burst from his throat. He drove into her, hard and fast. She arched up against him, welcoming him. They both paused, as if of one accord, her eyes locked with his, and she savored the stretch of her body to accommodate the fullness of him, the tight fit of him inside her, as if they'd been custom-made for one another. It was as if his heartbeat became hers, her breath became his, two separate parts merging to make a whole.

He grasped her thighs in his big hands and lifted her. Instinctively she wrapped her legs around him, pulling him deeper, harder still inside her.

Moving in tandem, she met his thrusts. Yes. Over and over and over, the sensations notching her higher and higher and higher. Beau, his eyes glittering, his features etched tight and hot, reached between them and found her clit, pushing her over the edge and plunging behind her as she free fell through waves of pleasure.

BEAU CAME BACK into the room after cleaning up and collapsed onto his back, bringing Natalie with him.

Her heart pounded against him, echoing his own frantic tattoo, and her hair spilled across his chest and shoulder. He'd known, somewhere down the line, they'd wind up in bed together but he really hadn't planned on this now.

"That was…" He searched for the right word.

"A mistake," she supplied, her voice muffled by his chest, her words vibrating against him.

"Hell, no. I was trying to decide between *fantastic* and *incredible*." Well, damn. Her take on it actually suited his overall purpose of driving her away, but in the gratification department he found he didn't like being considered a *mistake*. "That felt like a mistake to you?" He lay there and absorbed the feel of her skin against his, the press of her breasts against his bare chest. He idly smoothed his hand over the silky skin of her bare bottom. She immediately quivered against him and pressed her crotch into his. "Mistake, my ass."

Her soft laugh tickled the hair on his chest and she crossed her hands beneath her chin to look at him. She literally took his breath away. Her hair was a sexy mess and her lips were kiss-swollen. "It's a mistake from the standpoint that you and I shouldn't be doing this. I never mix business with pleasure—" at least she was categorizing them as pleasure "—and I'm not in the habit of jumping into bed—"

He captured a curl around his finger. "Then you're fine because this isn't a bed."

She rolled her eyes at him. "You know what I mean."

"Do you think I don't know that? Do you think I didn't know that from the moment you burst into my toter home on one heel? And tell me we didn't both know from that very second that we were going to wind up here together."

"But you're not my type."

Goddamn but he was getting tired of her hammering home that he wasn't what she wanted in a man. However, come to think of it… "You're not my type, either."

"Then how'd this happen?"

The efficient, everything-on-a-schedule wedding planner looked so adorably bewildered and confounded he had to chuckle. "Well, technically, I'm not sure if it started with that kiss or with the clothes coming off." He followed the indent of her spine down the smooth slope of her back with his hands. "Did you think about me last night after you left? I thought about you. I thought about calling someone to hook up with but that didn't work because I wanted you."

A pleased smile curved her lips. "You could have called me."

He explored the dimples at the top of her buttocks and the crease that bisected her lovely ass. He found he wanted to explore, to learn, to touch and taste every inch of her, which was something of a new experience for him. Typically, he had a good time, he made sure the woman had a good time, and that was that. With Natalie, he wanted to linger.

"We both know that wouldn't have got me anywhere. And you never answered my question." He cupped one cheek in each hand and kneaded. "Did you think about me when you left last night?"

She looked down as if suddenly fascinated by his chest. "Yes." She glanced back up and locked gazes with him. She rimmed her upper lip with the tip of her tongue. "I was wet all night."

Her frankness both surprised and delighted him. It also got the full attention of his dick. His phoenix was rising.

"Did you touch yourself?" he asked, teasing one finger against her from behind.

"Of course I did. Did you?"

"Uh-huh."

He'd started it, and she was laying it on the line. He found the whole conversation hot as hell.

How far would she take the conversation?

"Tell me about it," he said. "Tell me about touching yourself."

She deliberately licked her finger and then traced his nipple with the wet tip. She laughed softly as the contact hummed through his body and sent his cock into full erection against her. "You just want me to talk dirty to you."

"There is that," he said with a grin. "Guilty as

charged." He sobered. "But I really, really want to know what you did."

She levered up to a sitting position. "Put on a condom."

For once, he made short order of following directions, his hands not quite steady. She was unlike any woman he'd ever known before. He felt this need to be part of her, as if when he was joined with her, he was something more than just him.

And then all reflective thought evaporated as she slid her tight wet channel down on his cock, seating him deep inside her. "You were going to tell me about touching yourself," he prompted while he could still talk.

She paused and canted her head to one side as if in deep consideration. "I don't know…."

She-devil. She wasn't being shy, she was toying with him. "You know you want to tell me."

She rocked against him. "I don't know anything of the sort."

He cupped her breasts in his hands and rolled her nipples between his fingers. "C'mon, baby. Tell me."

Well, she was right. He did want her to talk dirty to him.

Her voice was low and sultry as she began to describe touching herself in graphic detail, using all the words men liked to hear and women were sometimes reluctant to say, accompanying her story with a slow ride up and down his dick.

Sweet and hot, and he gritted his teeth to keep from coming. "At this rate I'm never going to get the baseboards finished," she said with a teasing smile, sliding her slick folds along his length.

"Later." He grasped her hips and lifted her. "It's story time now."

"Where was I?"

"The good part…"

She sank back down on his erection, and he felt as if he'd just been hit with a shot of nitrous.

"Which was the good part?" she asked with a wickedly sensual smile.

Beau groaned and thrust up on her down stroke, eliciting a gasp of pleasure from her. "It's all the good part, so just start talking."

9

THE MUSIC of the cicadas filled the night when Natalie and Beau stepped out of the house. A sliver of a moon peeked over the tree line and a breeze whispered through the trees. His hand rested on her hip, and she was aware of the heat from his splayed fingers even through her clothes. The hallway light spilled out of the front door, leaving the rest of the night darker than ever.

He insisted on walking her to her car, and it hadn't gone unnoticed on her part that he'd held the door open for her on the way out of the house. She turned to face him, loath to open her car door and have the harsh dome light ruin the night's soft, velvety darkness.

He brushed his fingers over her jaw. "Do you want to give me five minutes to pick everything up here so you can at least follow me back to Dahlia or even Nashville?" he offered. "It's pretty dark and these country roads can be confusing."

Without thinking, she turned and pressed a kiss to his open hand, the marks of hard work lining his palm.

He was the oddest mixture of man. Arrogant. Infuriating. Thoughtful. His offer weighed in on the thoughtful side but she really needed some distance. She was torn. The truth of the matter was she didn't want to leave at all. She wanted whatever this was to-night to last, to never end. But nothing was static and tomorrow would come, bringing relentless change. So maybe she didn't want to leave but she needed to think, and that didn't include watching his taillights between here and home.

She tried to inject a light note. "Thanks for the offer, but I've never lost my sense of direction due to great sex before. I think it'll be okay." She delib-erately stepped away from the heat of his body, when what she really wanted was for him to wrap his arms around her and enfold her like a big, warm blanket. "I guess I'll see you bright and early tomor-row morning."

That was an understatement. She'd have to be up at the crack of dawn to make it back out here by six friggin' thirty. At least she'd be driving against rush hour traffic at that time.

"Wait." As if he'd read her mind, he gathered her close. He was solid and she could get so used to being right here, his heart beating beneath her cheek. "You've got to give me more than that, baby girl," he murmured as he buried his hands in her hair and bent his head.

With a blissful sigh, she wound her arms about his neck and finished pulling his mouth down to hers. His lips and tongue plundered her as if he were a pirate who'd just discovered a treasure chest. And there it was again, that low, insistent throb deep inside her that he awakened so easily. If she was going to leave—and she had to leave—she had to go now. She dragged herself away from him. "I have to go."

He scrubbed his hand through his hair, his face inscrutable in the dark. "I know."

"You know we've got to get some work done in the morning," she said, struggling to remind them both why she was here in the first place.

Even in the dark, she glimpsed his slow, knowing smile and it sent a rush through her all over again. They both knew work would come afterwards. "Then how about six-fifteen instead of six-thirty?"

Never mind, she'd be up well before dawn. And if she was crawling out of bed at four-thirty, they ought to at least make it worth both of their time. "How about six?"

She opened the car door and the dome light was more like a beacon.

"Six works." Another slow smile that tied her up in knots of anticipation. She got in and buckled up. Beau leaned in and brushed a kiss over her forehead. "Drive safe."

He closed her door and tapped on the window, reminding her to lock the doors. It was a testimony to her willpower that she didn't look back at him as she drove down the oak-lined driveway.

She didn't relax until she reached the main road and turned out of Belle Terre's entrance. She still couldn't quite believe Beau had declared her his. Both annoying and a turn-on—much like the man himself.

The dark country roads twisted and turned and she focused exclusively on driving until she reached the stop sign where she picked up the highway to the interstate. She dialed Cynthia.

"Natalie! I thought you were never going to call. I want to hear all about your enforced bondage but first I've got a surprise for you. Are you sitting down?"

"I'm driving." She put on her blinker and merged into the right lane.

"Oh, right. Guess who dropped by the shop today looking for you."

She couldn't think of any appointments she'd had today that she might've missed or even anyone she'd met as a prospective wedding client. Unless it was the cute little blonde, Alex Morgan, that she'd met…was it only last night? "Alex Morgan?"

"Who's Alex Morgan?"

So much for that guess. "A prospect and obviously not who came by."

"Try Shad Jackson. Looking for you."

Shadwell Jackson III. Newest junior partner at Jackson, Burns and Liswick Law Offices. Numero Uno contender, in her book, for the Prince Charming role. "Oh."

"That's all you can come up with? Oh?"

"Maybe he got engaged and wants me to handle the wedding."

"Or maybe he said he hoped you could make a cocktail party with him next Thursday night. He said he wanted to get on your calendar before anyone else beat him to the punch. I penciled him in." Cynthia sounded as if she was bouncing up and down, which she had a tendency to do when she was excited.

Natalie, however, wanted to bang her head against the steering wheel. Damn it all to hell…and back. Why now? Why not a month from now, when she and Beau Stillwell weren't, in all probability, still setting the sheets afire? Hadn't they just had a discussion, of sorts, about staking claims and not sharing? Beau wouldn't be happy if she was going out with Shad next Thursday, the same way she wouldn't be happy if he took one of those silicone-breasted Barbies to that burger joint, Headlights. The other option was to pull out of whatever it was they'd started before next week…and she just didn't know if she had the willpower to do that…not yet, anyway.

"Hello? Oddly enough this silence does not strike me as the 'I'm-so-excited variety.' What's up, Natalie?"

She still wore Beau's scent on her skin, the taste of him against her tongue, the feel of him imprinted on her cellular memory. She swallowed hard. "I can't go with Shad then."

"Look. I know how important financial stability and independence is to you. I know the Stillwell-Vickers gig is the break you've been looking for to put you on the high-end wedding planner map, but you work so hard. Go have a little fun. Don't worry about the repair thing at Belle Terre. God knows, I don't have anything going on after regular hours. I'll cover you on that. I can fill in at Belle Terre with Beau Stillwell next Thursday. Heck, I probably know as much about renovation as you do."

A possessiveness Natalie didn't even know was in her rushed to the forefront. Over her dead body. "I don't think so."

"Natalie? What's going on? Exactly what happened tonight?"

"Exactly isn't important, but I can't go with Shad."

"You didn't…you did. You made out with Beau Stillwell again."

Natalie laughed weakly.

"Jumping Jehoshaphat. You did more than make out, didn't you? You slept with him?"

"It was the best sex I've ever had." Granted she was sure he'd logged in lots and lots of practice, but still… And she didn't consider it kissing and telling if she was being complimentary about him in bed. "But go ahead and tell me how unprofessional that was because it was. Terribly. But, my God, it was great."

"Confession time. I did an Internet search on him after you left this morning. You know, since he races I thought there would be pictures. There were. He's gorgeous, Natalie." Yes. She was ashamed of the sentiment, but double hell, no way was she letting Cynthia anywhere near Beau. She quite seriously had no intention of sharing. "Not your usual type—certainly nothing like Shad, but the man has sexy down to an art. If he decided he wanted you, I'm not sure that even supergluing your legs shut would have done any good."

Natalie laughed again, and even she picked up on the faint note of near-hysteria. "Ouch. You know you come up with some gross imagery."

"Whatever. Look. Caitlyn's not going to freak out because you have a fling with her brother. It's probably a much shorter list of women who haven't or at least wanted to. And he's got love 'em and leave 'em written all over him. You're looking at a couple of weeks, tops a month. Enjoy it. Best sex of your life? How often does that happen? Go for it, but for God's sake, don't do something crazy like tell Shad you're seeing someone else. Just put him off for a while. You're busy, another commitment, that kind of thing. Heck, he probably came around because you didn't show up at the museum opening on Friday night. You can thank Beau for Shad going on the offensive."

Her head was spinning, emotionally she was a jumbled mess, and none of this was par for her course. "I bet Shad was a Boy Scout. And I bet he doesn't have any calluses." Funny how neither notion was as appealing as it had been three hours ago.

"Huh?"

"Never mind. Don't you think that's kind of…I don't know…not right to string them both along?"

"Then dump Beau because Shad's the safe one of the two."

Cynthia was absolutely right, even if she might have some subconscious, vested interest in Natalie foregoing Beau. The only safe aspect to Beau was the certainty that whatever they had was temporary. Prince Charming was always safe and Beau was no Prince Charming. Wasn't that part of the appeal of the whole Prince Charming persona? "You're right." But even now, when she should be totally sated, was totally sated, 6:00 a.m. felt like a lifetime away. "I'll dump him…a little later."

"Natalie—"

Another call clicked in on Call Waiting. Beau's name and number flashed up. "Look, he's on the other line. I'll see you in the morning after I've finished up at Belle Terre." She didn't wait for Cynthia to reply before clicking over to the other line. "Hi."

"Hi," he returned the greeting. One word, single syllable, and he sent shivers skittering over her skin. "I wanted to let you know…for in the morning…"

Dammit. She just passed her exit. "Yes?"

"I like my coffee black."

If he thought for a minute she was fetching him coffee… "Good. Make sure you order it that way."

His laughter exploded on the other end. "I knew you'd say something like that."

Now that she knew he was teasing, well, it had been pretty funny. She teased back. "Are you saying I'm predictable?"

"Not at all." His voice dropped to an intimate note and she knew he was thinking about her recounting her self-gratification while she rode him to an orgasm. "You're full of surprises. I was calling because I didn't know whether you'd rather have a cheese Danish in the morning or a blueberry muffin. Pammy's Petals makes the best stuff you ever put in your mouth."

She had the distinct feeling that he'd turn out to be the best thing she ever put in her mouth but she kept that thought to herself. "You're bringing breakfast?"

"No, baby girl, you're bringing breakfast. I'm just bringing the snack for afterwards."

Six o'clock couldn't come soon enough...and neither could she. "In that case, make it a cheese Danish. And pick up a small container of extra icing. I've got a sweet tooth."

AT FIVE-FORTY, Beau pulled up in front of Belle Terre. The impending sunrise brushed the horizon in shades of pink and orange. Was Natalie admiring the same thing? He knew a momentary pang of guilt that he had manipulated her schedule to wear her out. She couldn't have gotten home before ten last night, and chances were she hadn't dropped right into bed when she walked through the door.

He shook off his twinge of conscience and hauled out the quilt and the goodies from Pammy's. He'd make it worth Natalie's while.

He'd stayed later than he'd planned last night, checking out the fireplace in the front room—a building inspector had given it a good-to-go clearance but he'd wanted to make sure himself—and laying in wood for a fire. Belle Terre had come fully furnished, right down to the firewood stacked out back.

He struck a match to the kindling and spread the quilt on the large wool rug a safe distance from the snapping and popping fire, one of the benefits of seasoned wood. He placed the bag from Pammy's at one corner of the blanket and double-checked his jeans pocket. A four-strip of condoms? Check. Four was doubtful, but hey, even though he was no Boy Scout, better to be prepared.

He realized with a start that the unusual feeling in the pit of his stomach was nerves. When had he ever been nervous like this? He always wanted women to have a good time, to leave satisfied, but now, he realized with a start, he found he really wanted Natalie to walk through the door and be surprised. He wanted to earn a spontaneous smile of pleasure. And, he also realized, he was so damn sick and tired of her I'd-never-go-out-with-you-because-you're-not-my-type song that he wanted to teach her another verse. But, and it was a big but, he didn't want her to fall for him. That would be messy and sticky and that was why he pretty much stayed away from women like Natalie.

And…she was here…or else Tilson had pulled in, and if that was the case, Tilson could pull out pronto. Nope, it was Natalie's van. He watched from the window as she got out of her vehicle. She was wearing a coat. Good thing he'd built a fire to take off the chill in the tall-ceilinged room. She rounded the front of the van. Wait. That was a trench coat belted around her waist. A good look with those high heels, but when had the forecast changed to rain?

Dammit. He had two roofing crews scheduled today and if it rained, he was screwed. He double-checked the sky. Clear. It didn't look like rain but apparently Natalie knew something he didn't. What was he going to do with six guys he couldn't work today who depended on him to get in hours to feed their families? Goddammit, he should've done a late-night weather check instead of thinking about how he could please Natalie. He'd never lost his work focus like this.

The front door opened and closed and the tap-tap-tap of her high heels petered out on an air of uncertainty. "Beau?"

"In here," he said, trying to set aside the worry of how to keep two crews busy on a rainy day. He supposed he could haul them out here, but then that would put this project on schedule, which was precisely what he *didn't* want to happen.

She appeared in the doorway and he didn't have to work to summon a smile, especially when she saw the fire with the quilt spread before it. "Lovely," she said, her brown eyes widening with delight.

"No. I'm looking at lovely." Where had that come from? He never said stuff like that, but it had been a spontaneous reaction to…her. She was beyond lovely.

"Thank you." She crossed the room, her hips swaying beneath that raincoat, her legs bare and shapely in red heels. She stood between the fireplace and the quilt. "I need help with some decisions. I couldn't make up my mind this morning."

"I'm your man."

"For starters, the hair. Up or—" she reached up and pulled out a clip, sending her hair tumbling about her shoulders in a sexy tangle with a small shake of her head "—down?"

His throat went dry. "Down," he managed in a rasp. "Definitely down."

A secretive smile played about her lips. "Down it is." She tossed the clip to the floor. "Next—" she untied the sash with nimble fingers and started working the buttons free on her double-breasted trench coat "—the coat. On or—" she finished the last button and opened her coat "—off."

For a few long seconds he stood rooted to the spot, transfixed. Naked. Gloriously, hotly, sexily, erotically, totally naked. "Off. Definitely off. But keep on the shoes."

"I had a feeling you'd say that."

"Predictable?"

"Not totally." Her glanced flickered to the fireplace and the quilt on the floor. "Only in a good way."

She shrugged the coat back down her shoulders. "And look who's overdressed now."

Before he forgot and had to scramble for them later, he pulled out the condom strips and tossed them to the quilt's edge.

She raised an eyebrow? "Four? You must be a morning person."

"I'm trying to make up for my lack of formal Boy Scout training by always being prepared."

"Hmm." She let the raincoat fall to the floor and knelt at the edge of the blanket to open the bakery bag. "Did they have extra frosting?"

He was rock-hard already and she was worried about what he'd brought from the bakery. "Yeah. I bought one cream cheese and one vanilla."

"Which is your favorite?" she asked, hefting a lidded cup in each hand.

"Definitely cream cheese."

"Okay, then." She put the vanilla back in the bag.

He leaned down and unlaced his boots and then hopped from one foot to the other, taking off his boots and socks. He was going to have to find other footwear as long as Natalie was around.

"Yum. Still nice and warm and gooey." He looked up and damn near fell over. She was on her back, propped on one arm. She held the container of cream cheese frosting in the other hand. She'd coated her nipples in icing and was pouring a small trail down her belly and over first one hip and then the other.

Steadfastly ignoring him, she dipped a finger in the cup and raised her right leg in the air, smearing a generous helping from ankle to knee and then knee to inner thigh. He silently watched, taking off his clothes, while she repeated it on the other leg. He damn near lost it when she tilted her hips upward, drizzled it between her open thighs, and gasped as the warm icing found its target. She finally seemed to notice he was still in the room.

She dipped her finger once again in the frosting and brought it to her mouth. She deliberately licked the white glob off her finger with her pink tongue. She leaned back on both elbows, wearing red heels, cream-cheese frosting and an inviting smile. "Breakfast is served. I hope you like it hot, sticky and sweet."

10

"IF THAT WAS BREAKFAST, it boggles my mind to think what you'd turn out for a four-course dinner," Beau said with a smirk that turned her insides all wonky.

She ignored the wonky feeling and diligently scraped away, having cleaned up and changed into jeans and a T-shirt. "Don't sidetrack me. I've got to get this section finished before I leave this morning." However, she wasn't above shooting him a sideways glance from beneath her lashes and tacking on, "And that Danish was incredibly good."

He returned her look from where he was cutting lumber on a table saw in the corner. "I told you it was the best thing you'd ever put in your mouth."

Instinctively she dropped her gaze to the crotch of his jeans. "Second-best thing."

"Look at me again that way and you can forget all about finishing that section," he said with a mock growl.

He so easily tied her up in knots inside, it was gratifying to know she held the same power over him. She laughed. "Okay. I'll be good."

"Oh, you were very, very good." His low, seductive

voice sent a shiver through her that had nothing to do with the room's temperature. "That's the problem."

"It didn't seem like a problem earlier."

"It wasn't before. It's just now when you're insisting on actually working."

Lord, but he was great for her ego…actually, the way he'd licked and sucked every bit of icing off every bit of her, he was great for a lot of things. And if she had a remote prayer of finishing this section of scraping, she would not think about his clever tongue swirling that icing off her hoo-ha. It was much more prudent to focus on the food itself rather than the sex. "The Danish came from Pammy's? Is all of her stuff that quality?"

Beau nodded. "Her cakes are even better. Pammy did the cake for Caitlyn's college graduation. The woman can bake like nobody's business."

Natalie swatted away the instant flicker of jealousy his comment provoked. For all she knew, Pammy was married with six kids and a husband at home. And he'd complimented her baking, not her prowess in the bedroom. Natalie obviously needed more sleep than she'd got last night if she was going to react so ridiculously to such an innocuous comment.

"Caitlyn wants her to handle the wedding cake, the groom's cake and the reception pastries," she said. "I needed to stop by and wanted to sample something so this worked out well." She knew he was playing her by having her scrape baseboards. And in turn, she'd played him by making a production of being on her knees with her butt in the air. But she still hadn't figured out exactly what was behind this game he was playing. "Look, I'm seriously worried about scheduling and getting all of this done in the time frame we're looking at."

He shrugged. "Construction and remodel can be iffy. It's not unusual to have to adjust time lines."

"That's fine." He obviously wasn't too concerned but she was—enough for both of them. "But we don't have a lot of room to play with. Their schedule is tight. That's why I'm here."

He made a calm-down gesture with his hands. "I don't have a race this weekend so I'll be working out here if you're available."

She couldn't read him. Was he asking whether she was available for sex or whether she was available to scrape baseboards? "Cynthia, my assistant, can handle the rehearsal and dinner on Friday evening." They often traded duties. Both of them seldom needed to be in the same place at the same time. Saturday's wedding was Natalie's, however. "I have a wedding on Saturday. It'll be late, and by the time the day is over I don't think I'd be a whole lot of help anyway."

That slow, suggestive smile that sent a furrow of heat through her belly curved his mouth. "It sounds as if you'd probably need your feet rubbed on Saturday night." And oh, my, he had that sexy drawl down to an art form.

Hard as it was to turn him down, she knew she'd be tired, and driving under those conditions didn't seem wise. "I don't think I'd be up for driving to Dahlia. This wedding is going to be exhausting."

"My truck knows how to get to the big city." Despite his smile and teasing words, his eyes were serious.

This was notching things up a level. It was one thing to fool around at Belle Terre, where she wouldn't return once the wedding was over, and a totally different animal altogether to have him at her place, in her bed. Did she want him there? In about two seconds she came up with a resounding *yes*. And who knew how long whatever they had going on would last? Anything burning this hot was sure to burn out equally fast. "My feet would be a good place to start."

"How about I bring dinner? If you like Thai, I could pick some up on my way in. There's a good Thai restaurant off I-40."

"I've never had Thai." It was a bit of a surprise that he had. She'd sort of slotted him as a meat and potatoes kind of guy.

"I could bring something else."

"No. I'd like to broaden my horizons and try something different."

"Mild or spicy?"

He was serious and it was crazy the way her heart was racing over the prospect of him showing up with dinner and a foot rub. "Definitely spicy. I like chicken. I prefer noodles over rice. Beyond that, surprise me."

He glanced at her coat folded by the door and quirked his lips into a pulse-pounding smile. "Don't expect me to show up wearing just a trench coat. I'm not looking to be arrested. By the way, you drove all the way from Nashville wearing just that coat and those heels?"

She laughed. "No. I stopped at the convenience store right before you get off the highway and changed in the bathroom."

Beau offered a quick nod of approval. "Resourceful."

"I try."

"What time should I be there?"

"Eight would be good if you can wait that long to eat."

"Eight would be perfect. I just need your address. I can pull the directions off MapQuest." He felt in his pocket and then looked around. "Damn. I've misplaced my BlackBerry."

He retraced his steps into the front room. She got up from her cramped position on the floor and helped him check under the sofa, beneath the coffee table and the arm chair.

"Do you have it set on ring tone or vibrate?" Natalie said.

"Ring tone."

"Okay, hold on a sec and I'll call you." She grabbed her phone and scrolled down to his name.

Within seconds AC/DC's "Highway to Hell" began to play from beneath the quilt's edge. What… "Is that your general ring tone or is that special for me?"

He grinned, crinkling the corners of his eyes, and she had her answer even before he uttered a confirming word. "I thought you deserved your own."

She couldn't contain her laughter. She reclaimed her spot on the floor and picked up the scraper. "'Highway to Hell'? I'm not sure whether I'm flattered or insulted." Which was patently untrue. It was funny, and they both knew it. There was a spot by the floor that just wasn't coming off. Or was that a nick in the wood. She leaned down to see better.

"I meant it in the best way possible. And you know I don't spend a buck to buy a ring tone for just anyone."

"Yeah? 'Highway to Hell' certainly makes me feel special." She glanced at him over her shoulder and realized he was somewhat mesmerized by her extreme on-her-knees position. Bad idea that it was, she nonetheless gave a little wiggle with her tush.

Two strides and he'd closed the gap between them. He stood behind her and she could practically feel the heat radiating from him, the sexual waves vibrating between them. "Everybody's different. Cream-cheese icing makes me feel special."

He hooked an arm around her waist and hauled her up, wrapping his arms around her from behind. She sighed and tilted her head to one side when his lips found the sensitive spot behind her right ear.

She offered a token protest. "I'm never going to get this baseboard finished." Even as she said it, she wiggled her bottom against the burgeoning bulge behind her, feeling the onslaught of wet heat between her thighs that was ever present when he was within touching distance. She let the scraper fall to the floor once again and curled her hand around the sinewy bulge of his bicep. The scent of arousal clung to them.

He chuckled as he nuzzled her neck and unbuttoned her jeans, working down the zipper. Her muscles tightened in anticipation of his touch. "Of course you will…just not this morning."

BEAU PARKED in the alley behind his mother's shop and used the back door. There was no point in going through the front, and besides, there was something kind of emasculating about walking through the door of a store with dresses and nightgowns in the front window. When his mama summoned him to her place of business he was a backdoor kind of guy—even though he was proud as punch of her.

He waited in the back until her customers cleared out. She greeted him with her customary hug and kiss on the cheek. He couldn't remember a single time from the day his father had died that his mother hadn't had a hug and kiss for him when he saw her.

She cocked her head to one side and studied him, pursing her lips. "Something about you looks different. Did you get a haircut?"

He ran his hand over his head. "No haircut. Maybe it's just the spring air." Ha. Maybe it was Natalie and the great sex, but that was hardly the thing a guy said to his mother. Even if he was thirty-two.

She merely quirked an eyebrow as if to say she didn't believe in the restorative power of a spring day, but wisely didn't press any further.

"You needed me?"

His mother, one of the original steel magnolias suddenly looked as nervous as a cat on the proverbial hot tin roof.

"I wanted to talk to you about something. I wanted to mention it to you before I talked to Caitlyn. I'd rather you hear it from me first. I mean, I've always felt as if we could talk about anything—well, within reason."

"Mom, you can discuss anything with me."

She drew a deep breath and said in a rush, "How would you feel about me dating? I mean, I think it's been a suitably decent interval since your father passed, and both you and Caitlyn are adults now and, well, how would you feel about that?"

All that on an exhale. "I think the first thing you should do is breathe before you pass out and mess up your hairdo."

His mother smiled and gratefully picked up his thread of silliness. "Well, Lila's right next door if I need a touch-up."

That had been one of the main appeals for his mother in locating her shop here. She was right next door to her best friend's hair and nail salon. And the same clientele frequented both.

"You're a grown woman and I've always thought you had great judgment—well, maybe not the time you made me clean all the toilets in the house for a month because I lied about my book report in fifth grade, but other than that you've had a good head on your shoulders." She swatted at him and he ducked before wrapping his arm around her shoulders. "I want you to be happy, and if going on a date makes you happy, then I want you to go on a date."

"You don't think I'm too old?"

"You're kidding, right?"

"That's reassuring." She beamed a smile of relief. "I didn't want to say yes or no until I'd talked to both you and your sister. Natalie said she thought y'all would be okay with it."

"You talked to Natalie about this?" Was it just in his head or was she beginning to insinuate herself in the fabric of his life? Planning his sister's wedding—which was, in fact, her job. Playing confidante to his mother. Blowing his mind…and various and sundry body parts.

"She was here doing some shopping and the timing was just right. She's such a sweetie. Good head on her shoulders. Pretty, too." She gave him a pointed look. "How're the renovations at Belle Terre going?"

"It's slow going."

"Why'd you really want her to help you out there?"

"Well, as you just pointed out, she's smart, easy on the eyes, and I needed help."

That made his mother laugh.

"I'm honored you talked to me about this," he said, getting back to her dating. "There's just a couple of things I'd like to cover with you before I leave, though." He clearly recalled the "talk" she'd had with him shortly before his eighteenth birthday. Bless her heart, she'd spoken to him as if he was still an untried boy, unaware that he'd been having sex since he was fifteen. One of the cheerleaders had initiated him into the pleasures of someone bringing him to climax rather than his hand. He managed to keep a straight face. "Dating is one thing, but I'd prefer not to wind up with a little brother or sister."

Bright red flooded her face. "I'm past that—" She stuttered to a halt. "You knew that. You're just teasing me."

"It'd sure be the talk of the town."

"Your daddy had that same sense of humor."

"I know. But I'm not him." He'd made damn sure of it. *He'd* never leave the people he was supposed to care about the most in the world destitute. *He'd* never seek his out in the bottom of a whiskey bottle.

He supposed he could thank his father for teaching those lessons by negative example. He was a better man for it, but he was still mad as hell that his mother and sister had suffered. And it galled him that his mother still mourned the man who'd put his love of gambling and Jack Daniel's before her. His father didn't deserve her loyalty or her love.

"I know you're not, son." She looked beyond him,

as if looking at him was too painful. "You try so hard… I've never known whether to tell you or not, but I'm thinking maybe I should."

"Tell me what?" This didn't sound good at all.

"Your father…he had problems, Beau."

He'd thought she was going to tell him something he didn't already know, something he hadn't spent sixteen years trying to fix. "No kidding."

She suddenly looked every bit her age and weary beyond words. "Your daddy was a manic-depressive." She exhaled a long breath as if she'd handed over a heavy weight. "It was an illness, Beau. A mental illness. That's how we wound up so in debt. When he'd cycle down, he'd spend money we didn't have. And the alcohol just made it all worse."

His chest felt tight. "Why are you telling me this?"

"Because you need to know. It's past due, but it's just always been easier not to mention it." She drew an unsteady breath. "It's hard to admit mental illness in your family." Her eyes grew wistful. "He was so much fun when we first met, when we first married. And Lord, he was so proud of you." She looked at Beau. "He was sick, son. It was as if he had a cancer, but it was a mental cancer."

Oddly enough, that did put a different spin on things. Beau had assumed his father had made irresponsible choices, but if an illness was driving him, how much had actually been choice? He realized his chest didn't feel nearly as tight, and the tension that had been coiled deep inside him for sixteen years didn't feel quite as intense. "All the more reason for you to be happy now. So, just make sure you practice safe sex, Ma," he said on a teasing note. She hated being called Ma.

"Beauregard Jameson Stillwell, you're not too old for…well, I guess you are, but…."

"S'okay, Ma. I'll behave. And I guess I need to head out 'cause it sounds like I better go home and clean my shotgun…just in case."

She laughed and pretended exasperation. "You're a mess."

"I've been told it's part of my charm." He dropped a kiss on the top of her head and headed for the door. Whoa. He'd totally dropped the ball. He stopped and turned. "Wait a sec. Before I go home and start polishing my rifle, when are you going out, where are you going and, more importantly, who are you going with?"

"Well, I haven't said yes yet, so I don't know when or where. But Milton Lewis asked me out."

"Milton? You mean, Scooter?"

His mother sniffed. "I prefer to call him Milton, seeing as how that's his given name."

Scooter wanted to go out with his mother? Suddenly his comment about safe sex wasn't so damn funny. Neither was his crack about his mother having a baby. Not a damn bit funny. Not that there was anything wrong with Scooter, but this was a whole different ball game now that her suitor was actually someone he knew. Not just someone he knew but, damn…Scooter.

"Now you're scowling. You don't approve of Milton? You've spent nearly every weekend with him for the past seventeen years at the racetrack. Is there something I should know about him?"

"Nooo. Scooter's a nice enough guy…it's just…I never…well, I guess I never thought about him wanting to go out with you."

"Why? What's wrong with me? Do you think I look too old?"

Shit. He was making a mess of this. "No. Not at all. What I meant, I guess, was I never thought that you'd want to go out with Scooter."

"Why? Is he a womanizer? A playboy at the track?"

Scooter a womanizer? Good thing Beau wasn't eating or drinking because he would've choked. Obviously his mother saw Scooter in a whole different light. "Not hardly. He's a motorhead. I guess I just don't see him as your type."

"He's a nice man and he's always had a good sense of humor."

He was also only about an inch taller than Beverly and as bow-legged as the day was long. However, he was a good guy, and Beau was ninety-nine percent certain Scooter would treat his mother like a lady. At least, he'd better.

"You're right," he said. "I can't think of a reason why you shouldn't go out with him."

Except he didn't want to see his mother get hurt any more than he wanted to see Caitlyn make a mistake with Cash Vickers. But then again, Caitlyn had sounded so damned happy when he'd talked to her.

Beau had had no idea the extent of his father's problems. He hadn't had a clue that Scooter wanted to ask his mother out. He'd set out to get Natalie to quit, and now he couldn't wait to see her again.

Life as he knew it was going to hell in a handbasket all around him.

11

SATURDAY EVENING, Natalie gave a small sigh of satisfaction as the shaving-cream-adorned car carrying the bride and groom disappeared around the corner. Shanna Connors and Mark Tippens were heading to the Ritz-Carlton for the night and then catching a flight Sunday morning for a week of honeymooning in Bermuda.

"Good luck to him," Cynthia murmured at her elbow.

They stood apart from the guests, who had begun to drift back to the reception hall, others heading toward their cars.

Natalie exchanged looks with her assistant. She knew exactly what Cynthia meant. *High-maintenance* didn't begin to describe Shanna and her mother. Mark would need to grow a set of steel balls to deal with those two, and unfortunately, she didn't think he was in the steel-ball-growing business.

"How long?" Cynthia asked. Natalie had developed a nearly unerring knack for knowing which couples would and wouldn't make it.

"Two, three years tops." She eased one foot out of

her shoe and flexed it. She hoped Beau was serious about that foot rub. Her feet were killing her. "It'll take that long for him to work up the courage to leave."

Cynthia nodded. "Yep. Hey, I'll wrap up things here," she offered. "You head on home."

Natalie didn't understand it but Cynthia's favorite part of the whole process was tying up all the loose ends—making sure the cake top was boxed up and delivered to wherever the bride specified, getting the wedding dress to the cleaners and looking after the myriad other after-details that Natalie found so tedious. "Are you sure? I know you like that stuff but you'll have to deal with…" She let her words peter out, stopping short of calling Shanna's mother by name. Cynthia knew precisely who she meant.

"Not a problem."

"Then I'll gladly take you up on your offer."

They walked in tandem toward the parking lot. "You look beat," Cynthia said, more by way of concern than criticism.

"Thanks, that's reassuring. It's been a tiring week."

Getting up every morning at four-thirty and then not getting to bed until nearly midnight was exhausting…but worth it. She still hadn't finished scraping the foyer baseboard.

Sex was a great way to start and end a day, and as depraved as it might sound, the time in between dragged. And she was in a bad way because she'd been out to Belle Terre yesterday morning, but last night and today had been out of the question with the demanding Shanna and her mother.

A day and a half and she missed Beau Stillwell like crazy. Alarmingly, not just the sex but *him*—his arrogant, breath-stealing smile, his sense of humor, his take on world politics, which didn't necessarily coincide with hers but was well-thought-out nonetheless. And it was sheer madness because she'd been busy, busy, busy with wedding details, but missing him had been there still.

Cynthia's teasing smile held a wistfulness. "I'd tell you to get some rest but I think rest isn't on either your or his agenda. Go. Have fun. I've got this covered."

Cynthia was worth her weight in gold. Yet another reason to do a great job with the Stillwell-Vickers wedding, other than the fact they were one of the most in-love couples she'd ever worked with. When she got the resulting surge in business, the first place she was putting some of that money was in a raise for Cynthia. Natalie knew things had to be tight for her since her sorry jackass of a boyfriend had moved out. Cynthia didn't complain, but she was now footing all of her bills on her own. Plus, she flat-out deserved a raise.

If Natalie had any sense remaining, she'd call Beau and cancel. She'd go home, take a warm bath and crawl into bed alone for a good night's sleep. But all her sense had deserted her because to her way of thinking, there'd be plenty of nights to crawl into bed alone in the near future.

But not tonight.

BEAU SHIFTED the flowers, wine and small gift bag to his left hand and grabbed the handle of the shopping bag containing their dinner. Goddamn but he was nervous. He'd damn near licked every inch of the woman at some time or another in the last five days and she'd returned the favor, so why the hell his heart was pounding like some kid was beyond him.

Maybe it was because up until now when he'd seen her he'd been in his world. The drag strip, Headlights, Belle Terre. Now he was entering her turf. And he had to admit he was out to prove a point. Damn her, she'd wounded his masculine pride when she'd told him she wouldn't go out with him if he asked her—not that he'd planned on asking her at the time. True, he didn't have a college degree and he worked with his hands, but he wasn't going to be shortchanged. He could stand up to any accountant or attorney. Of course, in all fairness to her, he had come off as something of an asshole.

He'd parked in the delivery alley behind her place, next to her van. He couldn't say he particularly liked the idea of her parking back here when she got in late…and he'd made sure she got in late all last week. This wasn't a bad section of town, but it was a damn alley. He didn't like it, didn't like it even a little bit.

His step faltered as he considered that she could've been mugged…or worse. He was going to have to re-think his strategy of dragging her out to Dahlia to wear her out, because if something happened to her because he'd kept her out late, he'd have to bust some heads, starting with whoever dared to touch her and ending with his own for putting her in that position in the first place. And maybe he'd look up Black Jack, Alex Morgan's cop fiancé, and ask him to swing by this area more often or have one of his buddies check up on Natalie. If she lived in Dahlia, it'd be a different story. Outside of the drug ring that Drew Fisk had been running out of the drag strip, Dahlia was crime-free for the most part.

He rang a delivery buzzer at the back door. She'd told him her business was downstairs, and much like shopkeepers used to do, she lived upstairs. It made sense to roll two rents into one, even if it left her with-out a lot of neighbors to rely on.

Within a minute or two he heard her throwing the locks on the other side. She opened the door. "Hi," she said.

It was as if all the air in his lungs took a hike.

"You are beautiful, baby girl." He said the first thing that came to mind when he finally managed to breathe.

Her hair was piled on top of her head with tendrils framing her face, as if she'd just climbed out of a bath. She smelled fresh and warm, and her skin looked dewy soft against a black V-necked sweater and black slacks.

"Thank you. You clean up pretty nicely your-self," she said.

He'd traded the jeans, T-shirt and work boots for khakis, loafers and a blue golf shirt his mother had given him for Christmas because she said it matched his eyes. "Thanks."

"So, come on in. The stairs are this way."

"Would you mind showing me your shop first?" He wanted to see what she did, the place where she worked.

"Sure." It didn't take long because her shop was fairly small. She had as much stockroom as store-front. She carried an assortment of wedding paraphernalia—guest books, feathered pens, white gloves, champagne glasses and an extensive assort-ment of veils.

"Nice," he said, indicating the wall of veils.

"They're all one of a kind. I sell them on consign-ment. And that's it."

He nodded. The place looked like her. "It's warm and inviting, but elegant."

She dipped her head. "Thank you. So, you're prob-ably starving. Come on and I'll show you upstairs."

He followed her through the stockroom to a set of narrow, steep stairs. If his hands hadn't been full, he would've never been able to keep them off her de-lectable ass as she climbed the stairs ahead of him. Her apartment door stood open at the top. He stepped in behind her and she reached around him to close the door. He caught a whiff of her perfume and fresh scent.

"So, this is it. Nothing fancy but, for now, it's home. Decorated via early American thrift store." It was neat and tidy and, yes, obviously done on a budget. She chattered on, leading him into a small, damn near minuscule kitchen. He was pretty sure she was as nervous as he'd been when he arrived. "And the kitchen, as you can probably figure out, is this way." She took the take out bag and placed it on the counter. "Thanks for picking up dinner." She plucked the flowers out of his hand and put them next to the food. "And the flowers are beautiful. I'll have to find a vase." She looked from the wine bottle to the refrigerator to him. "Should I chill the wine?"

His attention wasn't on the wine. "I don't care. I missed you."

He reached for her, and she flew into his arms. "Oh, God, me, too."

And then they were tangled up in one another. He pressed kisses over her eyes, her hair, her chin, her mouth. She devoured him the same way, both of them murmuring almost incoherently between kisses and hands beneath clothes.

"Felt like forever…"

"Thought tonight would never come…"

"…need you…"

"…desperate…now…"

Scattering discarded clothes along the way, Beau found himself with the press of her mattress behind his knees. Natalie pulled back the comforter and sheet with one tug and pushed him to the bed, following him down. He sank into the soft feather mattress, the sheets cool beneath him, Natalie soft and, oh, so hot on top of him.

He rolled her to her back, pinning her arms over her head, and pressed hungry, openmouthed kisses down her neck, over her breasts, her belly, tasting the satin of her skin against his lips and tongue, until she was writhing beneath him and he was on the verge of losing control.

"Beau…please…" she gasped.

It felt as if it took forever for him to roll on his condom, his movements frantic and jerky with the need to be inside her. One thrust and his groan joined her wail as her silky slick channel welcomed him home. And in that one thrust, in that second of being buried so deep inside her the head of his dick nudged her womb, the near explosive franticness left him. Her lovely eyes widened and he felt the same sense of rightness, of peace settle through her.

An ache, a foreign humility filled his chest. He was honored to be here, in her bed, in her body. How the hell had he gotten so lucky? His Natalie, his baby girl.

"You are so very, very beautiful," he said softly as he began to make love to her, to pay homage, to offer his gratitude for what she was sharing with him. Slow, sweeping strokes that echoed that initial sweet homecoming.

"You are the most beautiful man I've ever seen."

Women had told him they liked the way he looked. He'd heard any number of compliments before, but they had all seemed superficial. However, with Natalie, there was nothing superficial about it…and it wasn't *him,* it was *them.*

"We're beautiful together," he said. "Look." He glanced down at where they were joined. "Me inside you. You around me. That's beautiful."

She looked at where his cock was buried inside her and her eyes were smoky when her gaze tangled with his. "Yes, it is." Slowly, deliberately, maddeningly, she canted her hips, taking him that much deeper inside her wonderland.

Beau lost track of everything except the feel of her hot, tight channel wrapped around him, the taste of her tongue in his mouth, the soft mewling sound she made in the back of her throat, the uneven rhythm of their mingled breaths, the scent of her, of them… He felt the first tremor go through her.

"Come for me, Natalie."

"No." She clenched her muscles around his cock as her orgasm began to roll through her. "I'll come *with* you."

And it was as if a storm roared through him and ripped him free of a weight that had anchored him, and in the aftermath of his climax he floated free, buoyant in her arms.

12

NATALIE LOVED the way Beau lay sprawled in her bed, as if he belonged there. She propped herself up on one arm and shamelessly admired the broad expanse of his chest with its smattering of dark masculine hair that gave way to trim hips. It was the body of a man who worked hard every day, who earned that flat, tight belly and those cut biceps by doing his job. He was hot and he was here and that's where she wanted him to stay.

"I don't want you to go," she said.

Beau turned his dark head on her pillow and looked at her, his blue eyes sated, content. "I don't want to go."

"Then stay." It was an invitation, not a plea.

He caught her hand up in his, threading his fingers through hers, offering that slow, sexy smile that robbed her of coherent thought. "If I'd known it was a spend-the-night party, I would've brought my pajamas."

She looked over his nakedness, slowly, deliberately, and offered her own smile. "It's okay. You won't need them. Do you really wear pajamas?"

"No. Not since I moved out on my own. Want to sleep in matching outfits?" This time he was the one to let his gaze slide over her. "His and hers?"

"Sometimes you're positively brilliant."

He grinned and her belly tightened. For long seconds she simply absorbed the feel of his fingers against her hand, the scent of their lovemaking mingled with the smell of her freshly laundered sheets, the devastating sexiness of him in her bed.

"Natalie…" He broke the moment, his tone more serious. "I don't want you helping on the renovations anymore."

Her heart picked up its pace and not in a good way. "But the schedule's already tight. I may not be that much help, but I've actually got a good bit done." *And when will I see you again if I'm not seeing you twice a day? Was he already tired of her? Was this letting her down easy? The beginning of the big dump?*

"I'll figure something out but I don't like you getting back late at night and parking in that damn alley." A scowl drew his dark eyebrows together. "And then it's dark when you leave in the mornings. I don't like it. I'll figure something out on the renovations."

She was so relieved he wasn't pulling the plug on them, whatever they were now, that she laughed aloud. "I'm fine. I carry pepper spray on my key chain and this isn't a high crime area."

"Baby girl, if anyone hurt you, laid a finger on you,

someone would be dead and I'd be rotting in jail because I'd kill the son of a bitch."

She swallowed hard. He meant it. Every word. She fully believed he'd do extreme bodily harm on her behalf. With her peace-love-and-happiness-to-all background she should have found the possessiveness, the threat of violence alarming. Instead, it made her feel cherished, something she'd never experienced before. Something warm and tender unfurled inside her.

"Beau, that's so sweet—"

He interrupted her. "No, it's not. It's not sweet. It's self-preservation. I'm being a selfish bastard. I don't want to go to jail and I don't want to have to kill anyone."

There wasn't even a glimmer of humor lightening the intensity of his eyes. He was one hundred percent serious. "I'm telling you, I'm not in any danger," she said.

"Not anymore, because you're not going to be getting back here after eleven o'clock. It's just not worth it. End of discussion."

Okay, his charm had just worn thin. "End of discussion?" She untangled her hand from his and sat up, pulling the sheet over her lap. "I don't think so. And it's not up to you to decide whether it's worth it or not. News flash—I'm not yours to manage."

He knifed up, as well, but didn't bother with the sheet. "Goddammit, Natalie, my sister getting married at Belle Terre in a couple of months isn't worth you putting yourself at risk. Caitlyn can just wait on that wedding if she has to."

"Goddammit back atcha, Beau." Who did he think he was? "Don't you get it? Don't you understand anything? Your sister is going to marry Cash one way or the other. I've seen a lot of couples in the last three years and I've got a great radar going as to who'll make it and who won't. The wedding I did today, I give them three years together at best. But Caitlyn and Cash—what they have is real and it's deep. They're both in it for the long haul."

His expression remained hard and set. He just wasn't hearing her.

"For God's sake," she went on, "the man bought her a plantation house because she wanted it. Because he wanted to give her a dream. Yeah, he's a rising star, he's on his way up, but he doesn't have that kind of money just lying around. If you don't have Belle Terre ready and I don't do my job, then you and I have robbed her of a dream."

"You really believe that?"

"I really *know* that." Maybe he was starting to get it, to understand. "And I've got dreams. You're smart. You've got to know that orchestrating the wedding Caitlyn wants will make my career." He was a businessman. He worked for himself. Surely he could relate to this. "Short-term, it'll mean I can give my assistant the raise she desperately needs and definitely has earned. In the long run, it means I turn this into additional retail space and buy a small house I can call my own. I grew up never having a thing that was all my own. This is my apartment but I share it with my business. Sue me if wanting financial stability and my own home is a sin."

He crossed his arms over his chest in an are-you-finally-through gesture and she totally lost it. No! She wasn't through yet.

"So, do not tell me what something is or is not worth to me. And for god's sake, don't sit in *my* bed, in *my* apartment, and tell me a damn discussion is over. Nobody crowned you king here."

The bedroom was so quiet she heard the hum of the refrigerator all the way from the kitchen. She waited, fully expecting him to get up and stomp out. If that was the way it went, so be it. She didn't care how good they were in bed together or how much she'd missed him in one lousy day and a half, he wasn't going to dictate to her. He might run his mother's and sister's lives, but he didn't run hers.

He sat there, his expression closed, inscrutable. Finally, he nodded, one curt up-and-down. "Okay. Points taken. The discussion is obviously not closed. Will you give me a few days to figure things out, during which period of time you will not, in my estimation, put yourself at risk by coming and going so early and so late?"

She'd fully expected him to storm out. She took a deep breath. He was still here and he'd made what she figured were huge concessions for him. And she realized, rather sheepishly, that she'd once again lost her temper with him, which was so unlike her, and been extremely profane, also unlike her, in the interim.

"I'll agree to that," she said. "And I'm sorry I lost my temper. I'm really not usually like that. You just seem to have this effect on me."

Beau chuckled and it was a relief to feel the tension between them dissipating. "Hot-wiring." He relaxed against the pillows propped against the white iron headboard.

"What?"

"Hot-wiring. It was one of the first things I learned to do with a car when I was a kid. You see a car you like and you don't have the key, so you just bypass the system. If you hot-wire it, you can take what you want. You hot-wire it and the ride is yours."

"Isn't that illegal?"

"Yeah." He smirked. "But I'm damn good at it. And I hate to break it to you, baby girl, but I've hot-wired you."

"You wish," she shot back.

"No, baby, I know."

"Has anyone ever mentioned you're arrogant?"

He pretended to ponder for a moment. "Nope."

"Consider it mentioned, then."

He wrapped an arm around her and pulled her onto his lap. "You know, I think we just had our first fight."

"No. I'd say our first fight was the first time we met."

"Okay. I'll give you that. But we just had our first *naked* fight."

"Do you always have to argue everything?"

"No. But I will argue that we just had a fight and now that means we need to make up." He dipped his head and nuzzled along her collarbone, sending all the right signals to all her right parts.

She dropped her head back, allowing him full access, and murmured. "As I mentioned before, you do have occasional, brief flashes of brilliance."

He stopped. Why'd he stop?

"Hold that thought, but for now, I really need you to argue with me."

"And that would be because…why?"

His smile sent a hot promise all the way through her. "Because then I'd have to tie you to the bed to make a point and have my evil, wicked way with your body."

The mere thought, the mention slicked her. She moistened her lip with her tongue, feeling all hot and bothered and breathless. "You wouldn't dare."

His eyes dared her. "Try me."

"We did not just have a fight. We do not need to make up. And you will not tie me to this bed and tease me to the point of madness before you have your evil, wicked way with me and screw me mindless."

"There you go. You've left me no choice. Now I have to tie you up and screw you mindless or you'll consider me a Boy Scout."

"What can I say? A man's got to do what a man's got to do."

And she knew just the man for the job.

BEAU WATCHED in fascination as the morning sun slanted through the bedroom blinds, illuminating Natalie's face. He thought he could watch her forever without getting tired. He'd been awake for an hour now, memorizing the curve of her brow, the arch of her lips, the slope of her nose.

Watching her sleep had given him lots of think time. He'd entertained the thought that maybe he was wrong about Cash and Caitlyn. The thought that even if he wasn't wrong, it was ultimately Caitlyn's decision and not his. And perhaps, the most important realization of all…that he could watch Natalie Bridges sleep for a very long time, perhaps a lifetime, and never grow tired of the show.

Natalie chose that moment to flutter open sleep-heavy eyes. Sexy right down to the very breath she drew. His sex drew its own deep breath, swelling with the influx of oxygen and the woman next to him.

"Morning, baby girl."

She gave a lazy stretch. "Morning. Did you sleep okay?"

"Great."

She snuggled into his side. "Have you been up long?"

"Awake for a while." He glanced down at his hardening cock. "Up, just now."

"I hope you didn't just lie here because you were afraid you'd wake me. I sleep like the dead. A habit I developed early on with the constant influx of kids in our house."

He knew that for a fact because he'd actually gotten up and done the bathroom ritual, complete with brushing his teeth—she'd rustled up an unopened two-pack last night—and then climbed back in bed with her.

He trailed a finger down her nose. "I was just enjoying the view."

She smiled and rolled to the edge of the bed. "Hit the Pause button, I've got to go to the bathroom."

He watched her cross the room naked, admiring the curve of her back, the indent of her waist, those legs that were so adept at wrapping around his waist or draping over his shoulder, and, best of all, the sway of her bottom. "The view just gets better and better," he called out as she walked out of the room.

She laughed over her shoulder. "Pause, big boy, pause."

Funny how the room seemed a little less bright, a little less warm without her in it.

He'd been so focused on her, he really looked at the room for the first time. The walls were a pale pink with white lace curtains flanking the one window. There wasn't much room for anything other than the white iron bed, a round nightstand and a mirrored dresser. It was uncluttered and intensely feminine, just like the woman herself.

Natalie waltzed back in, wearing a smile, her glistening breasts with their pert pink nipples and the triangle of dark hair between her thighs issuing a mating call to his dick.

She stopped at the foot of the bed on his side. A wicked little smile curved her mouth and glinted in her eyes. Oh, yeah. That look always meant good things were about to happen. Natalie climbed onto the mattress, between his legs and up his body, her hands and mouth stopping for sampling detours along the way, her hair a silken tease against him. She crawled all the way up him and then went back to the part of his anatomy that was throbbing with excitement and need.

She scattered teasing kisses along his thighs, hips, and below his navel until he was ready to beg her to touch his…finally. Her mouth on his cock sent a warm tingle rushing through him.

"Mouthwash," she said, shooting him a sassy smile. "Minty fresh."

She took her breasts in her hands, put them together and slid them down over the head of his cock. They were soft and pillowy and warm and slick and felt so good he groaned aloud. "Oh, baby."

"Ah, you do like it."

"*Like* would be an understatement. Is that oil?"

"Uh-huh. We both need a shower anyway so I thought now was the perfect time for things to get messy."

Messy was good. "Oh, yeah."

She rolled onto her back and looked at him through half-closed eyes as she palmed her oil-slicked breasts and tugged on her nipples until they were rosy and distended. She gathered her creamy globes in hand and pressed them together. She pushed her breasts up, leaned her head down and slowly, erotically tongued her nipple, and he thought his cock might explode then and there.

"You are every man's wet dream come to life. A lady in the street—"

She interrupted him with a laugh. "And a whore in bed? I try. So, climb on and make a mess."

13

BEAU LEANED AGAINST the kitchen counter and watched Natalie upend the leftover coffee into the drain, her short silk robe clinging to the rounded curve of her hips.

"I've been thinking—"

"I hope you didn't strain anything," she tossed over her shoulder with a smirk.

"Smart-ass." He smacked her butt playfully.

"Umm…" She made a little purring noise in the back of her throat. "Don't start something you don't have time to finish."

Well. "Does that mean I need to turn you over my knee one day?"

"Possibly. But right now I've got to get dressed." She settled the glass carafe back in the coffeemaker and dried her hands. "I told my mother I'd get out there today to share the love with Miguel."

That's right. Her new foster brother. She'd taken the call at Belle Terre. "Are you kicking me to the curb?"

It was only a few steps from the kitchen to her bedroom.

Jennifer LaBrecque   177

"Yes. Or you could come with me if you wanted to and we could go to Belle Terre afterward to get some work done."

"Damn. I think you may be more of a workaholic than I am." He shrugged into his shirt. Natalie had been right. Hanging his clothes in the bathroom during his shower had steamed most of the wrinkles out.

"No." He found it quirky and sort of endearing that she modestly turned her back to him to slip on her panties and bra. "I've just got a mission and that's to see your sister enjoy the wedding of her dreams." She opened the closet door and sorted through hangers. "And I'll make sure I leave in time to get back at a decent hour. I can be very determined."

He grinned, thinking back to her standing in the middle of his toter home telling him to kiss her ass. "No kidding. You tracked me down at the racetrack. Nightmare Natalie. Stubborn is more like it."

"Because you wouldn't cooperate and call me back," she said, her voice muffled by the clothes. "And my determination is simply one of my many endearing qualities." She slipped a sundress over her head and worked the back zipper up.

"Need some help with that?" he offered.

"I've got it."

He took over regardless, tugging the zip the rest of the way up. "I can't say *endearing* came to mind the first time I met you." He trailed a finger over her shoulder.

"Thanks." She tugged the dress down over her

hips. "Ha. You don't even want to know what came to mind when I met you."

"'Kiss my ass' was, I believe, the choice phrase that came from those luscious lips of yours." He finished tucking his shirt into his pants. "Do you need to check with your mother first before I just show up?"

Natalie laughed, picking her brush up from the dresser. "Er, no. One more warm body in the house won't faze her in the least. She'll probably just try to adopt you." He sat on the edge of the bed and watched her brush her hair. She looked at him in the mirror. "Be strong and just say no. Seriously, they're great. They're warm and loving but they are chronically disorganized. I'm a throwback in the gene pool. I'm telling you, it's mayhem there." She put the brush down and gathered her hair into a loose ponytail at the nape of her neck, fastening it with a long barrette. "You'll see." She turned to him as she clipped on silver hoop earrings. "And way back when, you were about to share a thought."

There was something intimately satisfying in watching her get ready. "Yeah, before I was so rudely interrupted."

She sniffed and stuck her nose in the air. Beau laughed at her theatrics. Underneath those prim suits she wore, his woman was a little on the crazy side. He liked it. "So, I was thinking about it and you know real estate's a helluva lot cheaper in Dahlia than Nashville."

She nodded and turned to the mirror once again, but she was listening. She picked up a tube of mascara or eye shadow or whatever the hell it was that women put on their faces.

He continued, "Even factoring in the costs of commuting, you'd still come out ahead." He'd worked it all out while he'd watched her sleep this morning. "And I happen to know a guy in construction who could work you a deal on remodeling this for retail space. For that matter, he could probably build you a house at close to cost. It'd take some finagling with his schedule, but once race season ended in November, his weekends would be free again."

He couldn't read her expression as she looked at him in the mirror. "And why would that guy in construction do that for me?"

"Because Dahlia's a hell of a lot safer than Nashville. That guy in construction is basically a self-serving bastard. He'd sleep a whole lot easier at night if you were tucked in your own little house in Dahlia." And he didn't want to examine it too much closer than that.

She brushed a soft pink gloss over her lips and turned to face him again. "But then I'd be beholden to that guy and I don't like being beholden to anyone."

Absolutely, breathtakingly lovely.

"You know, we have more in common than you realize. And you wouldn't be beholden to anyone. Just think about it."

She nodded. "I'll think about it."

That had at least gone a whole lot better than when he'd broached the subject of her not working at Belle Terre anymore. He didn't need her working at Belle Terre anymore, because as of this morning, he'd decided to pull all his crews out there.

Caitlyn would have her wedding on time.

NATALIE BOLTED the rear alley door behind them and then double-checked it. Beau's paranoia was catching. His truck was parked behind her van. It seemed a silly waste to take two vehicles.

"Did you ever fix that seat belt in your truck?" The sun was warm against her shoulders and back. It was a beautiful day. By all rights, she should've had another wedding today but the couple had cancelled when the bride succumbed to a case of cold feet a week and a half ago. Natalie and Cynthia had handled that, as well. It didn't happen often, but it did happen. And it had left her with today open.

"No." He shrugged. "Too many other things going on this week."

She rounded the van to the driver's side. "Then I'll drive. Plus, I know the way."

He folded himself into the passenger seat. "Control issues."

He was so good at making her laugh…when he wasn't busy pissing her off. "Whatever. Just buckle up."

She put the key in the ignition and turned it. *Click,*

click, click. That so did not sound good. She looked at Mr. Motor in the seat next to her.

"Baby girl, I believe your starter is history."

He was speaking a foreign language. "Is that bad?"

"It's not good."

She resisted the urge to bang her head against the steering wheel. "Can you fix it?"

"If I had some tools and a floor jack." He ran his hand over his stubbled jaw. "It's a whole lot easier to just lift it."

"I have no idea what you just said."

"Give me a minute or two and I'll hook you up." He climbed out of the van and paced on the sidewalk while he made phone calls on his cell. She sat in the van and mentally went over the bills she had due the next couple of weeks and what her cash flow should be.

Five minutes later, he opened the passenger door and leaned in, bracing his arms on the door frame. "I've got you taken care of. We're going to tow your van out to Scooter's and he's going to fix the starter. I'll drop you off at his place to pick it up late this afternoon. In the meantime, I'll drive us out to your folks."

She didn't want to come across as ungrateful but her budget was so tight it squeaked. "How much is the tow going to cost?"

"I did a little work for Darren Thompson, the guy with the tow truck, last year. He was short on cash at the time so we worked it out on trade. He owes me.

He said he'd be right out to pick it up. It's a freebie. And he'll flatbed it."

She didn't know what flatbedding it was but apparently it was good. It sounded sort of sexual, if you asked her, but then again, when she was around Beau, everything sounded sort of sexual. And she couldn't let him trade out a tow he'd worked for.

"But that's a debt he owes you, not me."

"Natalie, don't worry about it." There was a faint edge of exasperation to his voice. He really was used to being in charge. "You're actually doing him and me a favor. I never need a tow and he's just glad he can do this. It gives him the chance to pay up."

Fine. She gave up on that. "Well, what should I pay Scooter? He's doing this on a Sunday afternoon."

"You're actually doing Scooter a favor, too. He's had too much time on his hands the last couple of years since Emma Jean died. Replacing your starter gives him something to do and makes him feel useful. Plus, he likes you."

He had it all worked out. "I know what you're doing." He was taking care of her. The same way he took care of his mother and his sister. And he was doing it without her having to dip into her wallet.

"The only thing I'm doing is giving you a ride out to your folks and then to pick up your car. Pull the ignition key off and leave it under the floor mat. It's not as if anyone can steal it anyway."

She detached the key, slipping it beneath the mat,

opened her door and climbed out. "Uh-huh. You're fixing things." Heavy-handed. Arrogant. Sweet.

He grinned, totally unrepentant. "Put it down to early adolescent training." Beau opened the truck door on his side and offered a slight bow. "Your carriage awaits."

She laughed as she slid in ahead of him to the center seat, her heart beating a little faster. The seat right next to him. The one with a functioning seat belt. He climbed in behind her. His warmth and his scent seemed to enfold her. He was big, solid, sexy…and, for right now, hers.

His fingers grazed her hip when he fastened his seat belt, and her breath caught in her throat.

"Okay, where are we going?" he said after he cranked the truck.

"We need to head north on 65. Do you know how to get there from here?" She had no idea how familiar he was or wasn't with Nashville.

"Yeah. I've got it."

A few blocks later, they approached the expressway ramp. For all that she'd seen him drive like a bat out of hell down the racetrack, he was a very careful driver on the street.

She couldn't remember if Beverly had said his age or not. And if she had, Natalie didn't remember, so she asked him what had been niggling at her as he drove through the city. "Your mother said you kept the family afloat after your father died. You were how old?"

It was almost imperceptible but his face tightened and she could swear his body tensed next to her. "I turned sixteen two days after we buried him. The bank repossessed our house two weeks later. I promised him I'd take care of my mother and my sister." Another deceptively casual shrug of those broad shoulders that had taken on the weight of the world at an age when most boys were mainly concerned with a Saturday-night date. "I take promises seriously."

He made a right onto the ramp and merged into the northbound traffic.

"You're a complicated man," she mused aloud.

"No, I'm not. There's nothing complicated about me. I keep telling you, I'm ultimately a selfish bastard. I made a promise. If I don't keep it, then I feel bad about myself. Bottom line, I do what I have to do to feel good about me. Self-preservation."

"If you say so."

"I say so," he said.

He wasn't what she'd thought she wanted. He wasn't what she'd been looking for, but she could so easily fall in love with him. Heaven help her, she was already more than halfway there.

BEAU HAD TO ADMIT to being shell-shocked a couple of hours later when they left Natalie's parents' farm. "You're right. That was crazy. Cool, but crazy. It must've driven you insane."

"See, now you know what happened to me. Early-childhood-induced madness, hence my need for my own space and everything nicely scheduled and organized. I'm telling you, they were born in the wrong decade because they're hippies."

"They seem devoted to one another."

"Always. They met at Berkeley in the Seventies. What are the odds that two people from just outside of Nashville, Tennessee, would find one another in a liberal arts school in California?"

"How'd they wind up back here?"

"I think they envisioned themselves as being part of some Foxfire-like element."

He had no idea what Foxfire was, but he wasn't about to ask. He'd Google it when he got home. "You look like your mother. You're both beautiful women." It was like seeing what Natalie would look like in twenty years. Still beautiful. The notion gave him a funny feeling in his gut.

"Thank you." A sweet blush stained her skin. Amazing. He'd licked cream-cheese icing off her most intimate parts until she'd come and she hadn't blinked an eye, but let him tell her she was beautiful and she was embarrassed.

"You're welcome." Sudden inspiration struck him. "Look, let's skip Belle Terre today. I know you've got a schedule and I swear I'll take care of it, but I want to show you something."

She leered at him and he laughed, sliding his right

arm around her shoulders, steering with one hand on the wheel. "Baby, I'm always ready to show you that."

She snuggled into his side. "I'm always ready to have a look."

Despite her comment and the underlying sexual tension that always seemed to hum between the two of them, a comfortable, content silence stretched out as he navigated the switchbacks that cut through Tenessee's hills.

Half an hour later, he turned onto a dirt road and slowed down at the yellow flag at the edge of the ditch. "See that flag? My property starts there."

He hung a left and drove down the familiar, rough-cut road that wound through a mixture of hardwoods. "About a month ago, the dogwoods and redbuds were in bloom and it was beautiful."

"It's beautiful now."

"Just wait." He so wanted to show her his property. He'd had his eye on it for years and then last year he'd finally had the money to buy it. Now he almost had the money to build his house on it. His piece of paradise, bought and paid for.

He hadn't felt this way in years. He felt like a kid on Christmas Eve—both anxious and excited.

He rounded the curve and crested the hill and the clearing on the top of the ridgeline was there with the Tennessee hills spread out in all their blue-green glory. It was a view that never failed to pierce his soul.

He put the truck in Park and killed the engine.

"Oh." It was all she said. It was all she had to say. She looked up at him and her eyes shimmered with the sheen of tears. She felt it, too. He'd *known* she would get it.

"I know," he said quietly. He opened the door, got out and held out his hand. "Come on."

Natalie put hers in his and slid out on his side. To his way of thinking, he was never going to fix that seat belt.

The young spring grass was soft underfoot as they climbed the slight rise together. "This is where I'm going to build my house."

"It's so beautiful it makes me ache inside."

The sun glinted in her hair, picking out strands of copper and gold. A slight breeze rustled the leaves and swayed the grass. "That's exactly how I feel."

"When are you going to build it?"

"I thought I'd start this fall but it'll more likely be next spring, maybe summer." That was because, as of now, he was pulling all of his work crews off their jobs and sending them to Belle Terre. It'd screw with his cash flow, because all the jobs he pulled them off wouldn't pay until Belle Terre was finished, and it wouldn't be finished for a couple of months now. And he'd also turned the idea of trying to fit in a couple more races and picking up the money there.

But he'd come to the realization that he couldn't continue down the path he'd taken regarding Caitlyn and Cash. If Cash broke her heart, or even dinted it,

Beau would kick his ass to the Tennessee line and back, but marrying him was Caitlyn's choice. And *maybe,* not that he was totally convinced, he *might* have been wrong about Cash. He was willing to entertain the notion that his judgment had been clouded by overprotective instincts.

Both his mother and Natalie seemed to think Cash was okay, and Beau realized both women's opinions held a lot of sway for him. Somewhere in the course of the last week, Natalie had slipped under his skin, had become more than just a wedding planner to be gotten rid of. He respected her—her intelligence, her work ethic, her independence—and the two of them were explosive in bed together.

Running her ragged by dragging her out to Belle Terre now struck him as a supremely asshole plan. His crews would be there first thing in the morning. "There's been a slight change in plans. A blip on the radar, but nothing I can't handle."

She curled her fingers around his. Her hand felt tiny in his. "Will your house have a front porch?"

"Yep. Got to have a front porch. A back porch, too."

She nodded. "That's good. Porches are important, especially with this view."

"Absolutely. Porches are a Southern institution."

"Where's the front door?"

"Right here." He pretended to open a door. "Ladies first." She tugged on his hand and he followed her inside to where the foyer would be. "Den." He gestured to the open space to his left, still clasping her hand. "Kitchen, bathroom—"

"Show me the bedroom," she interrupted, her tone solemn, sensual.

He led her down the "hall" to the back right corner of the house. "Here," he said, facing the distant hills. "This is what I'll see when I wake up in the morning and what I'll see when I go to bed at night."

"Is this the bed?"

"Yeah, on this wall."

She nodded soberly, her eyes intense, a stillness about her that suited this place. Without looking away from him, she slowly, deliberately reached behind her and slid down the zipper of her sundress and slipped it off, laying it on the grass. She stepped out of her sandals and curled her toes into the green cushion.

His eyes locked on hers, he followed her lead and pulled off his shirt, spreading it on the soft spring grass next to hers. He stepped out of his pants as her underwear joined the other clothes. She stood waiting patiently, expectantly, while he took off his briefs.

Bare, she sank to the bed made of their clothes and stretched her hand out to him.

"Lie down with me."

14

NATALIE DIDN'T TRY to contain her sigh of content-
ment as they headed down the highway once again.

Beau ended his phone call. "Scooter has your van
ready. We can swing by and pick it up and then maybe
grab some dinner."

"Sounds like a plan."

She had never known such absolute, blinding happiness in her life. Of course, she'd never been in love
before, either. It was too late for heaven to help her.
She was done. Toast. History. She was totally, irrevo-
cably in love with Beau Stillwell. What had happened
in the meadow defied description. Their lovemaking
had been as spiritual as it had been physical. She'd
come so close to telling him she loved him then and
there, but it had been so close to perfect that she'd
simply loved him with her body instead.

He looked down at her and smiled and her insides
turned to gooey mush. Lord, she could look at him,
have him look at her that way, for the rest of her life.

"I'm never going to fix that seat belt," he said,
draping his arm over her shoulder, his fingers resting

right above her breast. The scent of their passion clung to his fingers.

"That works for me." *I love you.*

"I think it's supposed to rain on Wednesday." He sent her a boyish grin.

"Um, okay." Talk about a subject change.

"I could pick you up. You could wear that raincoat. You know, so you wouldn't get wet."

She got it now. She liked the way his mind worked. "Uh-huh. I could, couldn't I?"

"Damn. I wish it was going to rain tomorrow." He offered a mournful sigh.

Natalie grinned, shaking her head. "You're crazy."

He stroked his fingers along the edge of her breast. "You make me crazy."

Umm. She loved that husky, low-keyed tone his voice took on when he said things like that. And he made her crazy in a totally good way. "That's a two-way street."

He pressed a quick kiss to her hair and slowed down, putting on his blinker. "Here's Scooter's place," he turned left into a gravel driveway marked by reflective lights on stakes, "and there's your ride all ready to go."

Her van sat in front of a detached garage that was about twice as big as the frame house that sat slightly behind it. Scooter emerged from the shop and greeted them as she and Beau got out of his truck. A large tree—she had no clue what kind…tree identification wasn't her thing—shaded the area.

"Beau. Nat'lie. Got you all fixed up." He gave them a ready smile as he wiped his hands on a worn rag.

It was impossible not to like Scooter. "Thank you so much. What do I owe you?"

"You don't owe me nuthin'." Scooter shoved the rag into his back pocket, shaking his head. "I'm always messing around under one car or another. Might as well have been yours today."

It was a little chilly in the shade with the breeze blowing. Natalie crossed her arms. "But what about the part you put in? You can't pay for that."

Scooter nodded his head toward Beau. "Compliments of Stillwell Motors Racing."

"But—"

"Take it up with the boss there. I just did what the big man asked me to do."

Beau did a lousy job of looking innocent. "You cold? I've got a jacket behind the seat if you want it."

He could be infuriating, but at the core of him, he was a thoughtful man. "I'm okay. Thanks, though. And I will take it up with the boss later." She shifted from one foot to another. It'd been a long time and she'd had a big glass of iced tea just before they'd left her parents' house. And there was something about being chilly that intensified nature's call. She was in desperate need of facilities. "Um, is there a bathroom handy?"

Scooter scratched his head. "You don't wanna use the one here in the shop. It ain't none too clean, but the one in the house is in good shape. Just let yourself in the back door and it's the second door on your left."

"Thanks," she said, already moving in that direction. She had to *go*.

"It was the starter, right?" she heard Beau ask as she rounded the corner of the garage.

"Yeah. And I found a couple of loose belts that I replaced and changed out the spark plugs. I gave it a good going over. It ain't gonna leave her stranded anywhere anytime soon."

She smiled to herself as she crossed the neat lawn and let herself in the back door. In his own arrogant, high-handed way Beau had looked out for her, taken care of her. She could get used to being taken care of that way. Not that it would impugn her independence, but simply to know you had someone special to turn to. To know he had her back, the same as she would gladly have his back.

She let herself into Scooter's house. The kitchen smelled like vegetable soup and the empty can on the counter confirmed that'd been his lunch. A solitary bowl sat in the sink. A wooden sign, with *Emma Jean's Kitchen* written on a rolling pin—the kind you picked up at a country craft fair—was mounted over the doorway leading into the rest of the house. There was an ineffable sadness about the single bowl and the sign, and Natalie wondered if Beverly had agreed to go out with Scooter. She hoped so.

She took quick care of her business and checked

herself in the bathroom mirror while she washed her hands. Good grief, she had grass in her hair and a big grass stain on the back of her dress. Maybe Scooter hadn't noticed. She plucked the grass out of her hair, but there was nothing to be done about the stain. She retraced her route back to the garage. She was still on the side of the garage when she heard Beau.

"I'm fine with you going out with her, I just don't want her to get hurt," he said.

Natalie paused, unsure of what to do. She didn't want to interrupt what was obviously a personal discussion, but then on the other hand she was eavesdropping. She opted to do nothing. It wasn't as if she didn't already know about Beverly and Scooter.

"Beau, you know me well enough to know I'm not going to hurt her."

"Make sure you don't."

She winced at the hard note in his voice. She was pretty sure even the affable Scooter wasn't going to take that well. She understood Beau's protective instincts but he could come across as terribly overbearing sometimes. Of course, that's what made him the man he was—the man she'd fallen in love with.

"Look, I know you made a promise to your daddy. I never thought it was right for him to ask such of a boy, but I know you promised and you've been a man of your word. But you've got to know when to back off some."

Nope. Scooter hadn't taken it well at all.

"You're coming mighty close to crossing a line, Scooter. I'd suggest you back down."

"That ain't gonna happen. And you're one to talk, Beau. Because you've already crossed a line, and somebody has to check you on it and I reckon that somebody's me."

Good grief, it sounded as if they were squaring up. What would she do if one of them threw a punch?

"I haven't crossed any line."

"Yes, you have. Me and the boys know you don't want Caitlyn to marry Cash. I've known you for a long time. I knew from the beginning you thought him buying Belle Terre was a squirrely thing to do with his money. And I know ain't nobody ever gonna be good enough for your baby sister."

"You through?"

"Nope. Just gettin' started. I understood you not just taking it to her cause that sure wasn't gonna change her mind. And I sorta thought it was funny when you tried to trip that little gal up by not returning her phone calls—" Natalie realized with a start that Scooter was now talking about *her* "—and then trying to get her to quit by wearing her out, dragging her to Belle Terre twice a day." Son of a bitch. She'd known from the beginning he was up to something. The signs had all been there, but she'd chosen to ignore it, bury her head in the sand. "But I saw the grass in her hair and the grass stain on her dress, and you sleeping with Nat'lie to sabotage Caitlyn's wedding—that crosses the damn line."

Oh, God. She braced her hand against the side of the garage as nausea swept over her and she couldn't breathe. How could she have been so stupid? It had all been a sham, a scam. Bile rose in her throat. She would not give him the satisfaction of puking.

"You don't know what you're talking about. This is none of your business."

"I'm making it my business. Somebody's gotta stick up for Nat'lie before you break her heart."

She squared her shoulders, lifted her chin and willed her feet into action, wading in to wage war and fight her own battle.

"Thank you, Scooter." She walked over to Beau and wasn't sure who she surprised more when she slapped him on the face so hard her hand hurt. He didn't even flinch. Dear God, she'd never struck another human being in her life. But she'd never felt as if her soul had just been ripped out of her, either.

How had she ever imagined herself *in love* with him? At least she'd had the good sense not to profess undying devotion. "You are despicable. Loathsome."

At that, he flinched. "Baby gi—"

She would not cry. She let fury roll through her and scorch away the tears. "Never, ever call me that again."

Her handprint was bright red on his cheek. "Natalie, if you'll let me explain what—"

"Ms. Bridges, if you please." She stood ramrod straight. "And what is it exactly that you'd like to explain, Mr. Stillwell? Did Scooter get it wrong? You weren't trying to sabotage the wedding? And it'd be nice if you could manage the truth. If you're capable of the truth."

"The truth. I did set out to sabotage the wedding. Actually, I just wanted to delay it." He scrubbed his hand through his hair. "I don't want to see Caitlyn make a mistake. I worked damn hard to make sure she had stability and some financial security. I'm not sure Cash can give her either one. I figured with enough time, he would either prove himself or shoot himself in the foot. And he likes the women."

The urge to slap him again was so strong she stepped back from him. "And he loves your sister. You know what the problem is? You look at Cash and you see yourself. What? Like you don't like the women? Like they don't throw themselves at you left and right? But here's the difference, Cash loves Caitlyn." She put every ounce of betrayal and anger into a sneer. "I've met the both of you, and Cash Vickers has more integrity in his pinkie than you do in your entire body."

"I know it looks bad but—"

She stopped him with a raised hand and an unamused laugh. "I don't want to hear it. You played me. Plain and simple. Admit it. At least be man enough to own it."

"Okay. I'm owning it. I played you…at first. But dammit, listen to me now. I love you."

She felt as if she were breaking into a million pieces, but she refused to fall apart in front of him.

She laughed again. In his face. "Please. Please don't do this. I'm not really sure what your angle is with that, but I think you've already insulted me enough."

Scooter piped up. "Nat'lie, I've known him since he was running around naked as a yard dog, and I can vouch that he's never told a woman he loved her."

She shot Scooter a pointed look. "Has his sister ever been about to marry someone he disapproves of? See? That's what I thought." She rounded on Beau. "Was I supposed to be so overwhelmed by your skills in bed that I would forget about my job? Or maybe you wanted me to find this out and you thought I'd be so humiliated that I'd quit? Am I supposed to swoon now over your faux declaration of love and be so swept off my feet while you continue to play your manipulative games? Think again. If anything, I'm more determined than ever to see Caitlyn get the wedding she wants. And I told you early on, you're not my type. You're not what I'm looking for in a man."

"I've got three work crews showing up at Belle Terre in the morning," he said quietly.

She clapped, slowly, deliberately insulting. "Bravo. I'll be there to make sure they're doing their job and not just standing around."

"That's not necessary. I said I'd handle it."

It would be bittersweet going out there again but at this point she didn't trust him any further than she could throw him. "What? I'm going to take your word for it? Please. Your word means less than nothing.

Unfortunately, I'll have to see you at the wedding rehearsal and on the day your sister gets married. Other than that, however, I never want to lay eyes on you again. I think you owe me that."

His face took on that hard, set look she'd seen last night. "If that's the way you want it."

"That's definitely the way I want it." She couldn't get home soon enough to wash his scent and his touch off her skin. She walked over to her van and stopped at the door, turning to him. "Oh, and tell your crew I won't be there Friday morning. I have a date on Thursday night—a junior partner in a law firm. I anticipate a late night."

THURSDAY AFTERNOON, Beau straightened from where he was cutting a piece of baseboard that needed replacing when his mother walked through Belle Terre's front door. He'd set his equipment up in the front parlor. Four days into it and he and the guys had made a huge dent in the work. Right now, all the men were gathered outside, breaking for lunch. He didn't care about lunch. He wasn't hungry. And, much as he loved her, he didn't want to deal with his mother right now.

"I don't want to talk about it, Mom," he said, hoping to head her off at the pass.

She gave him her customary hug and kiss. "We're going to talk about it, Beau. Scooter thinks you're angry with him."

He ran a weary hand over his face. He hadn't slept in days. He thought he'd covered this with Scooter but apparently not. "No. I did a stupid thing and it bit me in the ass. In spades. I did this all on my own." He looked at his mother and the sorry-ass truth poured out of him. "I love her."

"That's what Scooter said."

"I took her out to show her my land and…Mom, she got it, she felt it there the same way I do." If he lived to be a hundred, he'd never ever forget making love to her in the grass, the sun warm against their skin, as she unwittingly claimed his soul, and he was glad to give it. In that moment, he'd become hers and he'd claimed her as his for all eternity.

Beverly's eyes widened. "You took her to the house site?"

"Yeah."

Tears gathered in her eyes and she put both arms around him and hugged. "Oh, son," she said, releasing him.

He had no pride left. He bared his soul. "When I'm with her…I don't even know how to describe it."

Understanding, sympathy and pain all glimmered in her eyes. "You don't have to. I loved your father the same way."

For the first time since his father died, mention of him didn't stir a cauldron of anger in Beau. He'd done a little online research and his father had been a classic case of manic depression. And Beau had finally realized that Monroe Stillwell had loved them but he'd been unwell and untreated.

"She said she never wanted to see me again and asked me to stay away. She said I at least owed her that. And she's right."

"I'm sorry, Beau. Give her some time."

He plowed his hand through his hair, jealousy clawing at his soul. "She has a date tonight. An attorney. A junior partner. The very thought is driving me crazy." The thought of her kissing someone else, laughing up at him, touching him, him touching her… It was like pouring acid on an open wound. "Remind me that getting knee-crawling, ass-kicking drunk is a very bad plan."

They both knew what had happened to his father. Beverly shook her head. "That's a disaster in the making."

"I know. And I've already screwed things up enough." Dammit. He just felt so useless doing nothing. Well, technically, he was busting his ass at Belle Terre, but at this point, the ball was in Natalie's court. He'd stated his case. All he could do was wait and pray for a change of heart. Well, actually there was one thing he did need to do. Put it down to stress that it hadn't occurred to him earlier. "I can't change things with Natalie, but I do know one thing I have to do."

15

FRIDAY MORNING, Natalie hurried down the stairs from her apartment. She'd been awake until nearly five and then had drifted off, only to find herself embroiled in a nightmare where she was sinking in quicksand and Beau kept throwing her a rope but she was too stubborn to take it. She'd been glad to wake up. And now she was late and sleep-deprived. Not a stellar start to the day.

"You look like shit," Cynthia observed, foregoing the customary "good morning."

"Thanks," she said on a sarcastic note. She hadn't missed the bags and dark circles under her eyes when she'd looked in the mirror this morning. She didn't need Cynthia to point out the obvious.

Cynthia quirked an eyebrow in inquiry. "How was your date with Shad last night?"

Natalie poured herself a cup of coffee, in desperate need of the caffeine. She settled down at her desk and looked at her day planner rather than her assistant. "I didn't go."

"Natalie! You stood him up?" She'd known Cynthia was going to react this way. "You stood up Shad Jackson III? You know you probably just blew your chances with him."

As if she gave a flying fig about Shad. Her time had been better spent soul-searching. Shad could never hope to be half the man Beau was. She'd been angry and hurt when she'd thrown that out at Beau, when she'd called and accepted Shad's invitation. She'd wanted to wound Beau, she'd wanted him to hurt as she'd hurt. She'd wanted to betray him as she'd felt betrayed. "I don't care. I'm not remotely interested in Shad. Going would've been a waste of his time and my time, and I would've felt even crappier than I already feel."

Cynthia took on a stern expression. "Natalie, you can't give Beau this kind of power over you. Be strong."

She was being strong. Figuring out just who and what her Prince Charming was and wasn't had required fortitude and taking a good hard look at herself. She'd always envisioned her true love to be someone like Shad. Sanitized. Safe. In retrospect, she realized she'd been looking for someone who didn't stir her too deeply, who didn't throw her into a tailspin with just a look. She'd also realized love, real love, wasn't safe at all. It meant opening yourself to hurt and heartache, and it was chaotic and messy.

"What if I was wrong, Cynthia? I was so hurt, so angry, I felt so betrayed…but…I don't know now. His crews are legitimately working. They'll be finished the renovations ahead of schedule. And what did he gain by showing me where he was building his house?" She wanted to cry every time she remembered making love with him there. It had been so tender, so special. How could that not have been real? "He didn't have to offer to help me renovate here and build a house in Dahlia."

Cynthia frowned over her tea mug. "But what if you were right?"

Cynthia was the walking wounded. "But what if I was wrong?"

Their conversation and her personal angst-fest were cut short by the ringing of her cell phone. Caitlyn Stillwell. Natalie squared her shoulders, took a deep breath and answered in her cheeriest professional tone, "Hi, Caitlyn."

"Beau called me last night." Caitlyn, true to form, cut straight to the chase.

She couldn't read Caitlyn's tone. "Really?"

"Yes. Really. The first thing I want to say is this call is strictly personal."

What else could she do but agree? "Okay."

"Beau told me everything. He told me about his reservations, his stupid plan, how you and Mama set him straight. Thank you for going to bat with him on our behalf. It's not easy to go toe to toe with him. He's used to being in charge."

"You're welcome. And I noticed," she tacked on dryly.

Caitlyn laughed on the other end. "I'd love to see you taking him on. He's used to women doing backflips to please him." Natalie could've lived without that reminder. "Well, everyone but me and Mama." Caitlyn's voice lost its teasing note, grew serious. "He gave us his blessing, Natalie," she said softly.

Tentative hope bloomed in her chest. "That's wonderful. I'm really happy for you."

Caitlyn sniffled on the other end. "You have no idea what this has cost him."

"Then tell me. I want to understand."

"Shortly after Daddy died, our house was foreclosed on." Beau had told her that. "We lost everything. House, furniture, cars. Daddy owed money to anyone and everyone." He hadn't told her that. "We moved in with Nana and Papa, which was pretty much miserable because Nana and Mama never got along. I was so little that I didn't really realize it at the time, but Beau was sixteen and he started driving a race car and winning and he worked at the IGA sweeping floors after school and he saved all that money so that after a year we moved out of Nana and Papa's house and into our own place."

She'd known he'd shouldered a heavy burden, but she'd had no idea it had been that heavy. Caitlyn wasn't through.

"Daddy dying changed him, Natalie. He's never owed a penny to anyone. Everything is paid for in cash. If he owns it, no one can take it away from him. That land he took you to is paid for. And just for the record, he's never taken anyone there other than me and Mama. He's fun, he's got a wicked sense of humor, but he's private. I don't know if you really understand what his taking you there meant. That's not a part of him he shares. And him sending those crews out to Belle Terre—it means he waits another six months to start building his house. He won't start building until the money's in the bank to pay for it. I wish Cash and I had the money to front him, but we don't. Once again, he put his dreams on hold for me."

Natalie took a deep breath, trying to steady her racing pulse, and then she said aloud what her heart had known all along. "I love him."

"Thank God. Now will you please put him out of his misery, because he is miserable."

"That makes two of us."

"Y'all are pathetic." Caitlyn sounded disgusted.

Natalie agreed.

"YOU'RE GONNA have to step it up to win," Scooter said as Beau levered himself out of the car after the first round qualifying. "You've got to get your head in the race."

"I'll make you a deal. You don't tell me to get my head in the race again, and I won't tell you to get your head out of your ass."

Darnell, Tim and Scooter all exchanged a look which didn't do a damned thing to improve Beau's surly disposition.

"Hey, man, why don't you go check out the ball game in the toter while we check the spark plugs?" Darnell suggested. The three of them exchanged another look.

Screw them. None of them was sitting around with his thumb up his ass while the woman he loved was out with some fancy-schmancy junior attorney who, in all likelihood, had totally screwed up the most important relationship of his life. Fine, he'd go sit on his useless ass in the toter.

He stomped off, knowing full well he was being a dickhead. He wasn't good at waiting, at "giving her space." She'd told him she didn't want to see him, but that was just too damn bad. He didn't believe for a minute that she didn't love him. That day, on his property. He knew what he'd seen in her eyes. She had a temper. She was stubborn as hell. And she was his. He was tired of sitting around like some dickless wonder. He was going to clean up and then he was going to Nashville. He was going to stake his claim for good.

He climbed the steps and slammed the door behind him for good measure. He dropped to the couch and pulled off his racing boots.

Out of nowhere, the pocket door between the kitchen and bathroom slid open. Natalie stood in the doorway, a towel wrapped around her, her hair a sexy curtain across her shoulders. "Can I help you?"

His mouth went dry. Hell, maybe he was hallucinating. God knows, he hadn't slept in days. "Natalie?"

She took a step toward him. "I'm sorry."

He wanted to touch her, take her in his arms, but he wasn't so sure that he could think clearly once he did that, and this was an important conversation. "For what?"

Her brown eyes bared her soul, handed it to him for safekeeping. "For not believing you. I've been so miserable. I love you. You're everything and more a Prince Charming should be."

"Natalie—"

She quieted him with a finger to his lips and just that touch sent heat spiraling through him. "Not Natalie. Say it. Please."

He took a wild guess at what she wanted to hear. "Baby girl."

Finally, he got something right. "You have no idea..."

"I have plenty of idea." And to hell with not touching her. He grabbed the edge of the towel. "Once again you're overdressed for the occasion." He yanked and tossed the towel to the floor and dragged her up hard against him. She was all soft skin and rounded curves and his dick was clamoring for attention. He still had important business to take care of with her. "I love you."

"I know." She smiled and reached between them, fondling him through his pants.

If she kept that up... "I know you know, but I thought it needed repeating."

He kissed the spot below her ear and she shuddered.

"I'll never get tired of hearing it," she said in that hot, breathy voice that fired his pistons. He cupped her buttocks in his hands and picked her up. She wrapped her arms around his neck and her legs around his hips and rocked against him with a wicked little smile playing about her mouth. God, he loved her mouth. He backed her up against the kitchen counter.

One long, hot kiss later he said, "I take it Scooter, Darnell and Tim knew you were in here."

"Uh-huh." She licked at the base of his neck. "I got here after you were already in the staging lanes. Tim brought me to the toter. Are you through racing for the day?"

"Uh-huh. What'd you have in mind?"

She ground her mound against him. "I've never done it with a guy in a racing suit."

He ground back. "I can help you with that."

"I've also never done it in a toter." She nipped at his jaw.

"We could kill two birds with one stone."

She batted her brown eyes at him. "Or we could do it twice."

"I like the way you think."

"Does that mean you only love me for my brains?"

Damn. How was he supposed to answer that? He opted for the truth. "Hell, no. I'm pretty fond of all of your parts. And I believe your motor's already running, baby girl."

"Hmm. That's because you were right."

"About what?"

"I've been hot-wired."

He grinned. It was good to know he was right…at least occasionally.

Epilogue

NATALIE SWIPED a tear from her eye as Caitlyn and Cash rode off into the sunset in a white buggy pulled by a pair of white horses.

"Absolutely beautiful," Beverly said, looking at the carriage and dabbing at her eyes with a fine handkerchief. Scooter patted her on the shoulder and winked at Natalie.

"Y'all done good, Nat'lie and Cynthia."

"Thanks, Scooter," Natalie said, not quite believing that they'd actually pulled it off.

Was that a look that passed between Beau and Cynthia? They'd become as thick as thieves once Cynthia had decided Beau wasn't the bad guy.

"Why don't you and Beau take a walk down to the river and let me get on with the cleanup," Cynthia said. "You know I like this part."

"But—"

"Shoo. Go."

"Tell me what you want me to do," Tilson said. He and Cynthia had met when Cynthia came out to Belle Terre one day. The two had been inseparable since then.

"C'mon," Beau urged, wrapping an arm around Natalie's waist and leading her around the side of the house. Even after three months, his touch still thrilled her. She suspected it always would.

They strolled in silence past the white tent on the lawn where the orchestra was packing up, down the sloping green hill to the swing that hung from a cottonwood at the river's edge. Of one accord, they settled next to one another on the swing.

Beau dropped a kiss on the top of her head. "That was a helluva wedding you pulled off, baby girl."

She leaned her head into the crook of his shoulder and smoothed her fingers over the leg of his trousers. He was heart-stoppingly handsome in his black tux. There wasn't a woman at the wedding who hadn't given him the eye. And that was just what it was like to date a hot hunk of a man.

"It was, wasn't it? But *we* pulled it off. You did a fantastic job with Belle Terre. We make a pretty good team, you and I."

She'd wanted nothing more than to be the one walking down the aisle with him today. She'd never been more sure of anything in her life.

"The best." He absently stroked his finger along the ridge of her collarbone. She loved the fact that he was always touching her. "I'm guessing you're about to be swamped with business."

"I'm thinking so. If things go the way I think they

will, we'll need to start renovating the upstairs of the shop in a couple of months."

The sun was dipping low in the sky and a mosquito buzzed past her ear.

"I wanted to talk to you about that," he said. It was that tone she'd come to recognize—the one he used when he was about to try to manage her.

"Okay?"

"If we're teaming up, I figured this was appropriate."

He reached into the pocket inside his jacket, pulled out a rectangular, flat gift box and handed it to her. Not the ring box she would've liked to have seen, but he was definitely up to something.

Puzzled, she opened it and lifted the lid. She burst out laughing. A brand-spanking new paint scraper lay nestled in tissue paper, a red ribbon attached to the handle. "You're crazy."

"About you. It's engraved on the other side."

She flipped the scraper over. Inscribed on the blade was Natalie Stillwell. And there, attached to the red ribbon, a ring.

Her breath seemed to lodge in her throat, and for a few seconds she felt dizzy.

"Marry me." In typical, wonderful Beau Stillwell fashion, it was a directive rather than a question.

Her hands were so unsteady she couldn't untie the bow with the ring on it. "This is just a ploy to get me to move to Dahlia so you can sleep easy at night."

He grinned, taking the scraper from her and working

at the ribbon. "There you go, making everything hard again. And I told you from the beginning I was a selfish bastard. I want you where I can keep an eye on you." He sobered, freeing the ring from the ribbon. "I want you to be with me, looking at those hills every morning when we wake up and every night when we go to bed. I want us to have babies together and I want us to sit on that porch and grow old together."

"That's absolutely beautiful." She was about two seconds from tearing up.

"There's a theme there. Together. Say yes, Natalie."

"Yes, yes and yes." She held out her hand and he slipped the emerald-cut diamond onto her finger. A perfect fit.

* * * * *

COMING ON
STRONG

BY
TAWNY WEBER

Tawny Weber is usually found dreaming up stories in her California home, surrounded by dogs, cats and kids. When she's not writing hot, spicy stories for Blaze®, she's testing her latest margarita recipe, shopping for the perfect pair of boots or drooling over Johnny Depp pictures (when her husband isn't looking, of course). When she's not doing any of that, she spends her time scrapbooking and playing in the garden. She'd love to hear from readers, so drop by her home on the web, www.TawnyWeber.com.

To the Writers At Play:
Beth, Kath, Janice, Sheila, Anna, Kimmi,
Terri, Stacey, Carla, Betty, Marlene, Lisa, Trish,
Tammy, Heather, Angi, Leslie, Mona,
Anne-Marie, Cheryl and Terry.
Wild, crazy, amazing.
I love you all!

Prologue

"I DON'T THINK I can go through with it," Belle Forsham said, one hand pressed to her chest. Beneath the beaded silk of her bodice, her heart raced like a terrified rabbit. "I mean, this is crazy, you know? What the hell was I thinking?"

"If I recall, you were thinking that Mitch Carter was the hottest piece of ass you'd ever seen," Sierra Donovan said absently, her attention focused on getting the fluffy white tulle arranged just so over Belle's blonde curls.

"I said I *thought* he'd be the hottest piece of ass," Belle corrected, frowning at the image in the mirror. It was like watching herself through a Halloween filter. "I haven't been able to find out how hot he really is, though, have I? Which is why I'd be insane to go through with this, isn't it? Like, you know, buying a poked pig or something?"

"Pig in a poke?"

"Whatever."

Sierra just laughed and, with one last fluff of the veil, stepped back to gauge the results. "You look so…virginal."

Her best friend's tone said it all. Virginal was the last image Belle had ever aspired toward. Then again, she'd never figured on being a bride, either.

Wild and free, that was Belle's motto. Or it had been, right up until she'd met Mitch Carter. Then mottos had been nudged aside for her new obsession. Getting Mitch into bed.

Mitch was her daddy's new VP of development. The man was gorgeous. Rich auburn hair, cinnamon-brown eyes and the tightest butt she'd ever ogled. He exuded an energy that fascinated Belle. Power, definitely, and drive. A kind of intense focus that promised a woman that once she had his attention, he'd give her the most incredible sex of her life.

And Belle wanted his attention. But while she'd practically panted at his feet, he'd barely acknowledged her. For a woman used to men drooling on her buffed and polished toes, he'd been a total challenge. She threw herself at him, he gave her polite acknowledgment. She flirted, he watched. She pursued, he evaded.

Hard to get? Hell, Mitch Carter was damn near impossible.

At least, to get into bed. For some bizarre reason, after about a month of chasing him, he'd turned the tables. To use his own words, he'd started courting her. She smothered a baffled laugh at the idea of it. They'd mostly attended business functions, family events with her father, the occasional romantic dinner.

Unable to pace in the voluminous dress, Belle fidgeted on the stool where she sat. Her fingers fiddled with her late mother's pearl necklace, so sweetly innocent as it circled with a heavy weight of expectation around her neck. Like the white dress and delicate veil, the pearls really didn't suit her. Of course, neither did marriage.

Three months of dating. A smoking-hot kiss at the end of the evening. A little touchy-feely to add to the thrill. But never more. God, she'd wanted more. Then he'd scared the hell out of her when, out of the blue, he'd popped the question. Marriage. He wanted to make an honest woman of her…which was just plain weird since he hadn't tried her dishonest ways first.

She'd been so hot for him, she'd agreed instantly. She'd rushed the wedding plans, pulled out all the stops and organized a ritzy society event in less than three months. Through all the planning, something she'd proven to be amazingly skilled at, she'd had one thought and one thought only.

Hurry it up so she could get to her wedding night.

But now, when faced with the actual nuptials, she wasn't sure it was the right thing to do.

"Sierra, am I crazy to marry Mitch after only knowing him six months? I mean, is this too fast?"

Her friend opened her mouth, most likely to offer some dumb platitude about bridal jitters. It wasn't nerves, though. Belle didn't know what it was, but the lead weight in her stomach made her feel trapped, terrified. She'd much rather feel jittery anxiety instead.

Then Sierra shrugged, her own worry clear.

"I don't know," she admitted, chewing off her lipstick as she started to pace the room. Her typical in-your-face honesty and her maid-of-honor duty to keep Belle from freaking out were obviously at odds.

"Does it matter, though? You've wanted Mitch since you first saw him and now you're getting him. Long-term, even. You'll have killer sex tonight and blow his mind. Happy-ever-after, all that crap—that'll come with time."

Crap, indeed. The last thing anyone would call Belle was naive, but compared with the cynical Sierra she was a wide-eyed romantic. Whenever she thought past the honeymoon, let herself focus on anything besides the killer sex she was anticipating, she felt ill. She understood honeymoons. They were all about indulging in decadent sex in as many ways, places and times as possible. But marriage? Oh, God. She pressed her hand to her stomach, hoping she didn't get sick all over her dress. Was she ready to get married?

Belle stared at her reflection. White satin, seed beads and tulle. It all went perfectly with the pearls. Sweet and innocent. Definitely not her style. Her first choice for a dress had been sexy and edgy, but she'd thought Mitch would like this better.

"I guess that establishes why I'm marrying him," she said slowly. She loved him. Or, at least, she thought she did. Or, at least, she figured what she felt was probably love. She was fascinated by his kisses and his mind. By the sexual energy that simmered just under the surface. She was willing to make a promise to Mitch and keep it. Add to that the fact that she was agreeing to tie herself to the guy before he'd given her a single orgasm…well, that had to be love.

So, yes, she was ready for marriage.

"But why is he marrying me?" she asked in a whisper.

"Why don't you find out?" Sierra prompted for, like, the millionth time. "Quit second-guessing yourself and trying to please him and just ask."

Confront him? Straight up ask for possible rejection? Hell, no. One thing Belle had learned watching her late mother's bout with cancer was "what you don't know won't hurt you until later." She'd rather take her chances with the unknown.

"I'm just saying, if you want to know why Mitch is marrying you, he's the guy to ask," Sierra said, her tone making it obvious she knew she was wasting her breath.

"He's marrying you because he loves you, of course."

"What?" Surprised, she and Sierra both spun around to see Belle's other bridesmaid, Mitch's sister Lena.

Average height, average features, pale-brown hair cut in an unfortunate bob that did nothing to hide her very high forehead, Lena looked nothing like her brother. Belle had first met her when the woman had flown in from Pennsylvania a week earlier. Where Mitch was dynamic, Lena was tepid. It was hard to believe the two of them were even related.

Belle wanted to like her, but it was a struggle. She'd first suggested Lena join the wedding party in an attempt to make nice with Mitch's family. But the other woman had a mocking, judgmental air about her that grated on Belle's nerves. She was trying to ignore it, though. After all, this was her new sister-in-law.

"He must be madly in love with you," Lena pointed out as she inched into the room. The pale-rose bridesmaid dress that looked so sexy on Sierra made Lena look like a fluffy pink marshmallow. "Why else would he give up on his goals to get married?"

What goals was Mitch giving up? Belle gave Sierra a confused frown, then looked at Lena.

"Well, sure, partnership with your father is a huge incentive since Mitch had only planned on a short-term association with Forsham Hotels. It was the last step in his plan to take his construction company to the next level." She said all this while gliding an ugly shade of nutmeg lipstick over her thin lips. Then she met Belle's eyes in the mirror and shrugged. "His own development firm. He was counting on the experience and, you know, connections to help him out. Of course, I don't have to tell you how ambitious and determined to succeed he is."

"Partnership?" Belle frowned. What partnership?

"You didn't know?" Lena's mouth rounded to match the oops look in her brown eyes. "I'm so sorry. Maybe he was saving the news as a wedding surprise."

"He's a vice-president, not a partner," Sierra said, sounding as confused as Belle. "I thought he didn't have enough money or land to bring to the table for that kind of a deal."

"Well, yeah. But Uncle Danny said Mitch was given one of those offers he couldn't refuse. I guess your daddy's backing a risky land deal with the agreement that Mitch develop it for him. Aunt Edna said he saw a perfect opportunity and made the most of it." Lena gave a little who-knows shrug and a wide smile. Neither hid the malice peeking out from her simpering demeanor.

All those family names blurred in Belle's mind. She'd been

so excited to be a part of a large family, for the first time since she was eight to have more than just her and her dad at the Thanksgiving table. But after meeting Mitch's relatives, she wasn't so sure. It was like coming up against a very large, very cohesive wall. And she was on the wrong side of it.

Lena babbled more family gossip and inane insights into Mitch's personality. Belle just stared, her mind numb.

A risky land development? Her father wouldn't go into a project like that with just anyone. It would require a family commitment. Had he offered to make Mitch family? Or had Mitch offered to marry her in order to get the deal? And what did that make her? The price he had to pay for success? An easy route to the top?

Recognition, denial and sharp pain twisted together in her stomach. She'd wanted to believe he was marrying her because he couldn't resist, because he was crazy for her. But she'd obviously been wrong.

It all made sense now. His reluctance for intimacy, his emotional distance. Her earlier bridal jitters turned to cramping nausea. He was marrying his way into a business deal.

Lena's overarched brows drew together above her gleaming eyes. "You look a little green. Are you feeling okay?"

"Of course she's not," Sierra snapped. "What are you thinking, coming in here and spewing ugly rumors like that? What kind of person goes around gossiping about her brother on his wedding day?"

"Stepbrother," Lena corrected with a pout. "My dad married his mom when we were teenagers. And you're the nasty one. I was just saying that Belle's lucky that Mitch loves her enough to give up his dreams of his own development firm to work for her father. I wasn't insinuating anything else."

Lena wasn't his real sister? Why hadn't he told her? Belle didn't know why, but that was the last straw. She stood, the stool pressing against her full skirt like the bars on a cage. She wanted to run, but where? To Mitch? Hardly.

"The hell you weren't trying to cause trouble," Sierra growled at Lena. Their voices seemed to be coming from a long way away, muffled by the buzzing in Belle's head. "You're intimating that Belle's father bought her a groom. Like she or Mitch would be that desperate."

"Desperate? No. But when you put it that way, the wedding does sound a little fishy, doesn't it?" Lena gave them a wounded look, then headed for the door. Once there, she glanced over her shoulder. "Of course, I'm sure Belle knows Mitch loves her more than any silly promotion. I mean, who gets married without hearing vows of love? And Mitch never lies, not even for a business deal."

Sierra's cuss words hit Lena's retreating back. The brunette stormed to the door.

"Sierra," was all Belle said.

"I'm taking her down. That bitch isn't getting away with ruining your day."

For just one second, Belle let herself imagine Sierra jumping Lena and pummeling the smirk off her face. For the first time in her life, she considered diving in to help instead of yelling encouragement from the sidelines. Unlike her friend, Belle hated arguments.

Before she could decide whether or not to encourage Sierra to chase the woman's passive-aggressive ass down, Belle's father strode through the door. Handsome as ever in his tux, he winked at Sierra, then gave his only child a doting smile.

"You're a beautiful bride, sweetheart. Mitch is a lucky man."

Lucky? Really. It sounded like Mitch and her dad were the lucky ones. After all, they'd made the deal between them. She felt like the booby prize. She sucked in a shuddering breath, trying to calm the nausea rolling through her system. It would be so easy to just go through with this. She wasn't stupid. She'd known Mitch didn't love her. She wasn't sure she loved him, although she'd been willing to convince herself she did. But, like this stupid school-girl wedding dress, she'd been trying to give him whatever he wanted. And he couldn't even give her the truth?

Tears stung her eyes as she mentally kissed happy-ever-after, *and all that crap*, goodbye. Which didn't suck nearly as much as being cheated out of her wedding night.

Belle swallowed hard and looked into the face of the only man she'd ever felt safe loving. "Daddy? Did you offer to make Mitch your partner?"

Oblivious as usual to his daughter's emotional state, Franklin Forsham shrugged and patted her shoulder. "Not to worry, sweetie. I won't work him too hard."

Belle's gaze met Sierra's. Sympathetic tears washed away the anger in her friend's vivid blue eyes.

Numb now, Belle looked past her father's broad shoulders through the open door to the archway leading to the chapel. She could see the swags of orchids and pink roses, hear the soft tones of the harp. Her storybook wedding awaited.

She couldn't do it. She wasn't a negotiating point or a piece of property to be acquired in a business deal.

"I can't go through with the wedding," she declared, gathering the slick folds of her white satin skirt in her fist. "I won't sell myself. I might be willing to change, to compromise, but I draw the line at being lied to and cheated."

"What are you talking about?" Franklin's face turned white, then red. Hands clenched, he looked like he wanted to hit someone. "Mitch cheated on you?"

Scared of the anger on her father's face, of the pain pouring through her, Belle just shrugged. Cheated on her, cheated her, what was the difference? Emotion choked her, heated tears washed down her cheeks. Unable to hold back her sobs, she threw herself into her father's arms.

This was the last time she'd ever let a man, or the promise of hot sex, mean a damned thing to her.

1

"I FOUND a replacement for Gloria, Mr. Carter. Everyone says this is the best event planner on the west coast."

Unspoken was the understanding that Mitch would accept nothing less than the best. Which was difficult, considering his luxury resort was six weeks from opening to the public and had been beset by one problem after another. The most recent was the loss of the woman he'd contracted to handle all the resort events.

"Call me Mitch," he absently told his new assistant. He motioned to the vacant seat opposite his desk, but she shook her head, preferring to stand.

She'd been here a couple of weeks, but Diana was still jumpy and nervous. He knew he was demanding of his employees and it definitely made it easier to demand if they were on a first-name basis, so she'd better get over her timidity soon. They were almost at the end of his Mr. Nice Guy two-week break-in period.

He took the papers she handed him and in one glance was thrown back in time. Shocked, Mitch stared at the glossy dossier. The black-and-white photo didn't do justice to Belle Forsham's fairy-like beauty. It didn't capture the gleam of her tousled blond curls, or the wicked tilt of her sea-green eyes. The shadows accented her sharp features, the light reflecting off her smile.

The best? Yeah, she was. Good enough to make a man stupid. He glared at that smile, irritated with his body's reaction. Belle Forsham was pure trouble. He knew she was, and still he got hard remembering the taste of her lips. He tried to dull his body's reaction by visualizing himself standing, alone, at the altar.

Yeah, the anger definitely dimmed his desire.

"Mr. Carter?" Diana interrupted his pathetic obsessing. "Do you want me to contact Eventfully Yours? They're perfect for the job given the scope of the resort's needs and what you are looking for in an event planner."

"I'd rather not work with this particular company," he said, making it sound like he'd put some thought into the decision. In reality, no thought was required. Despite how often she showed up in his dreams, usually nude, Belle was at the bottom of the list of women he wanted to see. And she was definitely the last one he'd consider depending on for any aspect of his success.

After all, who knew better just how undependable she was? He tossed the file on the pile on his desk, the banner on her dossier catching his eye. He sneered. *Society's Planning Princess,* indeed.

"But…I don't understand. Everyone says they're the best. They've worked for a dozen A-list actors, some of the top musicians in the country and any number of politicians. They've arranged club openings, publisher parties, award-ceremony after-parties."

"They're not what I'm looking for," he snapped.

Diana's face fell, making her look like a sad chipmunk. Obviously sticking with her own version of the dress-for-success theory, she wore a tidy suit, stockings and ugly shoes. The overall image was serious efficiency, which was supported by the fact that she did a damned good job. Mitch wouldn't have hired her otherwise. He just wished she'd loosen up. He glanced down at his own jeans and workboots and gave a mental shrug. So she didn't have to loosen up to his level, but a little less formality wouldn't hurt.

"Let's look at the other event planners," Mitch instructed. "Sometimes a reputation is based on perception, rather than how good the firm actually is. I need more than gloss to make this work. If Lakeside is going to succeed, I'm going to need clever, resourceful and intuitive."

He pushed away from his overloaded desk and strode to the wide bank of windows that looked out to the lake. Almost completed, this resort was the culmination of all his dreams. Ten acres of verdant hills, lush gardens and what he secretly referred to as the enchanted forest, Lakeside was going to be the brightest jewel in his development crown and his first venture into hotels. So far he'd launched a half-dozen business parks, a mall and a couple of small restaurants. All of which he'd turned for a sweet profit.

But this resort was more than ambitious. For a guy who'd started out swinging a hammer, it was a huge coup. To kick this venture off here, in Southern California, was ballsy, given that he'd torched his bridges with the top hotelier on the west coast six years ago.

"I need a creative wizard with killer contacts. Someone who gets what our clientele will want, who can make the resort a posh getaway for the wealthy. If I'm going to turn this into the most talked-about hot spot of the rich and famous, I'm going to need someone who kicks ass."

Diana's mouth worked for a second, then after an obvious internal struggle, she thrust out her chin and pointed to the abandoned dossier on his desk.

"But that's what I've been trying to tell you, *Mitch*. Belle Forsham is all of that. Her events are the most talked-about, the most outside-the-box successes of the last two years. She seems to know everyone, do everything. She…" Diana stopped, wrinkled her nose and took a deep breath before continuing. "She kicks ass."

Amazed she'd finally used his given name, Mitch gave a snort of laughter at the uptight way she said *ass*. Amusement faded as he glanced again at the photo of his ex-fiancée.

When had she gone into event planning? And how the hell had she stuck with it long enough to be such a success? He had to admit, though, she had the intelligence and creativity to make it happen, although she'd always tried to hide the brains behind a flirty flutter of her lashes. She was definitely a social butterfly. He recalled the guest list for their aborted wedding. It had read like the who's who of *People* magazine.

It was the memory of that damned wedding, the humiliation of standing alone in front of all those gawking and snickering witnesses, that cinched it. Mitch ground his teeth, long-simmering anger burning in his gut. Belle might have great ideas, be clever and well-connected. But when the chips were down, she couldn't be counted on.

"She's a flake," he finally said.

"She's the best." Diana held up a sheaf of papers, all recommending Eventfully Yours. "Everything I've heard, all the research I did says that Belle Forsham is the It Girl of events. She's the hottest thing on the west coast."

Ambition fought with ego. The good of his company versus the biggest humiliation of his past. His need to see Belle again, to see if she was still that intriguing combination of sexy and sweet, battled with his desire to keep the door to that part of his history nailed shut.

Mitch looked over the resort grounds again, the gentle beauty of the sun-gilded lake beckoning him. Reminding him to do his best. A lot was riding on this deal. He'd sunk all his available resources into making this resort the most luxurious, the most welcoming. None of that would matter without guests with big enough wallets to indulge themselves.

He'd screwed himself into a corner once because of Belle Forsham. Or because of his desire to screw her, to be exact. He'd never wanted a woman the way he'd wanted Belle. But she'd been his boss's only child and off-limits. His old-fashioned upbringing and his worry that he'd be disrespecting Franklin if he had wild monkey sex with the guy's daughter had inspired him to the dumbest proposal of his life. Well, that and his idiotic belief that he'd fallen in love with her.

He'd handled it all wrong. He could see that now, but that didn't change the fact that she'd dumped him at the altar, and because of her he'd lost both his job and the respect of his mentor. Which bothered him almost as much as never having the wild Belle-against-the-wall sex he'd wanted so badly.

And he was supposed to welcome her back in his life? Was he willing to make a deal with the sexiest little devil he'd ever known in order to ensure his success?

He thought of his team. They were just as invested in the resort as he was. Because Mitch had little experience in the resort business, he'd brought in two managers—one to oversee the hotel, the other to run the three restaurants. He was the money man, the one with the vision, but he needed each of them on board to handle the hundred-plus employees and make sure the day to day of the operation ran smoothly while he made his vision a reality.

He glanced at the family picture behind his desk. He knew his family took great pride in his accomplishments, just as they had huge expectations for his success. Expectations that included supporting his grandmother and providing jobs for four of his cousins in his company. Those expectations were both a source of pride and a noose around his neck. He had to succeed.

The resort already had enough problems. On top of the usual

construction glitches and startup issues, they'd been having a run of bad luck. Losing his event coordinator was just the last in a long string of unexplained setbacks. Could he afford to blow off the perfect planner out of pride?

Damn. He sighed and pushed the file on the desk toward Diana.

"Check her availability."

"THERE'S ONLY one man who'll satisfy you. Quit stalling and go for it, already."

Belle Forsham stopped pacing across the lush amethyst carpet of her office to roll her eyes at her best friend and business partner. The office was a quirky combination of trendy accessories, sexy textures and practical lines. Much like Belle herself.

"It's not like chasing some guy down for hot sex, Sierra. This is serious. We're talking business here. My father's business. Or should I say, the end of my father's business."

"Exactly. You want to save Forsham Hotels, you need to get help." Sierra flipped open the pink bakery box she'd brought in for their morning meeting and, after a careful perusal, chose a carrot-cheesecake muffin.

Not even looking at the other offerings, Belle automatically went for the fanciest muffin. Rich, chocolaty and decadent, just the way she liked it. Except she was so stressed, she put it down after one bite. Why waste the indulgence?

"I don't need help," she lied.

"Yes, you do. It's not like you and I can plan an event that will save your dad's butt," Sierra shot back, referring to their company, Eventfully Yours, as she licked cream-cheese icing from her thumb.

They were *the* elite event planners on the west coast, catering to the rich and famous from southern California up to Monterey. Combining Sierra's fearless attitude and Belle's knack for creative entertainment, the two women had hit the Hollywood scene hard and strong four years back. Eventfully Yours had grown from organizing themed play dates for sitcom divas' Pomeranians to arranging intimate soirees for A-list actors and five hundred of their closest friends.

"You know, now that I think about it, I really shouldn't be going behind my father's back," Belle stalled, sitting on the edge of her inlaid rosewood desk. "He'd be the first to say his heart attack is no reason to treat him like an invalid. If he wanted to make a deal to save the hotels, he'd do it himself."

Used to Belle's habit of squirreling out of anything that made her uncomfortable, Sierra just stared. It was that uncompromising, see-all-the-way-into-her-soul look that Belle hated. Whenever Sierra narrowed her blue eyes and shot her that look, Belle felt like a total wuss.

"Don't you think if my dad wanted to deal with Mitch Carter, he'd approach him himself?" she asked, playing her last excuse.

"Right. Your dad, upstanding guy that he is, is gonna go begging help from the man he fired from a dream VP position and partnership in one of the primo hotel conglomerates in the U.S. The same guy his daughter ditched at the altar."

"Exactly," Belle exclaimed, jumping up from her perch on the desk to throw her arms in the air. "Given our sucky history, why would you think Mitch wants anything to do with me?"

Sierra arched a brow, then gave a little shrug. Taking her time, she dusted the crumbs off her fingers, shifted in the plush chair and curled her long legs under her. Raising one brow, she tapped a manicured nail on her bare ankle.

"This is the guy who refused to have sex with you before marriage. I figure he has some twisted belief in things like honor."

Sierra rolled her eyes at her own words. Always the cynic, she didn't understand the concept of selfless honor. Of course, neither did Belle. But it sure sounded sweet.

"This would also be the same guy who, despite having the perfect opportunity to make your daddy's life a living hell when you ruined their deal, simply shook hands and walked away."

Walked away and left her daddy holding a piece of investment property that, because of zoning and development legalities, was now taking his business down the toilet. But considering what Belle had done, that wasn't really Mitch's fault. Was it?

"So he's freaking hero material," she muttered. "So what?"

Belle slid off her heels so she could pace faster. Nothing slowed down a good pace like four-inch Manolos. The way her luck was running, she'd stumble and break the heel. And she needed to move around and try to shake off the nasty feeling that had settled over her when she'd been reminded of how badly she'd treated Mitch. That he'd broken her heart was no excuse. She knew that now. But knowing it and being willing to do something about it were definitely two different things.

"Exactly," Sierra agreed. "He's hero material. Which means he's hard-wired to ride to the rescue. Even after all that crap went down, Mitch never badmouthed you or your father. If he knew how bad things are now, maybe he'd offer some advice. Or best case? He'll step in, checkbook at the ready, and save the company."

Belle grimaced.

Mitch definitely lived by his own code. Over the last six years he'd developed a reputation as the man with the magic touch. Mr. Money, a real-estate developer with an eye for success, he was known in the industry as a fair man who played by his own rules, uncompromising, intense and dynamic. People appreciated his generous willingness to share his success, but behind the scenes, there were whispers of ruthless payback to anyone who crossed him.

Which didn't bode well for Belle, since she was the one seen as most deserving of Mitch's revenge. Mutual acquaintances still joked that she'd better watch her back. She knew better, though. She'd never mattered enough to him to merit that much attention.

"He won't deal with me," she assured Sierra, playing her trump card.

"You don't know that." The way Sierra said it, as though she had some naughty little secret, made Belle nervous.

"Yes, I do." Belle took a deep breath and, with the air of one confessing a mortal sin, dropped her voice to a loud whisper. "I never told you, but I tried to see Mitch. Two years ago. Remember when I had that car wreck?"

Eyes huge with curiosity, Sierra nodded.

"I was shook up and had some weird idea that being hit in a head-on accident on a one-way street was a sign that I should make amends for all my wicked ways." She met her friend's snort of laughter with a glare. "I figured ditching Mitch topped my wicked list, so I sucked up my courage and went to apologize."

"No way," Sierra breathed. "And you didn't tell me?"

"There was nothing to tell. He was supposedly out of the country."

"Supposedly?"

"Well, I went back a couple weeks later and his assistant said he was out with the flu."

"So?"

"So isn't it obvious? He was avoiding me."

"He left the country and got the flu to avoid you?"

Belle rolled her eyes. "No, that was just BS. He was probably there in his office telling his assistant to make something up so he didn't have to see me."

Sierra's expression clearly said "you've got to be kidding."

"Don't give me that look. It could be true."

"Only if the roles were reversed. You're the one afraid of confrontation, Belle. Not Mitch. If he were in the office, I'm sure he'd have taken five minutes to personally tell you to kiss his ass."

"And you want me to go chasing the guy for favors?" Belle ignored the confrontation issue. It was true, after all. "We both know he doesn't want anything to do with me."

Sierra hummed, then slid off the chair and crossed to the leather bag she'd tossed on the credenza. She pulled out a file folder with what looked like a printout of an e-mail clipped to it.

Waving the file at Belle, she arched a brow and asked, "Wanna bet?"

"Spill," Belle demanded, making a grab for the folder. Sierra whipped it out of reach with a laugh.

"You really need to have more faith in your impact on people."

"According to you, people are only out for what they can get," Belle shot back.

"Exactly. So while Mitch might happily punish you when it's convenient, the tune changes when he needs something."

"And he needs us?"

"No. He needs you. This gig is right up your alley," Sierra claimed. Which meant it was totally social. Sierra handled the big corporate and studio events, the types of things that required juggling numbers, working with specific images or ground rules. In other words, the more traditional events that relied heavily on organization. Belle's specialty was the over-the-top hedonistic fantasies. And since she'd indulged in so many fantasies about Mitch Carter, the idea of having another shot at sharing a few with him sent her pulse racing.

"Spill," she demanded. She tried to ignore the excitement dancing in her stomach, making her edgy and impatient. This was crazy. Mitch hated her. He had to. But maybe, just maybe, this was her shot at making amends. At fixing the past and helping her father. And maybe, just maybe…at finally getting into his pants.

She'd blown it before, stumbling over that silly marriage idea. But she was older and much more experienced now. This time she'd be smarter. If she and Mitch did find common ground, all she wanted was sex. That, and help for her dad.

She took the file from Sierra with a smile of anticipation. Belle read the e-mail. Then she read it again. The excitement curdled in her stomach.

"A resort grand opening? That's more your gig than mine," Belle said, trying to ignore the disappointment that settled over her like an itchy wool blanket.

"That's what they say they want. But check out the details I found."

Knowing her friend's instincts were usually spot-on, Belle opened the file. It just took a glance, a quick flip through the papers and plans for her to see the perfect hook to turn his lush resort into the hottest, most exclusive getaway on the west coast.

Mitch's background was in development. And he was damned good at it. But he was thinking too traditionally for this resort. It wasn't a run-of-the-mill hotel and shouldn't be treated that way. Given the remote beauty of the location, yet its easy access to L.A., it could be the nice luxury vacation place he had outlined. Or it could be the chicest spot for decadence in southern California. Indulgent weekends, clandestine trysts, decadent fantasies. All there, for a price. All guaranteed to be unique, elite and, best of all, private.

Her blood heated, ideas flashing like strobe lights through her mind. Excitement buzzed, but she tried to tamp it down. There was nothing worse than getting all stirred up, only to be left flat. It was like foreplay with no orgasm. Amusing once or twice, but ultimately a rip-off.

"This e-mail isn't from Mitch himself," she pointed out. "And his assistant isn't offering us the position, she's only checking availability."

"So? Since when have we waited for an engraved invitation to charm our way into a job?"

Good point. The two women had spent their first year in business clubbing and hitting every social event they could wiggle or charm their way into on the off chance of finding clients. Once at a fashion show someone had mentioned a director's wife with a penchant for poodles and Motown. The next day Belle contacted the director and suggested he throw his wife a surprise party, with the musical dog theme. Such ballsiness paid off both in contacts and jobs as they'd built Eventfully Yours.

But this was different. Mitch probably hated her. Then again, why would he be willing to work with her if he was holding a grudge? Belle sighed, not sure if her reasoning was sound or pure bullshit.

"We have an opportunity to kick ourselves to the next level with a job this exclusive," Sierra said quietly as she settled back in her chair. "Better yet, you have a chance here to settle up some past debts, get some of that fabled closure. Are you going to let semantics stop you?"

Was she? Belle glanced at Sierra, noting the assured confidence on her friend's angular face. Sierra wouldn't push unless she thought it was really important. She might be a relentless nag when it came to the success of Eventfully Yours. But she was a good friend and would never sacrifice Belle to snag a client. Even one as potentially huge as MC Development.

Belle had spent the last six years regretting her screw-up. She should have faced Mitch herself instead of running like a wuss. Hell, she should never have agreed to marriage in the first place. She'd known better. Sex, as incredible as it might have been, was no reason to go off the deep end. But she'd been afraid to push the issue, then after the altar-ditch, too hurt and upset to face his anger.

Ever since, she'd tried to find a guy to replace him, both in her bed and her fantasies. None had stuck, though. Probably because she'd never actually had Mitch. This might be her chance to get over him, once and for all.

She glanced back at the files, the panoramic photo of the resort and its welcoming lakeside forest. She wanted to see it in person. Even more, she wanted to do Mitch, right there on the edge of that lake. Outdoor sex in the woods, like something out of a fairy tale. The orgasm she was imagining was probably mythical, too. But she didn't care. She wanted to find out.

Despite the nerves clawing at her, she set the file down, slipped her shoes on and grabbed her purse.

"Shopping?" Sierra asked, sliding her feet into her shoes, too.

"We'll start with lingerie. I heard about this new place called Twisted Knickers. The designs supposedly take provocative to a whole new level."

FOCUSED ON his conversation, Mitch strode past Diana's desk with his cell phone glued to his ear. His assistant waved her hand, trying to get his attention, but he held up one finger, then pointed to his office door. He'd talk to her when he was done.

"I don't want any more excuses," Mitch ordered his foreman. "The electrical has to be finished by the first of the month." This damned week had gone downhill fast. There'd been even more building delays, his designer had gone into labor two months early, and now electrical problems. To top it off, he'd talked to three event planners so far and none had come close to sparking his interest. He was wound so tight, he was ready to snap. "The plumbing is already three weeks behind. If we lose any more ground, we won't open on schedule. If that happens, we're screwed."

He listened to his foreman's justifications with half an ear as, still ignoring Diana's increasingly frantic gestures, he

opened his office door. As always, the view of the lush green
woods through the window beckoned him. Maybe he'd go for
a run, shake off some of the tension. He'd rather have a long,
sweaty roll in the sheets, but he couldn't afford the distraction.
Not when everything was on the line.

One more step into his office and Mitch felt like he'd been
hit in the face. Maybe it was sex on the brain, but even the air
shifted, turning sultry and suggestive. He breathed in, his lungs
filling with a musky floral scent.

Instant turn-on.

Seated as she was in the high-backed leather chair facing
the window, all Mitch could see were long, sexy legs ending
in strappy black do-me heels. He tried to swallow, but his
mouth had gone dirt-dry. Those were wrap-around-the-shoul-
ders-and-ride-'em-wild legs.

Damn. Talk about distraction.

Mitch flipped his phone closed, not sure if he'd said
goodbye or even if his foreman was still talking. He stepped
further into the office, deliberately closing the door behind
him. Two more steps into the room, and he could see around
the high leather back of the chair.

Gorgeous. The impact was like getting kicked in the gut by
a black belt on steroids. Swift, intense and indefensible. The
first time he'd seen Belle, she'd been twenty-one. He'd thought
then she couldn't possibly be more confident in her own sexual
power. He'd obviously been wrong, since she was now a master
of it. Or was that mistress? And why did that make him crave
studded black leather shorts?

Six years had added layers of polish, maturity and assurance
to her already powerful sexual charisma. Mitch's gaze reluctantly left those delicious legs to travel upward. He noted the
flirty green skirt, the same shade as her eyes, ending a few
inches above her knees. A wide leather belt accented her waist

and emphasized her lush breasts in the gossamer soft-white blouse. Mitch let his eyes rest there for just a second, millions of regrets pounding in his head. He wished like hell that once, just once, he'd tasted their bounty.

He was sure if he had, he'd have easily kept her out of his mind. The only reason he'd never found another woman to replace her was that he'd blown the fantasy of sex between them all out of proportion.

He felt her amusement before he even looked at her face. Belle was used to being ogled, so he didn't waste time on embarrassment. He wondered briefly at giving her that much power this early in the game, but he couldn't seem to help himself. That there was a game afoot was implicit. The question wasn't who would win, either. It was how much it would cost him to play.

She arched one platinum brow, amused challenge clear in her eyes and the dimple that played at the corner of her full lips. Her hair was shorter now, angled to emphasize her rounded cheekbones and the sharp line of her jaw.

"Well, well," Mitch drawled, moving around to lean on his desk while he faced the biggest mistake of his life. "If it isn't my long-lost bride."

2

"LONG-LOST bride-*to-be,* if you please," Belle corrected precisely.

She had to work to keep her smile in place. As much as she'd have preferred to avoid reference to their past, she'd known Mitch, for all his gentlemanly reputation, wouldn't sidestep the issue. She took a little breath before she lifted her chin. Since she had to deal with it, she'd face it head-on.

Or at least make him think she was dealing with it just long enough to flirt her way off the topic.

"Don't you look gorgeous," she commented with a wink. Since he'd made no attempt to hide his visual tour, she let her eyes take their own leisurely stroll, appreciating the view from head to toe.

Damn, he really had gotten better with age. His hair, still that deliciously rich auburn, was a little longer, a little less formal. His face was leaner, his shoulders broader. She was tempted to ask him to turn around so she could decide if his ass was any tighter. But it was awfully hard to beat perfection, so she doubted it.

"The years have definitely treated you well, Mitch."

Beneath her husky words and confident smile, her insides felt as though they were on a wobbly roller coaster. Despite that, she slid to her feet in one slow, sensual motion. His cinnamon-brown eyes blurred as she stepped forward. Heat flared between them, the same heat that had lured her from interested to obsessive so long ago.

Then, so quickly she wondered if she'd imagined the desire, he blinked and the look switched to simple curiosity. Belle had to fight to keep her smile in place. Damn him, that's how he'd always twisted her into knots. One second she'd been sure he was hot for her, the next he had total control.

Not this time.

Instead of the expected move, another step closer so she was in body-heat distance of him, Belle shifted her weight. Her hip to one side, she lifted a shoulder and gave a flutter of her lashes.

"Well?" she asked.

Mitch just arched one brow. His shoulders, she noted, were stiff, as though he was preparing himself. For what? she wondered. A handshake, a hug or, even worse, a big sloppy kiss.

She was tempted. But lurking behind that polite curiosity in his eyes was something edgier. Perhaps he was just waiting to verbally rip into her. Instead of intimidating her, that just added to the excitement.

"Well, what?"

Some insane impulse urged Belle to blurt out an apology. To tell him how sorry she was for the pain she must have caused. To confess her immaturity, her lack of consideration. Luckily, nerves trapped the words in her throat.

"Did you miss me?" she asked instead. Getting Mitch to deal with her, to give her the contract and with it the opening to butter him up so he'd help her father, was going to be hard enough. Why throw fuel on the flames? Especially when she was much more interested in starting a whole new fire.

"About as much as I miss the Macarena," he shot back.

Belle snickered. Then, unable to help herself, she laid her hand on his forearm. "It is good to see you again."

Eyes narrowed, he glanced down at her hand, then back at

her face. With a shrug, he gave a half smile and jerk of his chin. Only an optimist would call it a nod. Belle, being a glass-half-full kind of gal, took heart.

"Why are you here?"

"Right to the point, hmm?" Belle used the seconds it took her to return to her seat to take a deep breath. Control was crucial here. She had to play it just right.

With that in mind, she leaned back against the soft leather and gave Mitch a warm smile.

"I've got something you need," she told him.

"I'll pass," he responded instantly. "I tried to get it once before and look how that worked out."

Belle hid her wince. Whether the pain in her chest was from a singed ego or her bruised heart she didn't know.

"Maybe you were using the wrong inducement."

"Obviously," he said. Apparently resigned to the fact that she wasn't going to explain her presence until she was good and ready, he moved around his desk to take a seat.

"Oh, please. Let's be realistic. I was young and hot for you. For what I imagined would be incredible sex between the two of us. I wasn't looking for marriage, but that was the price you put on yourself." Talk about role reversal. She might be a jerk for her way of handling the situation, but he was a bigger jerk for being willing to use *her* lust to advance *his* career. But if she wasn't holding any grudges, why should he? "We'd have been much better off if you'd just gone for the kinky affair I was hoping for instead of insisting on milking the free cow."

"Why buy the cow if you can get the milk for free," he corrected.

"There you go," she said with a smile. "Except we were both after something other than milk, weren't we?"

She'd wanted sex, he'd wanted a foot up the career ladder. Neither one of them came off lily-pure, so she didn't bother pointing that out. Instead, she leaned down to pull a file out of her black leather portfolio.

"I understand you need an event planner."

Mitch's jaw tightened, but he just gave a dismissive shrug. His shirt rippled over arms that looked very intriguing. She'd bet there were some sweet biceps under that pristine cotton. Her teeth itched to take a nibble and see just how hard his muscle was.

"I might have considered a planner for the grand opening, but I'm not overly attached to the concept," he hedged.

Which meant he wanted one, he just didn't want it to be her. No problem. She'd change his mind.

"That's smart," she said, leaving the file in her lap instead of handing it to him. "Your grand opening should make a statement, of course. But you want that message to integrate with Lakeside's theme, its purpose."

"This isn't Disneyland," he pointed out, rolling his eyes.

"No, but you would do well to look at the success of theme parks like that. They have a clear message. A purpose that fulfils the guests' specific needs. Everything they offer, every single thing, supports that purpose."

"My resort has a purpose. You grew up in the hotel business, you already know this."

"But you're not trying to launch a hotel here, are you? You aren't targeting the average vacationer, honeymoon couple or getaway guest."

"I'm not?"

Even though he phrased it as a question, his tone was pure let's-humor-the-airhead. She was used to people taking one look at her blond hair and sexy image and judging her by stereotypes. Since it usually worked to her advantage, Belle didn't mind. At least, she told herself she didn't. It wasn't like Mitch knew her well enough to understand her or anything. So she fell into her typical lure-'em-in-and-close-the-deal mode with a flutter of her lashes.

"Are you? What do you see this resort offering?" she asked off-handedly.

"Offering? What any resort offers, of course. First-class luxury accommodations. Relaxation and pampering. The perfect getaway."

"I can get luxury and pampering at my father's hotels for half the price," she pointed out.

His eyes flashed at the mention of her father. Uh-oh, not a good sign. But instead of commenting, he just pointed out the window.

"Not with this lavish view, prime location or decadent opulence. Lakeside is top of the line. Luxurious suites, each with its own fireplace and bar. Three-hundred-count Egyptian sheets and down comforters, one-of-a-kind artwork and a stunning view from every room. We have the hottest golf course, three four-star restaurants, a ballroom, spa, designer shops."

Belle pressed her lips together to hide the smile brought on by his fervent recital of his resort's brochure. He sounded like a momma defending her baby against the crime of mediocrity. Good, that meant he was heavily invested in making Lakeside the biggest success possible.

"Let's cut to the chase, hmm?" she said once she was sure she could keep the triumph from her tone. "To really make your resort stand out, to make it a certifiable success, you need a hook. If you want the wealthy southern California clientele to flock here like flaming moths you're going to need to offer something a little more exotic than nice sheets, a golf course and hot stone massages."

"Moths to a flame," he corrected.

"Exactly," she agreed with a wink. "And like those moths, the wealthy and famous will swarm here. With the right incentive, of course."

"What do you have in mind?" he asked, sounding reluctantly intrigued. His gaze fell to the papers in her lap.

She tapped one red-tipped fingernail on the file and smiled.

"To use that Disney analogy again, I'm talking about a theme park for adults. Wealthy adults. Or better yet, famous wealthy adults. Ones who are looking for a grown-up park to play in."

Belle leaned forward to put the file on his desk. Mitch's gaze dropped to her cleavage. From the heat in his eyes, the way they went dark and intense, she figured her Twisted Knickers leather-and-lace demi-bra had just paid off.

"You want to make this resort a standout, you need to cater to the rich and famous. If you want them lining up to get in here, you need to offer them the one thing they want more than anything else. The one thing they'd pay almost any price for."

Keeping his eyes locked on hers, Mitch used one finger to pull the file toward him. He didn't flip it open, but sat there with his hand over it as if considering whether it was even worth the effort.

"And that is?" he finally asked.

"Sex, of course."

MITCH'S JAW dropped. This was a multimillion dollar venture, prime real estate, and he had everything on the line—his money, his company and, even more important, his reputation.

"You're suggesting I turn my luxury resort into a sex club?"

He didn't know why the idea surprised him. Everything about Belle made him think of sex. It always had. From her husky voice to her bedroom eyes and on down that gorgeous body to her suckable toes.

But he'd screwed up his career once because he'd been obsessed with her. Blinded by the dream of having it all, he'd tossed aside his own plans to accommodate her and her father's wishes, and ended up with nothing. It'd taken him three years to rebuild his reputation, another two to regain lost ground. He wasn't about to screw up again.

"Actually, I doubt you'd be able to pull off the sex club," she replied with a long look that made it clear she'd love to see him try. "There are some fabulous ones around that make good money, of course, but that's not quite the niche I had in mind."

It took physical effort to keep himself from asking her just how familiar she was with these *fabulous* sex clubs. He managed, just barely, to smother the biting jealousy that clawed at his gut when he imagined her hitting those clubs with another man. Or, given the clubs, other *men*.

Dammit, six years ago, that ugly green monster had goaded him into proposing marriage instead of taking her up on the wild sexual affair she'd offered. He hated—not just disliked, but viciously rip-the-head-off-whoever-it-was hated—the idea of some other man touching Belle. She was the only woman in the world to inspire him to want to brand her. To make her his and his alone, in every way possible. For a man who considered himself evolved beyond caveman idiocy, it had been a blow to the ego. Not enough of a blow to stun the jealousy monster, though.

To distract himself from the images, and from the memory of her lush, lace-clad breasts, clearly visible when she'd leaned across to hand him the file, Mitch tilted his head in question.

"What exactly are you proposing?"

"Private sex," she said in the same tone she'd use to share a national secret.

"Huh?" He didn't get it. The rooms had locks. There were no video cameras around.

"The paparazzi and gossip hounds have declared open season on celebrities. They have no degree of privacy anymore. Not only actors and musicians, but any big name in the industry. Before you relocated here, you were based in New York, right?" At his nod, she continued, "You probably see it, or would if you paid attention, on the east coast. But it's nothing like the insanity here in southern California."

"What does that have to do with sex? Or, how did you put it? Private sex?"

Belle arched one brow. "Everything. Haven't you ever wanted some hot, wild getaway sex at a luxury resort?"

Hell, yeah. He wanted it now, as a matter of fact. Mitch did a quick mental tally of how many bedrooms were complete here at the resort. He could do Belle in fourteen hot, wild ways without using the same room twice. Even more if they went vertical. And that wasn't even counting the private cottages scattered around the resort grounds.

"Your rich and famous are welcome to come have sex here," he told her. "We're an equal-opportunity resort in that regard."

Her look made him laugh. Like a crack in her perfect image, she went from glossy sex kitten to cute and adorable in the wrinkle of her nose.

"I'm glad to know you have no restrictions on sex," she responded, her tone husky and blatantly interested. "I hope that applies to your personal life as well as your resort?"

"The only restriction I follow is to avoid trouble." His grin fell away as he remembered that Belle was pure trouble, inside and out.

She tut-tutted. "Safe sex? How boring is that? The only time those two words belong together is in reference to health precautions."

Images of swings, leather and handcuffs—without the cushy fur lining—flashed through his mind. His body stirred in instant reaction. Damn, maybe he needed to rethink this keeping-Belle-at-a-distance thing? After all, she was here, he was here. They had no commitment beyond the moment, were free to do as they liked. Maybe instead of cursing the past, he should take her up on the offer of pleasure so clear in her eyes.

Fourteen rooms.

Wild sex.

Handcuffs.

And then show her on her way.

"I take it you'd rather have unsafe sex?" he asked with a slow, teasing smile. Mentally watching his caution trampled by lust, Mitch waved good-bye to good sense and gave Belle a look that said just how unsafe he'd like sex to get between them.

Her expression didn't change, but a faint flush washed over her chest, letting him know she wasn't unaffected. His mouth watered to taste her there, just above the curve of her breasts. The rational, ambitious voice in his head warned him not to get dragged down by his dick. She was trouble. She'd proved that by almost ruining him when she'd walked out. His dick didn't give a damn.

"I like sex," she corrected, "without rules and restrictions."

"I like the sound of that. Tell me more."

"What I really want is a chance to show you."

Rock-hard and ready to sweep his desk clean for a hot, fast preview, Mitch bit back a groan. Principles fought lust. Need smothered angst.

Then Belle stood, took two short steps to his desk and leaned forward. One leg bent, she rested her knee and hip on the desk. Right there on the redwood surface where he'd just fantasized about stripping her bare.

Her scent, something that reminded him of a moonlit garden on a hot summer night, wrapped around him with long, delicate fingers. When she leaned closer, it was all he could do to keep from grabbing her. Better to let her make the move, he told himself. Less liability for going along than for doing the grabbing. He swallowed, his mouth ready to taste her, his tongue craving the feel of hers.

Inches away, she stopped. Mitch frowned. No kiss?

She arched one brow, then tilted her head to indicate the file lying on the desk between them. Of course. He snickered at himself, a mocking reminder that this woman was trouble.

A sardonic smile curving his lips, he took the hint and flipped open the file. Might as well give it a cursory glance so he could refuse her services before they got horizontal.

It didn't take long for Mitch to take in the file contents. Event outlines, yes. But more than just party ideas, the proposal included a general marketing plan and focus strategy.

A chill ran up his back when Mitch skimmed the vision statement. Either she was a hell of a lot savvier than he gave her credit for or she had an inside track to his company's information. Because this statement was the twin of his own, with a few tiny exceptions.

Vital exceptions in terms of marketing direction, focus. And, he had to admit, probable success.

Why couldn't she be just a pretty face and hot body? Her proposal was outstanding. The risk was minimal, the possible benefits innumerable. Damn. Mitch ground his teeth in frustration as the businessman in him overrode the horndog.

"This is a great plan," he reluctantly admitted. "By focusing on the paparazzi-hounded stars, we can provide the perfect getaway for the rich and famous. We'd amp up the security, spread the word that this is a photo-free zone." As ideas started to flow, Mitch grabbed a pen. "Special training for the staff, non-disclosure agreements, legal repercussions."

"Privacy is vital, but it's just one benefit," she cautioned. "Don't lose sight of the bigger picture. Yes, you want to bring in the Hollywood crowd. Once word gets out that you're offering a safe haven from the voracious press, combined with the buzz about how fab your resort is, I guarantee they'll be interested. But that's not going to be enough."

Mitch barely heard her, he was so focused on getting his

flying thoughts on paper. Then Belle slid another folder on top of his notes.

He should have known. She was an event planner, and her initial plan hadn't mentioned a single party or gala. His eyes narrowed as he read the event outline.

"You do want to turn my resort into a sex club," he exclaimed in shock.

"Not exactly," she denied, with a shrug that reminded him that her breasts were less than a foot from his mouth. Luckily her words were enough distraction. Almost.

"I'm suggesting you focus on indulgence of the most decadent kind. Couples' massages, chocolate baths, midnight champagne dinners by the lake. All romantic enough on their own, but you'll offer a few extras. I've got tons of ideas, and I'll share them if we go to contract on this. But basically, you'll have to take your standard resort offering and sex it up. Make it hot and inviting with just a hint of depravity. You do that and I guarantee you'll reel in the jaded Hollywood crowd."

"Depravity? Like what? On-call hookers and pole-dancing lessons?"

"There's nothing depraved about pole-dancing," she chided. "I do it and it's great exercise." She gave him a heavy-lidded look that promised all sorts of pulse-raising benefits. "Someday I'll show you."

Did nothing faze her? Mitch had to laugh.

"The difference between a high-class sex club and a luxury resort offering decadent indulgence is vast, Mitch." Her tone turned serious as all teasing flirtation left her face. "A sex club is cheap, base. It's all about the pickup, the kink, the instant satisfaction. You'd be offering a safe haven for your guests to indulge themselves in all ways, including their sexual fantasies. Masquerade balls, a menu that includes reputed aphrodisiacs, a lingerie shop in the lobby. Pure luxury in perfect keeping with the rest of your resort's offerings. Nothing tacky or low-class."

Decadent indulgence? She was right. That would definitely mesh with the extravagant luxury he'd planned to offer. As far as hooks went, it was certainly fresh. Definitely better than anything his marketing department had come up with.

But it meant focusing his business on sex. And working with Belle. Two things that he'd learned the hard way should never go hand in hand.

Mitch leaned back in his chair, both to show control and because he needed to put some distance between him and Belle's hypnotic scent. He glanced at the Eventfully Yours contract, then gave her an assessing look through narrowed eyes.

"This plan has potential, I'll give you that," he acknowledged. "But I have to ask, what's to keep me from handing you back this contract, unsigned, and running with the plan on my own?"

"Ethics, of course." Belle's look was pure, pitying amusement. "You're one of the good guys, Mitch. You believe in helping others, not screwing them over."

He pulled a face. Yeah, she had him there.

"Besides," she continued as she studied her well-manicured nails, "you can't pull it off without my contacts. At least, not to the level necessary to be the kind of success you're looking for. And then there's the fact that if you do try without me, I'd take the plan to three hotels and resorts within driving distance and offer them the same idea. People are going to try to copy you down the road, but if you lose the exclusivity right out of the gate, you're guaranteed failure."

Damn. So she was hell on wheels as a businesswoman. Mitch knew he should be disgruntled, but he only felt an odd sort of admiring pride.

She read the frustration on his face and laughed. With a wicked look, she leaned forward and patted his cheek.

"Don't worry, you'll love working with me. I'm…fabulous," she purred. The innuendo made Mitch want to whimper.

"You realize if I give you this contract, sex between us is out of the question." He tossed the words out like a drowning man going down for the last time. *At least while they worked together,* he amended in his head. He wasn't stupid or delusional. He knew, sooner or later, they'd be doing the nasty. But he planned on calling the shots, and working together would make it much later than his body wanted.

"If that's the way you want it," she said agreeably. From the wattage of her smile, she was just as happy he'd issued the ultimatum. Damn her.

Mitch frowned, wondering if he'd miscalculated Belle. She came across as hot and sexy. Her nature, her demeanor and vibe were pure sensuality. Was it all an act? A hot front shielding a cold core? A tool to twist a guy by his dick so she could easily lead him around?

"You're fine with that," he clarified.

"Of course," she said, sliding off his desk. With a quick twitch of her hand, she straightened her skirt and made sure her blouse was tucked into the wide leather belt circling her tiny waist. He clenched his teeth to keep from drooling as she bent over to pick up her bag, and wished like hell he'd refused outright to work with her.

He forced his gaze from her ass to the folder, contents and plans spread over his desk blotter. No, he couldn't regret considering her for the job. Her take on the resort's events and focus was the most dynamic he'd ever seen.

He could wish they'd done the dirty on the desk first, though. Mitch stifled a sigh and came around to the front of his desk to escort her out.

Belle turned to give him a wide smile and held out her hand. Seal the deal with a handshake, he supposed.

When he took her delicate palm in his, she dropped their hands so, enfolded, they rested on her hip. Then she closed the distance between them until her breasts were a hair's-breadth away from his chest. Mitch's erection returned, granite-hard.

Her gaze locked on his, Belle leaned forward. Up on her tiptoes, she used her breasts against his chest for balance. She wrapped one hand around the back of his neck and gave a gentle tug, pulling his mouth down to meet hers.

Both fascinated and turned on, Mitch let her take the lead. She was the most sexually confident women he'd ever met. Yet beneath it all, he sensed the same sweet vulnerability that had hooked him six years before. The sweetness, he knew, would be his downfall if he wasn't careful.

Not willing to show her how strong her power was, he held himself still as her lips pressed, soft and lush, against his. His hands itched to pull her close, to press her tight against his body so he could feel her curves surrendering.

Then her tongue, so soft and seductive, traced the line of his mouth. A quick flick to the corners, a soft slide across his lower lip. Blood roared through Mitch's head, drowning out all caution. When her teeth nipped, just a little, at his lip, he lost it.

His hands dove into her hair, holding her head still as his tongue took hers in a wild dance of pleasure. Slip, slide, intense and delicious, he gave way to the power of their kiss.

More, was all he could think. He had to have more.

He didn't know if it was that desperately needy thought or the sound of his groan that pulled him back to sanity. Unable to do otherwise, knowing it would likely be his last chance to taste her for God knew how long, Mitch slowly ended the kiss.

With a moan of approval, Belle stepped away. Her eyes, blurry with desire, stared into his as she ran her tongue over her bottom lip and gave a sigh. Then her mouth curved in a smile that screamed satisfaction.

"You'll give me the contract," she assured him, her words a husky promise. "And we'll have incredible sex. And in the end, you'll be thanking your lucky stars you were smart enough to do both."

3

"I BLEW IT," Belle insisted, pacing her office. The plush carpet warmed her bare feet as she stomped from one end of the room to the other. "I got so caught up in the sexual game, in wanting to show Mitch what he'd lost by wanting some business deal more than me, I lost sight of why I was there."

"Chill," Sierra said, ensconced behind Belle's desk while working on a seating plan. "You haven't blown it. Mitch is a by-the-book kind of guy. When he's ready to reject both of your propositions he'll have his assistant e-mail you."

Despite her anxiety, Belle snorted and gave a rueful shake of her head. No patty-cake from Sierra, nope. The brunette shot from the hip, to hell with the fatalities.

"You think he'll have his tidy little assistant send me a no-thanks-on-the-sex e-mail?"

"Nah," Sierra said as she frowned at the sketch, then checked her guest list. "He'll make it all businesslike. You know, something like, 'I appreciate your time and creative proposal, but have decided it doesn't suit my needs. As clever and inventive as your suggestions are, I don't feel that's the right direction to take at this time. Oh, by the way, I'm not hiring you for the event gig, either.'"

The rejection sounded so realistic, Belle almost rushed to her laptop to see if Sierra was reading it verbatim.

"Did you hear something?" she asked suspiciously.

Sierra just rolled her eyes.

"We've been friends since training bras and boarding school, and in all these years, I've never seen you turn stupid over any guy but this one," Sierra pointed out. "Maybe we'd be better off if he does turn the deal down. I don't think he's good for you."

"He tasted good," Belle muttered. Tasted good, felt good, looked good. Her breath shuddered as she remembered how amazing his kiss had been. She'd only intended to prove a point, tease him a little. He'd been the one with the point, though. Hard and long, pressing into her thigh.

God, she was going crazy with wanting him.

"You're doing it again," Sierra reminded.

Belle glanced over at her friend, surprised to see she'd pushed aside her seating chart and was unwrapping a butterscotch candy. Sierra only resorted to sugar, and only in tiny amounts, when she was really stressed. Given the half-dozen unwrapped pieces in front of her, she was definitely worried.

"Doing what again?" Belle asked.

"Getting stupid," Sierra repeated. "It's like an automatic shutoff button gets flipped whenever you get near Mitch Carter. Your brain goes into hibernate mode."

Belle rolled her eyes and dropped into the chair opposite Sierra. "Don't be silly. I'm just hot for the guy. You've seen him, he's gorgeous. Sexy, smart and fun. That doesn't make me stupid, that makes me horny."

"I've seen you horny before. You don't blow business deals over horny," Sierra said, chomping down on the candy with a loud crunch.

Belle winced at the sound. That had to hurt the teeth. Then her eyes went round as Sierra unwrapped another and popped it into her mouth.

Best friends since they were fourteen, the two women knew

each other inside out. Belle had never considered anyone else to go into business with. Guilt trickled down her spine. And now she was stressing her friend into a sugar coma.

"I didn't blow it," Belle defended. At least, she didn't think she did. "I might have gotten a bit carried away, but a little flirting won't affect the deal. He loved my spiel. He was impressed with our ideas. Whether we get it or we don't will depend on whether he's open to the sexual angle or not. For the resort," she quickly added.

Sierra chewed up another hard candy without replying. She gave Belle a long, considering look, then unwrapped another piece.

The look was a familiar one. She'd worn it when she'd talked Belle into taking a chance on their business. She wore it when she told a client their request was over-the-top crazy. She always wore it when she told Belle her outfit sucked or her ideas were lame. It was her truth-at-all-costs look.

Belle hated that look.

For the good of her own ears and Sierra's dental bill, Belle reached over and scooped up the remaining candy.

"Belle, you barely knew this guy and you were willing to toss aside your principles and beliefs. For what? A piece of ass."

"I'm not some dumb tramp," Belle snapped back. "I might have been distracted during that meeting, but I'll be damned if I gave away a single principle and I sure as hell didn't ignore my beliefs."

Whatever that was supposed to mean, she fumed. God, if she didn't hate confrontation so much, she'd yell at her friend. Tell her to quit being so negative, so mistrusting. Instead she sucked in a deep, calming breath and reminded herself that this was just Sierra's way.

"I meant six years ago, when you agreed to marry the guy just so you could get in his pants," Sierra corrected with a roll of her eyes. "You weren't interested in happy-ever-after back then. But you gave in despite your better judgment. And look how that turned out."

Belle winced. She'd rather not think about it. "Please, do you think Mitch would be crazy enough to propose to me again? All he wanted was a leg up the ladder, and he doesn't need that any longer."

"You don't say anything about whether you'd be crazy enough to accept a proposal," Sierra pointed out.

"I didn't think I had to state the obvious. I gave up believing in fairy tales or happy-ever-after. I'm hot for the guy, okay? That's it. I know better than to risk anything other than a little time and some sexy lingerie."

"I hope so. I really, really hope so," Sierra said, her words dripping with doubt. "Because your history says otherwise."

A chime snagged her attention and Sierra glanced at the laptop. She clicked the mouse a couple times and heaved a sigh. Belle's stomach dropped to her toes at the look on her partner's face.

"Okay, here's the deal," the sleek brunette said in her no-nonsense tone. "If we get this contract, I need you to make me a promise."

Belle eyed the computer, her fingers itching to grab it and see what message had prompted Sierra's ultimatum.

"What's the promise?" Belle hedged. She wasn't about to agree to anything crazy, like keeping her hands off Mitch. Yes, she might lose a few brain cells around him. But she was an intelligent woman, she had extras.

Replaying those excuses through her head, Belle heaved a sigh and privately admitted they were bullshit. This job was huge, and not only to Eventfully Yours. If she pulled it off, made friendly—but not *that* friendly—with Mitch, there was a good chance he'd help her dad.

Belle thought back to the call she'd had that morning from her father's secretary. Her dad was stressed again, and even though he was supposed to be home recovering from his heart attack, he'd spent the last four days running to the office trying to find some way out of the mess he was in. Between a series of bad investments, the real-estate crash and a sucky economy, Forsham Hotels was sinking fast. A wave of helpless frustration washed over her. She had to do something, anything, to get Mitch to talk to her dad.

Maybe Twisted Knickers lingerie carried chastity belts.

Sierra took a deep breath. Belle was nodding before her friend could even issue the request. Fine, no sex.

"As soon as you can, hell, the first day if possible, you haul Mitch Carter into the nearest closet and have wild monkey sex with him," Sierra commanded. "Have as much sex as possible. Do it as many times in as many ways as you can. Get it all out of your system. Do it on the ceiling if you have to. Use toys and kinky leather getups."

Belle's jaw dropped. She shook her head, sure her hearing was faulty.

"For the good of Eventfully Yours, for the good of your thought processes and, most of all, for the good of my sanity, I'm begging you—" Sierra placed both palms on the desk and leaned forward, her face intense "—do him. Immediately."

It took all Belle's strength to lift her chin off her chest. Sierra was a dyed-in-the-wool cynic, but she'd never been this…well, pragmatic about deliberately seducing someone.

Belle kind of liked it. Even if it was insane.

"You're kidding, right? I thought you were worried about my poor judgment with Mitch?"

"I'm worried about your judgment when your head is clouded with unrequited lust," Sierra shot back. "Once you've screwed his brains out a few times you'll be fine."

"Fine?"

"I've read studies that list all the ways sexual frustration hinders a person. This exact situation wasn't on the list, but I'm sure it qualifies. Once the sexual curiosity is sated, you'll be your normal, savvy self and kick butt with this deal."

"So this is for the good of our business?" Belle's tummy did a wicked somersault.

Shouldn't she feel excited instead of nervous? Sierra was the voice of reason, so her encouragement made the whole idea seem…well, weird.

"Sure," Sierra returned with a shrug.

"We got the deal?" Belle pointed to the computer and whatever message Sierra was hiding.

"We've got a shot at the deal. He wants a meeting to discuss it." She spun the laptop around so Belle could read the message from Mitch's assistant. Lunch meeting, tomorrow afternoon. Come prepared to negotiate.

Excitement buzzed through Belle's system like electricity. Her stomach tumbled, nerves and anticipation warning her to eat ahead of time. Yes. This was her chance, her shot at everything she wanted. She'd show him the fine art of negotiation…her way.

Belle gave a wicked laugh of delight. "Never let it be said I'm not willing to give my all for the cause."

While she didn't quite share Sierra's anxiety that she'd blow the deal or do something stupid, she wasn't about to turn down a direct order to hunt down the hottest guy she'd ever lusted after and screw his brains out.

As a waiter topped off his coffee, Mitch patted the pocket where he'd tucked the faded cocktail napkin with its gold foil inscription of his and Belle's names and their former wedding date. He'd spent two days dissecting Eventfully Yours's proposal with his management team, listening to their analysis and opinions. The unanimous belief was that of all the proposals, this was unquestionably the strongest. The best. And in Mitch's opinion, the biggest pain in the ass.

Not because the plan would be difficult to implement. All that meant was he had to work harder, smarter, than the average guy. Since he'd built his reputation doing just that, he never shied from difficult.

Proof positive was right here, he thought as he looked around Spago Restaurant. Airy, bright and lush, it was one of the top restaurants in L.A. He'd have had to save up for a month just to bring Belle to have a drink here when they were engaged. But not anymore. Six years and a driving need to prove himself to her, to everyone—including his former father-in-law-to-be—who'd thought he'd marry his way to success, had given him a much stronger edge.

So no, he didn't blink at taking on the difficult. But this plan came with his personal version of kryptonite: Belle Forsham. The one woman guaranteed not only to bring him to his knees, but to make sure he loved the hell out of being there.

Working with her could be a disaster. If he let himself get off track, the results would be ugly. He had everything on the line here. Not only the resort, but his investors' money and trust. To say nothing of his reputation. Sex with Belle wasn't worth risking all that. Which was why he was only agreeing to part of her proposal. The events, specifically.

As intriguing, and probably lucrative, as the sex themes had been, he didn't trust himself to deal with her on that level. She was simply too much temptation. He was afraid she'd use those themes to take that hot kiss one or two—or twenty—steps farther.

So—he fingered the napkin again—he'd keep her at arm's length. Business, pure and simple. Hell, he'd been burned once, he was a smart man. He knew how to keep his fingers—and other body parts—to himself. If he was otherwise tempted, he had his talisman as a reminder that Belle was off-limits.

Suddenly, as though someone had pushed a button, his body went on full alert. His senses flared as he glanced across the restaurant, not surprised to see Belle making her way toward him. Sleek and sexy in a simple spring dress of the palest pink, she sauntered between the linen-covered tables, her eyes never leaving his. Standing as she approached, Mitch eyed her half smile, the hint of naughty amusement igniting his body to instant lust.

His body would just have to get over it.

"Thanks for meeting me," he said as he gestured to the chair the waiter held out. "I'm sure you have a busy schedule."

Her green eyes narrowed as if she were trying to read his tone, then Belle gave a little shrug and murmured her thanks to the waiter.

"My schedule's never too busy for you," she returned, spreading the napkin over her lap without releasing his gaze. "Unless, of course, you're planning a wedding or something. Then I might have to run."

Mitch's jaw sagged. The mischievous humor gleaming in her eyes assured him he hadn't heard wrong. Leave it to Belle to poke fun at something taboo. It wasn't just her smile that was naughty.

"I don't think you'll need your sneakers anytime soon," he deadpanned. "My tux is at the cleaners."

Her laugh rang out, garnering a few indulgent smiles from other diners and sparking an irritatingly warm feeling in Mitch's belly.

"Whew. Good thing, since I don't even own a pair. Let's have lunch and talk business, instead. Okay?"

On cue, the waiter stepped over and handed Belle a menu. She barely glanced at it before ordering iced tea and salad. Interesting. Either she dined at four-star restaurants often enough to be blasé about the famous menu or she really was focused on business. Mitch wondered if she'd been here before, and what kind of men she dated. Irritated at his train of thought, he shoved aside the jealous curiosity and gave the waiter his order. The only thing he needed to know about her activities of the past six years was in reference to her business.

"Your assistant said you had questions, wanted to discuss Eventfully Yours's proposal in more depth?" she said, her tone professional. Her look, though, was pure sex. Glossy lips pursed, she let her gaze do a slow, appreciative slide over his face and chest. Mitch was grateful the table was between them, both preventing her from going any further and keeping his reaction hidden.

She arched a brow in query. The gleam in her eyes told him she knew she was sending mixed signals and was looking forward to seeing which ones he chose to pick up.

"I do have questions," Mitch said, his tone neutral. He wasn't going to play her game, but damned if he'd let her know that. Keeping her guessing was his only shot at maintaining the upper hand. And with Belle, he needed all the control he could get. She was like a wily dominatrix, luring him in with sugar and spice but hiding a whip and chain behind her back.

With that in mind, he pulled out his file of questions, suggestions and ideas. Through the rest of the meal he and Belle hammered out details for the grand opening, as well as a series of smaller pre-events that would build buzz for the resort. He was again impressed with her savvy suggestions, especially as she expanded on her proposal, filling in the crucial details that she'd held back initially.

Damn, she was good.

By dessert, she'd gone from good to mind-blowing.

"You're going to want to redesign the landscaping here and here," she said, poking at the sketch of the resort's property with one blunt fingernail. "If you bring in some fully mature trees, a few more bushes, you'll have a perfect sex-in-the-woods setting. Guests will love that, and if you set it up right they'll think it's their little secret."

Definitely mind-blowing. And thanks to comments like that, all he could think of were other things he'd like her to blow.

"You've obviously considered everything," he said. He wondered if keeping him in a constant state of arousal was planned as well. Glancing at the amused awareness in her eyes, he figured it was. "Now about your suggested themes…"

"I noticed you kept changing the subject when I brought them up." There was no judgment in her eyes, only curiosity. "So, what? You're going to go vanilla?"

"Vanilla?"

"Safe and tame."

Ahh, there was the irritation. Mitch grinned in relief.

"Let's just say I don't think the two of us focusing on sex is a good idea," he returned.

"Chicken?"

"Prudent."

Belle rolled her eyes. "Safe sex again?"

He couldn't deny it. After all, the safest sex was abstinence.

"Because of our past association I think we should discuss our history and clear the air," he said instead. "I want us both to be on solid ground, which means we need to deal with any past resentments or issues."

For the first time in memory, Mitch watched Belle's expressive face close up. Like a door slamming, it simply went blank and unwelcoming. Then, so fast he wondered if he'd imagined it, she gave a roll of her eyes and flashed her sassy smile.

"The past is over, Mitch. I promise, I'm not bringing any old baggage to the table." She leaned forward, and for the first time since she'd waltzed out of his office two days earlier, touched him. A whisper-soft brush of her fingertips over the back of his hand. Gentle, teasing, easy. Heat flared, instant and hot, in his belly. "Any desire I have to chase you around is definitely fresh and new, not a leftover itch."

"You don't own sneakers, remember?" he snapped, equal parts irritated that she'd so easily closed the door to their past before he could find out why she'd really run off and relieved not to have to admit to his own part in their failed history. "So we'll just keep chasing off our list of things to do."

"Then what's the problem?"

"Like I said, given our history, I think it's wise to keep the sexual temptation to a minimum." He'd rehearsed and re-hashed his next words multiple times since he'd decided to work with her, but Mitch still had trouble voicing them. "I've also written up the contracts event by event, rather than the job as a whole."

"Care to clarify that?" He'd had no idea her husky voice could turn to ice.

"I have everything riding on the success of this resort. That success will depend greatly on how well the events are handled. I have to depend on these events happening. As amazing as your proposal is, I can't afford to tie myself up for more than one event at a time given the circumstances of our last…association."

If he'd reached across the table and slapped her, she couldn't have looked more shocked. Mitch felt like a first-class bastard. Belle's luscious mouth parted as if to challenge him, her eyes sparkling with fury. Then, as if a switch had flipped, she sucked in her bottom lip and gave a jerky little shrug.

"No way. I'm sorry, but these mini-events are back to back, each one leading up to the grand opening. Eventfully Yours won't take the job without at least the pre- and grand opening events contracted." Her tone was pure business, her eyes shuttered.

The fairness of her words, spoken in that even, businesslike tone, made Mitch realize he was the one letting the past get in the way.

"That's fine," he agreed. "We'll contract for the five smaller events and the grand opening."

"Great. Unless there are any more grudges you're harboring, I'd say we're good to go."

"No grudges." At least, none he'd admit. "Like I said, just being prudent."

She rolled her eyes again, but the gesture didn't hide the hurt lurking in the sea-green depths. Mitch frowned, irritated that the sight made him feel like a jerk.

"Then we have a deal," she said, her tone making it clear she was glad to close the history book. Mitch was surprised, since most women were only too happy to discuss the past in all its gory details. "I'll be at the resort a week from Monday. Given the distance from L.A. and how much work is involved, I'll require a room on-site, of course. A suite would be best as I'll set up office there."

Belle opened a file, made and initialed a few adjustments on the contract to reflect his changes. With a flourish, she signed her name, then slid the papers back in the folder.

She handed it to him with a wink. Apparently she'd regained her good humor.

"I think I'll put you in one of the cottages," he returned. "Unlike the suites, they're already furnished and should suit you perfectly."

"How far are these cottages from your on-site office?"

"You can call me anytime you have questions," he assured her. And the distance would make him think twice about dropping in to visit.

Her brow creased, her eyes rounded. "You're starting to make me think you're harboring more issues, Mitch. Are you planning to avoid me the entire time I'm working with you?"

Not Belle, per se. Just sex with her. Mitch winced. There was no way he wouldn't sound like a pompous ass, but he had to make things clear.

"Please don't take this the wrong way, Belle. But I'm not going to sleep with you. We're doing business together, and business and pleasure just don't mix."

"Hmm, interesting. Too bad you didn't think that six years ago when you tried to mix your business with my daddy's and in the process ruined my pleasure."

He frowned, but before he could respond, she gave a quick shake of her head and a brittle, dismissive little laugh. "Now that does sound like I'm the one harboring some of those issues you're worried about. Let's start fresh, okay? I'm not the same person I was before and I'm betting you aren't, either."

He opened his mouth to retort, but closed it again. All of a sudden, he wanted to clear the air, to ask her the reasons behind her bridal dash. But to do so meant acknowledging emotions he'd locked away. Admitting mistakes he regretted. And worse, bridging the chasm of mistrust that the past kept firmly between them. As long as it was there, he knew they'd never have a shot at intimacy.

He slid his hand into his pocket and fingered the wedding napkin. Between his talisman and that chasm, he'd be safe from screwing up. He couldn't afford to lose again.

"I've changed a lot in six years," was all he said.

"So have I," she assured him as she laid one warm, smooth hand over his. Energy, mostly sexual but with a subtle layer of something else Mitch couldn't define, shot through his body at her touch. The most platonic connection, and he was hard, hot and horny. It boggled the mind to think what his response would be if they had full body contact. Chasm and talisman, he reminded himself.

"I hope you're not upset," he said, telling himself it was guilt and not lust making him want to pull her onto his lap. "You're a gorgeous, sexy woman. You don't need to be chasing a guy."

"Who said I'd chase you?" she asked, her tone light and amused.

Mitch frowned. He knew he hadn't misunderstood her signal or her flirting words.

"Like you, I'm much smarter than I was six years ago. Smart enough to know better than to chase a man. Especially a man like you."

Mitch opened his mouth to deny that she'd chased him before, but she continued before he could get a single word out. "You say we won't have sex. I say we will. Simple difference of opinion and only time will tell which one of us is right. And if you're too uptight to do two things at once successfully, that's fine. I can wait."

"What the hell are you talking about?" he asked, watching nonplussed as she slid her folder into her briefcase and got to her feet. "What two things?"

"Rock your resort opening and have wild monkey sex with me," she shot back as she turned to leave. "When it happens, I won't have chased you to get it. You'll be the one doing the chasing…and the begging."

4

BELLE GLANCED over the guest list for the pre-opening event and added two more names. Actors, politicians, celebutants. She needed to scatter in some high-profile musicians, but she wanted to do a little more research first.

Almost two weeks had passed since her lunch with Mitch and she'd yet to spend any time alone with him. The first week was understandable. She'd been working from her office in L.A., finalizing things and tying up loose ends so she could spend the next few weeks here at Lakeside. The resort was a hundred miles from her office, and it was only practical that she work on-site for the duration. She'd figured the bonus would be seeing Mitch day in and day out for the next three weeks. Not only would she relish the sexual thrill, but she could drop a few hints and feel him out on the topic of her father.

But since she'd arrived to find her cozy cottage ready and waiting, he'd been avoiding her. And he wasn't even trying to hide the fact.

The perfect host, he'd had fresh flowers waiting in her room. But he'd sent his assistant to help her settle in. He'd remembered her preferences, making sure she had hot tea and a basket of muffins delivered each morning, but he'd avoided seeing her unless there were at least three other people in the room.

Today she was supposed to tour the grounds, the suites and

the spa. And knowing Mitch, he'd send his rabbity assistant to do the honors.

She thought of her promise to Sierra. Do him. Fast, furious, as soon as possible. So far, she was failing dismally. Sexual frustration was never comfortable, but she was a big girl and could handle losing the game. But Mitch hadn't even manned-up enough to play. She recalled his declaration that sex between them was off-limits. This must be his way of making sure she knew he was serious.

Well, so was she. And seduction wasn't going to work. It hadn't when they'd been engaged, it hadn't when they'd met again a couple of weeks ago. She obviously needed a new plan.

Nibbling on her second blueberry muffin, she punched a button on her cell phone, leaving it on speaker.

"Morning," Sierra answered cheerfully. "I take it you haven't died of sexual frustration yet?"

"I'm surviving," Belle said dryly. "Barely, though. I need your help."

"Sorry, sweets. You're not my type."

"Ha-ha. I need ideas, you dork. Mitch is running scared. He's avoiding me except for e-mails and the telephone. Try as I might I can't even get him to have phone sex with me."

"Shit," Sierra muttered. Belle heard the clink of glass against glass and knew her friend was topping off her coffee. Sierra always thought best when highly caffeinated.

"I need a plan," Belle said, stating the obvious.

"No kidding. Otherwise I'll be shopping for some ugly bridesmaid's dress again."

"Hey, the dress wasn't that ugly."

"Anything in Easter-egg pink is ugly and that's beside the point." Belle could hear the tap-tap-tapping of Sierra's nails against the coffee cup. "Give me a rundown of what you've done on the job while I think."

Belle thought best while lounging in a bubble bath or lazing in the sun, something that allowed her to relax and let the ideas flow. Sierra, though, was the opposite, needing noise and activity to find her solutions.

Pulling her notebook toward her, Belle went over the timeline and to-do list. On the off chance she managed to convince Mitch to consider the theme idea, she'd ordered sex-toy samples, sketched out three separate theme ideas and started the plans for the pre-opening event. To garner word-of-mouth buzz and set the tone for privacy, she'd suggested that Mitch hold a low-key non-advertised event before the media caught wind of the resort's offerings. It would offer that semblance of privacy while giving their potential guests a taste of just how special a stay at Lakeside would be.

"Quit flirting," Sierra said, interrupting Belle's recitation of the tentative guest list.

"I was reading in my most serious tone," Belle responded with a sniff. "I can't help it if my voice excites you."

"Ha. Seriously though, your last encounter with Mitch, you tossed down the gauntlet. I don't blame you, of course, but still, the guy is definitely running scared."

Belle wrinkled her nose and pushed away what was left of her muffin. The idea of Mitch wanting nothing to do with her ruined her appetite.

"I told him I wouldn't chase him and I'm not," she defended, her tone stiff. "But is it asking too much that he meet with me without the chaperones?"

"You need to change tactics, lull him into complacency then reel him in."

"Lull him from afar?" Her pouty tone was only half-pretend.

"He's going to have to meet with you sooner or later," Sierra assured her. "Once he does, turn the tables. Play the professional card. You know, pretend you're there to work, to do a job."

This time Belle really did pout. "I *am* here to do a job."

"Yeah, yeah. But we both know you have ulterior motives. He's not stupid, so he probably suspects it, too. So confuse him."

"Professional?"

"More focus on the job, the reasons you're there. Including needing Mitch's help for your dad." Glass clinked as Sierra got even more coffee. "Less focus on how cute his ass is."

What, was she blind? Belle wanted to argue, but knew there was no point. Too much was at stake. Not only the job itself, but Eventfully Yours's reputation and her father's business. Mitch had made his disinterest plenty clear; she'd respect his decision.

"Have you talked to him any more about the theme program?" Sierra asked, obviously taking Belle's silence as agreement to her plan.

"I haven't seen him to pitch it any further," Belle reminded her.

Silence.

Belle sighed. "I'll send him an e-mail. He seems to like those."

She and Sierra wrapped up a few more details then hung up, leaving Belle to feel like a total slacker. Sierra was right. She'd been so focused on her attraction to Mitch, she'd let her priorities slip. Well, no more. She grabbed her pen and started a list of what she needed to do to set things right.

Before she could write more than a few things, though, her cell phone chimed the "Boogie-Woogie Blues."

"Daddy," she greeted in answer. "How are you feeling?"

"I'm feeling sick and tired of being asked that question, princess," Franklin Forsham growled.

"People ask because they care, not out of some twisted desire to be irritating. You need to rest and give yourself time to recuperate. Quadruple bypass is nothing to blow off."

"I'm sitting on my ass instead of golfing, aren't I? That's

recuperation enough." The pain of that was clear in his voice. Frank Forsham loved nothing more than a good game of golf. Belle glanced out the window at the gorgeous tree-studded view. Off in the distance the sun glinted, jewel-like, off the lake, and beyond that was what Diana had claimed to be a first-class golf course. Not big enough to bring in the major tournaments, but challenging enough to keep the guests entertained.

Her father would love it. Maybe after she got him and Mitch together, he'd come play a few rounds. She didn't consider it naive to believe it would happen any more than she considered herself overoptimistic to think she and Mitch would get together. Faith and hard work. She figured as long as she had both—and some hot lingerie—she was set.

"Of course, I wouldn't be able to golf anyway, given the state of things here," he grumbled, stealing her attention back from her idyllic imaginings. "Damned market is only getting worse. Forsham Hotels hasn't been hit this hard since the early seventies."

Belle listened to her father's description of the state of his company. She knew enough about business to realize he was actually making light of how bad it was. Worse, though, was the tension she heard in his voice. He was supposed to be recovering, not working himself into another heart attack.

"It'll turn around and everything will be fine, Daddy," she said, even though they both knew it was an empty promise. But as always, Franklin didn't expect any real input or contribution from her, so he let the comment go unchallenged. She was his pretty little girl, no more, no less. Belle had long ago given up the idea of proving herself to him. But maybe, just maybe, he'd respect her a little if she saved his company?

"Come by tonight, we'll go to dinner," he ordered.

Belle glanced at her to-do list. Even if she rescheduled the tour, her plate was full. Added to that, it would take her an hour and a half to drive back to L.A., longer if she hit traffic. She flipped the page in her planner, noting an early breakfast meeting with the spa manager.

Then she thought of her dad, alone in that big rambling house.

"I'll be there at seven," she promised. "I wanted to talk to you, anyway."

"About?"

"Um, I sort of ran into someone from the past and thought you'd like to hear about him."

"Him?"

She hated it when he did that. Single-word questions, then silence that made her feel as if she had to spill tons of details to fill the empty space.

"Mitch Carter," she said. Then she cringed and waited.

But not for long.

"That cheating sonofabitch? I thought he'd run back to the east coast where he belongs."

Belle winced. "Dad, I told you, Mitch didn't cheat."

"Harrumph."

"He didn't. Really. He just sort of misled me. I'm sure he thinks I did much worse, leaving him at the altar like that."

"He was a lucky man and he blew it."

Belle pressed her lips together. She had to get her dad to quit hating Mitch or there was no point in pushing Mitch to help him. Leave it to her to be stuck between two stubborn men.

"Let's talk about it over dinner, okay?"

"Let's not. I don't want to discuss the cheater or that debacle that was your wedding. Especially not when it's thanks to him that I invested in that damned property. His connections and contracting license were supposed to get us past the stupid zoning regulations. Thanks to his duplicity, I'm stuck. Can't build, can't sell."

Her father continued to mutter. Belle's stomach twisted.

She'd told her father the day after the wedding that Mitch hadn't been with any other women, that she hadn't meant to imply anything like that. But her father had blown up at her, ranting about the humiliation and misplaced trust. Too horrified to ask if he meant his trust in Mitch or his trust in her, she'd gulped down her explanation and run from the room.

Her father's attitude didn't bode well for her little save-Forsham-Hotels plan. But she'd worry about convincing him later. For now, she needed to focus on getting Mitch to listen to her. That was enough of a challenge.

With that in mind, she bade her father an absent-minded goodbye, promising to see him that evening. As soon as she hung up, she grabbed the cottage phone and dialed star-seven.

"Diana? Hey, I need to postpone the tour until tomorrow, okay?"

"Is there a problem?" Mitch's assistant asked in her hesitant tone.

"Not at all. I just have to run home for the evening. An offer came up that I couldn't refuse."

"Business?"

"No, dinner…" With her father? No, just in case Diana shared the excuse with Mitch, she didn't want to bring her father into the mix until she'd had time to butter them both up. "A dinner date."

"WHAT IN THE HELL do you mean, the program crashed?"

The hotel manager winced, then he gave a helpless shrug. Tall, skinny and blond, Larry looked like a morose scarecrow. Mitch had hand-picked him to run the resort because he handled the staff like a gifted choreographer and knew hotels inside out. And, theoretically, hotel computers. "We don't understand what happened. I've spent the morning on the phone with tech support—they're baffled, too."

The computerized reservation program was supposed to be bug-free, idiot-proof and have both on- and off-site backups. "You recovered the lost data, right?"

"We're working on it. The system has a backup, but somehow, well, the battery went dead."

Mitch closed his eyes and shook his head. Continual construction delays. The pipes had burst in the pool room, there was a gopher infestation on the golf course, and now this? Seriously, who had his voodoo doll and why the hell were they jabbing it so hard?

The only person he'd recently pissed off was Belle. And he couldn't see her going the voodoo route. She was too direct for that. She'd rather see him on his knees begging. Or maybe just on his knees.

"Get it fixed," he instructed tiredly. As soon as the manager left, Mitch lifted his phone and punched a button.

"Do you believe jobs can be cursed?" he asked as soon as Reece answered.

"Nah, that's the kind of thing suits like you come up with as an excuse for falling on their ass."

"Well, my ass is definitely getting bruised," Mitch acknowledged. "I'm starting to think it's more than a learning curve."

"You don't really believe that curse crap, do you? You want me to fly you out a witch doctor?"

"If I thought it'd make a difference, I'd have you hand-deliver one."

Reece laughed, although Mitch was only half joking. "Gotta hand it to you, cuz, you're the most hands-on guy I know. Guess that's why you're kicking butt. You stick your fingers in every pie you deal in, swinging a hammer as easily as you make those slick deals."

Not quite *every* pie. Mitch had been doing his damnedest to avoid the sweetie pie that was his ex. Not trusting himself around her, he'd justified his absence by putting Diana in charge of the events projects. And Belle was the Party Princess, after all. She didn't need his supervision to plan a successful event.

"Seriously, what's the deal?" Reece, or Cowboy, as Mitch's cousin and security guru was aptly nicknamed, sounded as concerned as he ever did. Which meant his drawl had slowed and the teasing humor had left his voice.

Mitch listed the resort's problems-du-jour, from construction to rodent infestation to computer crash. He was explaining about the staff issues when his cousin interrupted.

"Your event gal quit? Just like that? The hot little redhead who loved to party? What happened?"

"She's in rehab."

"No shit? What're you going to do about that opening weekend party you were so hot to have?"

"If I can't stop this streak of bad luck, there won't be an opening," Mitch hedged, not wanting to mention Belle's involvement in the resort. Since Reece had been his best man, he had a pretty vivid memory of her. "I'm willing to accept a few problems here and there, but not this level of misfortune."

"Sabotage?"

"That sounds so paranoid."

"It ain't paranoia if they're out to get you," Reece pointed out.

"Right."

The two men were silent for a minute, then Mitch heard Reece shuffling some papers. That his bronc-riding cousin was working in an office amused Mitch. A go-getter Kentucky cowboy, Reece was more suited to riding horseback than riding a desk. Rather than putting his military time to use in law enforcement, he'd opened his own security firm.

"Did you get the note I sent you about new requirements for the resort?" Mitch asked.

"Something about catering to the fancy-ass folks there in Hollywood?"

"That's it. Why don't you send a guy out early? He can start assessing for the upgrades, and poke around a little at the same time."

"Two birds with one stone. Good plan."

They nailed down the details, then hung up. Mitch let his head fall back on the chair, his eyes, as always, going to the view.

Ever since he was a kid, he'd dreamed of a place like this. Oh, not the rich and fancy angle, but of owning something huge, something major. He'd wanted to make his mark, to be special. An only child, he'd been one of seventeen cousins. The last words his dad had spoken to him before he'd died were to tell him to be the man, to take care of his mom and show the world what he was made of. Even at five, Mitch had taken those words to heart.

They'd sparked his desperate need to prove himself. To be important.

Starting out in construction as a teen, he'd worked his way up the ranks in his stepdad's company by the time he'd entered college. He'd graduated with a degree in business and been left the construction firm when his mom and stepdad had died just before his twenty-third birthday. Like Reece said, he'd worked every aspect of his business, from swinging the hammer to marketing property to making deals. Within five years he'd launched his development company and figured he was well on his way to the big time.

But he'd wanted more. Enter Forsham Hotels and the biggest mistake of his life.

Which reminded him…

Mitch pushed away from his desk and strode into Diana's office. As soon as she saw him, the mousy brunette held out a sheaf of papers.

"Larry sent these up," she said.

"Obviously his team hasn't figured out the problem yet," he observed, flipping through the pages of techno-speak as if he had a clue what they said. With a shrug, he tossed the report back on Diana's desk and asked, "Did Belle have a list of suggestions after her tour?"

"Um, not yet." Diana busied herself with shuffling the tech report, then clipping the pages just so.

"She's writing it up?"

"No, I don't think she is."

Mitch's earlier irritation, still bubbling away just below the surface, threatened to erupt.

"I suppose there's a good reason why she hasn't done what I specifically asked?"

"Well, maybe because she had to cancel," his assistant mumbled, bending low to put the tech report in the bottom filing-cabinet drawer.

"Why the hell did she cancel the tour?"

"She had a, well, a date," Diana said, her face almost buried in her keyboard.

Either she'd figured out how irritated he got when people wasted his time on the job or she was still afraid to look him in the face when she gave him bad news. Either way, her timidity pissed him off even more.

"Get her on the phone," he snapped. When Diana winced, Mitch sighed, feeling like he'd kicked a puppy. "Please."

"She's already left the resort. She said since she had to drive into L.A. anyway, she'd leave early and go into town to meet some vendors, store owners and suppliers to look into possible liaisons for the resort."

If Diana's face got any closer to the keyboard, she'd smash her nose on the *H* key. Mitch swallowed a growl and tried to remember all the organizational qualities that made her a great assistant. Maybe he'd better take to carrying a list in his pocket?

"Get her on her cell, then," he barked, this time not bothering to temper his tone. Diana was just going to have to get over her fear, because he didn't have time to baby her. And damned if he hadn't been right about Belle being a flake. Less than a week here at the resort and she was already slacking off.

Date. Fury bolted through him like lightning. Fast, furious, deadly. It was because she was screwing off, he assured himself. Not because she might be screwing some guy other than him.

Reece was right. Mitch had built his success by taking part in every aspect of his business. Every single thing. Which obviously needed to include his luscious ex-fiancée. This hands-off approach wasn't working. Not for the resort, and definitely not for his resort's event planner.

"Her phone goes direct to voice mail," Diana said, dread clear in her tone.

Images of Belle and some faceless guy sent that bolt of fury right through him again, ripping a hole in Mitch's gut.

"I'll deal with Ms. Forsham and the tour tomorrow," he decided. "No more of this letting her do things her way. I'm stepping in and showing her who's boss. From now on, she'll answer to me."

5

HUMMING her favorite pop star's latest song, Belle strode through the resort lobby with a swing in her hips and a smile on her lips. Her heels tapped a pleasing counter-beat as she crossed the polished marble and breathed in the rich scent of fresh flowers from the atrium.

Gorgeous morning. It was weird how good she felt waking up in the enchanted forest, as she'd taken to calling the wooded view outside her bedroom window. Throw in tea and muffins on the tiny, private deck, and she'd managed to shove aside all her worries about her father and grab a positive attitude.

After all, she was a smart woman. A talented woman. A woman on a mission. And she'd succeed. Although it would be a lot easier if she could get Mitch to face her instead of pretending she didn't exist. Maybe her e-mail would help? As soon as she'd gotten back to the resort last night she'd drafted an outline of her pitch, detailing the many reasons why this resort should be themed to cater to the sexual needs of its guests.

Now to see if he responded.

Of course, there were advantages to not dealing with Mitch face-to-face. One of which was wearing jeans and a tank top instead of dressing like a fancy professional. She still wore a crystal-trimmed satin bra under the turquoise silk tank, though. Nothing overt, just a flirty hint of femininity. Her pep talk with Sierra fresh in her mind, she had a solid game plan. Professional and polite, all flirting—except lingerie-style hints—were now off-limits.

That reminder firmly in her head, she gave the manager a finger wave and winked at his trainees as she passed behind the check-in counter to make her way back to Diana's office.

And even though she knew she shouldn't, she gave a little prayer of thanks for her fancy bra when she saw the delicious treat awaiting her.

The only thing better than seeing Mitch Carter first thing in the morning would have been seeing him a little sooner. Like as soon as she'd opened her eyes.

Like her, he wore jeans with his T-shirt. Belle had noticed early on that while the rest of the staff dressed upscale casual, Mitch didn't bother with the upscale part. His rich auburn hair, shoved back off his face, was just past the need-for-a-haircut stage and curling toward his collar.

Her fingers twitched with the desire to touch that hair, to feel it beneath her palms and see if it was as silky and warm as she remembered.

"Mitch," she greeted him with a smile. "This must be my lucky morning."

"Following your lucky night, I suppose."

Belle frowned at the angry snap in his tone, but just shrugged.

"It could have been luckier, of course," she returned, since she'd have much preferred to spend it with him than driving back from L.A. at midnight. "But I had a great time."

"I'll bet."

She made a show of looking around the room, empty but for the two of them. "Just us? I was starting to think that was against the rules or something."

As soon as the words were out, she winced. So much for professional. But, she realized, looking at his stormy face, she was a little hurt at Mitch's blatant avoidance of her, even if he was a total grump-butt in the morning. Someone must have missed his caffeine fix. Belle couldn't recall ever seeing Mitch so out of sorts. It would have been endearing if she didn't feel as if she was blindly stepping into the path of a natural disaster.

"Rules? Don't you just ignore those? Things like showing up to work, agreements and contracts? What, too much like a wedding ceremony for you?"

Anger blasted Belle's amused confusion to bits. She had to grind her teeth to keep from snapping back at him. Lips pressed tightly together, she glared. How dare he?

Mitch arched a brow, challenging her to defend herself.

Belle opened her mouth to yell back, then closed it again, swallowing hard. She hated ugliness and fights. Her parents had fought constantly. Right up until her mother was diagnosed with cancer, every little thing had been an argument. She knew better now, but in second grade, she'd been sure her momma had been argued to death.

Mitch was pissed, most likely because she'd left yesterday. She debated telling him she'd gone to see her father, but didn't see how making him angrier would help anything.

Instead she plastered on her social smile and, with a wink, wiggled her sandal-shod foot toward him. "No sneakers, remember?"

She took his twitching lips as a good sign and opened the leather portfolio she had tucked under her arm. She pulled out the list of local recommendations she'd come up with, along with an outline of the mini events. And, with another glance at the lurking fury in his cinnamon eyes, she steeled her spine and added the theme-pitch outline as well.

"Although both our agreement and contract show these reports due next week," she said, handing them to him, "they're almost complete now and I'd like your input before I go any further. Maybe we can sit down and hammer out some details?"

"I've scheduled the morning to give you the tour you blew off yesterday," he returned.

His words were short, but the curt edge had left his tone. Hearing it gone, Belle felt some of the tension melt from her shoulders.

"Then let's tour," she agreed. "I'm sure I'll have more questions when we're through and we can handle them all at once."

Jaw tight, Mitch gave a stiff nod. Belle hid a sigh. No wonder he and her father had once considered partnership. They were both grumpy SOBs when they wanted to be. Another shock, since she'd have sworn during their engagement that Mitch was the most affable guy in the world. Just went to show how blind she'd been.

"I'll tell Diana we're going," was all he said. But he took the papers with him as he strode into his assistant's office.

Her body tight from the stress of not yelling at his bad-tempered self, Belle dropped into one of the plush chairs outside the main office and heaved a huge sigh. She didn't know which was worse: the way Mitch's irritation pushed her to face her fear of confrontation, or the fact that he was even sexier when he got all intense and uptight like that.

Either way, the man was bad for her control. Part of her wished hard for a pair of sneakers. The other part, the mature businesswoman, steeled her spine and gave thanks that she and Sierra had agreed that professional was the new plan.

An hour later, she was recalling the sports store in town and wondering if sneakers came in pink. Since they'd arrived in the dining room, she'd spent more time sketching pictures of Mitch's butt in her notebook than making notes of the menu plans, rotation of celebrity chefs and floral arrangements.

"Are you getting all of this?" he asked, his words rightfully suspicious. "You look a little distracted."

"The meals I've had since I arrived are excellent, so obviously your chefs are top-notch," she said as if she'd been paying full attention, "but I agree having guest chefs and rotating your menu will keep things fresh. I think, too, that you might want to incorporate some type of theme that works with each chef. For instance, when you bring in the latest Italian wonder, integrate a taste of Italy into the entire month at the resort. Decor, events, that kind of thing."

Mitch's eyes lit up at her suggestion, but he didn't comment. Instead he gestured toward the door and the next stop on their tour. Belle didn't mind, though. She knew she was getting through to him. This was how she liked to do business. Face-to-face. Or, she thought with a tiny sigh as he strode ahead to open the heavy oak door for her, face-to-butt.

God, she wanted him. It was killing her to hold back the flirtation. Instead she kept dropping subtle suggestions and hints that supported her idea to slant the entire resort toward a sexual theme. She wished she could blame her lusty awareness on that, but she knew all the credit went to Mitch.

She reached the door and was surprised, after all his careful avoidance, that Mitch had barely opened it. She had to brush against him to get through. As she did, her eyes met his and she raised a brow.

"The door's stuck," he muttered. "I've got a carpenter coming to look at the hinges."

"Mmm," was all she said. That was the fifth problem they'd encountered so far on the tour. Slipshod construction, a computer failure, a missing stove and, if she hadn't been mistaken, a few too many holes on the golf green.

For a brand-new resort set to open to the public in four weeks, it was a little disconcerting. She knew the hotel business inside-out and a few start-up problems here and there were normal. These seemed excessive.

As they made their way out of the restaurant and toward the

spa and gym, Belle slanted Mitch a sideways glance. She'd thought he was the best. Her daddy had thought so, too, as did everyone she'd talked with. Everybody couldn't be wrong. Could they?

"Do you usually take such a personal hand in your developments, Mitch?" Like the rest of the resort, the mosaic-covered walkway was a combination of art deco and lush greenery. Plants, perhaps echoing the woods beyond the resort, were tucked in every corner, graced every curve. The decor was rich, intense, reminiscent of the Erté statues she'd seen in the foyer.

"My name is on the project, my money is invested in it," he said simply. "I'm going to be involved from the ground up."

Admirable. And, she frowned as she noticed wilting trellis roses, a little concerning. Mitch, who seemed to notice the browned roses at the same time, swore.

"My nana swears that a little water fixes that particular rose problem," Belle joked.

Mitch glared, then pointed to the ground beneath the roses. Belle saw the broken sprinkler heads. Brow furrowed, she stepped closer.

"They look like someone kicked them." A few times, she noted, taking in the destroyed plants surrounding the black plastic. Her first thought was kids, but there were no kids around Lakeside. "Vandals?"

"Maybe. The gardeners keep finding this type of destruction. All minor stuff, just enough to be a pain in the ass."

"This isn't the first vandalism problem?" Construction problems, personnel issues and now vandalism? What was going on? Sure, one or two could be blamed on start-up woes. But all three? Who had Mitch pissed off?

"There've been a few similar landscape issues, along with some missing supplies. The linen shipment disappeared from the

laundry room, showed up a week later in the generator shed."
The frustration in Mitch's tone was echoed in the cold anger in
his eyes. Belle was glad that look wasn't aimed at her. "Nothing
I can take to the police as proof there is an actual problem."

"You don't have video out here, right? I remember that
being one of the things that factored into my idea to run with
the sex theme. You offer so much privacy, it's a shame not to
use it. Then again," she waved her hand at the poor rose and
wrinkled her nose, "if you're going to waste my plan anyway,
maybe you should put in some kind of security measures."

"You have quite a few ideas for someone who can't tear
herself away from her hot sex life to do her job," he snapped.
"Why don't you focus on not screwing up these events and let
me worry about handling my resort."

Belle gasped. Fury such as she'd never felt before flashed
hot and bright. She didn't even think to temper it, instead giving
in to the wave of anger. "How dare you? Who the hell are you
to question my work?"

Normal restraint disappeared, leaving Belle freer than she'd
ever felt before. She threw her notebook to the ground, the slap
of leather against tile ringing out like a gauntlet.

Two steps was all it took to put her up close and personal
with Mitch. Her sandaled toes butted up against his work boots.
She glared into his shocked face.

"I'm damned good at my job and have never screwed up a
single event. Can you say the same? No," she plowed on before
he could respond, "I don't think so. If you have an issue with
my work, just say so. Although how you'd have a freaking clue
is baffling since all you've done for the last week is hide."

"I—"

She swung her arm up in an arrogant, speak-to-the-hand
gesture she'd never thought she'd use and cut him off. Anything
he said was only going to piss her off more.

"And for your information, my sex life currently sucks." She slapped her palm against his chest to push him out of her way. She knew it was shock that made him step back, not her strength. She didn't care, as long as he moved. "Just so you know, I blame you for that, too."

MITCH'S MIND reeled between regret at his unfair accusation to astonishment at Belle's reaction. But as she shot that final slap, both physical and verbal, his jaw dropped.

His fault? The hell it was.

Her hair was a silken wave that hit him smack in the face as she spun around to leave. Before she could take more than a step, Mitch grabbed her arm and pulled her back.

Anger, frustration and a pounding desire all beat at him. All the practical excuses and sane reasons he'd taken to reciting daily in an effort to avoid temptation flamed to cinders when he met the fury in her stormy sea-green eyes.

"We need to talk," he said in a low growl. With a quick look at the deserted landscape, he decided it was still too exposed for the chat he had in mind. So, his hand still gripping the soft skin of her arm, he pulled her with him toward the pool's linen room.

"We don't have jack to discuss," she snarled, trying to tug free. "I don't want to talk to you and I guarantee you don't want to hear what I have to say."

"On the contrary," he snapped, pushing the door open and pulling Belle with him into the dimly lit room. It was the size of a small shed. Neatly folded towels filled the shelf-lined walls and the air was warm with the scent of laundry detergent and sunshine. "We obviously have a lot to say to each other."

Belle tugged her arm free and glared. Her breath shuddered in and out, drawing his eyes to the lush bounty he'd been trying to ignore beneath her silky tank top. Mitch's gaze traced the curve of her breasts to the sweet indention of her waist, emphasized by a jeweled belt before the silk gave way to denim.

All week, hell, for the last six years he'd dreamed of her long legs wrapped around him. Of those hips welcoming him. Caution screamed in his head, a blaring warning that he was treading on thin ice. He'd promised that he'd keep his hands off her as long as she worked for him. Too much was at stake.

Apparently unaware of Mitch's inner struggle between desire and his vow to stay the hell out of her pants, Belle planted her fists on her hips, tugging the silk tighter against her breasts in a way that showed a narrow strip of her bra. Sparkling jewels caught the faint light like a treasure beckoning.

"What the hell is your problem?" she asked, her tone as angry as the look on her gorgeous face. "When did you turn into a caveman?"

"We needed to talk," he repeated. "We both have jobs to do. Given all the problems I've had, the last thing I need is you stomping off in a snit."

"Snit?" She actually hissed the word.

Getting turned on by her anger was probably a bad sign.

"Look, I overreacted, okay? But I promised myself I'd keep my hands off you. Which isn't easy with all your blatant flirting and come-ons, I'll have you know."

From the sneer she shot him, it was a piss-poor explanation.

"Want to remind me of when I begged you to put those hands on me?" she asked. She gave him a long, slow, up-and-down look that jacked his already cranked-up libido into full gear. "Did I touch you? A little pat on the ass? Flirty suggestions or come-do-me looks?"

Mitch arched a brow, about to remind her of their first meetings two weeks before. Catching the look, Belle rolled her eyes and flicked her hand toward him. "Bullshit. Anything that happened before we signed our contract doesn't count. You said the only way you'd be comfortable with us working together was if it was all business. I complied."

He hated that she was right. She'd been totally professional. At least she had until she'd blown off the previous day's tour to go on a date. Mitch mentally winced. Was that the real reason for his anger? Was he jealous? Pitiful, especially since he had no right to be.

Mitch's brow furrowed. Damn. It was one thing to be pitiful, but he had no right to take his anger out on her. He ground his teeth and tried to shove the emotion aside. He owed Belle an apology.

Ramming his hands in his pockets, Mitch stiffened his shoulders, battled down the fury and opened his mouth to offer up his apology. Before he could say a word, though, she was off and running again.

"Just because you're too sexually uptight to handle a hot relationship doesn't mean you should take your attitude out on me," she snapped, stabbing at him with her finger.

Mitch's apology turned into a glare but she just rolled her eyes.

"Oh, please. Even if we accept your silly excuse about our past and your business being too touchy to allow anything to happen between us, there's still the rest of it," she scoffed. "Admit it, you're too uptight to consider an incredibly innovative and exciting proposal that would guarantee your resort's success."

He'd had enough. Enough of her accusations. Enough of the sexual frustration that kept him churned up and crazy. Enough of being practical and self-sacrificing for the good of the many.

Screw it all, he was sick and tired of denying himself. For once, he was taking what he wanted.

He gave a low growl. Belle gasped. Before she could do more than blink, he moved, grabbing both her wrists and pinning her, arms overhead, to the smooth wall of the linen shed.

Heat, lust, anger all tangled in his system as he pressed his body close to hers. Like a drug addict grabbing for his fix, he closed his eyes in ecstasy even as he hated himself for giving in to the need.

But damn, it felt good.

Mitch didn't wait for Belle to recover. Instead he took her mouth in an intense, wild kiss. Passion flamed hot and furious between them as she opened her lips to his seeking tongue. Her welcoming moan sent a shaft of desire through him. His downfall felt deliciously decadent.

SHOCK FADED as Belle gave over to the power of Mitch's kiss. She had no idea what had incited the move, but she loved it. Loved the feel of his lips, soft and slick as they moved over hers. The power of his tongue as it tangled and wove, inviting hers to join him in the sensual dance.

Her breath came in pants now. Between the heat of his kiss and the wild excitement of feeling trapped by his hands holding hers prisoner, her panties were damp. She'd never gone for the submission thing, but Mitch holding her captive made her wild to let him have his way with her.

She squirmed a little, needing Mitch to hurry, to do something to relieve the building tension in her belly.

"More," she murmured against his mouth.

"Wait," he murmured back.

She groaned as he slid his lips from hers, already missing the hot dance of his tongue. She sucked in her lower lip, wanting, needing, to taste him.

Mitch traced kisses, hot, wet and exciting, down her throat. Belle groaned when he reached that spot, just there where her neck met her shoulder, and nibbled.

She tugged at her hands, needing to touch him. To feel his shoulders under her fingers, his chest and biceps. She just wanted to grab him and hold on while he took her for a wild ride.

Mitch wouldn't let go. Instead, he shifted so he held both her hands in one of his. Belle thought briefly of how large his hand must be to wrap so neatly around her wrists. The realization made her grin, then, unable to help herself, she pressed her hips closer to his, a quick undulation to check out the myth.

Yummy. If the very hard, very large length pressing against her thigh was any indication, that myth was based on reality. A reality she wanted to see, to feel and get to know up close and personal.

"More," she demanded again. The need in her belly was getting tighter, more urgent. "Quit playing and show me what you've got, big boy."

Mitch chuckled, as she'd hoped he would. But even better, he used his free hand to test the weight of her breast, then in a swift move he released her hands to tug her tank top and bra straps down one shoulder.

Belle's breath caught, her gaze locked on his face. She'd never worried about being judged before, but Mitch was different. She felt she'd wanted him, just like this, all her life. Lust and pure masculine appreciation were clear on his face. That look was as much a turn-on as the feel of his dick, hard and throbbing against her thigh. Tension fled, leaving only desire and need as he met her eyes. Their gazes locked as Mitch traced his finger over her areola, then flicked her hardening nipple.

She gasped.

His gaze dropped to her chest, color heating his cheeks. He bent and touched just the top of his tongue to the aching tip of her breast. Belle wanted to cry at the torment.

But she'd be damned if she'd beg again. Instead she shifted, wrapping one leg around his hip so she could press her wet, hot core against his thigh. The move lifted her breast higher. Mitch showed his appreciation by taking her nipple in his mouth, sucking, licking and nibbling.

Belle whimpered, her breath coming in pants now. Her head fell back against the wall, eyes closed to the dim light as she gave herself over to the wonderful feelings Mitch's mouth was inspiring. She didn't even notice that he'd let go of her wrists until she felt one hand under her butt. That hand lifted, controlled her undulations as he pressed her closer. The other tugged the second bra strap down to bare both breasts.

His mouth still tormenting one nipple, he worked the other with his fingers. Belle groaned her approval, pressing tight enough that the seam of her jeans added to the spiraling pleasure.

Mitch released his grip on her butt, shifting just a little so Belle could wrap both legs around his hips, his dick pressed against her throbbing core. The denim between them only added to her wild excitement.

Holding a breast in each large hand, he pressed them together. His thumbs worked her nipples as his mouth moved, wet and wild, first tormenting the left, then the right. Belle's hips jerked. She pressed closer, her ankles grabbing tight to his butt.

Heaven. When he nipped, teeth sharp yet gentle, at her wet nipple, she cried out in pleasure and lost control.

Gasping for breath, she came hard and fast. Lights exploded behind her eyes, her body melted with the power of the orgasm.

"Ohmygod, ohmygod, ohmygod," she chanted as she rode the wave. Mitch kept her up there, his tongue still working, his hand back beneath her butt to support her as she collapsed in delight.

Tension—hell, all feeling—fled her body as she sank into the afterglow of a first-class orgasm. Her legs numb, she dropped her feet to either side of Mitch's, but didn't shift away from the throbbing power of his dick where it pressed against her belly.

It took her a minute to realize he'd stopped his torment of her breasts. When she did, she lifted her head and opened her eyes to meet his.

She had to laugh. His grin was pure male ego.

Then it faded. Belle heard voices outside and realized his crew had probably shown up to fix the sprinkler problem.

Seeing she'd regained control, Mitch stepped away, visibly working to regulate his breathing. Belle stared through foggy eyes, satisfaction throbbing in her belly, between her legs. Damn, she felt great.

"Your turn?" she asked, her voice husky with pleasure.

She watched him swallow, then glance out the narrow window.

"The last thing I need my gardeners seeing is my bare ass," he said with a grimace.

Belle smirked. The chances of the gardeners peeking in were slim at best, but she didn't bother calling him on the flimsy excuse.

"I'm not uptight," he insisted. Belle kept silent, letting her arched brow speak volumes.

Well, he hadn't *felt* uptight, that was for sure. But then, he hadn't dropped his drawers, either. Rather than giving him the agreement he so obviously wanted, she just shrugged and adjusted her clothing, again not saying anything.

She hid her grin when she heard his teeth grinding from across the tiny shed.

"I'll read your proposal again," he suddenly promised. Shocked, Belle met his eyes. "If it's as solid as I remember, I'll submit it to my management team."

She didn't want a job—any job—based on sex, or in Mitch's case, unrequited sexual need. But she did want a chance.

"Why?" she asked.

"Because you're right. The idea is solid, it meshes with what I'm trying to do here. So it's worth considering."

"And if your team agrees?"

"We'll modify your contracts."

Belle nodded. Then she moved forward, close enough to feel the assurance that he was still hot, hard and excited. "And what about us?"

Mitch winced. "It'd be stupid to screw up a business deal over sex."

"It doesn't have to be like that," she returned, noticing he didn't say they wouldn't have sex. "Think of it this way. My proposal for your resort is based on sexual thrills. Don't you owe it to your clientele to try them all first?"

Mitch's eyes went round, then crinkled with laughter. "Why don't we see how the proposal goes first?"

Belle grimaced, thinking of what the last proposal between them had cost her. But she was smarter this time and definitely nowhere near as naive.

With that in mind, she gave Mitch her most wicked grin and stepped closer, letting the back of her fingers brush over his still-straining erection.

"You take me up on my proposal—business, pleasure or both—and I promise, you won't regret it."

With that and a quick butterfly kiss, she turned to saunter away. She felt the heat of his gaze on her swaying hips and let her grin fall away. Now she'd better figure out how to make damned sure *she* didn't regret it, either.

6

"WHAT KIND of sexy food did you have in mind for the room-service menu?" Mitch asked the people around the board table. This was their first group brainstorming session on the resort's new theme and he wasn't doing so well. It was a struggle to use the same tone he'd employ to discuss the type of artwork they'd carry in the lobby or how many brands of scotch the bar should have on hand. In other words, to keep this discussion at the level of pure business.

Damned hard, too, seeing the woman sitting across from him who had cried his name as he brought her to an orgasm in a towel closet three days before. The look she was giving him, pure flirtatious amusement, told him she was waiting for a repeat performance.

"Probably just two or three items," Belle said, her delight at the conversation, and probably at his apparent discomfort, clear in her tone. "The trick is going to be choosing the right ones. You might want to tie into your revolving-guest-chef theme with these. Keep a standard on the menu at all times, say oysters, since their reputation is so tried in food."

Mitch exchanged confused frowns with his manager, then asked, "Tried and true?"

"Exactly." She shot him a grin before leaning over to dig through her satchel and pull out files for everyone at the table. Their current discourse on sexual turn-ons was being shared with two of his managers, his head chef Jacques, and Miles, the resort's head of security. A nice, intimate group with which to brainstorm kink.

Belle had put them all at their ease, though. From the minute she'd walked into the room in her demure black skirt and red sleeveless turtleneck, she'd had his staff in the palm of her delectable little hand. A couple of jokes, a personal comment to each guy to let him know she'd done her research and appreciated the job he did, and they'd all relaxed.

And, given the topic, relaxation was key. At first, nobody had wanted to jump in with an opinion, so it'd been just Mitch and Belle talking sex. But after a quarter of an hour or so, the group hadn't been able to hold back. Now the opinions and ideas were flowing fast and furious, which gave Mitch time to sit back and watch Belle at work.

He glanced at the list she'd handed out. Title: Aphrodisiacs. He couldn't help but laugh. Belle winked at him.

"The room-service menu should otherwise be standard, of course." She glanced around the table and all the men nodded in agreement. Mitch suspected they'd have nodded if she'd suggested adding popcorn and Popsicles to the menu, they were so equally fascinated and out of their element. "But for the restaurant menu we can get more creative. Maybe cultural or thematic—Mexican chocolate, oysters Rockefeller, Greek honey cakes. That kind of thing."

"Graphic desserts?" offered Larry.

"Too bachelorette partyesque," Belle rejected with a grimace. "Think classier. Something that convinces people this isn't a gimmick, that it will really work."

"Asparagus and arugula salad?" he offered.

"There you go," she said, pointing her pen at him in approval before making note of his suggestion.

Mitch snickered when Larry preened as though he'd just been given a gold star.

Damn, she was good. She definitely knew what she was doing. Her society-princess title had been well earned. She orchestrated the meeting like a cocktail party, introducing this idea and that, making sure everyone had a chance to interject their comments before rearranging and serving the concepts back to them on a platter.

Who knew watching a sexy woman using her brain to work a room could be such a turn-on. Mitch wasn't a chauvinist pig, he respected women for more than their bodies. But he'd had no idea Belle had so much more going on.

He thought back to their engagement. He'd never seen her as a real person, just a princess to be won. And then there was their towel-closet encounter. While she'd obviously enjoyed the end results, he doubted she was impressed with his finesse and gentlemanly behavior.

Mitch grimaced. Maybe he was a pig.

"Now that we've covered the menu, let's see if we can nail a few of the special amenity details," Belle suggested, launching the discussion in a whole different direction.

Since most of those details were sexually explicit, Mitch had to work to keep his expression neutral.

"Do you really think handcuffs are necessary?" he asked as Diana brought in a tray of coffee and snacks. Apparently Belle had left word that she needed a midafternoon pick-me-up and his assistant was only too happy to oblige. Mitch couldn't say he blamed Diana, since he'd willingly do quite a few things, most cheap and kinky, to see Belle's smile of gratitude flash his way.

"Of course you need handcuffs," Belle said, her green eyes flashing wicked delight at odds with her matter-of-fact tone. "The key to having this work is to keep the sexual offerings classy by making them a standard amenity. If a guest has to call down to the concierge and ask for sex toys, it ruins the spontaneity."

From the bemused looks on the faces his staff as Belle passed around a tray of cookies, Mitch figured they were as speechless at that image as he was.

"And our goal is spontaneous sex?" he finally asked, giving up all pretense that he wasn't completely out of his element.

"That is precisely our goal," Belle said, her eyes hot and intense as she nibbled at a chocolate cookie. "The more spontaneous, and the more sex, the better."

Mitch went from intrigued to rock-hard in two seconds flat.

"You'll need to specially train your front desk and your concierge," Belle continued, talking to Larry. "Given the target demographic, you want to support the high-end thrill and excitement of a sexual getaway. Few people looking for the privacy to indulge their sexual fantasies care to explain to a concierge whether they prefer their handcuffs fur-lined or solid metal."

"Good point." Mitch frowned as he made a note on his report and muttered, "Apparently I'm going to need to find a supplier of kinky toys."

Belle pulled a paper from her file and handed him a complete list of companies, color-coded by fetish.

Helpless to do otherwise, Mitch snorted with laughter. Damn, she was good. Belle shot him an impish smile that said she knew what he was thinking and looked forward to proving just how good she could be.

BELLE LEFT Mitch's boardroom, doing a little happy dance as soon as the door swung shut behind her.

"That went well, I take it?" Diana asked, a hint of something Belle didn't understand in her tone.

"It was fabulous," Belle returned, too curious about the

other woman to feel embarrassed. "I think this is going to rock. Everyone had great ideas. It's got success written all over it."

From Diana's grimace-faking-it-as-a-smile, Belle figured the other woman might have some issues with the sex stuff. Leave it to Mitch to hire a prude as his assistant, Belle thought affectionately. But she'd brought him around, and she was sure she could bring Diana to accept the concept as well.

With that in mind, she pulled a chair up close to the woman's desk and leaned forward with her friendliest look.

"This must be fascinating," she said conversationally. "Being in on the ground floor of opening such a great place. I mean, you're surrounded by luxury, an incredible view and a hot boss. And once the place is open, it'll be like free cable. The inside scoop on famous people and clandestine sex. Not a bad job, huh?"

Diana looked at her as if she was a two-headed dog and both sides were missing a brain. Uptight *and* no sense of humor? Poor Mitch.

"Or not," Belle muttered, wondering if she had any common ground with this woman. She surveyed Diana's polyester blouse, navy slacks and flat pleather sandals. Probably not.

Belle glanced at her watch and sighed. How much longer was Mitch going to be?

"So tell me, Diana, how's the resort shaping up?" she asked after a few minutes of miserably uncomfortable silence. She didn't really care about the answer but was desperate for some conversation.

"Falling apart is more like it," the other woman mumbled into her computer screen.

"Beg pardon?"

Diana slanted her a sideways look and shrugged. "You know, it's just one problem after another. I've never been in on the— how did you say it?—ground floor of a resort opening before. But I'd imagined it'd be a little smoother, if you know what I mean."

Belle's brows shot up. "You mean things like the sprinklers and construction hitches?"

Diana winced. "Sure, those and the gophers and the computer crashes and the laundry mix-up and the lost supplies and, well, I could keep going but you get my drift."

Funny how the woman lost her quiet reserve when she was reciting all the resort's issues. Belle frowned and gave a one-shouldered shrug. "I'm sure that's all part and parcel to opening a new venue."

At least, she assumed it was. Her father's hotels had never hit so many hitches, but then he'd been at it a long time. This was Mitch's first hospitality venue, so maybe he just hadn't found his stride yet?

"Maybe," Diana agreed doubtfully. "I mean, I've heard such amazing things about Mr. Carter. He's got a reputation for being such an expert."

Diana's tone made it clear that she wasn't buying the rep any longer. Doubt washed over Belle. Was Mitch the guy to help her dad? She'd been so sure. As Diana said, he had a stellar reputation for being Mr. Amazing when it came to business. She frowned. Was that rep wrong?

"Can you excuse me for a minute," she asked Diana. "If Mitch comes out, just let him know I had a call I forgot I have to make."

"You can make it here," Diana said, pointing to the phone.

"Um, no thanks." Belle waved her cell phone and gestured toward the hallway. "It's…private."

The other woman gave her an ohhh-one-of-those-calls look and shrugged.

Once alone, Belle punched a button and paced impatiently while waiting for Sierra to pick up.

"We might need to rethink a few things," she said as soon as her partner answered.

"Which few?"

Belle explained the resort issues she'd discovered, both on her own and the ones Diana had shared. "So now I'm wondering if Mitch is really the right guy to help daddy."

"What about the Eventually Yours gig? Do we need to pull out?"

Pull out? Belle considered the question. They couldn't. They'd tied up a lot of time and energy in this project. If it went belly-up, they would definitely hurt. But not enough for her to consider ditching Mitch. He believed in the resort and had so much more at stake. She wanted to give him her support, even if he didn't realize it. The only thing she was risking was her time and energy. Yes, Eventfully Yours might take a hit, but as long as she came up with some other idea to help her dad, she could handle it.

"I gave my word, I can't back out." Her fear of failure faded a little as she made the statement.

At Sierra's snort she pulled the phone away from her ear and rolled her eyes.

"I've matured," she claimed, talking into the speaker again.

"Matured my ass. You just want to get in his pants."

"That's beside the point," Belle mumbled. So what if she did? Was that the only reason she wanted to stick with the job? No, of course not. She believed in it. She'd had a great time in their brainstorming session and the ideas they'd all come up with were awesome.

With that in mind, she squared her shoulders, shook off her nerves and claimed, "This is business and we signed a contract. Besides, I really haven't seen any hard evidence to make me believe Mitch isn't all his reputation says. Just little things that could easily be chalked up to normal start-up woes."

"You wouldn't have called me if you weren't worried."

"Not worried. Cautiously concerned about the big picture, you know?" And she hadn't wanted to voice her doubts about Mitch's success aloud. It seemed so disloyal.

"You mean you don't want to let your lust for this guy blind you a second time."

Belle pulled a face and, feeling like a slug, mumbled, "I'd rather just depend on us, if you know what I mean. As long as you're okay with the decision."

Sierra was silent for a second. Belle heard the cellophane crinkle of a candy wrapper. Then, "Eventfully Yours can handle whatever happens. The real question is, what do you want to do about your dad? Find someone else to help him? Like who? You're the one with all the hotel experience."

Blinking away tears of relief at her friend's understanding and support, Belle paced and considered. "Let's just see what we can come up with ourselves, okay? I don't want to make any decisions yet. I just, you know, needed a sounding board and to get your brain in on the action."

"What are you going to do while my brain works?"

Mitch strode out of his office just then. Unlike the businessmen her daddy worked with, who always did the suit-and-tie thing, Mitch seemed to have left that phase behind him. Other than their meeting at the restaurant when they'd signed the contracts, he always wore jeans.

As Mitch turned to respond to something Diana had said, Belle sighed. Damn, she loved a guy in jeans.

"Continue with plan A," Belle said as her eyes met Mitch's when he turned around.

"Jump his bones?" Sierra confirmed.

"You know it." With that, Belle pushed the disconnect button and slid her phone into her bag.

"Ready?" Mitch asked, referring to their plans to tour the golf course and wooded picnic area.

"I need to change," she said, waving her high-heeled sandal-clad foot his way. "Let's stop by my room and I'll get some flats, okay?"

They headed outside toward her cottage.

"I don't think I ever saw you in jeans when we were dating or engaged," she commented.

Mitch's look of surprise must be due to her bringing up the past, Belle figured. But while she wasn't about to play the blame game, it was silly to pretend they didn't have a past. Maybe if they melted the ice with easy chit-chat, she'd be able to work up the nerve to apologize for abandoning him at the altar before her job here was done.

"Six years ago I had too much to prove to let myself wear jeans," Mitch finally said.

Intriguing. "And did you?"

"Did I what?"

"Prove your point? And what was it? That denim makes your ass look great, but you wanted to be taken seriously so you denied the world the sweet sight?"

He snorted and shook his head. They'd reached her cottage, so he gestured for her to precede him to the door. Belle glanced back to see if he was going to answer and caught him checking out *her* ass. She grinned. Well, tit for tat and all that.

"Hardly," he said, shrugging an apology for the ogling. Belle just winked back to let him know she didn't mind. "I wanted to play with the big boys. Hotels, entertainment. I figured nobody would take a hammer-swinging kid seriously so I went the businessman route."

"Trying to be a wolf with silk ears?"

He frowned, then after a second corrected, "Wolf in sheep's clothing? Or silk purse out of a sow's ear?"

"Both." She smiled up at him as she pushed open the door. "But I heard talk before you showed up in those fancy suits. Nobody thought of you as a kid or as less than a driving force. They were looking forward to working with you. You had a great rep."

At least he had before she got a hold of him. Belle winced and, before he could respond by pointing out that exact fact, she gestured to the bowl of fruit on the small kitchenette table. "Help yourself to a snack while I change, hmm?"

And off she scurried, like a scared little mouse, guilt pounding at her like a sledgehammer on speed. In the bedroom, she dropped to her bed and stared at the ceiling while reciting all the reasons she'd screwed up and why he had the right to hold them against her. Then, once they were out of her system, she shot up and tugged open the plantation-style closet doors to grab a denim skirt and casual blouse for their tour.

MITCH BLINKED at the closed door, wondering what the hell had just happened. One second he and Belle had been having a friendly jaunt into the past. The next she was offering him a banana and running away.

Apparently that was the theme of their relationship, that running thing.

He sighed and glanced around the cottage. *California casual* was the term the decorator had used—light woods, soft fabric, bare tile floors. The space was open and airy with a few plants here and there to make it welcoming. As comfortable as it had started out, in less than a week, Belle had made it her own.

Colorful scarves over the chairs added rich splashes of green and turquoise. A wooden bowl filled with engraved stones sat on the coffee table. Mitch walked over to pick one out. *Perseverance,* he read. Motivational sayings? Belle?

He noticed a small framed poster on the wall. Stone in hand, he stepped closer to read about the ABCs to Achieve Your Dreams.

Wild. He frowned at the closed door and tried to adjust his image of her, a flighty sexpot with great planning skills, with the idea that she bought, let alone used, motivational tools.

It was then that he saw it. A small, fluffy, pink, stuffed

bunny rabbit. As spotless as the day he'd won it for her at a corporate fund-raising carnival, it sat in the rocking chair looking fat and content.

Mitch grinned at the sight and, tossing the stone back in the bowl, lifted the bunny for a closer look.

"Don't mess with Mr. Winkles," Belle said, coming out of the bedroom. Her tone was light, but there was still a lingering frown around her eyes.

"I can't believe you still have this," he said with a laugh, holding up the stuffed animal. "I never took you for the sentimental type." He considered, then added, "I never thought our time together was something worthy of sentiment, to tell you the truth."

As soon as the words were out, Mitch winced. He sounded like an ass. But, well, the truth was, he'd never allowed himself to think about their time together as anything but a business deal gone bad. It hurt less that way.

She gave him the glare of death, but in a blink, the look was gone. Had he imagined it? Maybe.

Then she snatched the toy from his hands as if he'd stolen it. That's when it hit him.

"Are you embarrassed?" he asked with a grin. "There's no reason to be. I think it's sweet."

Her porcelain skin flushed crimson and the death glare returned in full force. She gripped one hand so tightly around the rabbit's neck, it'd be stew meat if it wasn't a stuffed toy. Mitch winced. From the look on her face, she was imagining his throat between her fingers.

"Sweet, my ass," she shot back. "I'm not sentimental over our time together. Believe me, the last thing I need is a constant reminder of my mistake."

Mitch's spine snapped straight, his amusement fleeing at that one word. *Mistake.*

Oh, yeah, there had been mistakes. But they were his. It'd taken him six years to make up for the business ones, and damned if he needed his personal ones thrown in his face by the woman at fault for all of them.

"Mistake? Care to clarify that?" he asked, his tone the one he reserved for embezzlers, liars and cheats. Icy-cold and precise.

"Oh please, like you don't know." Her sneer was a work of art. Angry, but still disdainful enough to hide the hurt he'd glimpsed earlier. And he'd called her sentimental? "You can pretend all you want that we're business buddies here, but we both know damned well what happened."

"Us and a couple of hundred guests," he shot back.

Belle rolled her eyes. "That's your own damned fault," she declared. "If you hadn't put such an insane price on your body, we'd never have ended up in that mess."

Mitch had fallen off a fifth-story girder once, his safety rope keeping him from serious injury. That was the only time he recalled ever being this close to speechless. He stared, mouth open. "My body?"

"I wanted sex," she declared, pointing the bunny at him like a pistol. "Simple, uncomplicated sex. But no, you had to turn it into something else. Complicate it. You ruined everything, and for what? Ambition?" Disdain dripped from her words like battery acid, burning Mitch.

He clenched his jaw, struggling to find a response. Anger pounded at his temples: fury at the past and at the woman in front of him for reminding him that he'd never measured up.

He'd spent his entire career trying to prove himself. To prove he was man enough to take care of his mother after his dad had died. To prove he was worthy of the trust his stepfather had later showed in him. And then to prove that he wasn't going to fall apart when he'd been left with the responsibility of his stepdad's construction company.

And then he finally thought he'd found his perfect woman. The one he'd seen as proof that he was man enough for anything. And she'd walked out on him.

Mitch had never admitted, not to anyone but himself in the dark hours when it was just him and his thoughts, his fears that Belle had found him lacking. That she'd decided he wasn't rich enough, wasn't talented enough, wasn't worthy enough.

It was the last one that really grated. All he'd wanted from the moment he'd set eyes on the sassy blond was to sweep her off her feet.

Mitch glared at her, all grown up now and just as sassily sexy. He should have swept when he had a chance. Maybe if he'd knocked her feet out from under her she wouldn't have run away.

Well, he'd blown his chance once. He wasn't stupid enough to blow it twice.

"You wanted sex?" he ground out, anger and lust sharp and jagged in his system. "Fine, I'll give you sex."

Two steps was all it took to pin her between the hard, needy length of his body and the wall. Belle's shocked gasp was lost against his mouth. Her sea-green eyes glared into his as she gave a low growl. Being a smart man, Mitch kept his tongue out of the game just yet. But he used his lips to full effect.

And his hands. Because, if he did say so himself, he was damned good with his hands. He skimmed them over her hair, a gentle glide down her shoulders then a quick, barely-there flick along the sides of her full breasts, crushed against his chest. He gripped the gentle curve of her waist for just a second, then gave in to the need and scooped his hands under the sweet curve of her ass.

Mitch groaned as the move pressed her tighter to the throbbing length of his dick. God, he wanted her.

Tossing off all restraint, all the rules he'd tried so hard to live by, he let himself go. His hands gripped Belle's butt, squeezing her soft curves one more time before he pulled her between his thighs. One hand slid up to cup the back of her neck, holding her head in place when she tried to jerk away from his kiss.

Feeling her heart pounding in her throat, he told himself it was passion and, desperately needing to taste her, he risked it all and slid his tongue along the seam of her full, soft lips.

Her shuddered gasp was barely discernable, but he felt it. Both against his mouth, and in the way she pressed herself tighter against his erection. Her wiggle was a tiny thing, but damn, it felt great. His grin was fast and triumphant before he took her mouth in a wild ride. Tongues dueled and tangled in a dance of passion. Quick, deep kisses that hinted at dark pleasures and intense emotion. He gave over to the power of tasting her, feeling her. Belle, the one obsession he'd never been able to shake.

A voice whispered in the back of his head to slow down. Mitch told the voice to shut the hell up. In pure defiance he shifted her, one quick move, to straddle his hips and gave a guttural groan when she wrapped those long, delicious legs around him. Mitch pressed, once, twice. Belle mimicked his rhythm, taking on the slow, intense undulation.

Desperate now, he released her hip and neck to cup her breasts. The heated warmth filled his palm. Her soft whimper turned to a moan when he flicked his thumbs over her pebbled nipples.

Need pounded now, a heavy dark beat. Mitch gave in to it, releasing her mouth as he pulled her blouse over her head. Seconds before he lost himself in the lush bounty of her breasts, he met her eyes. Head supported by the wall, her blond hair a cloudy pillow behind her, Belle stared back. Desire, power, pleasure all shone in her gaze.

Mitch's ultimate dream, here in his hands, the taste of her rich on his tongue. The image he had of him and Belle—the poor kid in patched jeans and the princess—flashed through his head. *You've come a long way, baby,* that voice said. But, he vowed, not nearly as long as he planned to make Belle come.

7

WHO KNEW confrontation could feel so good? Belle's breath trembled, the wall a hard pillow behind her head, and she closed her eyes and let the delicious sensations wash over her in powerful, throbbing waves.

Her fingers slid, caressing their way through Mitch's hair as she pressed his face closer to her breasts. The contrast of his mouth, so soft and moist and warm, and his cheek, roughening just hours after his morning shave, drove her nuts.

Fingers stroked, squeezed, in rhythm with her movements. Belle hitched just a little so her skirt shifted up higher, out of the way. Ahhh, she pressed closer, her silk panties moist and hot. They added to the intensity of his rough jeans against her swollen nether lips.

She wanted to squirm, to ratchet up the power. She wanted hard and fast and intense blood-pounding sex against the wall.

But Mitch was in charge, and despite the wall and the absolute control he'd grabbed early on, he was taking it slow. Damn him.

With deliberate care, he scraped his teeth over her aching nipples. Belle gasped and gripped his hair tighter, needing more. His tongue swirled, taunted and teased the tip of one breast, then switched to the other to continue the torment. Belle ground herself against the hard length of him.

"More," she moaned.

"Soon," he said, his breath hot against her damp flesh. Belle squirmed again, losing the rhythm. Her frantic movement made Mitch groan, the smooth stroke of his tongue turning to an almost desperate sucking motion.

Oh, yeah. Heat, fast and furious, shot through her body like a bolt of lightning. Pleasure bordered on pain as his mouth ravaged her breast, his hand gripping the other in a heated caress. Yeah, that's what she wanted. Her head fell back again, her eyes closed as she gave herself over to the sensations. Her panties were soaked now as she rode up and down the rigid length of his turgid, zipper-covered dick.

"I'm not doing this alone—again," she panted. "This time I want you with me."

"I'm right here."

"Naked," she insisted. She'd spent six-plus years wanting to get her hands on his naked body and she didn't want to wait a second more. "I want to see you. Touch you. Taste you."

He groaned and gave a little shudder, but didn't stop.

"After," he said.

After?

Mitch shifted, bringing one hand down between their bodies while the other still caressed the nipple he wasn't sucking. His fingers stroked the wet silk between her legs, sending a jolt of pleasure through her. Belle gasped, her thighs trembling as he worked her swollen clitoris through the fabric.

He played her body like a virtuoso, bringing her higher and higher with every flick of his tongue, brush of his fingers. As her climax built, she knew which "after" he was referring to.

Then he slid the fabric of her panties out of the way. He danced his fingers over her slick folds, pressing, sliding, driving her crazy. Stars danced behind Belle's closed eyes, her body on overload. Mitch's tongue teased her nipple, then sucked it deep into his mouth as he worked her with his fingers.

One finger in, then out, was all it took. Belle exploded. Her thighs tightened, her fingers grabbed Mitch's shoulders as the orgasm shook her body. Spirals of pleasure danced through her system, spinning higher, wilder as she flew over the edge.

She slowly floated back to earth, her breath soft pants as she became aware of Mitch again. His mouth pressed into the curve of her throat, he held her tight against his body. As her thoughts coalesced, she felt the tension and strain in his shoulders, the bunched muscles of his back. And, she realized, that ever so deliciously hard muscle throbbing behind his zipper.

Twice now he'd made her come with all her clothes on, not taking anything in return. While she wouldn't deny the thrill of being taken against the wall—twice—she still wanted a little more active role in screwing Mitch's brains out.

With that in mind, as soon as she thought they'd hold her, she let her legs slide down Mitch's hard thighs, sighing at the sensation of denim against bare flesh. Feet on the floor, she felt her knees try to buckle, making Belle grateful to be sandwiched between the wall and Mitch's body.

Time to upgrade this event to a couples theme…

"Off," Belle purred, needing to feel skin. Years. She'd waited years for this opportunity and she'd be damned if she was going to waste a single second of it. Not even to bask in the afterglow of a rockin' orgasm.

Her hands slid up his forearms, the soft hair tickling her palms. As she passed over the rolled-up chambray sleeves, she paused to squeeze his rock-solid biceps. She wanted to see those muscles. Now. She pulled at Mitch's shirt to get it out of her way. Buttons flew everywhere. She didn't care. Her eyes were focused on the prize, on the broad planes of his smooth, golden chest.

"Mmm," she murmured as she took in the sight. She let Mitch deal with getting the shirt off his arms. She was busy appreciating the view. Golden skin stretched over the nicest set of pecs she'd seen since ogling the big screen. Like the first fall leaves, a dusting of mahogany hair trailed down his chest. Belle swallowed, her eyes landing on the very large, very hard package pressing against the worn denim of his jeans. Yowza and come to momma. She placed one hand against his hard chest while she smoothed the other over his shoulder, down that bicep again. Mitch wrapped his hands around her waist, but she barely noticed his caress, so focused was she on the tactile wonderland of his body.

She leaned forward, pressing her face to the warmth of his chest, breathing in his cologne, then turned her head just a little to flick her tongue over his flat nipple. He swiftly sucked in his breath, his abs going concave.

Belle grinned her appreciation before letting her head fall back to look into his face.

"You're gorgeous," she told him. "Sexy, buff and delicious. I plan to taste every single inch of you."

His eyes seemed to lose their focus at her words. Releasing her waist, he shoved his hands into her hair, fingers gripping the back of her scalp. He pulled her up to meet his mouth. Hot and wild, his tongue ravaged hers. Belle wasn't about to give up control, though, so she met him thrust for thrust, then sucked his tongue into her mouth in a way that made him groan and reach for her naked breasts.

"No," she gasped, moving away before he could work his magic and distract her again. "My turn."

And she made the most of it. In little, nibbling bites and long wet kisses, she worked her way over his chest and down his belly.

Dropping to her knees, she pressed her cheek against the bulge in his jeans and, glancing up to give him a wicked grin, reached around to squeeze his butt. Mitch's laugh eased her tension, and with an answering wink she released the catch on his pants and eased his zipper down.

A quick shove was all it took to bare his straining dick, right there at mouth level. She sighed in appreciation at the sight, sure that very tasty treat was going to bring her untold hours of pleasure.

Like a yummy lollipop, she ran her tongue up the length of his shaft and grinned when he grabbed her shoulders and groaned. Oh, yeah, she was definitely going to enjoy this. With a sigh of pleasure, she wrapped her lips around the smooth cap, and after a couple of teasing swirls of her tongue, quit playing and gave him the best head she could.

After a couple minutes of service, Mitch's fingers dug into her shoulders in a gentle signal that he was reaching his limit. She briefly considered pushing him over that limit, sending him right off the cliff, but then realized there were so many more delights to be had. Why rush things?

With a smooth slurping motion, she released him and leaned back on her hands. Mitch watched her like a man possessed, waiting to see what her next move would be, a wicked grin playing at the corner of his mouth.

"How're you at numbers?" she asked, her breath shuddering as the spiraling heat reignited in her belly. Pressing her fingers against her damp, aching mound, she pulled them away to show him the wet evidence of her desire.

"You mean like sixty-nine?" At her nod, Mitch reached down and took her hand, dropping to his knees as well and sucking her fingers into his mouth. Belle whimpered at the action, the tension between her legs ratcheting even higher. "I'm damned good, as you're about to find out," he promised.

"Do that again," she instructed, "just, you know, somewhere else."

Mitch's grin flashed. In a quick move, he kicked off his

shoes, tugged his socks and jeans off, too. Naked, he lay back on the floor and gestured.

"Gimme," he said. "But get naked first."

Belle glanced down at herself—on her knees, her blouse long gone, her bra scooped under her breasts, pressing them up and together in a way that made them look much larger than they actually were. Her skirt was bunched around her waist like a belt, and her panties but a tattered memory of silk and lace.

She stood, placing one foot on either side of Mitch's hips and giving him a clear view of her wet, pink folds. Like a magnet, his eyes flew to the sight and his grin fell away. He reached for her but she shook her head, so he settled on running his hands up and down her calves, accented by the high heels she still wore.

She smoothed her skirt back in place. He frowned, then watched as she flipped the hook and zipper open. Belle shimmied, her breasts swaying with the movement. Mitch's eyes went opaque. She pushed the tight skirt down her hips, and bending one knee to bring her legs together, she dropped the skirt to the floor, then kicked it away.

Almost naked now and loving Mitch's full attention, Belle stood, legs spread, and gently scraped her nails up her thighs. She passed her hand over the damp curls between her legs, pausing to flick one finger over her clit. The movement made Mitch's dick jump as though it was jealous. She loved his eyes on her. It was almost as good as his hands, although not nearly as sweet as his mouth. She felt like a sex goddess, the way he looked at her. She slid her hands up her torso, cupping her breasts and squeezing them. Head falling back, she closed her eyes and let the sensation, hot, intense and powerful, wash over her.

Her fingers tweaked her aching, turgid nipples, amping up her desire, preparing her for the thrust of Mitch's tongue. As if he heard her thoughts, suddenly his mouth was between her legs. Belle gasped, then gave a keening cry as he skipped all the preliminaries and thrust his tongue inside her.

Her knees buckled again, but his hands were there on her ass to hold her up. She looked down and almost came at the sight. Her nails teased and circled the pointy pink tips of her nipples, and there below Mitch half sat, half lay, his eyes staring into hers as he used his tongue to drive her crazy.

She wanted to come. Two more seconds and she would. But she'd promised herself the next time she'd be taking him down with her. Calling on a willpower she'd have sworn didn't exist, she stepped away from the best tongue job she'd ever had and pointed to the floor. Mitch frowned. Belle arched her brow. Not bothering to take off her shoes, she gestured to the floor again and ran her hands over her breasts in promise.

Mitch lay back, his dick as rigid as a redwood, waiting for her. As gracefully as possible, Belle dropped down, one knee on either side of his hips. Her wet bush rubbed against his dick, tempting her to simply shift and take him inside her. But she wanted more, she wanted to drive him so crazy he never forgot her. She wanted him to want her so bad, she became the most important thing in his life. Even if it was only for the moment.

Needing the connection, she let herself fall forward so her hands braced on either side of his head, and kissed him. Dark and drugging, the kiss tasted like musky sex.

With one last bite at his lower lip, she sat upright, then swung her legs around so she faced backward. Falling forward to brace her elbows on the floor on either side of his hips, she wrapped one hand around the base of his straining dick and, knowing he was waiting, feeling the tension in him building, swirled her tongue over the silky head. Mitch groaned and grabbed her hips, his fingers digging erotically into the soft flesh. She swirled again, then pulled just the head into her mouth, sucking it like a lollipop. He got even harder and she felt him groan, a warm gust of air between her thighs. Then his mouth was on her. He licked, then sucked her clit into his mouth, causing Belle to shudder.

Determined to make him come first, and hanging on to her control by the thinnest thread, she poured everything she had into giving him the best, the hottest and sexiest blow job of her life. Lips, teeth and tongue worked magic as she sucked and swirled, taking him deeper. His tongue mimicked lovemaking, spearing her in then out, as his finger massaged her swollen lips.

Belle couldn't take much more. While still sucking, she scraped her teeth, gentle as could be, up the length of him. Mitch stiffened and grabbed her hips. She did it again. His fingers tightened, then proving those rock-hard biceps were well-deserved, he lifted and flipped her around so she faced him.

He reached up and wrapped his hand around the back of her neck, pulling her mouth down to meet his. Wet, sliding, open-mouth kisses added to the intense, needy ache in her belly. While driving her crazy, Mitch reached over to pull his jeans to him and grabbed a condom out of his pocket.

Releasing her mouth, he let his head fall back to the carpet and handed her the foil packet. "Ride me," he demanded.

In quick moves made jerky by impatience and need, she sheathed his straining erection in the ribbed-for-her-pleasure condom and rose to her knees.

One leg on either side of his hips, she locked eyes with Mitch. Excruciatingly slowly, she lowered herself one delicious inch at a time on his rock-hard cock until she'd taken all of him inside her.

With a shuddering moan, she ran her hands up the sides of her body, her skin so sensitized the barely-there move made her want to scream with pleasure. She slid her hands over her breasts and up her throat, then speared them through her hair. Lifting her arms overhead, she gave silent thanks for the delicious treat she was about to enjoy.

Then she set out to pleasure the hell out of herself. Riding him, slowly at first and with ever-increasing strokes, she let the tension build. Tighter, deeper, need coiled low in her belly. Belle's gaze stayed locked on Mitch's, watching his eyes to gauge his pleasure. Fingers meshed as they held hands, their focus completely, totally on the sensations building in both of them as Belle rode him.

Her climax just a breath away, her body started to shake as she tried to hold off. She needed to see him come first. Had to know she could give him as much pleasure as he gave her. With that in mind, trying as hard as she could to hold off the pounding orgasmic waves, she swirled her hips, adding a deep undulating move to each thrust.

Mitch's eyes went dark, then closed for a second as he fought for control. Belle's breath hitched and she did it again. He hissed, his gaze meeting hers once more.

She licked her lips and, their hands still entwined, raised one his to scrape her teeth along his knuckles, to run her tongue over his palm.

Mitch exploded. His guttural cry of pleasure set hers free. Belle felt the power of his climax, her own body shuddered with wave after wave of the most incredible sensations.

Panting, she dropped onto his chest. Mitch's arms wrapped around her in a hug that was more emotional than sexual and brought tears to Belle's eyes. Just orgasm overload, she assured herself as she struggled to catch her breath.

"Now aren't you sorry you didn't take me up on my offer earlier?" she teased, trying to lighten the mood.

"Better late than never," he said with a laugh, his own breath sounding labored. "And keep in mind, I only get better with age."

Didn't that image simply boggle the mind? Belle shifted her legs so they lay alongside Mitch and hummed at the mini climax she felt at the move.

"Tell you what, gorgeous. If you only improve with age, you're going to be off the charts by the time you're forty."

Mitch snickered but Belle fell silent, realizing she wouldn't know. She'd be nowhere around in eight years when Mitch hit that milestone. Some other woman would likely be reaping the rewards of his age-improved sexual games. But not Belle. She'd thrown away—or rather, run away from—the right to know.

The idea made her miserable. Her stomach pitched and her eyes filled. Blaming it on emotional overload brought on by four orgasms in a row, Belle sniffed and rolled away to hide her tears. What now? Did she pat him on the ass, hand him his jeans and get back to business? It sounded so cold when all she wanted was to curl up in his arms and be held.

"Getting that good takes a lot of practice," Mitch mused, wrapping his arms around her from behind and tugging her back against his hot, naked body. "I have a few ideas I've wanted to try out on you, with you."

The painful tension eased from Belle's body, only to be replaced by tension of the sexual kind. Much happier with horny over weepy, she turned in Mitch's arms and grinned. "Do tell. I'm always intrigued by self-improvement programs."

He laughed and in a single move stood and scooped her up in his arms. Belle linked her hands behind his head and cuddled, a soft glow of joy settling in her chest.

"We need a mattress for what I have in mind," he told her, heading for the bedroom. "Something soft and comfortable, since next time I want you on the bottom."

"Sounds prosaic," she teased as he dropped her on the bed.

"Prosaic, my ass," he growled, kneeling at the bottom of the bed to take hold of her foot, still shod in her strappy sandal. A few quick flicks of his fingers and he'd unstrapped first one, then the other. Sliding his hands up her body in a way that left yummy tingles, he reached her mouth and planted a quick, hard kiss on her lips.

Before Belle could respond, he rolled away and shot a swift glance around the room. Her open closet apparently offered exactly what he was looking for, because he leaped from the bed and grabbed two belts and a silk scarf.

Belle's jaw dropped when he grabbed her wrist and, using a soft suede belt, tied it to the headboard.

"You're kidding," she breathed, scared, intrigued and totally turned on, all at the same time.

He didn't answer, instead holding out his hand and waiting. With a silent gulp, her breath coming a little faster as her body heated, Belle put the fingers of her free hand in his. Mitch tied it to the headboard as well, then lay on the bed next to her.

His gaze moved over her captive body like a caress. Her nipples peaked at his look, damp heat pooling between her legs. He stared for so long, she started to squirm.

Meeting her gaze, Mitch's eyes were hot and intense, filled with sexual promises. Belle pressed her lips together to keep from whimpering.

"I've wanted to tie you up for what feels like forever," he said softly. "Keep you here, at my mercy where you can't run or hide. Now that I have you, I'm going to touch you, kiss you, taste you." He ran the length of silk fabric between his fingers, then trailed it along her hip, over her quivering belly, and draped it gently over her aching breasts. "I'm going to use my tongue and my fingers. I'm going to drive you crazy."

Then he shifted, pulling the fabric from her breasts so the silky texture teased her nipples. Belle gasped and pressed her thighs together to ease the building pressure.

"And I'm going to do it all while you're blindfolded," he told her. Belle's gasp was lost in his mouth as he kissed her sense-less while wrapping the jade-green silk over her eyes and tying it gently behind her head.

Belle planted her bare feet on the mattress, raising her pelvis in supplication. Mitch moved so he was between her wide-spread legs, his hard dick brushing against her aching center, but not relieving any tension, not entering her. She felt him lean forward, the mattress dipping on either side of her as he sup-ported himself.

Holding her breath, she waited. Damp and hot, his tongue licked one nipple, then the other. A gentle gust of air teased the already hard peaks into aching stiffness. Belle couldn't hold back her whimper now. She needed something, anything.

"Do me," she begged.

"My way."

His way was killing her.

Still keeping that delicious pressure against her clit, he shifted. His hands cupped her breasts, pressing them together, his thumbs working her nipples as his mouth worked them in turn. Sucking, nibbling, licking. Teeth and tongue, just rough enough to make her crazy with need.

Oh, man. She was going to come before he even reached her aching center. She just knew it. And, she realized as the orgasm exploded behind her eyes, she just loved it.

Later, much, *much* later, wrapped in plush towels warmed by the heated towel-bar, Belle and Mitch fell to her bed in a state of exhausted pleasure. Her eyelids drooping, she glanced at the clock and yawned. Five hours ago, they'd stopped off here so she could change her clothes for the tour.

And now she was floating on a cloud of sensual satisfaction like nothing she'd ever felt before. A tiny frown, all she had the energy for, creased her brow. If she hadn't messed up, she could have been floating like this for years. At least a few, she told herself, knowing the trophy-bride role wouldn't have worked for long.

Her thoughts ran like a snag in a favorite sweater, irritating and ugly, ruining her mood. If she'd been a trophy then, what was she now? Why was Mitch with her? Sudden lust? Tension seeped down her spine. What if she fell for him again? It'd hurt badly enough before, when she'd known it was only infatuation. What if this time, now that they'd had the incredible sex and she was able to deal with him on a one-on-one adult level, she really fell hard? What if he broke her heart?

Panic tightened the muscles across her back, her breath starting to hitch.

Mitch's hand curved around her waist, pulling her closer. His warm breath on her back was all it took to melt the icy fear. Determined not to ruin what had been the best sex of her life, she shoved her fears aside and let her mind empty.

"We missed exploring the grounds," she murmured sleepily.

Ever the gentleman, Mitch tugged the blankets over them before curling up behind her and draping one arm around her waist.

"Tomorrow," he said, his voice sounding as worn out as she felt.

Tomorrow. They had tomorrow. Belle drifted off to sleep, the satisfied smile on her face due more to that promise than the fact that she'd just had the most incredible sex of her life.

8

"IT WAS…incredible. Totally amazing," Belle rhapsodized over the phone. Her mind was still filled with the memory of her and Mitch, naked. Two hours had passed since he'd left her bed after a hot bout of early-morning delight and she could still taste him. She shifted, just a little, and her unused-to-such-wild-sex body felt the reminder of him inside her.

"But, I don't get it—when I'm with Mitch, I totally lose control," she admitted to her best friend from the very bed where she'd had that wild sex. Now, though, it was man-less as she carefully applied a second coat of blushing burgundy to her toenails.

"Well, good sex will do that to a gal. I thought you'd have realized that by now," Sierra returned grumpily. Belle felt a surge of guilt at the worry she was causing her partner.

Not enough to drop the subject, though.

"Ha-ha," Belle deadpanned, capping the polish and setting it on the bedside table. "I mean, I keep…" She trailed off, needing to talk about it but realizing how stupid she'd sound.

"Keep what? Having premature orgasms? Screaming in ecstasy loud enough to bring the gardeners running? Welcoming your climax with a litany of filthy porn words?"

Belle's jaw dropped. Not at the words, but at the tart tone. She pulled the phone away from her ear to stare at it in shock, then flipped over on the bed so she lay on her stomach.

"Something's wrong," she decided aloud. "Is there a problem with Eventfully Yours? Are you okay? What's going on?"

Silence. Then she actually heard Sierra shrug, the fabric of whatever she was wearing brushing against the phone. "No problems. Nothing's going on. Company is fine."

Shorthand for Sierra didn't want to talk about it.

One of the cornerstones of their lifelong friendship was knowing when to push the other and when to back off and let her stew. Belle's telltale clue to leave Sierra alone had always been how many millimeters her lower lip stuck out. A champion pouter, Sierra was open to commiserating if she had the lip out. But if she'd sucked it in, concentration-style, she was off-limits.

Belle silently cursed the distance between them and tried to figure out what to do.

"What lipstick are you wearing?" she asked.

"What kind of question is that?" When Belle didn't say anything, Sierra admitted, "I'm not wearing any right now."

Chewed it all off. Definitely off-limits. Automatically backing away from the confrontation, Belle shifted back to the original topic. "I feel like an idiot," she admitted, "but I keep losing my temper with Mitch. You know me, I don't get angry. This is so bizarre."

"You do, too, get angry," Sierra pointed out. "You just don't allow yourself to express it. You'll end up with ulcers if you don't learn to let go of some of that, you know."

"Apparently I've found my release valve."

"Sex'll work every time," her partner agreed. "But since I'm not getting any, I'd rather talk about something else, okay?"

Sierra would never be in danger of ulcers. Despite her unwillingness to share whatever was bothering her, she never bottled up her emotions. Why bother, she usually said, when it was so much more fun to let them spew all over like a well-shaken bottle of soda.

Except now, when she seemed to be holding them in even better than Belle ever had.

"Okay, so, um, did you get my notes about the sex-themed ideas?" Belle asked, obediently changing the topic. "I'm going to need additional staff to help set up for the pre-events. I think Mitch said something about his security team running checks on everyone to guarantee a complete media blackout."

"We've got two dozen independent contractors on file who've passed top security screenings. That should be enough, shouldn't it?"

Belle glanced at her leather portfolio, flipping pages with the pad of her finger so as not to smudge her fresh polish. "That should work, in addition to Lakeside's serving staff."

The two of them went over details for the upcoming opening, plus ideas for possible follow-up contracts, such as holiday-themed sex and weddings à la kink.

"I talked to a couple of bigwigs when I was handling the CEO gig last week," Sierra said after they'd wound up business. "You know, just a few questions about who they think the top developers are, what they'd do in today's real estate climate and economy, that kind of chit-chatty thing."

Belle sat up and drew her knees to her chest. She glanced at the tab in her notebook titled Dad and grimaced. She'd been so busy getting mad at, then getting on top of Mitch, she'd forgotten the most important reason she was here.

"And?"

"Things just suck right now. They all said the same thing your dad did. It's not the time to build. In their opinion, anyone sitting on a big fat piece of land is stuck with it for the next little while."

"The next little while will bankrupt Daddy."

Sierra gave a sympathetic sigh. "I know."

Out of the blue, Belle thought back to the contract she'd seen on Diana's desk. There was a luxury spa in the resort lobby—fancy and very upscale. And oddly enough, it was not owned by the hotel but was leasing the space from Lakeside. Was that an option for her dad's hotels? An additional income? It was worth looking into.

"Let me talk to a couple of people," she told Sierra. "I thought of something earlier, but I need to get some details to figure out if it even makes sense."

Belle stared out the window at the gorgeous golf course. Morning sun washed it in gentle light. Lush, green and exclusive. Her father's hotels were lovely, but not in the same category as Lakeside. This resort would cater to an elite clientele, whereas Forsham's catered to upscale business travelers, wedding parties and couples looking for indulgent getaways.

Maybe the spa angle was the answer to increasing the cash flow until the real estate market turned around and her father could sell the properties without losing everything. She watched the gardeners putter along the green in a golf cart, stopping every ten feet or so to check on the bizarre gopher population explosion, and sighed.

"I'm going to dinner with Mitch tonight," she said. "I'll see if I can get some hypothetical advice or something."

Sierra made a sound that could be taken as agreement, then said, "Just be sure you ask him before you throw your next fit."

"What? Why would I throw a fit?"

"I thought temper tantrums were your new foreplay."

"Ha." Belle started to laugh as she hung up, then stopped. What if he was only interested in her when she was pissy? Did he only want her because she was a challenge now? Unlike before when she'd tried to serve herself up on a platter?

She told herself she was being silly. But still, her initial reaction was to pick a fight as soon as she saw him. That wasn't fair, though. She had to know. Which meant she'd be an absolute doll all night, flirt to her heart's content with nary a hint of anger or confrontation, and see how it went.

Hell, no, she wasn't going to take the easy way out. Belle gathered all the confidence she could and squared her shoulders. She'd have him begging for sex again and she'd do it with a smile on her face.

"REECE?" Mitch frowned as he crossed the lobby to greet the tall guy in the cowboy hat. "What're you doing here?"

Unselfconsciously, he gave Reece a quick man-hug, the arm-around-the-shoulder kind that he knew wouldn't embarrass his ex–Green Beret cousin.

"I thought I'd drop in, check the place out," Reece said in his slow drawl.

"Check up on your investment, you mean?" Mitch asked, referring to the fact that all the family members were stockholders on the MC board of directors.

"Nah, just wanted to see what kind of trouble your sorry ass has been getting up to." Reece made a show of looking around. Mitch followed his gaze, taking in the towering potted plants, the glossy marble-inlaid floor and ornate rosewood check-in desk. Reece gave a nod. "Long way from home, cuz."

"Ain't that the truth." Mitch pulled back his shoulders and grinned with pride. "You think the whole family will turn out for the grand opening blowout event?"

Reece pulled a face and gave a slow shrug. "Not so sure about that. I mean, if I read your reports right, you're shifting focus from a ritzy resort to a sexually charged amusement park for the rich and famous. Might be a little racy for Grammy Lynn, if ya know what I mean."

Mitch snickered. "Grammy Lynn sent me a list of suggestions to make sure we were offering enough sexy options."

"I shoulda known." Like everything else about him, Reece's grin was slow and easy. That smile deceived the enemy into thinking he was slow, women into thinking he was easy. They soon found out they were wrong. He was also loyal, tenacious and brilliant, but few people outside the family knew that, since Reece had a habit of keeping everyone at arm's length.

Mitch stood visiting with his cousin, feeling on top of the world. Family, success and hot sex. What more could a man want? The image of Belle as he'd last seen her, naked except for a very satisfied smile, flashed through his mind. Mitch shoved it right back out, figuring a hard-on while discussing the resort's sex themes might give the wrong message. Besides, he was still trying to sort through how he felt about last night. Awesome sex aside—and damned if it hadn't been the most awesome of his life—his mind was a mess. He ricocheted between sexual satisfaction, concern over being led around by his dick, and terror that it'd meant nothing to her. Hell, he felt like a teenage girl PMSing.

For the twentieth time since leaving Belle that morning, Mitch shoved the worries aside and forced himself to focus on the here and now.

So he asked about Reece's business. His cousin had opened a security firm after leaving the service. While he consulted and supervised security for MC Development, there was definitely not enough business in Mitch's little world to keep a man like Reece busy. Instead he kept his wits sharp working as a for-hire bodyguard, defense trainer and, as Mitch liked to rib him, all-round spy.

"Seriously," he asked when he'd been brought up to date on everything, "what're you doing out here? You didn't say anything about a visit when we talked the other day."

"I had some stuff to go over with you, wanted to take a look around. Maybe meet your planner and discuss the security list you sent on her behalf."

Well, shit. Mitch hummed. He'd known his family would have questions once they found out Belle was his new planner, but he'd figured he had plenty of time to come up with a reasonable explanation. And more important, plenty of time to get used to—and over—the wild sexual intensity that flamed between them before he was faced with the threat of it being extinguished by the past.

Maybe he could keep Reece and Belle apart? Tell her he'd meet her later, have Larry haul his cousin around for a tour?

Keeping his smile in place, Mitch felt his mind race with possibilities. Despite the mind games he was playing with himself, things were going too well right now. He wasn't ready to give this pleasure up. He'd dreamed of being with Belle for years, wanted her for what felt like forever. Bottom line, he wasn't letting reality—in any form—intrude on this time with her.

Not even his cousin.

BELLE WALKED out of the spa into the resort's lobby, a satisfied smile on her face and three pages of notes in her portfolio. Apparently, MC Development rented space to all the little boutiques in the resort. Which not only cut back on their overhead, but brought in a tidy little income as well.

With a purr of pleasure, she raised her hand to her nose and sniffed the rich, floral fragrance on her silky smooth skin. Smelled good, felt great. The owner, Kiki, was a savvy businesswoman with an eye for success.

Belle had a feeling they'd get along great, and she'd know for sure the next day when they had lunch together. That was enough time to run her idea past Sierra, work up an outline and make a quick phone call to Daddy.

And, she thought as she spied Mitch across the lobby, even more important, time for that couples' massage and chocolate bath she'd talked the spa owner into booking for them, despite the spa not being open yet.

With that in mind, she sauntered toward Mitch, her heels making a snappy sound as she crossed the marble floor. She focused on his jean-encased butt, so sweet and tempting, and wondered how long it'd be before she could bite it. Again.

For now, she settled on a pat when she reached him. "How'd you like to get naked and play in chocolate?" she asked, coming up behind him.

Mitch spun around, a look of appalled bewilderment on his face. Quick as lightning, he grabbed her hand off his ass and, with a gentle squeeze, shook it as if they were distant business acquaintances.

Hurt and confused, Belle tried to figure out what his problem was.

The sound of male laughter clued her in. She glanced around Mitch's shoulder and saw a lanky, Southern hunk seated on the white-leather couch and realized she'd embarrassed Mitch. At least she hoped that look had been embarrassment and not distaste for her suggestion.

Putting on her best society-princess smile, she stepped around Mitch and held out her hand in greeting. As the guy got to his feet, she gave a mental frown and tried to place him. He looked vaguely familiar.

"I'm Belle Forsham, and I'm afraid I've reached my limit of naughty offers for the day, but I hope we can be friends anyway?" she greeted in a light, joking tone.

"Reece Carter. It's a pleasure to meet you." It wasn't the touch of his large hand engulfing hers that clued Belle in. It was Mitch's supportive one grazing the small of her back. "Again."

A buzzing rang in Belle's ears, and her breath stuck somewhere in her chest. Carter. Mitch's cousin. The cousin, she remembered, that Mitch considered his best friend and had asked to be his best man. That's why he looked so familiar. He'd attended their kyboshed wedding and probably thought, with good reason, that she was a flaky bitch from hell.

Gathering what little nerve she had and taking strength from Mitch's warmth, she looked into Reece's midnight-blue eyes, but she saw no trace of judgment. Just an odd sort of waiting. The steady gaze made her stomach hurt. Maybe censure would have been better?

Mitch's cell phone rang and he excused himself, stepping away to take the call. She didn't know why, but Belle wanted to grab his belt loop and follow him to safety.

She offered Reece a hesitant smile. He didn't return it. Instead he gave her a long, intimidating stare that let her know without words that yes, he definitely remembered what she'd done and flaky bitch from hell was the nicest way he could think of her.

Belle wondered how fast she could run in these heels.

"I hear your naughty suggestions are going to be the highlight of this resort," Reece finally said.

Oh, fun, talking sex with a guy who completely hated her. She'd rather take her chances with her heels, but for Mitch's sake, she knew she couldn't.

Belle swallowed twice, trying to wet her tongue. She stretched her lips into a smile. "They'll make Lakeside the go-to playground of the rich and famous. I'm not sure how much Mitch has shared, but we have some great ideas that I know will lay a solid promotional foundation."

Realizing she was babbling, Belle stopped and pressed her lips together. She barely heard Mitch rejoin them and take over the description of their plans for the resort. She wanted, no needed, to leave. Now.

"Gentlemen, I'm so sorry, but I have to run," she interrupted.

Mitch frowned at her. "I thought we were having lunch." He looked at his watch, then gestured to his cousin. "Reece'll join us. We can go now if you're hungry."

She'd really been looking forward to eating with Mitch. Lunch and a little footsie, some flirting and maybe a quickie nooner for dessert.

"Um, I can't. I'm sorry, but I forgot I need to run by your office and talk to Diana about a few things. I need to use her fax to send off some contracts, too."

Belle knew she was a rotten liar and now apparently so did the men standing in front of her. Mitch gave her an angry look that slowly shifted to suspicion, staring at her as if she was an intriguing puzzle with a few vital pieces missing.

"We'll do dinner instead, then," he said after a few moments. He used his business voice. The one that let her know he was speaking as the guy signing her contract, not the guy who'd done her doggy-style before breakfast.

"I'll look forward to it," she lied before turning to make her way across the marble foyer toward the questionable refuge of Mitch's office. It had been a stupid lie, since the men could easily and justifiably follow her, but her brain had stalled. When she saw them head toward the restaurant, she heaved a sigh of relief.

Not willing to be proved the liar she was, she decided to go visit Diana anyway. Just CYA.

She scurried down the hallway and into Mitch's assistant's office. Except Diana wasn't there. Belle gave a huff of frustration and debated her options. She could just go to her cottage, but that meant losing her witness. She could wait for Diana, but, well, she really didn't like the gal enough to waste who knew how long twiddling her thumbs.

Or, she eyed the fax machine, she could send a fax as she'd said she would. That would turn her lie into a truth and make it all right. She grinned at her twisted justification and, flipping open her portfolio, grabbed the specs from the spa and penned a quick note to Sierra to outline her idea. She'd planned to e-mail them all, but hey, faxing meant she didn't have to type up all the specs since she didn't have a scanner.

She rolled her eyes at the continual justification.

"Hey, Belle."

She turned and saw Larry in the doorway and grinned. Perfect. "Hey, Larry, how's it going?"

"I'm glad I found you. I pitched an idea to Mitch about bringing in a live band each month and he said to get together with you to expand on it."

They chit-chatted as she set her stuff on the armoire housing the office equipment and slid her papers into the fax machine's paper feed. Punching in Eventfully Yours's number, she listened to the manager's ideas and considered tasteful ways to integrate the sex themes.

Before she could offer any feedback, Larry glanced at his watch and shrugged. "Lunch over, I've gotta run. I'll send you a memo about this, okay?"

She nodded and said goodbye as she gathered the faxed papers from the tray.

Well, that had worked out nicely. Despite being bummed at being cheated out of her lunchtime sexual romp, and very nervous over the arrival of Mitch's cousin, Belle was feeling pretty good as she sorted the specs to put back in her portfolio.

As she filed them, she noticed a crumpled ball of paper stuck under the fax tray. She tugged the wad out and, about to toss it in the trash, noticed the word *gopher.* Had Mitch found a way to get rid of the pests? She smoothed the page flat and glanced at it. A memo typed on Lakeside's stationery.

Then she read it from beginning to end.

Confused, she turned it over, looking for what she didn't know.

Was someone deliberately causing damage to Mitch's resort? She looked at the typed to-do list.

Damage sprinklers, reroute laundry, break bench slats. The list went on and on. Brow furrowed, a sick feeling in her stomach, she scanned the rest. And right there, gophers on the golf course.

She bit her lip and wondered briefly where the hell one imported gophers from, then shook her head. Did it matter? Someone was doing all of this deliberately. Messing with Mitch's property, trying to screw up or ruin the launch of the resort. She flipped to the second page and noticed a handwritten note. Her stomach sank as her vision wavered in shock.

Keep up the good work. This is exactly what Mitch asked for. Inflict as much damage as possible before the end of the month.

It was signed with the initials L.N.

"YOU DIDN'T mention your event planner was the little blonde who turned your world upside down a few years back."

"Belle?" Mitch grimaced and took a drink of his coffee to buy time. "I sent the specs on Eventfully Yours. I'm sure you read her qualifications."

"Glowing. And nary a mention that she'd once planned the event that left you doing a solo act at the altar." Typically, Reece's voice held no judgment. Just a musing sort of curiosity.

"She's the best planner on the west coast. Her company is perfect for what I want here, and she's already proved her worth by coming up with the theme idea that you yourself claimed was brilliant," Mitch defended. When Reece just stared, Mitch rolled his eyes and shrugged. "Let's face it, she was right to call it quits six years ago. Getting married was insane. I was the one in the wrong, marrying her to seal that deal with old man Forsham."

And to prove to everyone, including himself, that he was enough of a hotshot to score the boss's princess daughter. Mitch might admit that to himself, but he wasn't about to tell his cousin. Not that, nor the fact that he'd straight up used Belle's desire, their sexual attraction for each other to manipulate her into the engagement.

"You trust her?" was all Reece said.

Mitch shrugged. "In business, sure." In bed, too. "I'd think twice if it involved rings or ministers though."

Their waiter arrived with lunch and both men fell silent.

Hoping the topic was over, Mitch picked up his knife and fork and cut into his Baja grilled chicken. Reece lifted his Angus burger, but before taking a bite he gestured with it and claimed, "Your girl's nervous about something. Might be the past. Might be more. I'm going to do a little checking."

"Don't bother," Mitch said, his brow furrowing. "I trust Belle, okay?"

"Glad to hear it. Trust always makes the sex hotter, I'm sure." Reece's grin was quick, wicked and knowing. "But someone's deliberately screwing with you and this resort, cuz. And I find it mighty curious that you're having all these unexplained problems right about the same time your ex shows up. Can't hurt to poke around."

All Mitch heard was *deliberately*.

"You're sure it's sabotage?" he asked, all defensiveness over his past mistakes forgotten.

"Looks like."

"Check everyone." Fury flashed like a strobe light behind Mitch's eyes. *Deliberately.* He'd worked his ass off to get this far and someone was trying to ruin him. He clenched his fist, anger burning in his gut. He'd be damned if they'd get away with it. "I want whoever is behind this caught and strung up."

"And if it's the pretty blonde?"

Frowning, Mitch thought of Belle. Her smile, the laughter and fun she had teasing him. Mr. Winkles and the vulnerability she tried so hard to hide. The sexy way she walked across the room and the mewling sound she made when she came.

"It's not her," he declared, trying to shrug off the idea. "But before you tell me it's your job to check everyone thoroughly, I'm saying go ahead. Just don't be surprised to find out you're wrong."

Worry pounded at his temples until Mitch forced himself to think the situation through. Once he did, he was able to relax a little. After all, Belle might be a lot of things. A little flaky, impulsive and quick to react without thinking. Sexy, flirtatious and sweet, definitely. But the one thing he was positive about was that she wasn't a liar.

9

"YOU STILL haven't explained why we're here instead of your cottage." Mitch asked for the third time as he followed her down the short hall to one of the guest suites the next evening.

Belle glanced back at him, a thrill of excitement flashing at the sight of his version of evening casual. Jeans, a black button-up shirt and, her gaze dropped to his feet, dress shoes. He looked so good, even better now that she'd seen him naked. She sighed. The man was simply delicious.

And, she glanced at his face, so not the kind of guy who'd play some elaborate scam to screw over his own company. She'd asked him to trust her to make dinner arrangements, and had been gratified—and a little shocked—when he'd readily agreed. She figured this was the perfect time to do some subtle questioning, just to assure herself he was as innocent as she thought.

It had to be her own doubts that had her imagining the suspicion in his voice. Belle tried to shrug off the weird feeling, telling herself it was paranoia brought on by Reece's surprise arrival and the papers she'd found in Diana's office.

"It's a surprise," she told him again. With a deep breath, she reached into her purse to pull out the room card. Her tummy spun with nerves and she missed twice before she could get the flimsy card into the lock. She'd never been this nervous to present an event or theme to a client before.

Of course, she'd never planned to get the client naked before, either. She didn't know if it was that, or nerves over playing Mata Hari on a quest for secrets that made her feel so intimidated.

It definitely wasn't because they'd had the most intensely wild, passionate sex of her life or that it left her feeling emotionally naked and vulnerable. Worrying about that would be ridiculous, especially since she couldn't do anything about the vulnerability unless she was willing to stop having the incredible sex. And that was out of the question.

She told herself for at least the hundredth time since yesterday to quit obsessing. And while she was at it, just to put Reece-the-intimidating out of her mind and forget about the note and the suggestion that Mitch had asked for damage to be done to Lakeside. It just didn't make sense for him to ruin his own resort.

Belle shook her head as if she could knock the thoughts out of it. With a deep breath, she focused instead on the previous night, the great sex, and the hot lovin' she had planned for tonight. Whew, much better.

With a deep breath and a little wiggle of anticipation for what she hoped was about to come—namely her—Belle pushed open the heavy door.

"We're doing dinner here tonight," she said as she entered the dimly lit room. Hurrying before Mitch could get a good look around, she grabbed the lighter and lit the bank of candles on the dresser. "I thought we'd have a preview of what your guests can expect when they stay."

"Really?" Excitement, curiosity and a hint of naughty pleasure were all packed into that one word.

His tone instantly settled her nerves. Belle pasted on a seductive smile and turned to face Mitch. Leaning one hip on the dresser, she gestured to the room.

"What you see before you is a typical, luxurious resort suite. Comfortable seating, antique furnishings, good art. Quality all the way, which your guests will expect." She tilted her head toward the table in the corner, set up to her specifications. "A delicious private dinner for two, wine and a decadent and one-of-a-kind dessert. Yummy by any standard, but we're hinting at something more. Something, dare I say it, sexy?"

Mitch's lips twitched but he kept his expression intrigued instead of amused. "Sexy?"

"Just a hint," she demurred, stepping to the table and curving her fingers around the handles of the domed silver covers she'd instructed the kitchen to find. She wanted that movie-star ambiance. Lifting the covers, she set them aside and gestured again, this time toward the loveseat next to the table.

Oysters, asparagus, lobster and a spice-encrusted steak. This time Mitch didn't bother to hide his grin. Instead he stepped forward, and after a quick glance at the table pulled her into his arms for a kiss that put the ninety-dollar-a-plate meal behind them to shame.

Belle gave herself over to the kiss, needing it in a way she couldn't even explain to herself. Maybe because it was the first one since he'd left her curled up naked in her sheets, or maybe it was just the nerves, but as soon as his lips touched hers, her entire body relaxed in one huge sigh of relief. She was silly to suspect him.

A kiss and a grope later, Belle peeled her fingers off his ass and they settled on the plushly cushioned loveseat for their meal.

"This is fabulous," he said after a few bites of his steak. "Not just the private dinner, but the whole setup. The candlelight and roses, the view—" he gestured to the open balcony window and the moonlit copse of trees "—it all adds to the romantic ambiance."

Pleased, Belle glanced around the room. That worked perfectly with her theme. Romance went hand in hand with sexual fantasies.

But the theme would be pointless if whoever made that list hit their goal and Lakeside went belly-up before the end of the year. Belle squared her shoulders, remembering her private mission for the evening. Dig.

"So, how's it all coming for the resort's opening?" she asked as they ate. "It's just a week until the first party, three weeks until the doors open to the public. Is everything ready to go on your end?"

A tiny frown came and went, but Mitch just shrugged and nodded. "It's coming along. Things will move a little smoother now that Reece is here."

Was that because Reece was Mr. Security? Did Mitch know who was behind the problems and had brought his cousin out to catch them? Or was Reece here to stop any further incidents? For about the hundredth time, Belle considered showing Mitch the list. But, as always, she recalled the comment about the damage being something he'd requested and held back.

"You've run security checks on all the resort employees, haven't you? Including management?" That memo had definitely been sent by someone who wouldn't be questioned hanging out in Diana's office.

"Sure, a check is standard and we sent around those confidentiality agreements you wanted, too." The look he gave her, curious and just a little suspicious, let her know it was time to change the subject.

"Wait till you see dessert," Belle said, shifting so her thigh slid along his. The move pulled the hem of her dress higher, leaving bare thigh pressed to the rough fabric of his jeans. "Since I thought it'd be better to postpone the chocolate spa treatment until, um, later," like, after Reece had left, "I came up with a fun after-dinner treat that has a similar effect."

Tearing his eyes from her silky thigh and its hint of the

naked delight barely hidden by her dress, Mitch looked at her and frowned. "Chocolate spa treatment? What's that?"

"I met with your spa owner to discuss some ideas I had." Like finding out if Kiki, who was looking to launch two more spas, might want to consider renting space in a Forsham Hotel. But that wasn't her point. "She and I came up with a dozen or so sexy themed services she'll offer and I booked us to try the couples' chocolate spa treatment."

Belle had also noted that none of the "accidents" had affected the spa or any of the other privately owned businesses. Only Mitch's direct holdings.

"Sounds…intriguing," he said with a grin. Setting his fork down, Mitch rested his hand on her knee. His warm fingers sent a tingle of excitement up her bare thigh all the way to the heated core between her legs. She wanted to shift, to encourage him to slide his hand higher and discover for himself that she was commando under her slinky black dress. But she was on a mission. Besides, part of the fun was anticipation, so she forced herself to be still.

"Why'd you cancel the appointment?" he asked.

"I…" She'd been so distracted by Reece's appearance, and then her discovery that someone was deliberately trying to tank the resort, she'd forgotten to confirm a time. Belle tried to come up with a decent excuse, but his fingers were making a slow, hot trip north and she couldn't think straight. "Um, you have family here."

Mitch's jaw dropped. Belle frowned. She didn't so much mind shocking him, but she did mind that his fingers stopped their delicious journey.

"What?" she asked when he started laughing, not sure why she felt so self-conscious all of a sudden. It wasn't as though she'd confessed that she'd spent months practicing her signature as Mrs. Belle Carter.

"I'm just surprised," he admitted. "I mean, I would have sworn you didn't have a shy bone in your body."

"I don't," Belle snapped, offended.

"And yet now that we're not having anonymous, hotel-employees-are-totally-discreet sex, you're taking it into hiding?"

"Did you want to ask your cousin to come watch?" Belle shot back without thinking. "Or maybe videotape us doing it in the shower to show at the next family reunion?"

"Most of the family will be here for the pre-event next week," Mitch mused. "We can show it then. Really kick off this sex theme with a big bang."

She stared in slack-jawed shock, irritated embarrassment forgotten.

"You'd actually show your family sex tapes?" She couldn't even read romance novels in the presence of her father, he was so uptight about the topic.

"Nah, I was teasing. They don't want to see my naked butt move to some porn soundtrack." Mitch grinned and gave a rueful shake of his head. "But they are amazing, especially my grandma. She pretty much raised all my cousins and me."

"And your sister?" Remembering Mitch's snotty sister from their abandoned wedding, Belle hid her grimace in a fake smile. She'd spent months regretting not letting Sierra kick her rude ass.

"Sister?" He frowned, then his face cleared and he shook his head again. "Lena? We lived in the same house for a year or so when my mom first married her dad, but then she left for college. After our parents died, we grew apart. We reconnected right before I went to work for your dad. I'd decided to merge her late father John's construction company with MC Development and I needed her signature."

Belle remembered the bland woman's taunts as if it were yesterday. Of course, she'd replayed her "runaway" reel in her head a million times, so that actually felt like yesterday, too. Lena had been so cocky about her knowledge of Mitch's character.

"Most of my family is on the board of MC Development, except her. I offered her a chair, but she had other things going on. Other than Lena, who never really hung out much, the family is really tight. When I was growing up, my grandma was the family babysitter. Even after she remarried, my mom was a working woman. All my aunts were, too."

The love he had for his family was clear in his voice. Belle felt a twinge of jealousy. Sure, she loved her dad, but they weren't tight like Mitch's family seemed to be. Would she have been welcomed in if they'd gotten married? The thought of what she might have had made her want to cry, so she gestured to Mitch to keep talking.

"The family all lived within four blocks of each other so instead of after-school care, my cousins and I went to Gram's house." Mitch went on to describe his childhood and random details about what various cousins and family members were doing now. From the sound of it, each and every one would be arriving at the resort the following week.

Belle felt like throwing up her perfectly delicious lobster. All of them. Here. Knowing exactly what she'd done to Mitch, how she'd run away on their wedding day. Wouldn't parading naked down Rodeo Drive be easier?

"So that's why you cancelled the chocolate and sex massage?" Mitch asked as he finished the last of his dinner. "Because you didn't want my cousin to know we're practicing what you preach?"

Embarrassed heat washed over Belle from the top of her forehead to the edge of her bra. She hated when she blushed. The color totally clashed with her hair.

Trying to save face, she just shrugged and pointed out, "This is what your clientele would be dealing with, you know? They want to have wild, uncensored sex and the oddest things cause inhibition. You might want to talk to your cousin about making sure the resort's security is solid. That'll be crucial if you want to pull this off."

Mitch's arched brow told her he hadn't missed her blatant avoidance of an answer, but he let it pass. "I've set up a meeting between you and Reece for tomorrow," he said.

Belle licked her lips. Meet with Reece? Alone? Um, no. Even though he'd been perfectly cordial through dinner the previous evening, she hadn't forgotten that threatening look he'd given her when they'd first met. He obviously had it in for her, and while he might be willing to play nice in front of his cousin, she had no doubt the gloves would come off in private.

"Can we make it the day after?" she asked, buying time as she stood and made her way over to the second room in the suite. Time for dessert. Or at least a change of topic.

Mitch just shrugged in answer. His attention, she realized, was on the bedroom. The bedroom containing her pièce de résistance, the culmination of her sex-themed evening. Her nerves returned. Fingers laced together, she tried to keep herself from bouncing in her high heels as she waited for his reaction.

MITCH FELT like he'd died and gone to heaven. A delicious dinner, Belle, and from the look of the bedroom and glimpse of the bath he could see from the doorway, a very hot night yet to come.

Like the romantic dinner, the dimly lit bedroom screamed romance. A midnight-red trail of rose petals lay strewn over the floor and across the cool, white expanse of the turned-down bed. Every surface held candles waiting to be lit. He squinted, trying to see the array of items displayed on the silver tray on the nightstand. The thick, knobby curve on one of the things worried him a little. Belle had talked about sex toys for the guests, but he wasn't sure he was ready to play hide the dildo with her. The light glanced off something metal—handcuffs, he realized. He'd just have to cuff her to the bed before she hauled out the Rabbit vibrator.

He glanced at Belle, who was trying to read his reaction. The moonlight shone through the window, casting a glow of pearls over her skin and blond hair, tousled and sexy for their date. But the luminescent beauty that tugged at his heart was all hers.

She nibbled her sweet lower lip between her teeth, brows raised in question. Mitch could see the nerves in her sea-green eyes, that underlying worry he'd been so surprised to find in such a confident woman. He supposed that was why she was so good at what she did. She cared, really cared about her clients loving her work.

Not that he saw this as being about business, of course. What was between them was all personal. No matter how she tried to wrap it up as justifying her contract. Or how much Reece tried to argue that Belle was only after some weird revenge by sabotaging his resort.

"I take it this is phase two of our evening?" he asked.

"The dessert phase," she responded seriously.

Mitch glanced around again, but didn't see anything resembling food. "I take it we're each other's treat?"

Which suited him perfectly. Feasting on the sweetness of Belle's body was an ideal ending to a delicious dinner.

Her eyes danced in delight as she giggled, but Belle shook her head. "No, no. I wouldn't cheat you out of a yummy ending to such a special dinner. Dessert is waiting."

Mitch followed her gesture toward the bathroom, then glanced back at her in question. Hardly his idea of the ideal eating place.

"I need a couple of minutes to get everything ready," she said, sounding a little breathless. He hoped it was anticipation and not amusement. "While I'm preparing the surprise, why don't you think about preparing yourself for a little fun?"

He looked over at the dildo, even bigger now that he could see it clearly, and arched his brow. She followed his gaze and laughed aloud. "No, no, that's just a sampling for the guests. You don't want to judge what they might indulge in. You just want to give them plenty to choose from."

"And your choice is?"

"You," she said, the laughter fading as she stepped close and pressed her hands against his chest. He automatically reached up to curve his fingers over her breasts so lovingly encased in filmy black fabric. Her nipples perked under his palms, her breath hitched just a little as she stepped up on tiptoe to meet his lips.

Mitch tasted the rich lobster, butter and the sweetness that was all Belle as he sank into the kiss. Tongues danced a slow, wicked waltz, making him painfully aware that the bed was waiting just a few feet away.

Needing more, he curved one hand behind her neck and felt the hooks that held her halter dress together. With a flick of his fingers, the fabric loosened and skimmed down her body.

"We'll call this a taste of what's to come," she purred with a satisfied look on her face. Belle stepped away, wearing nothing but a strappy pair of black sandals and gorgeous smile. "While I get the next course ready, why don't you undress? I hate to be the only naked body enjoying the treat."

Screw the treat. Mitch wanted her. Now. He reached out to grab her but Belle danced away, surprisingly nimble in such high spiked heels.

"No, not yet. Go undress." She gave a little wave of her fingers toward the other side of the room. "I want to do this for you, okay? For you, with you. You'll love it."

With that and the mouthwatering view of her naked ass as she scurried from the room, she was gone.

Mitch sighed and, after a quick recitation of the first twenty

U.S. presidents, managed to return the blood from his throbbing dick back to his brain.

Deciding she was right and naked would get him inside her hot, wet body sooner, he stripped. From the bathroom and dressing area he heard the rush of water in the tub, the clinking of glass and, at one excruciating point, her moan of delight.

"She'd better not be starting without me," he muttered as he left his jeans in a pile with the rest of his clothes.

Naked and rock-hard, Mitch strode across the room. When he reached the suite's dressing area, he noticed the carved, tufted rosewood dressing bench had been covered in thick towels. Next to it was a small glass table, a bowl and two spoons. The bowl was filled with what looked like ice cream and some kind of topping, making Mitch's mouth water as he thought about eating the treat off Belle's naked belly.

Steam poured from the open bathroom door, the scent of peaches and heat filling the room. Like a dream, Belle stepped out of the steam naked. Droplets of water dotted her bare flesh, one trailing a wet caress to the tip of her right breast.

Mesmerized, Mitch walked across the room, not breathing until he reached her. He bent down and sipped at her wet nipple, making her mewl like a kitten begging to be petted.

His hands moved easily over her damp skin, up and down the planes of her back twice before he pressed his fingers into the curve at the base of her spine to bring her tight against his body. His sips now turned to nibbles. One hand slid around her waist and down between their bodies to cup her damp and, he realized in shock, very bare sex.

Mitch pulled back from his feast to see the discovery his fingers had made.

"Well, well," he said with a grin.

Belle giggled, then arched one brow in a vampy look. "A smooth surface was better for what I have in mind."

"Later," he dismissed, wanting to run his fingers and tongue over that silky expanse of bare flesh.

"Uh-uh," she corrected, stepping back. "Keep your hand on your bird and not in my bush."

"A bird in the hand is worth two in a bush," he corrected absently, shooting her a grin. "Besides, you're bushless now."

Belle's giggle made Mitch feel like a million bucks. The simple fact that here she was, the princess of his dreams, naked, laughing and totally focused on him— Well, it blew his mind. Mitch recalled how excited he'd been to buy the resort, to see what he'd thought of as his dream actually come true.

But he looked at the woman staring up at him; amusement and happiness clear on her face, and realized this was his real dream come true.

"Come see why naked is better." Oblivious to the shocked realization that'd just kicked Mitch in the face, Belle grabbed his hand and pulled him back to the dressing area, where she'd set up the towel-covered settee and dessert.

Telling himself he'd overreacted and to focus on the naked woman and incredible sex in store for him, Mitch shoved aside the emotional bomb and watched Belle. His mouth watered both at the richly sweet scent filling the air and the sight of her naked ass as she swayed across the room, still wearing those sexy do-me heels.

Wiggling her brows at Mitch and giving him a look that was a combination of flirtation and amusement, Belle sat in demure nudity on the cushioned bench. She lifted a crystal bowl filled with ice cream, peaches and what looked like a caramel sauce.

"Freshly made vanilla-bean ice cream, brandied peaches and caramel," she told him as she held out the bowl for him to see. Then she puffed out her lip in an exaggerated pout and gave a tiny shrug. "But it's so rude to eat out of the serving bowl, isn't it? So you'll be my dessert plate and I'll eat off you, hmm?"

His cock jumped at the image of her eating dessert off his body and it was all Mitch could do not to grab the bowl and pour the sweet confection over himself.

"What about my dessert?" he asked, the gentlemanly part of him struggling to overcome the powerful urging of his dick.

"You'll get to eat all you want later," she promised. When he started to protest, she made a tut-tutting noise and shook her head. "Ladies first, remember."

He told himself it was manners that stifled his protest, but they both knew it was the fact that she took his hands and pulled him forward so his dick was level with her breasts.

Visions and ideas flashed through his head, each one more erotic than the last. But before he could act on any, Belle shook her head again and dropped to her knees so he was now level with her mouth. She lifted the bowl and with a wink she blew him a kiss and poured.

Mitch groaned at the sensation of cold ice cream and warm caramel sauce sliding over his straining head. Then Belle added her hot mouth to the mix. His hips bucked, and unable to help himself, Mitch tunneled his fingers through her hair and held on as she blew him and his control all to hell.

His orgasm hit hard, fast and intense, and Mitch growled with pleasure when Belle didn't stop sucking, licking or nibbling away at her dessert. Everything went black, his knees almost buckling as he gave over to the pleasure pumping out of his body.

It took him a solid minute to regain his senses. When he came back to earth, he realized Belle had stopped sucking and had laid her head against his belly and was giving him a hug, her arms wrapped around his thighs.

He smoothed a caress down the back of her tousled hair, causing Belle to pull back and grin up at him.

"Now that was a tasty dessert," she purred. "Shall we follow it up with a relaxing bath and wash off the stray peaches?"

"What about mine?" he asked, wanting nothing more than to taste her juices mixed with hot caramel.

"Help yourself," Belle said with a wink.

Mitch noted a peach stuck to her shoulder and grinned. He scooped it up with one finger and popped it into his mouth, then proceeded to enjoy the clean, smooth pleasure of peaches, Brazilian style.

Ten minutes later Mitch sighed with pleasure as he held her back against his chest and sipped champagne in the huge spa tub.

"So what do you think of this particular theme?" she asked, her face still flushed from her climax.

"It's perfect. Traditional yet just kinky enough to appeal to the average guest," he assured her. "Like everything else you've come up with, it's perfect."

"Wait till you see the setup for the kinkier guests. You know the ones—seen it all, done it all." He felt her laugh as her shoulders shifted against his chest. "The leather goods, floor-to-ceiling poles and edgier sex toys arrived this afternoon."

"I can't wait to try them out," he assured her before taking a drink. The explosion of bubbles, alcohol and peaches filled his taste buds and Mitch sighed. Damn, life was good.

"Hmm, I think that means I deserve a reward," she mused. Wicked humor lit her green eyes, but before she could take charge of their lovemaking again, Mitch set down the champagne flute and grabbed her hips.

A quick move and he had her pressed against the opposite side of the tub, her breasts just above water level and her butt up in the air.

His fingers went to work on her nipples as Mitch sucked and licked the trail of water up her spine until he reached the back of her neck.

His body holding her in place, he slipped into the glorious

wet pleasure of her body from behind. Belle's moan was breathy, lost in her soft pants of delight.

The steamy heat, the slickness of the water added another level of decadence to their lovemaking. Mitch took his time, building her pleasure with long, even strokes countered by tiny flicks of his fingers over her wet, turgid nipples.

When Belle couldn't handle it anymore, her pants becoming whimpers and her body pressing tighter against him, he pulled out, turned her in one swift move and pulled her right back down on his throbbing dick. The move, so hard and fast, sent him over the edge and his explosion of pleasure brought her right along. His mouth took hers as they came together. Belle's gasping cry of his name added an emotional edge to his orgasm.

He scooped her slippery slick body out of the frothy bubbles and, still kissing her, carried Belle into the other room. Uncaring that they soaked the sheets, he dropped to the bed, pulling her with him. He couldn't release his hold on her, not even to grab a towel, to pull up the blankets. He didn't want to let go of Belle.

Ever.

His last thought before sleep wound its way through his sexual haze was that he couldn't wait to introduce Belle to his grandma. Six years ago, he'd used the excuse of their rushed wedding as his reason for not bringing her into his family circle. The truth was, he'd been afraid of losing her.

This time, he knew it'd work out.

This time was forever.

10

"KNOCK IT OFF, Reece," Mitch snapped the next afternoon. His glare should have slain the man in his tracks, but his damned cousin was made of tougher stuff. "I don't want to hear this crap. It's bullshit, you're wasting my time."

"Cuz, I know you don't want to hear bad about your ladyfriend, but you have to face facts. Someone is screwing you over and everything is pointing in her direction."

"Belle isn't behind the sabotage. It was happening long before she signed on. There's no reason to suspect her." He slammed his fist on his desk. Mitch's vision blurred as fury filled his brain. "What's your problem with her, Reece? Are you holding on to a grudge on my behalf? Do you hate blondes? Is Belle just too much for you? What exactly is the problem here?"

The fury did a slow burn as his cousin just sat there calmly, staring in silence. The contrast of his own anger and Reece's composure only added fuel to Mitch's frustration.

Then, stretching his jaw to either side, Reece pulled off his cowboy hat and contemplated the curve of the brim before setting it back on his head. Preparing for battle. Mitch recognized the move and steeled himself to win. Because there was no way in hell he was backing down.

"Look, I know you're into the gal and I'm not saying I have a personal issue with her." At Mitch's glare, Reece shrugged and admitted, "Well, other than the whole screwing-you-over-and-leaving-you-standing-there-with-your-dick-in-your-hand thing, I don't have a personal issue with her."

Mitch thought about defending his dick-holding practices as his business, but realized it'd be a waste of time. Family defended family, end of story.

"But you have to be realistic. Your resort is seeing problems and this gal has a history of problems. She also knows the hotel business inside out. She's the daughter of a guy who thinks you screwed him royally. And, well, bottom line, she's female."

Mitch squinted. "Care to justify that last one?"

"She's a woman. Women do the strangest things. Who knows, she might have spent the last half-dozen years stewing over whatever it was that pissed her off enough to leave you at the altar and is just now implementing her revenge."

The flames of his fury were doused as if they'd been hit by a deluge of water. Mitch just shook his head in pity. "You still reeling from your divorce, cuz?"

"Nah, I'm over the hangover now." Reece shot him a grin that Mitch had seen turn women from disinterested divas into panting groupies. Mitch was probably the only person who knew that grin was hiding a pained heart. Not broken, but bruised. Even Reece would be surprised at the news.

"Shawna aside, since she was in a class by herself, I just don't get what goes through their pretty little heads sometimes," Reece continued with a shrug.

Mitch didn't comment. There wasn't much to say since he'd never cared two damns about what went on in a woman's head until Belle had showed up—this time, he forced himself to acknowledge. Their first round, his only interest had been in proving himself, in snagging the biggest prize in the game.

"You said you wanted me to investigate." Reece's grin fell away as he leaned forward to rest his elbows on his knees. The look he speared Mitch with was all business. "That means man up and listen to the results of that investigation, regardless of what your dick wants to hear."

Mitch set his jaw and with a jerk of his head indicated his cousin offer up those results.

Reece stared for another few seconds, then lifted a file folder from the seat next to him. He held it up for Mitch to see, then without opening it tossed it on the desk.

"You've had a series of e-mails coming out of the resort. Not unusual," he said before Mitch could scoff, "except that each one is going to the same IP address and each one is deleted from your server. A few a week, sometimes more, never less."

Mitch frowned and laid his palm on the file.

"Interviewing the staff and repair crew involved in each incidence, I think it's clear the problems the resort's faced in the last month have all been deliberate. The lost linens, the destruction of property, even the gophers."

Mitch pulled his head back in shock. How the hell did someone come up with that many gophers?

"The gophers, by the way," Reece continued, pointing a finger at the file folder under Mitch's hand, "were actually shipped direct to the resort. Ballsy move, that."

Mitch pulled the folder toward him but didn't open it.

"From what I've gathered, the person behind it is a woman."

Mitch glared, but waited for the justification he knew was coming.

"I say that because all of the destruction was smallish, things easily broken by someone of a slight stature." He went on to list the items to support his supposition. While he listened, Mitch flipped open the file folder and scanned the reports of property damage. With each one, his anger and frustration mounted.

"You really think all that is definitive evidence it's a woman behind the problems?" Mitch asked, his tone dismissive. He had small guys on the crew and in his management team. He was sure it could have been any of them.

"Nah, that's all circumstantial." Reece leaned out of his chair and across the desk to flip the pages in Mitch's hand to a manifest. "That the gophers were delivered to and signed for by a woman is definitive."

Mitch stared at the loopy and decidedly feminine scrawl on the delivery manifest. Two dozen gophers, signed for by Janie Doe. He hated that his brain was scrambling to remember Belle's signature. He glanced at the date on the invoice. The same as the date of her first visit to talk him into hiring her. Mitch felt sick, but told himself it wasn't her. His gut knew it wasn't, but there weren't many women at the resort yet, especially not ones with enough authority to commandeer a direct delivery without being questioned.

"This doesn't point to Belle," he stated unequivocally, tossing the folder down. The pages fanned over his desk but he and Reece both ignored them.

"Her old man is in trouble—financially sinking and the cause is pretty much your fault," Reece said, his voice quiet with resignation. Mitch knew his cousin figured he'd just delivered the death knell to Mitch's relationship and felt rotten about it. "That deal the two of you cooked up, then you bailed on when your princess ran off has him tied up financially, and with real estate tanking, he's screwed with no way out."

"That sucks." And it did. Hugely. Mitch hadn't heard a whisper about it, but he wasn't surprised. Franklin Forsham was good at keeping things hush-hush. Regret washed over Mitch in a heavy wave. He'd been an asshole to leave Franklin in a lurch like that. Sure, he'd been humiliated and feeling justified in slapping out at anyone named Forsham, but the bottom line was it'd been bad business. He considered the current real estate climate, the tightened zoning laws in California and the probable debt Franklin had incurred holding the property all this time and winced.

"That totally sucks," he repeated. "But how does that make Belle the culprit in Lakeside's sabotage? In the first place, the problems started before she got here. Second and more significantly, she's under contract with me. The success of her business hinges on the success of my resort."

"Maybe. Or maybe she's more interested in her daddy's business right now." Reece grimaced, then pulled some more papers from that damned file. "I was chatting with Kiki, the gal who runs the spa here." In other words, flirting and looking for a good time. "Turns out Belle made her a very interesting proposition."

Mitch's mouth watered as he remembered the Brazilian treat he'd enjoyed the night before. "So?" he asked.

"It seems she's trying to lure Kiki away from your resort." Mitch's smile dropped away as Reece continued. "She's offering her gigs at her daddy's hotels. Same deal you have, but a few extra perks."

"That doesn't put her behind my resort issues."

"True," Reece agreed. Then he handed Mitch the papers he'd been holding. "Copies of the e-mails sent through the resort server from Belle to her partner."

Mitch started to point out how wrong it was to invade her e-mails when the words caught his eye.

The plan is in motion. Daddy will be thrilled.
Check timing of all of this. Can't let the cat out of the closet or Mitch will know.

Cat out of the closet. It was totally Belle-esque. His stomach fisted at the idea of her screwing him over with such calculation.

She'd walked out on him once without giving him the benefit of the doubt, not caring that she left him looking like an idiot. She was clever enough and resourceful enough to pull off revenge at this level and confident enough not to bat one long, mink eyelash.

But despite all the proof Reece was pitching, regardless of how many papers he stuffed in that file pointing the finger at Belle, Mitch wasn't going for it.

With a smile at odds with the subject, he settled back in his chair and finally identified the feeling he'd been struggling with since he'd walked into this office and seen his past waiting for him. He was in love with Belle. He had been six years ago, although he'd called it ambition. He was now, although he'd been trying to tell himself it was lust.

Love. Mitch shifted his gaze out the window to stare at the expanse of trees and gopher-infested lawn. Who knew it would feel so confusing?

But confusing or not, he loved her. Which meant, bottom line, he trusted her.

She might only be in this for the sex. She might still run away at any time, Mitch realized as his heart sank a little. He swallowed the bitter taste of fear at the possibility and told himself he'd deal with it later. The truth was, he wasn't blind to Belle's issues. But he knew screwing him at the same time she was screwing him over wasn't one of them.

"You're meeting with Belle tomorrow to talk security for the grand opening," he told Reece. "If you need to ask questions to make you feel like you're doing your job, go ahead. She's clean. But keep digging because the real culprit needs to be stopped before they do any more damage to my resort."

"You're gone, cuz." Reece shook his head in a pitying, you're-so-stupid kind of way.

"Totally gone," Mitch acknowledged, shoving aside the doubts. "And I'm loving every minute of it."

"I'VE GOT IT, the answer to our problem," Belle claimed in her daily phone call to Sierra. She tucked the cell between her chin and shoulder as she sliced a peach. They were now officially her favorite fruit.

"A blow-up doll with remote-control hands?" Sierra shot back.

Belle rolled her eyes at the phone. "Hardly. If we're using remote control I plan on operating something much more interesting than hands."

"Right. So what's our problem and then what's the answer?"

Sierra was usually so on top of things, but she'd been distracted during their last few phone calls, forgetting to send papers and contracts, just sort of disconnected from everything as far as Belle could tell.

Taking her snack to the table, Belle frowned in frustration. Questions were pointless. Sierra answered them all with annoying assurances that everything was just fine.

"Kiki's in," Belle explained. "She's really excited to take her spa to the next level and sees aligning with Forsham Hotels as the way to do it. Besides all the info I already sent you, I just found out she's courting a contract with one of the big-name beauty suppliers for an exclusive label."

"Do you think that's enough to help your dad?"

"I hope so. She'll pay top dollar for the square footage, but she'll also bring in a huge clientele. Between the label and her own promotion, they're going to skyrocket." Belle considered. "I have to convince Daddy, but if it works, he'll be able to switch all his on-site boutiques and stores. Rather than entities he runs and assumes the business expenses for, he can let his tenant take on the employee, inventory and liability risks. He'll cut his own expenses by at least an eighth."

Belle nibbled on her peach as they went on to brainstorm a few more ideas and kick around ways to pitch the proposal to her father. Finally deciding Belle would do it over Sunday brunch the next weekend, they wound up the topic.

"What about Lakeside?" Sierra asked. "Have you talked to Mitch about borrowing Kiki?"

"No," she said slowly. "I just didn't think it was a good idea until we'd worked out all the particulars."

"In other words, you don't want to rock the nookie boat until you're sure your dad's on board."

Belle was glad her shamed flush couldn't be seen over the phone.

"Kiki doesn't have an exclusivity contract," she defended.

"Doesn't mean Mitch expects her to be stolen away by his bed buddy."

"She's not being stolen. After she set things up here, she planned on leaving a manager in charge anyway. Besides," Belle justified, "it's good insurance for her. If someone really is playing some game here and the resort is going to suffer, she needs a safety net."

"Speaking of which, what'd you find out?" Sierra asked.

Glad to change the subject, Belle thought of the list she'd copied from Diana's office the day before. Someone was deliberately trying to ruin the resort. Was it Mitch? Despite the note and e-mail address, she couldn't believe it.

"It's not Mitch," she declared. "Why would he ruin his own venture? There just isn't anything in it for him. His board of directors is made up entirely of family. It's a family-held corporation, even."

"So?"

"So, nothing means more to him than family. This guy has a total *Brady Bunch* mindset."

"Are you sure you're not just trying to rationalize the fact that you're not done playing in his pants?" Sierra asked.

Pulling a face, Belle dropped to the couch and huffed out a

breath. "Do you really think sex is that important that I'd risk everything for it?"

"You did before."

Belle frowned. It wasn't sex, she wanted to say. It was Mitch. Just Mitch. Sex with him was her only excuse to intimacy, she realized. And didn't that make her a pitiful lovestruck idiot?

"Look, I need your input then. How'd you like to see the resort firsthand?" she asked after tucking her notes into her portfolio. "Come out, get a feel for the place, see Mitch in person and give me your opinion on what's what."

"You want me to come out there? Why? What'd you do?"

Belle rolled her eyes and made a huffing sound of irritation. "I didn't do anything. At least, nothing I need you to come fix. You have doubts about Mitch, I want your feedback. And I thought you'd enjoy getting the lay of the land, so to speak, before we kick into high gear next week preparing for the first event."

"Well, I'm grateful you don't want me to come fix your sex life," Sierra said with a laugh. "And you've already got a solid lay, so to speak, so I doubt you need me there."

"An upside-down head needs twice the help," Belle pointed out.

"Two heads are better than one," Sierra corrected with a sigh.

That she was desperate for Sierra to pinch hit for her in the security meeting wasn't going to fly as a reason, even if it was pure truth. She was totally freaked to face Reece alone. Even worse, she was terrified he'd ruin what she'd found with Mitch.

But she wasn't telling Sierra that.

"I'd love to have your take on who's tanking the resort, and maybe while you're here you can see if there's anything I could add for the first party, the one for Mitch's family and board, next week," Belle claimed instead. "I'm just a little nervous about pulling this off given that someone is trying to screw things up. It'd help to have a second set of eyes."

It was a flimsy ploy and she knew it. Belle orchestrated events for thousands on her own and never needed hand-holding. She cringed, waiting for her partner to call her on it and trying to figure out how to get out of dealing with Reece. Pretend to be sick? Really get sick? Family emergency and run home? She had to do something, anything. She so did not want to deal with the hot cowboy. Not when she knew he was just waiting to get her alone and confront her about the past.

"Okay, I can be there tomorrow morning," Sierra agreed after a long silence.

Belle kept her squeal of triumph to herself. "You can?"

"Sure. You want my help, I'll come give it. Why the shock? We're partners. That's what we do, help each other and tell each other crap."

Interesting theory, since Belle knew damned well Sierra was keeping *crap* from her. But confronting her friend was pointless, so Belle kept that a silent observation.

"Great." Never one to ruin a miracle by asking too many questions, Belle rushed on, "Since you'll be here anyway, you can take the meeting with the head of security and go over all the details, okay?"

"I should have known there was a catch." Sierra laughed. "Fine, I'll take the meeting."

Noting a movement out of the corner of her eye, Belle glanced out the window at the golf course. Mitch and Reece strode across the green expanse. Although both wore jeans and work shirts, the two men couldn't look more different. Yet they seemed to be solid friends in addition to having that family con-nection that was so important to Mitch.

Family. Since it was just her and her dad, Belle didn't quite get the whole clan feeling Mitch seemed to embrace. But she definitely knew how important it was to take care of her loved ones. Worrying over her father was proof of that.

Belle gave herself a second to appreciate Mitch's gorgeous ass, encased lovingly in denim, before she glanced at his leggy cowboy cousin. A sneaky plan formed in her head.

Six years ago she'd thought Sierra and Reece looked great together. Both tall, dark and gorgeous, they'd been striking at the pre-wedding festivities. If Reece had Sierra to distract him, it would keep him off Belle's back while she tried to figure out who was behind the dirty deeds at Mitch's resort.

It had nothing to do with the fact that Belle was so far gone over Mitch that she wanted everyone to experience the wonders of coupledom. Or if it did, she forced herself to admit, it was only because good sex was something her best friend deserved.

"Great," she told Sierra. "You're so much better at those details than I am and this security guy is hot. You'll have fun."

She figured Sierra was due for a hot, wild fling and Reece Carter was the perfect man to show her friend a sexy time. Belle couldn't wait to watch the sparks fly.

Sparks, hell. It was like watching an inferno. Belle gaped as Sierra and Reece did everything but get naked and duke it out on the boardroom table.

"The resort has enough staff to handle the opening," Reece said in his long, slow drawl. "We don't need to bring in outside help and deal with more of those damned confidentiality agreements and clearances. Besides, how many people does it really take to serve a plate of mini hot dogs and tacos?"

"Don't worry about those mini hot dogs, cowboy," Sierra said with a wicked smile. "Nobody's going to hold yours against you. Besides, we figure the guests will have a little more refined taste. That means gourmet food, circulated while it's hot and fresh. And then there's the resort's theme—"

"Waste of time and money," he muttered, scrawling something over his notes. "People don't need silly games to have a good time."

Belle started to defend the themes and Mitch shifted his chair, leaning forward at the same time to comment. But before either could utter a word, Sierra gave a deep, patently fake sigh and shook her head.

With a pitying look, she tossed her long, dark hair over her shoulder and made a tut-tutting noise. "Are you afraid of games in sex, cowboy? Or is it the idea of other people coloring outside the lines that bothers you?"

"I'm all for a good time," he said with a look that made it clear to everyone in the room just how good a time he'd like to show Sierra. "It's when the good time veers out of easy and into complicated that I see it as a problem. Nobody should have to work for fun. Games just mess it all up."

Belle had the feeling she was missing half the conversation. The best half, if Sierra's breathless little laugh was anything to go by.

"As long as nobody's trying to slap handcuffs or nipple clips on you, what do you care?" Sierra asked. Then she gave him a taunting look. "Or are you afraid to play?"

"Sweetheart, I wrote the book on how to play. And," he said slowly, leaning across the table with a wicked grin, "how to win. You want a peek at a few pages, you just let me know."

"I'm trying to cut back on my fiction," Sierra told him with a wink.

Belle glanced at Mitch. He was staring, jaw slack, at the battle of verbal foreplay.

"So," Belle said bravely, breaking in to what should have been a simple security discussion. "I can see the two of you have this in hand so I'm going to take Mitch and do a walk-through of the weekend plans."

They ignored her.

Belle offered Mitch a helpless shrug. With one last look at the warring pair, now standing and facing off on either side of the table, she grabbed Mitch's hand and pulled him from the conference room.

As the door thudded shut behind them, Mitch started to ask a question. Before he could do more than mutter "oh, my God," they noticed Diana standing at the fax machine, her eyes huge.

"Guess you heard that," Belle said with a wince.

"Is everything okay?" the assistant asked quietly. "I needed your signature on some orders, Mitch, but it was so loud in there I figured I should wait."

"Security is a touchy issue," Mitch quipped as he strode over to take the file and pen from her.

Belle laughed and sat on the edge of Diana's desk to wait. She tried to think of something to say that would calm the other woman, who was visibly agitated, but all she could come up with were dirty jokes. Trying to get control of herself, she glanced away. Her gaze dropped to the computer monitor, where bubbles bounced across the screen.

Across the bottom of the open Word files was one with a stylized header. Belle noted how pretty the gold MC lettering was as the purple bubble shifted to turquoise. MC? Mitch's logo wasn't that girly, was it?

Before she could ask, he handed Diana back the papers and pen. "Stay out of the boardroom," he instructed his assistant as Belle joined him at the door. "If you hear furniture breaking, call the cops."

"But only furniture," Belle cautioned. "Groans, yells or screams should be ignored."

They were halfway down the hall before Mitch glanced at her in question. "Groans?"

"Oh please, they're so going to be doing it up against the wall before the day is over."

She'd taken another two steps before she realized he'd stopped cold.

"Doing it?" he asked blankly.

"*It.* The vertical vibration. The dirty deed. Riding the wild stallion. Bumping uglies." He still stared. Belle laughed and grabbed his hand to get him moving again. "Jeez, Mitch. What'd you think that was in there?"

"I thought it was hate at first sight," he muttered.

"With all that sexual innuendo? Hardly." They stopped at the front desk and Belle offered her thanks and a smile to Larry, who handed her a large picnic basket. Mitch took it from her and gestured for her to precede him out the door.

She waited until they were in the golf cart on their way to the woods to continue sharing her theory. "Heck, the sexual sparks and tension were so heavy back there I was getting turned on just being in the room."

"Are you sure that was them and not me?" he asked, glancing over as he steered the machine toward the trees. "I'd like to think you get hot and horny just being in the same room."

"You'd like to think that, hmm?" Belle laughed and patted his thigh before getting out of the now-stopped cart. "I admit, you do have a way of turning my thoughts to sexual escapades, whether you're in the room or not."

She reached for the basket, but he beat her to it. With a wink and a quick kiss, he gestured for her to step back and let him set up their lunch like the gentleman he was.

Belle settled against a tree trunk and looked out over the clearing, her entire being filled with a sense of peace and happiness she'd never felt before. She didn't know if it was the result of a week of incredible sex, her feelings for Mitch or the utter beauty of the woods. Whatever it was, she felt great.

She was curious though.

"Is your family going to have a problem with the sex angle?" she asked, watching him spread the thick red blanket over the lawn, then place the picnic basket on the corner before kicking off his shoes.

He laughed and held out his arm. Belle slipped off her sandals and settled on the blanket, where Mitch immediately grabbed her and rolled so she lay flat on top of him. He bunched the blanket up as a pillow and settled his hands on her waist with a sigh of contented pleasure.

"Believe me, my family has no issues with sex. From my youngest cousin to my gram, they're all pretty open-minded. Remember that list of sex-theme ideas I gave you? Those were straight from my family. Including this picnic, which was decidedly the tamest."

"Yeah," she said, her attention more focused on tracing his lips with her fingernail and reveling at the sweetness of the moment than their discussion. "There were some good ideas there. I tend to think a little bigger, and Sierra a little kinkier, so those were a nice balance."

"Kinkier? We left kinkier with my cousin?"

Delighted, Belle met his gaze and grinned. She was so in love, she realized. And even though it could be the biggest mistake of her life, right at this moment, she didn't care. She wanted to jump up, scream from the treetops how incredible Mitch was. Equal parts happiness and terror made her light-headed. Okay, she realized as the ringing in her ears turned to a buzz, maybe the terror had an edge over the happiness.

There were so many reasons why this was insane. Why falling for Mitch was a horribly bad idea. Their history alone made believing they had a shot at happy-ever-after a total fairy tale.

But for right now, just this moment in time, she didn't care. She was giving happiness free rein and wringing every drop of joy from this interlude. And since joy translated so easily to sexual energy between them, she wiggled her hips a little. Mitch's body reacted instantly.

She melted at the humor in his cinnamon-sweet eyes and leaned closer. "That's okay. I've got bigger here with me," she said, referring back to his concern over his cousin being left with a kinky Sierra.

The humor left and Mitch's gaze went dark with desire. One hand slipped from Belle's waist down to cup her butt and press her tighter to him. The other combed through her hair.

"Why don't we see how much bigger we can get?" he said as he pulled her mouth to his.

Just before their lips met, Belle whispered, "And when we're done, I have a whole basket of aphrodisiacs there to prep you for the next round."

11

BELLE TRIED to stop her hands from shaking as she carefully lowered herself into Diana's office chair.

"It's not booby-trapped, you know," Sierra hissed from the door where she was standing lookout. "Just sit down and get to it."

Belle rolled her eyes at her partner in crime. Her exasperation was more calming than the deep-breathing exercise she'd been trying since they'd decided to break into Mitch's assistant's office.

Her stomach constricted again.

No, *break in* was the wrong term. It was business hours. Broad daylight. Just because Belle had carefully timed her visit to coincide with Mitch's trip to the airport and had arranged for Diana to pick up a special order that suddenly couldn't be delivered didn't mean it was wrong.

"Get on with it," Sierra snapped. "We don't have that much time."

Belle glared, but before she could say anything, her lookout did a hurry-up motion with her hand. Figuring finger gestures were next, Belle bit the bullet and, with a cringe, started peeking into file folders.

"You're positive she's the dirty dog who's screwing Mitch over?" Sierra asked as Belle carefully repositioned the laundry invoices in their file.

"No," Belle shot back. "I already told you, I'm not positive. But every bit of evidence I've found has been right here in her office. And since I refuse to believe it's Mitch himself, that leaves her. Now stop bugging me and keep watch."

Finished with the folders on the desk and not brave enough to start on drawers, Belle moved the mouse beside Diana's computer. The floating bubble screen saver cleared and her gaze flew to the bottom of the screen. Of course, there was no incriminating document open today. Clueless but determined, she randomly opened and scanned document files. While she did, she considered the question. At least Sierra had stopped arguing that it might be Mitch. After meeting him again, spending the last few days in his company, she'd been totally won over.

The same couldn't be said for her opinion of Reece, Belle had noticed. After that first explosive meeting four days ago, they'd retreated behind a wall of polite iciness. So much for sexual tension. Instead of being engulfed in heat, they'd straight up frozen each other out. When she'd tried asking Sierra about it, her friend had claimed instant irritation as the culprit and stated she was taking the high road and ignoring the idiot.

Frustration built as the seconds ticked and Belle came up empty-handed. Sierra hissed. Terror slapped Belle and her gaze flew to the door. Instead of a bust, though, Sierra made another hurry-up gesture. Belle opened her mouth to retort but Sierra put her finger to her lip for silence and raised both brows. She was having way too much fun with this covert crap.

With a curl of her lip, Belle mentally flipped her friend off, then went back to her snooping. Her silent cuss-fest halted when she found the recycling bin and stabbed the mouse button to open it.

Gobbledygook. Most of the files had recognizable names, but a few were weird combinations of numbers and symbols. All had the current date. Did that mean Diana emptied the recycle bin daily? The extent of Belle's computer knowledge ended when she hit Send on her e-mail, so she had no clue. She clenched her teeth in a silent scream of frustration. She should have let Sierra check the computer, but if one of them was going to get caught, Belle needed to take responsibility.

Helpless to do anything else, she started opening random files.

And found what she was looking for in her third gobbledy-gook.

"Holy shit," she whispered as she read.

"What?"

Belle waved Sierra to silence as she right-clicked, trying to find the print command.

"Belle," Sierra muttered.

"I'll tell you in a second," she said, brows furrowed as she tried to find the print icon. She hated this new operating system, she had no idea where anything was.

Aha. She clicked.

"No." Sierra's words had gone from a hiss to full-out panic. "Now—you have to move now."

"What?" Panic was a stifling blanket of intense black heat as it poured over Belle. Her gaze flew to the printer, spewing pages, and back to Sierra's freaked-out face.

"That damned cowboy is coming up the hall," Sierra hissed, her eyes flitting around for someplace to hide.

"Damn."

Belle stood so fast the chair flew back and hit the wall. But the move didn't make the printer spew any faster. How long was that file? She gnawed at her lip, dancing in place. Did she hit Stop and leave it in the queue, tipping Diana off? Did she grab and run? Did she...

She caught herself actually wringing her hands and gave a little scream of frustration at the printer.

"Hold him off," she ordered.

"What? You're crazy."

She glared at Sierra and pointed toward the hallway. "Now. Get his attention, drag him off to look at a horse or something. I don't give a damn what you do, but keep him out of here."

Sierra huffed and glared. But Belle watched thankfully as she turned on her heel and with a quick shake of her shoulders sashayed down the hall. As the door swung shut behind her, Belle sent up a brief prayer for the cowboy's virtue and cleared the files from the computer screen. Finally, the last page printed. She grabbed the stack of papers, folded them and then looked down. A-line skirt, camp shirt, sassy heels. No purse, no pockets, no hiding place.

She glanced at her breasts. Too small, shirt too tight not to notice the sharp angle of folded pages. Oh to be a C-cup and have hiding room.

With another glance at the door and knowing that as good as Sierra was, if he wanted in this office, Reece would be storming in any moment, she slid the pages into the waistband of her skirt right at the small of her back. Tucking her shirt over the top of them, she winced and realized she'd have to walk sideways down the hall to keep them hidden. Of all the times to forget her portfolio.

But a girl had to do what a girl had to do. So she smoothed a shaking hand over her hair, pasted her biggest fake smile on and headed for the door. Opening it just a smidge, she peeked out.

Nothing. No Sierra, no Reece. Belle frowned and tried to angle herself to peek the other way. Still nothing.

Had Sierra really dragged him off to see a horse?

Did she care? Nope, Belle just heaved a sigh of relief, and with a quick grab for an empty file folder on the cabinet, retrieved the pages from her skirt, tucked them in and opened the door.

She couldn't wait to get back to her cottage to see who was behind the dirty deeds. Belle grinned, gave a finger wave at the concierge and practically skipped through the foyer. Wouldn't Mitch love her when he realized she'd saved him, too? Hey, she'd take any way she could to get into his heart.

MITCH WATCHED the rush of bodies hurrying through Lakeside's foyer in satisfaction. Waitstaff bringing food to the registration desk for the guests. At the concierge station, uniformed men were polishing the brass of the luggage carts. Housekeeping was running a damp mop over the marble and berating the waiter for dropping a crumb. Mitch grinned. Crazy busy preparation for the party that night. He loved it.

"What do you think?" he asked Larry, who was checking items off some list in a frantic way. The only person Mitch knew who was more list-obsessed was Belle. Totally beyond his comprehension, but he was damned grateful for the results.

"Timing, check. Food, check. Housekeeping, check. Flowers… where are the flowers?" Larry asked in a panicked tone.

Mitch nudged him, then pointed to the bouquets flanking the registration desk and the three people setting other arrangements around the foyer. His manager's lips moved as he counted them. Then he nodded and made a mark on his clipboard.

Assured that things were under control, Mitch grinned and slapped Larry on the shoulder before heading over to the desk to sample the appetizers.

Before he could eat more than one brie-stuffed mushroom, Reece strode up, his face set in hard lines. He reminded Mitch of a gunfighter taking his stance to draw.

"What's wrong?" Mitch asked when his cousin came closer. "Did you have a row with one of the cousins already?"

The investors, aka their entire family, had been arriving all day for tonight's event. He'd been fielding congratulations and backslaps all afternoon and he was loving it.

"We need to talk."

Mitch's smile didn't falter. He was in too good a mood to be worried about his cousin's recent doom-and-gloom attitude.

"So talk."

"Privately."

"Look, I don't have time for a covert exchange of information. I've got a lot going on here, in case you didn't notice. The entire family flew in. I picked Grammy Lynn up at the airport a couple hours ago. She's up in her room now laughing over the sex toys. The party is in three hours, so you should think about getting yourself ready."

In other words, Mitch didn't want to deal with this shit now. His focus was the party, a small-scale practice run for the special invitation to the press and A-listers grand opening starting the next week. They were still serving an aphrodisiac-inspired menu, hiring a live band for dancing and inviting couples to participate in the sex-themed offerings. But as much as he loved them, Mitch didn't think his family would appreciate caviar and Cristal. Not when they knew the costs came out of their investment.

"Belle was in your office," Reece said in a low voice.

"So?"

"Snooping around, using the computer." Reece's tone changed. "Her and that high-maintenance friend of hers."

Mitch sighed. "Again with Sierra? You don't have to maintain her, so what's the problem."

"No woman is worth the energy it'd take to maintain that one," Reece mused. He rocked back on his heels and shoved his hands in the front pockets of his jeans while he contemplated the idea. "Although she's one helluva short, sweet ride."

"Giddyap," Mitch muttered as he took the clipboard from Larry. After glancing at the liquor-delivery invoice, he signed his name and returned it with a nod of thanks. "You said *is?*"

Pulled out of his reverie, Reece stared blankly. "Huh?"

"*Is* a wild ride. Not *would be,* not *seems like. Is.* Care to fill me in?"

His cousin stood stock-still, no expression on his usually affable face. Then he shrugged.

"That's not the point," Reece stated. "Those women had no reason to be in there. I think they were up to something."

Mitch sighed.

"Look," Reece said, stepping around so he was face-to-face with Mitch. "You don't want to believe it, that's fine. But security is my job. Let me do it my way."

"Do what your way? Giddyap?"

Reece's eyes flashed rare anger. Mitch braced himself, even though he knew the punch wasn't coming. His cousin never lost his temper.

"Mitch," called a woman's voice.

Both men glanced over to watch a stunning, heavyset woman cross the foyer in khaki capris and a white military-style shirt.

"Lena, you made it," Mitch greeted, glad to see his stepsister. They exchanged a hug before she turned to Reece and, a hand on either bicep, pulled him close for a half hug.

"Royce, how are you?" she asked. She tossed her dark hair behind her shoulder and gave him a toothy smile.

"It's Reece, and I'm doing pretty good. It's nice to see you again."

Mitch doubted that. Reece had complained more than once about Lena back when Mitch's stepdad and mom had been alive. The two families hadn't blended well, though not for lack of trying on the adults' part. But Lena hadn't ever quite fit with

Mitch's bevy of cousins. Reece in particular had developed a tendency to leave the room as soon as she entered. Probably because she'd thought he was—how'd she put it? Mitch frowned then remembered. The bomb.

He gave a silent laugh and watched her pour the charm on his cousin and realized that whatever was bugging Reece must be major, since he wasn't excusing himself to leave.

Apparently Reece's monosyllabic responses outweighed his appeal as the bomb, so, after a minute of attempting to catch up, Lena turned her attention back to Mitch.

"I'm so excited for you. I just took myself on a tour around the grounds and, wow, Mitch. This is one gorgeous property."

"Thanks."

They discussed the resort's amenities while Reece loomed like a silent nag behind them. Since she wasn't an actual investor or on the board, Mitch hadn't considered Lena when he'd told Diana to arrange for his entire family to come out. He rarely saw the other woman, but since he'd loved her father and the old man had always been there for him, he'd readily approved her addition to the guest list.

"It's so great to see you both," Lena gushed again. "But I'm going to go ahead and pretend I'm a posh guest here and do the registration thing, then relax a little bit before the fancy soiree this evening."

The men offered their goodbyes, and, as Lena turned to leave, she tossed an invitation over her shoulder. "Reece, you be sure and save me a dance. I'd love to revisit old times."

"Old times?" Mitch teased under his breath as she left.

"Whatever," he muttered back.

Mitch laughed in delight. This was going to be one helluva fun evening.

"You need to let me do my job," Reece said when they were alone again.

Mitch shrugged. "We've been through this already. Go ahead, do your job. But don't screw with my event and don't be making any unfounded accusations. You nail someone, you better be damned sure you have the right person and enough proof to make a case."

"You'll have your proof by the end of the night," Reece assured him.

The words were right, but the feeling in Mitch's stomach was all kinds of wrong.

BELLE DISCONNECTED her cell phone and was just tossing it in her evening bag when Sierra came into the cottage.

"What took you so long?" she asked. "We're due on-site in five minutes."

She spent ten seconds admiring her partner's vintage Vera Wang dress before she glanced at Sierra's face. Belle frowned.

"You're chewing on your lip," she mumbled.

"So?"

The brunette's tone was not only confrontational, it had do-not-disturb vibes all around it. Belle wanted to know what had happened that afternoon, where Sierra had hauled Reece off to, that kind of thing. But it didn't take a half-assed Sherlock Holmes like herself to put two and two together and realize wherever it was, whatever they'd done, Sierra wasn't happy about it.

"So, nothing," Belle said, backing down. No point in starting a fight. "Do you want to see what I found?"

Sierra took one eager step forward then grimaced and shook her head. "We don't have time. Give me the summary."

"The file was a detailed list of instructions on how to cause trouble for the resort. Everything from those animals in the golf course to the cancelled meat order are listed there."

"Diana typed up a list?" Sierra's tone made it clear how dumb she thought that was.

"No, they're instructions from the person she works for." Belle checked her hair in the mirror one last time and adjusted the strap of her ice-blue evening dress. Bias-cut silk, it hugged her curves in ways she hoped Mitch appreciated. "Apparently she's supposed to delete any files from the computer each day, too. Thanks for the idea to send her on that wild goose chase to pick up the replacement supplies. Otherwise she'd have emptied the recycle bin and I wouldn't have proof."

"Who's behind it?"

Belle paused, still trying to believe it herself. Then she shrugged and said with a frown, "L.N. Larry Nelson. Mitch's manager."

"No," Sierra breathed, her blue eyes wide with shock. "He seems so geeky and devoted. Are you sure?"

Belle cringed at the question. She felt so defensive even making the accusation. Like a traitorous bitch.

"I don't have proof positive," she defended. "But his name is mentioned here and these are his initials. He's also on the access list and was involved with the computer crash."

"That's pretty sketchy," Sierra pointed out with a grimace. "Remember at one point you thought it might be Mitch based on that first note?"

"I never believed it was Mitch," Belle defended angrily.

"Right, I know. But it looked like it. All I'm saying is this isn't enough to hold up in court, if you know what I mean."

"I know." Belle's defensiveness dropped away. She thought of the list. Only half the items on it had been crossed off. Some looked like they were supposed to take place after the grand opening. The ones about contacting the paparazzi would ruin the resort.

She shoved a hand through her curls and tried to think straight. They were silent for a few seconds, Belle trying to figure out how to tell Mitch what she'd found and wondering how angry he'd be with her for snooping, Sierra undoubtedly imagining how this was going to affect their contract.

"Have you told him yet?"

"Told Mitch?" Belle's stomach tensed again, fear dulling her anger. She swallowed twice before answering. "No, I haven't had a chance yet."

"But you're going to, right? As soon as you see him?" Sierra's face set in stubborn lines.

"I'll tell him later," Belle hedged. Her friend glared. "What? I'm supposed to grab him just before the party he's throwing for his entire family and tell him to turn around so I can point out the knives two of his most trusted employees shoved in his back? Warned is unarmed, as they say."

"Forewarned is forearmed," Sierra said with a roll of her eyes. "That's stupid. You're sidestepping the confrontation. Just talk to the man, Belle. You get naked and eat fruit off each other, for God's sake. You can tell him."

"I was talking to my dad just before you came in," Belle said, changing the subject. Sierra sighed, but didn't say anything. Belle ignored her blatant disapproval. She wasn't going to push for a confrontation at the party. That'd be crazy. She'd wait until tomorrow, sit down with Mitch and show him the proof. She took two deep breaths to calm her nausea and focused on distracting Sierra.

"He met with Kiki and they're good to go. He's offered her space in two of his hotels for her spa and he took your suggestion to make the same offer to some boutiques. He even has a meeting on Monday with Cartier and Tiffany's to bring in some bling."

Sierra paused in reapplying her lipstick to grin, genuine pleasure edging out the disapproval in her bright-blue eyes. "That rocks. It sounds like he figures this is the right track?"

"His people crunched some numbers and estimate the changes

will keep things afloat until the real estate market levels and he can get out from under that property."

"And…" Sierra shot her a long, narrow look. "You're nervous about something. Is he okay?"

Belle bit her own lip now and pressed her hand to her stomach to calm the flutters. "I invited him to the main event."

"Here?" Her eyes huge, Sierra gave a silent whistle. "Did you tell him whose resort you're opening? Aren't you afraid of an ugly public blowup?"

"I told him. He was…" *Ugly* would be the best word. But Belle had stood up to him. She'd almost puked, but she'd stood her ground. "I told him I'm serious about Mitch and they need to mend the fence I kicked down. He agreed to go to dinner with Mitch and me next week."

Sierra dropped her lipstick into her beaded black purse and the two women made their way out the door. "Mitch is cool with this?"

Belle wrinkled her nose. "I hope. I'll ask him over whipped cream."

The two women walked through the garden, lit with fairy lights, past the fountain with its cushioned benches and into the ballroom.

Staff was putting last-minute touches on the flowers and lighting candles at the small tables around the room. The bar staff was setting up the champagne fountain while two bartenders organized their stations on either side of the room.

"You need to tell him," Sierra said as they stood in the entrance.

"You need to back off," Belle shot back. "If we're going to play show and tell, maybe you could fill me in on the cowboy?"

Silence.

Then her friend shrugged and shook out the skirt of her dress.

"It looks good, everything is on schedule," Sierra said with a glance at her watch. "An hour till show time?"

"Yep," Belle agreed. "You're in charge of keeping an eye on Larry."

Sierra wrinkled her nose, but nodded. "Let's rock this party."

And later tonight, after a vigorous bout of hot, sweaty sex, Belle would tell Mitch his assistant was in cahoots with his manager to destroy his resort.

12

"LADIES AND gentlemen, welcome to Lakeside," Belle said from the raised dais, the microphone carrying her words to the glittering corners of the ballroom. "You're all going to enjoy an incredible stay at this gorgeous luxury resort, and for you couples here, you're in for one wild time."

Mitch watched the nudges spread around the room and grinned. Belle was like a sexy fairy up there on stage, wooing and entertaining his family and friends. She described the features of the resort and the quote-unquote "normal" special events they had planned for the next three days.

"And for those, shall we say, more adventurous among you," she added, her tone changing from charming to flirtatious, "we've got a few special treats."

Her emphasis on *special* had the room laughing. "As you know, Lakeside is going to be much more than a posh vacation spot for the rich and famous. Only at Lakeside can paparazzi-weary A-listers come for complete and total privacy. For relaxation. For romance. And best of all, for great sex."

At her last words, the entire room broke into applause. Belle waited for the wave of chatter to die down before going on to describe some of the more exotic extras the resort would offer. She also listed a choice few the guests would be able to sample for themselves tonight.

Mitch's grandma elbowed him in the side and lifted her champagne flute. "Good job, sweetie. She's got style."

"She came up with a great plan for the success of the resort," he said, unable to take his eyes off Belle as she descended from the stage and stopped to speak to Larry, then to Sierra, who for some bizarre reason had been clinging to the manager all evening. Mitch liked Larry well enough, but wondered if he should warn him about Belle's business partner. If Reece couldn't handle the giddyup kink of that sultry brunette, there was no way Larry could.

Belle, looking serious and intense, was speaking to some guy Mitch didn't recognize. Must be one of her people, he guessed. Mitch's gaze slid over her tousled blond curls and he sighed. Damn, even in a room filled with glitz and glitter, she still sparkled.

"She's caught your eye again, that's for sure," Grammy Lynn noted.

Mitch just shrugged. Why deny the obvious? He tore his gaze from Belle to look around for Reece. His cousin was at the far end of the room talking to one of the security guys. Mitch frowned. Had something else gone wrong? He caught Reece's eye and raised a brow in question. Reece gave an infinitesimal shake of his head and nodded toward the lake, visible outside the open French doors.

Good. Preparation for the tour details. The tension left Mitch's shoulders as he returned the nod. Just then, Belle sauntered over, a gorgeous smile lighting her face.

"Phase one complete," she said, sounding happy. A tiny purse dangled from her wrist and Mitch had to wonder if she had one of her infamous lists all folded up in there. She offered his grandmother a warm smile and said hello, reminding Mitch that he was being rude.

He reintroduced the two women, feeling a little ashamed about the last time they'd met—the non-event of their wedding.

"I was just complimenting my grandson on how well you've put this all together," his grandmother told Belle after the introductions. "When he first mentioned this to the board, I was worried it'd be tacky. You know, like that penis confetti at my niece Jenny's twenty-first birthday party."

He grinned at Belle's wince when Grammy Lynn said *penis*. For such a sexually adventurous woman, Belle was oddly prim in some situations. Satisfaction and happiness settled around him like a comfy blanket as Mitch watched his grandmother and Belle fall into an enthusiastic discussion. In five minutes, they covered parties, the perfect cake and, as Belle's initial inhibitions faded, the right way to display condoms.

Before they could start exchanging sex tips, he laid a hand on Belle's forearm and gave his grandmother a warm smile.

"We need to start the tour," he told his ladies. *His ladies.* He liked the sound of that. Knowing the message it'd give, he slid his hand down Belle's arm to wrap his fingers around hers. She shot him a panicked look and subtly tried to shake his hand off, but he didn't let go.

"So it's like that, is it?" his grandmother said in satisfaction.

"No."

"Yes."

They answered at the same time, then Belle gave him one of those what-are-you-doing-are-you-crazy? looks. Before he could say anything else, she unwrapped his fingers from hers so she could put her hand out to shake Grammy's.

"I'm not… We're just…" She glared at Mitch. He just rocked back on his heels and grinned. "It was a pleasure talking with you, Lynn. I'd love to have brunch tomorrow and hear more of your ideas."

With that and one last searing glance at Mitch, she gathered the silky fabric of her skirt in her hand and swept away.

"You gonna make it to the vows this time?" Grammy asked.

Belle subtly crooked her finger at a waiter, who immediately approached her, carrying a large crystal dish on a tray. Mitch watched her hand each set of guests who'd signed up for the sex-theme tour an envelope. She spent a few minutes with each couple, chatting, putting them at ease with her jokes and natural warmth. Damn, she worked the room as easily as she'd worked his heart.

"You bet," he said, his gaze still locked on the sweet sway of Belle's hips as she moved between couples. "I'm a lot smarter this time."

HER SMILE large enough that she figured her cheeks would ache in the morning, Belle handed the second-to-last envelope to one of Mitch's cousins and his very pregnant wife.

"I've been looking forward to this weekend for months," the petite redhead told her as her husband tore into the envelope. "But when Jase told me about this little sideline, I'll admit, I went into impatience overload."

She leaned closer and dropped her voice to a whisper. "This last trimester has me so horny, Jase is going to have to go on early paternity leave to keep up with me."

"I had no idea pregnancy had such a stimulating side effect," Belle said, intrigued. Before she could decide if she wanted more details or not, Jase showed his wife the invitation. From the looks of it, they'd drawn the rose garden adventure. Pure fairy-tale fantasy, complete with a rose bower and fairy lights. Belle gave a silent sigh of relief. As horny as she seemed, Belle doubted a ride in a golf cart over a gopher-ravaged golf course at night was good foreplay for a pregnant lady.

With a giggle and a promise to chat the next day, the couple hurried out of the ballroom. Belle smiled and gave a rueful shake of her head. She felt like a madam sending her couples off for a night of decadent debauchery.

This whole evening was incredible. She loved Mitch's family. Fun, easygoing and interesting, they'd all welcomed her as if the wedding fiasco six years ago had never happened. Well, all except that one weird guy who'd tried to get her to agree to meet him for a private talk when she'd left the dais.

One last envelope to go. She had no idea what the sexual treat hidden in the heavy card stock was, but she couldn't wait to find out. She saw Sierra across the room holding court among the single guys, including Larry, and headed that way.

She'd made it halfway when she came face-to-face with her worst nightmare. Belle's vision wavered as fury hit. The woman who'd ruined her wedding. Belle wanted to scratch her eyes out.

Pleasant and distant, she told herself. This wasn't the time or place to tell Mitch's stepsister what a nasty, rotten bitch she was. Belle clenched her teeth so tightly she thought they'd crack and forced a smile on her face.

"Well, well," drawled the stocky brunette. "I'd heard you were in charge of this little sexcapade, but I thought it was the family's idea of a joke. What kind of kinky things did you have to do to con Mitch into trusting you?"

"Lena," Belle said, her voice pure ice in an attempt to smother the fiery anger. "I'm surprised to see you here. You have an odd habit of showing up at Mitch's celebrations with an eye toward ruining them."

The other woman gave her a toothy grin and looked around the room with a disdainful shrug that shifted her blue beaded evening dress in unattractive ways.

"This party is already doomed. Why would I waste energy?"

"Doomed, is it?" Unable to help herself, Belle stepped forward until she was close enough to smell Lena's oversweet perfume. "Why would you say that?"

Lena's brown eyes narrowed and she flipped her hair over her shoulder with a look of disgust. "It's a no-brainer, isn't it?

You're in charge." She arched her brow. "Things are bound to be unfinished. Did you plan to escape before or after the champagne runs dry?"

Belle hissed.

"Ladies, dessert is being served," Sierra said, her tone dulcet. The hand on Belle's waist squeezed in warning. "Lena, why don't you go on in? I'm afraid I need Belle's help for just a second."

After a ten-second stare-down, the woman shrugged and left. It was all Belle could do to keep herself from going after her.

"Well, this is a fine turnaround," Sierra said with a tense laugh as Lena flounced away. "You looking like you were going to kick her ass and me being the voice of reason."

"Scary," Belle agreed as she tried to shake off her anger.

"You can't go after her," Sierra cautioned. "You're too emotional. If you blow up, it'll make you look like a fool and ruin the event." Sierra's voice trailed off and she gave a quick glance around. Nobody was paying any attention to them, so she just shrugged and said, "You have a fit and you'll play right into her hands. You've won over Mitch's family, and that's saying a lot considering they all thought you should have been strung up for leaving him. Don't ruin that. Just avoid her."

Mitch.

Belle took a deep breath and smoothed a hand over her silk-covered hip. With a second deep breath she looked around to find him in conversation with Reece. She pressed her lips together to try to keep from growling and forced the anger aside.

"Escape, my ass," she muttered, clenching the envelope in her fist. She gave Sierra an angry shrug and instructed, "Cover the dessert reception, please."

Then she stormed across the room to get her man.

"Belle, no," Sierra warned, hurrying to keep up with her. "Do not ruin this event. You'll regret it."

Belle kept going.

"Don't let her win. Again."

Belle stopped so fast she was surprised there wasn't smoke coming off her Manolos. "She ruined my wedding."

"No." Sierra stepped around Belle so they were face-to-face and gave her a long, serious look. Her voice was low and apologetic. "She didn't. She pushed the buttons, but the problems were already there. You know that."

Belle was about to protest, but when her friend just raised a brow, she dropped her gaze to the marble floor. Sierra was right. Belle didn't want her to be, but she was. Belle had ruined her own wedding, pure and simple. Shame washed over her as she blinked to clear the tears from her eyes. She wanted to leave, to go to her cottage, curl up under a blanket with Mr. Winkles and pout. But she couldn't. This wasn't the time or place to have a girly breakdown. Mitch was counting on her, and she was counting on herself.

"Okay, you're right. She didn't do anything," Belle finally conceded.

Sierra's arched brows drew together over angry blue eyes. "Oh no, I didn't say that. She's a selfish, conniving bitch and we're going to haul her out to the woods and kick her ass when this is all over."

Belle's surprised laugh faded as she watched Lena and Diana greet each other like long-lost friends. A quick hug and the two women put their heads together, talking at the same time. She'd had no idea they even knew each other. Were she and Sierra the only ones in the room not family or close friends?

Before Belle could speculate, a hand curved over her hip and someone dropped a kiss on the side of her neck. With a gasp of surprise, she spun around. It was Mitch, of course. Who else would it be? she asked herself as she tried to calm her racing heart.

"What?" he said with a laugh. "You two look all guilty. Like you're planning to rob a bank. Or…" He glanced around the room, then noted the envelope in Belle's hand. He reached out so they held it together. "…talking sex."

"Definitely sex," Sierra agreed with a nod. She puffed out a little breath, her only sign of nerves, and gave Mitch a warm smile. "And speaking of sex, if you'll excuse me, there's a man I'm interested in."

Belle wanted to grab Sierra back and force her to stay with them until she'd got her thoughts under control. Between worrying that Diana and company had some trap planned for the evening and the shock of seeing Lena the bitch again, Belle's nerves were shot.

"Care to share?" Mitch said in a low, sexy tone as he leaned closer.

"Um, share what?"

He laughed again and moved her hand. She glanced at the envelope and grimaced. As hot as Mitch was in a tux, for the first time since she'd set eyes on him, she wasn't interested in having sex with him.

"You know, it's probably tacky for the host and the event planner to sneak off and have nookie," she said, giving him a wide-eyed look.

"It's a nookie kind of night," he pointed out. He slid an appreciative look up and down the length of her body. Belle felt as if he'd stripped her naked and licked his way down to her toes. Hot, damp excitement sparked inside her. "And there are no peaches on the dessert menu."

Unable to say no when he gave her that cute, little-boy grin, Belle giggled and released her hold on the envelope. "You're going to have to give other fruits a chance, you know."

"Nah, why mess with perfection? Besides, I have a bowl of peaches waiting in my room for later," he promised, his attention on ripping open the envelope. When he read the card inside, a huge grin split his face. "The lake? In a boat? Right on."

So in love it hurt, Belle burst into laughter, and even though she knew she should suggest they go to his office and talk, she let him whisk her out of the room.

MITCH FELT damned good. He'd impressed the hell out of his family with the resort. The party had rocked. And now he was taking his woman out to play water games. Life didn't get much better than this.

"Wow," he said as they approached the lake. The long, wooden dock was lined on either side with jars, each one containing a flickering candle. Rather than a motorboat, she'd gone the safer route and had a large rowboat tied to the end of the dock. As they got closer, Mitch could see there was a bottle of champagne chilling, glasses and what looked like some kind of dessert.

"Peaches?" he asked hopefully.

Belle grinned and shook her head. "Chocolate-covered strawberries."

Mitch watched her balance on one foot, her hand on his arm as she slipped off one shoe, then the other, before stepping onto the grass. He took the strappy sandals from her and, dangling them from one finger, clasped her hand in his and led the way to paradise.

He wasn't sure if she was tired after all her work on the party or if someone had upset her, but Belle seemed a little distant and disconnected, as though she didn't mind humoring him, but would rather be anywhere else but here.

Wanting to help her relax, he dropped her shoes in the grass and wrapped his arms around her. One kiss turned into two, deepening as Mitch lost himself in the glory of her mouth. He felt the tension leave her body as Belle relaxed and leaned into him, her tongue dancing around his in sensual delight.

Mitch's hands curved over the smooth fabric of her dress, smoothing his way down her hips and over her butt. She drove him crazy. He pulled her close to grind his hardening dick against her silky warmth.

Releasing her mouth, he trailed wet kisses over her jaw, down her throat. When he reached the curve of her neck, Mitch buried his face there and breathed in the delicious scent of her.

He slipped the tiny straps of her dress off her shoulders, his mouth giving the delicious peak of her breast a nibble. Before he could do the same to the other breast, he was blinded by a flashing light.

"Do her on the grass," a male voice yelled. Insults and degrading suggestions flew through the air.

More lights. Click and whir. Belle screamed. Mitch pulled away, pushing her behind him as he tried to see into the dark woods. Fists clenched, he ran forward to find out what was going on. Before he could take more than three steps, a golf cart flew across the lawn, grass flying behind it as it suddenly braked.

Wrapping a protective arm around a shaking Belle, Mitch watched his cousin Reece leap from the cart and grab someone at the edge of the woods.

"Oh my God," Belle breathed as they watched him do some intense martial arts move and kick an object from the guy's hand. Then with a flying leap, he sent the other person flying backward, where he smacked into a tree with a loud thud.

Two more golf carts flew by, security staff jumping out to grab the guy and haul him over to Mitch. Reece sauntered over, scooping up his dropped cowboy hat on the way and smacking the dirt off it before putting it back on his head.

Mitch almost laughed at his cousin's nonchalant attitude, then he caught sight of the creep being held by the scruff of his jacket.

"Who the hell are you?" Mitch demanded. He wanted to haul off and punch the guy in the face, but the idiot was still dazed and bleeding from his lip, thanks to Reece's roundhouse kick.

Dammit, his cousin got to have all the fun. Mitch consoled himself with the promise that he'd have one hell of a time prosecuting the guy.

"Don't worry about that," Reece said. "The question isn't so much who he is but who called him out here."

"Paparazzi?" Belle asked in a small voice, sounding shaken by the lightning-fast change from passion to violence. God, Mitch thought, if the guy had shown up ten minutes later, his shots would have been X-rated.

Obviously thinking the same thing, Belle took a deep breath and seemed to be fighting the need to cry. She gave Mitch a watery smile. "At least he didn't get any incriminating shots, right?"

Mitch frowned, but before he could reply, his cousin stepped between them.

"What if it had been someone else? This is exactly what you're promising your guests they'll be protected from, isn't it?" Reece stepped close and dangled the broken camera pieces from his index finger. "This could have been any one of our family members. While I'm sure cousin Jenny's lakeside frolics wouldn't make headlines like some movie star's, it'd be pure misery for her to see them splashed across a gossip rag."

"This is what security was supposed to prevent," Belle snapped. "All those meetings, all our discussions. Confidentiality agreements, key codes, alarms. And yet this dirtbag still managed to get in here? This entire plan hinged on the guarantee of privacy. What the hell happened?"

"Someone tipped him off," Mitch accused. Fury blurred his vision at the betrayal. He stepped forward and grabbed the guy's collar.

"Who the hell hired you?" he growled.

The guy muttered through swollen lips, "The party gal."

Shocked, Mitch almost dropped him. "Belle?"

"Don't know her name. Just had the phone call that this was some big fancy A-lister gig with a lot of money shots. Sex, partying. I was told to come on out. She put my name on the guest list, texted me to tell me where to hide."

No. Mitch reeled at the words. Reece grabbed the guy from his slack hands and wheeled him around.

"Bullshit," Reece claimed. "You're saying Belle Forsham hired you? Tipped you off? What?"

"Don't know her name. Just that she's the gal in charge of the party" the guy snapped defiantly. "We talked by phone, e-mail. I never saw her before."

"He's lying," Belle called out. Horror filled her voice, tears glistening on her cheeks.

"Why would he lie?" Reece wondered aloud.

"I don't know," Belle cried. "Why don't you ask him?"

"I don't think we need to ask anyone except you, Ms. Forsham." Reece's words were quiet, bland. But his accusation hung in the air.

"Me? Why the hell would I do this?" Anger snapped in her eyes.

"You could be working to discredit the resort," Reece said in his slow drawl. "Your dad's hurting, needs money. You might have thought putting Mitch out of business would keep away some competition."

Belle shook her head. "You might want to go back to security school, cowboy. So far you're batting zip. First you let that camera-toting idiot in here, despite all the supposed precautions. Then you accuse me of something impossibly far-fetched. This resort is no competition to my father."

"Sure it isn't," muttered someone behind Mitch. "She

screwed him over once, she's obviously doing it again. This time she's getting pictures, too."

Belle gasped, her eyes filling. But instead of letting the tears fall, she lifted her chin and faced the crowd that had formed around them.

Shaking off the feeling of fury and betrayal, Mitch followed her gaze and saw her glare at Lena. Mitch frowned. He glanced at his stepsister, whose grin looked evil in the glinting moonlight. Belle opened her mouth as if to say something, then she shrugged and turned to leave.

"Where do you think you're going?" he asked.

"Away." He could hear it in her voice, the need to escape. To get away from the whispers and judgmental eyes.

"This isn't settled, Belle."

She gave him a dirty look. "What's to settle? Did you want to wait for one of your kinfolk to go grab a rope from the golf cart so you can hang me?"

"You're overreacting," Reece said quietly. "This isn't a lynch mob."

"Could have fooled me," she shot back.

Mitch realized that his family and friends were all looking pissed enough to justify her accusation.

He took Belle's arm and pulled her away from the crowd, up toward the ninth hole where they could talk without all the commentary.

"Belle, tell me what's going on," he asked when they reached some semblance of privacy. "The truth this time."

"I told you the truth. You're choosing to believe that guy over me." She gestured to the photographer Reece was tossing into the golf cart. "You're so busy obsessing over your image, over your need to prove yourself perfect that you won't even consider that you're wrong."

Mitch bristled at the accusation. To hell with that. He wasn't trying to prove a damned thing. He was just protecting his investment. He recalled her reluctance to come down to the lake earlier. Had she been having second thoughts? Or had it been because her plans were derailed when they'd gotten the lakeside envelope? God, he was the world's biggest idiot.

"Is that what you think?" he asked. "That I'm obsessed with image? Well if I am, you sure blew it all to hell with this little stunt. Again," he accused. Mitch spared a glance at his family, here to watch another of his dreams smashed to hell.

Belle gave a bitter laugh and shook his hand off her arm. She took a step backward as if she couldn't stand to be close to him. Mitch wanted to grab her and yell that he wasn't the guilty party here. He'd be damned if she'd make him feel bad that she'd been busted at her own game.

"You go ahead and believe that," she said. "It's easier for you to blame me than figure out the truth." She gave a wave of her hand toward the crowd and swallowed, her jaw working and eyes blinking rapidly. "I thought I could trust you this time. I thought you were different. My God, I was such an idiot."

Spying her shoes on the grass, she leaned over and snatched them up, then tilted her chin at him. "There is no advantage to me ruining my own business reputation. There is no point in busting my ass to make this event, this entire themed resort, come together perfectly if I was going to just screw it all up in the end."

She stepped closer and punched her index finger into his chest. "Someone is fucking you over and it's not me. Why don't you grow up and quit flexing your dick and go find out who it really is?"

With that, she stomped up the hill toward the golf carts parked haphazardly all over the ninth hole.

Her words echoed in his head. His family's voices faded into background noise.

Brow furrowed, Mitch watched Belle slam the golf cart into gear and drive away. Part of him wanted to yell to her to wait. He wanted to run after her and fix things. But his family was all standing around. And they'd just seen Belle make him look like a loser idiot in front of them. Again. He let her go. Confusion and pain clawed at his gut. Belle had used him, used this event, all for publicity?

Once again, he'd lost the princess. And once again, he'd lost face in front of his entire family as she screwed him over.

Mitch tried to console himself that at least this time he'd had a whole bunch of hot, wild, kinky sex. But all that did was remind him of what he'd lost. Of what he'd never actually had.

Wasn't he a pitiful chump?

13

BELLE STUMBLED into her cottage, tears streaming down her face. She stopped cold when she was hit with a faceful of bright light and heavy metal music.

Damn. She'd forgotten Sierra would be there.

"You're back early," her friend yelled over Black Sabbath. "What happened? All that rocking the boat make you seasick?" She was one to tease, given that she was twisted around like a pretzel with her ass in the air.

"Paparazzi," Belle said shortly, not able to find her usual razz about Sierra being the only person in the world who practiced yoga to Ozzie. She scrubbed the tears off her face with the back of her hand.

Sierra fell sideways with a crash. "What?" she asked, rubbing her shoulder. She finally took a look at Belle's face and jumped up to slap the stereo off. "Oh, my God, what's wrong?"

"Paparazzi," Belle repeated, throwing her shoes across the room so hard they knocked a teacup off the table, sending it to a shattered death on the tile floor.

She glared at the mess, and not even caring that she was barefoot, stormed over to the couch. She dropped to the cushions, drew her knees up for comfort and waited.

She didn't have to wait long. Two seconds later and Sierra was right there, wrapping her arms around Belle. Belle took a shuddering breath, but before she could spill the details of the horrible encounter and Mitch's betrayal, someone pounded on her door.

"Belle, I want to talk to you."

Her body went numb at the sound of Mitch's voice. Sierra stood to answer the door but Belle grabbed her damp T-shirt and gave a shake of her head.

He pounded again.

"Now."

Her chin flew up and anger, drowned out earlier by her tears, rekindled.

Sierra took one look at her face and yelled back, "Get lost."

Silence.

Sierra gave a satisfied smirk, but Belle knew better. Ten seconds later the pounding started again. Confused, angry and hurt beyond belief, she still knew she had to face him. But not yet.

She went to the door and, after flicking off the overhead light to help hide her ravaged face, she set the security chain, then opened the door.

Mitch's fury was clear through the small opening. It was all she could do not to start crying again at the sight. Determined to cling to some form of dignity, she took a deep breath. Before he could say a word, she held up her hand. "I'll discuss the situation with you in a half hour," she told him. "I'm not dressed for this and I'm not prepared to talk to you yet."

"You're not negotiating a contract, Belle." The disdain in his voice was so sharp, she wondered if she'd be left with a scar.

She inclined her head toward him and gave a one-shouldered shrug. "No, but this is business, isn't it? If you want to talk tonight, I'll come up to your office in a half hour. Otherwise it will wait until tomorrow."

She watched his jaw work and knew he was struggling for control. His anger, so clear in the set of his shoulders and furious glare, shouldn't turn her on. But, sicko that she was, it did, just a little. Her heart whimpered at the uselessness of the realization.

"Fifteen minutes," he finally said.

"Thirty," she repeated.

He snarled and lifted his fist as if he were going to pound it through the door. But he didn't. Instead he growled, "Fine."

Belle didn't wait for him to leave. She shut the door and, knowing it would only add to his fury, flipped the locks with a loud snick.

She turned to see Sierra staring, the shock in her blue eyes echoed in her slack jaw.

"What?"

"Just wondering where you're hiding those brass balls. Your dress is awfully revealing."

Belle gave a watery laugh and collapsed against the door. Her fury-induced adrenaline washed away, leaving her limp and miserable.

"We're just getting hot and heavy on the dock and out jumps a blood-sucking photographer snapping pictures, calling dirty suggestions." Belle shivered at the memory. "It was horrible. Then, before I could take that in, up squeals Reece like the cavalry, grabbing the guy and beating the hell out of him."

Sierra's fascinated curiosity turned to derision and she shook her head. "Leave it to him to get all macho," she muttered. Then she glanced at the clock, grabbed Belle's arm and tugged her toward the bedroom.

"Talk while you're changing. We have twenty-five minutes."

"The paparazzi said it was me, the party girl," Belle whispered. "He said I'd hired him. Arranged all this."

Sierra sucked in a sharp breath. Then she let out a low, vicious growl that would do a momma cat proud. "Someone's setting you up."

Belle shrugged and started changing.

"And there was that smug-faced bitch, Lena Carter, just gloating over the whole ugly mess," Belle summed up as she finished recounting the horrible scene while reapplying foundation to cover her blotchy, tearstained skin.

"Lena Norris," Sierra corrected, her voice muffled by the sweater she was pulling over her head.

Belle lowered the makeup brush and stared at her friend's reflection. "What?"

Sierra settled the black cashmere sweater in place and pulled her hair free, then met Belle's eyes in the mirror. "Norris. She's not one of the Carter clan. I found out tonight when I read the guest list over Larry's shoulder."

She and Belle exchanged a long, comprehending stare.

"L.N.," they said together.

Stunned, Belle dropped her makeup brush on the counter and sank onto the wide edge of the spa tub. That nasty vindictive woman was behind all this?

"What a bitch." Sierra gave a little growl and shook her head. "I can't believe it. I thought she had it in for you, but it's actually her own brother she's been trying to screw over all these years."

Belle tugged on her short suede boots and considered the idea. God, she'd been a gullible idiot.

Six years ago she'd scurried away at the first sign of conflict instead of talking to Mitch or her father. As always, she'd been so sure she'd be rejected if she confronted the issue. Shame washed over her. Apparently she was a wimp as well as an idiot.

But not this time. She sucked in a deep, fortifying breath and squared her shoulders, trying to find courage. Hell, Mitch had already rejected her, so she had nothing left to lose. And one hell of a lot to gain by outing that obnoxious bitch, Lena.

"She's planning on ruining more than a wedding this time," Belle pointed out, anger making her hand shake as she tried to apply lip gloss. "Mitch's business is her goal this round."

Belle tried to focus on that, but she couldn't quite get over the indignity of being so easily manipulated. She wanted to beat the hell out of Lena. And not some girly slap-fight, either. She wanted to gut-punch the other woman.

"What a dirty sneak," she muttered.

"Exactly."

Belle let the fury of it all propel her out of the room. "C'mon," she called back to Sierra, who was hopping from foot to foot trying to put on her platforms. "I have to tell Mitch. As soon as he hears this, we can sit back and watch him deal with that duplicitous bitch."

Belle had never been one to contemplate revenge before, but suddenly the idea filled her with a grim satisfaction. She couldn't wait to see Lena pay for everything she'd done. To Mitch, to the resort. To Belle.

Five minutes early, Belle stormed into Mitch's office, Sierra hot on her heels. It was like walking into an ice-filled court-room. Belle shivered, her momentum stalled at the implacable coldness on Mitch's face. Like a judge, he sat behind his desk, the position of power loud and clear.

There was a movement by the window and Belle's gaze shot to the prosecutor du jour. The fiery anger in Reece's glare was the only heat in the room. Nerves snapped and snarled in her stomach, the little voice in the back of her head warning her to give it up and run. Get the hell out of there before they verbally shredded her.

She'd actually taken a step back before she realized what she was doing. No. Belle squared her shoulders and forced herself to stand still. They wanted to judge, that was fine. She was here for justice.

Knowing the only way she'd get through this was to block Reece's intimidating presence out of her mind, Belle focused on Mitch. It took her two deep belly breaths to get the nerve, then she stomped over to his desk and slapped her hands on the surface.

It was a good indication of how angry he was when he kept his gaze locked on hers instead of letting it drop to the view highlighted by her low-cut blouse. *Okay, fine.* She told herself she wasn't worried that her one real weapon had already proved ineffective.

"Look, I know who's behind all your problems," she said quietly. His blank stare didn't change, but Belle pressed on. "Just hear me out and we'll get to the truth of this whole mess."

"Truth?" Mitch snapped. She winced as his frigid tone sliced at her. "Or excuses?"

Tears threatened again, but Belle blinked them away. She felt Sierra come up behind her. Her friend didn't say anything, just stood a little behind and off to the side, giving silent support. It was all Belle needed. With a deep breath, she handed Mitch the papers she'd found in Diana's office. He didn't look at them, just slid them aside and kept his eyes on hers. With a quick glance at Sierra, who nodded, she went on to describe how they'd searched through Diana's computer files.

Through it all, the men said nothing. Mitch just sat there, his hands steepled as he stared at her emotionlessly. Reece lounged against the windowsill, one cowboy boot tapping impatiently.

Finally, Reese straightened and walked toward the door. "You're accusing Diana?" he asked as he passed her.

"I found the information in her office," Belle shot back, her tone pissy and defensive. It was like they hadn't even heard what she said. She gave Reece the evil eye, to which he only raised a brow.

"We talked to her," Mitch said quietly. Belle glanced back at him. His face was still blank. Her fingers twitched nervously. She couldn't read him at all and it was starting to scare her. "Turns out you're right."

Belle opened her mouth to argue with him, then closed it. "Right?"

"She's not the mastermind, obviously. Diana's just a very good, very efficient assistant." She knew him well enough to recognize the betrayed hurt beneath his bitter words.

"Mitch, I'm sorry," Belle murmured.

Instead of accepting her sympathy, he just gave a snort of disbelief.

Belle's brows drew together.

Before she could say anything else, though, Reece opened the side door to the boardroom and gestured to a security guard on the other side.

Suddenly nervous but not sure why, Belle looked at Sierra. Her friend shot the security guard and his big gun a concerned look and rubbed a quick hand over the small of Belle's back in support.

But the only person to enter the room was unarmed. And, from the look of her, totally broken. Diana's hair, styled so carefully for the party, hung in a stringy curtain around her tear-ravaged face. She shot Belle a fearful look, then took the furthest seat away from everyone.

Reece sat opposite her, his long legs kicked out in front of him in a pose so relaxed it was a total insult to the situation. Belle wanted to beat him upside the cowboy hat with Mitch's desk blotter.

"Diana, you go ahead and repeat what you told Mitch and me earlier."

"I'd rather not," she mumbled into her lap.

"That's too bad," Mitch said shortly. "It's talk to us or talk to the cops. Take your pick."

She gave a deep, shuddering sort of sigh, then, twisting her hands together in a way that was painful to watch, started in a hesitant voice, "I told you already, I admit to helping sabotage Lakeside."

"On whose orders?" Mitch demanded.

The tension in Belle's shoulders loosened, anticipation and a weird sort of vindication surging through her. Yes, now Lena would get what was coming to her.

"Hers," Diana mumbled, the word so quiet they all had to lean forward to hear it.

Sierra and Belle exchanged confused looks.

"You mean Belle?" Reece asked in a low, empty tone.

"What?" Belle couldn't believe the question.

"Yes," Diana whispered.

The room tilted just a little and Belle felt her stomach pitch. "You're so lying. I didn't do a damned thing."

Diana just shrugged. Reece took off his cowboy hat and ran the brim through his fingers before putting it back on. Belle's gaze, filled with confusion and panic, flew to Mitch. He didn't believe this crap, did he?

He stared back at her, his eyes steady and furious.

Apparently he found the crap perfectly believable.

Her heart cracked, tiny tentacles of pain radiating through her system. She should have known. She never should have let herself feel anything for him. Tears burned the backs of her eyes as she tried to figure out why Diana would tell such lies. And more importantly, how Mitch could so easily believe them.

"Since when did you start taking orders from Belle?" Sierra snapped.

Diana gave a helpless little shrug, her gaze locked on her toes. "Since she offered me a job with her father's hotels."

Belle's gasp drowned out Sierra's hiss at the lie.

Showing the first spark since she'd come slinking into the room, Diana ignored them and threw an accusing look at Mitch before continuing. "She promised me her father runs a normal office. I'd be managing a successful hotel, not ordering disgusting sex toys."

Belle narrowed her eyes. "The sabotage was happening long before I showed up with my disgusting sex ideas."

Diana gave a tiny smirk and inclined her head. "That was the plan, wasn't it? And why I pushed your business so hard when you lured away the last event planner."

Belle stared in shock. "Oh my God, you don't really think they're going to believe this, do you? You are sitting there telling straight-up lies and you think you can get away with it?"

"Why would I lie?" Diana countered. The look in her eyes made Belle realize that this little mouse had sharp teeth and deadly claws. "I'm already being brought up on charges. I've lost my job, my reputation and, since you blew it, I'm sure I've lost all the recompense you promised me, too."

"I didn't promise you a damned thing," Belle growled, her hands fisted on her hips.

"Did you have contact with Diana before you came to Lakeside?" Reece asked.

"Of course." Before she could explain that it had been Diana who'd contacted Eventfully Yours for the job, Reece continued.

"Did you come to Lakeside for any purpose other than to secure a job contract?"

How could she answer that? If she admitted she'd come for her father, they'd only see it as more guilt. But she couldn't lie, either. Belle wet her lips.

"Did you?" Mitch asked quietly.

"I, well, yes, I had other reasons. Mitch and I had a history. I wanted to see him again."

Reece's passive demeanor cracked just a little, showing a hint of derision. "Really? The man you left at the altar? You had a sudden hankering to what? Stroll down memory lane?"

"Of course not," Belle said with a scowl. "We had unfinished business. I wanted to see Mitch," she looked at her ex-fiancé and shrugged. "I tried to see you a couple of times before, but never got past first base. We had stuff to talk about, a past to deal with."

Belle tried to find the words to apologize for running off on him, for the humiliation and devastation of leaving him at the altar. But there were too many people in the room, too much nastiness going on. Instead she just shrugged.

"So you admit it," Reece said. "You had motive, means and opportunity before you showed up here."

"Oh. My. God," Sierra snapped. "What is this, a bad Sherlock Holmes novel? Get a magnifying glass or get over yourself."

"I had an apology to make," Belle said softly. She saw Mitch's eyes widen in surprise and wanted to scream with frustration. What? Did he think her so much a bitch that she'd have no regret about what had happened?

Belle pressed her lips together. With every fiber of her being, she wanted to throw her hands in the air and say screw it. To walk—no run—out of the office and escape this nasty scene. Then her gaze fell on Mitch. Beneath the palpable fury emanating from him she saw something else. Pain.

Tears, so easily held at bay for herself, welled up for him. Regardless of how she felt about the unfounded accusations, the ugly mistrust and rotten character assessment, the bottom line was he was the one being hurt.

And she was the one being used to hurt him. She needed to focus on that, to let it excuse his actions. But as much as she tried, she couldn't. The truth was he didn't trust her. And without trust, they were nothing but fuck buddies.

"This is the second accusation thrown at me tonight," she said quietly through the pain of her realization. "Both of them are complete and total bullshit. If you knew me at all, if the last few weeks we've spent together had meant a damned thing to you, you'd know they were bullshit."

Belle stepped away from the desk and, because she was suddenly freezing, wrapped her arms around herself and shook her head at Mitch. "But you're too busy worrying about your image. The only thing that matters to you is that people think you're Mr. Perfect, that your family holds you on some stupid pedestal."

His fist clenched on the desk, Mitch didn't say anything.

Fury driving her words, Belle continued to spew uncontrollably. "The fact that it makes no sense doesn't seem to matter to you and your vigilante cowboy here. If I wanted to screw you over, there are a dozen ways. None of them include busting my butt to create and implement a creative and unique hook to help you succeed."

Belle shoved a hand through her hair and saw it was shaking. Hell, her entire body was shaking, she was so upset. Her breath came in gasps now, her vision blurred around the edges.

"If you want to blame me, you have a good ol' time with it. But the person you should be looking at is your sister." Even through her pain, Belle winced at the raw delivery and its effect on Mitch. His face paled, his mouth dropped open. All in all, he looked as though she'd just kicked him in the 'nads.

Oh God, look what confrontation got her. A big fat lot of pain and misery. She hadn't changed their minds about a damned thing, and now she'd hurt him. Belle pressed her hand to her mouth to hold back a scream of frustration and shook her head.

"I can't do this. You go ahead and believe whatever you want. If it helps to make me the culprit here, go ahead. I'll send you my lawyer's name. We'll deal with it that way." She had to get out of the room. She could barely breathe through all the tension and pain pounding in her chest.

She felt Sierra's arm on her shoulder and leaned in, needing the support of at least one person in the room. She drew strength from her friend, then straightened and gave Mitch a long, clear look.

"You're right, though. I wasn't completely honest with you. I did show up here hoping for more than a contract from you. I came here hoping you'd talk with my father. Give him some advice and ideas." She felt like a traitor admitting her self-serving motivation, but figured the truth couldn't be anywhere near as debilitating as the crap they were making up.

"But once I got here, once I got to know you again—no," she corrected, "got to know you period, then my reasons changed. All I wanted was to see you succeed, Mitch. To see the resort succeed."

Behind her, Diana gave a watery snort. Belle spun around, not sure if she was going to scream at the bitch or beat the hell out of her. Before she could do either, though, Sierra launched herself past Belle, claws outstretched.

Diana squealed and jumped back, lifting her feet into the seat with her as she tried to curl up in a ball.

Reece grabbed Sierra around the waist and swung her away from the whimpering traitor.

Belle's nerves were jangling and raw at the violence, both in the room, and churning inside her.

Mitch just sat there watching, his face impassive.

"You don't believe her, do you?" she asked, her words barely discernible as Sierra screamed obscenities at Diana and Reece tried to calm her.

"I don't like being used," Mitch finally said as Reece and Sierra's swearing died down.

The implied accusation tore her heart in two.

"You're one to talk," Belle sobbed. Finally unable to hold back the one ugly truth that had eaten at her heart for more than six years, she said, "When have you done anything but use me?"

Saying the words aloud was like opening Pandora's box. Pain, misery and a million and one self-doubts all came flying out at her. Vicious and biting, they ripped at her. The look on Mitch's face, judgmental and angry, proved that she'd never stood a chance.

Belle tried to speak, but her throat was constricted with tears. She just shook her head and turned away.

It wasn't until Reece handed her a handkerchief on her way out the door that she realized she had tears dripping off her chin.

14

MITCH WATCHED Reece escort Belle into the foyer of the hotel, his heart stuttering a little at how gorgeous she was in the morning light. Apparently she took the phrase *dress to kill* seriously. A short, fitted skirt hugged hips his fingers itched to hold and her blouse wrapped around her torso enticingly, highlighting her cleavage. Power heels in a kick-your-ass red completed the look.

Her face was set, like a beautiful ice carving. Her eyes, though, sparkled with fiery anger. God, he loved her. His gut hurt at the idea of how much pain he'd caused her last night. As soon as she'd left, he'd told Reece it was a set-up. He was sure of it. Despite the mountain of proof Diana had offered—e-mails, faxes, Belle's signature on everything, he knew she hadn't done it.

Starting with the papers Belle had left him, they'd spent the entire night digging for the answer. An answer that had hurt like crazy but one that Mitch knew was true.

Now all he had to find out was why. And that, he figured, Belle had a right to know, too.

As they reached him, he murmured his thanks to Reece, who nodded and tilted his head to indicate that he'd be waiting in the restaurant.

"How fun. We've gone from unsubstantiated accusations to goon patrol?" Belle commented, giving him a dirty look.

"Am I so worthless that you can't just come talk to me directly? You need to send your big security chief to fetch my criminal butt?"

Mitch opened his mouth to explain, but one of his aunts walked past just then and yelled an enthusiastic hello. He grimaced and shut his mouth again. He'd almost blown it. This was too important to screw up with a lame explanation. He had to show her. To show her and his entire family that Belle was innocent.

Belle frowned in confusion when he didn't say anything. Then she glanced at his departing aunt and got one of those you-are-such-a-pig looks on her face. "Oooh, I get it. I have cooties. You need to distance yourself from me so you don't tilt any further off that precarious pedestal you're perched on."

Even though he knew he was being a jerk and that she had every right to be angry, Mitch couldn't stop from giving her a narrow-eyed look and asking, "Alliteration so early in the day?"

Anger spat from her sea-green eyes and her mouth thinned. She looked like she was going to slug him. Mitch realized he was a sick puppy when the idea turned him on. God, he had it bad when any sign of passion from her, even non-sexual, got him all hot and horny.

"Let's walk," he suggested.

"Let's not," she returned. "You were too rude to talk to me privately before I'm escorted off the premises, so you can tell me what you want right here."

Mitch grinned and took her arm to pull her to his side. Yeah, she was one helluva turn-on. "C'mon, I'll show you."

Her fury was clear in the snap of her heels against the floor and the stiff set of her shoulders. Of course, the sharp elbow in his gut was a good indicator, too.

But she didn't pull away as he escorted her into the packed restaurant. She hesitated in the entrance, her step hitching just a little. Realizing she must think he was furthering that public-lynching thing she'd accused him of last night, Mitch shifted his hold, releasing her arm to wrap his hand around her waist.

Her accusation about him using her echoed in his head. Had been echoing through the long night. She was right and he hated himself for that. He'd hoped that publicly vindicating her would start to make up for his previous dicklessness, but once again, he'd miscalculated.

"It'll be fine," he whispered. He knew Reece wanted the element of surprise on their side. That for the trap to work hinged on Belle's unscripted reactions. But he couldn't stand seeing her suffer. If it meant only that he, Reece and the culprit knew the real truth, that was fine. He realized he didn't want the public vindication at the cost of Belle's feelings.

"Look, let's go to my office," he said softly, watching the nerves play over her features at the sight of his entire clan gathered in the dining room. The need to protect her over-whelmed him. Whispers carried around the room, fingers pointed and angry looks flew at Belle. Mitch shot a blanket glare at everyone.

He'd been a total idiot to give in to Reece's plan. All he'd thought of was to publicly prove Belle's innocence. To push Lena to admit in front of everyone here that she was behind the problems. Not to vindicate himself, but so nobody, ever, could doubt Belle again. He hadn't thought the scheme through enough to realize what she'd have to endure in the process, though.

"Let's go," he repeated. "We'll talk there."

Some of the tension left her body as she leaned into him just a bit. She started to nod. Then something, or someone, caught her eye and she went steel-straight again and gave a little growl under her breath.

"That *bitch* is eating my afterglow special?" she asked.

Mitch followed her gaze and pulled a face. He glanced at

Reece, seated across the room at the table next to the afterglow special, and grimaced.

Guess the show was still on. Belle pulled away with a hiss and stalked across the dining room. Yep, show on, whether he wanted it to be or not. He shoved his hands into his pockets and, body tensing for battle, followed her across the room.

Belle, apparently the consummate hostess even when blinded by spitting fury, sidestepped his family's snide comments and rude questions graciously. But she didn't slow down.

Thankfully his legs were longer, so, by the time she reached Lena's table, Mitch had caught up. Mitch joined her as she sat, uninvited, at the damask-covered table.

"Lena," he greeted quietly. He watched his stepsister's eyes, knowing they gave the only clue to what was really going on behind that wide forehead of hers. They showed curiosity. He had to admire her. She was so damned sure she'd won, she didn't feel a speck of fear.

"I realize it's a public restaurant, so to speak," Lena said in a haughty tone, "but I think I have the right to enjoy my breakfast without being interrupted by a traitorous sex-peddler."

Mitch glanced out the dining-room window at the gorgeous view of his beloved woods. The woods that had made him buy this property. The ones that made him feel like he'd finally made it. The woods where he'd been made to look like a loser idiot. And not, he knew, turning his gaze to Belle, by the woman he loved.

No, he had family to thank for that.

"I'll give you sex—" Belle started to rage, leaning across the table.

"Really, Lena?" he interrupted, laying a hand on Belle's knee. She shot him a furious look. Her anger turned to confusion when his eyes asked her to trust him. He was asking for the moon, he knew. That, the sun and a few planets, given that all he'd ever done was betray her.

But damned if she didn't give it anyway. With a tiny furrow of her brow, she gave an infinitesimal nod and released her breath.

"I'm surprised you can sit there eating like you haven't a care in the world," he continued, gesturing to her almost-empty plate as well as the two side dishes she'd apparently enjoyed. "Are you so sure of yourself that you aren't the least bit worried?"

Lena scooped up a bite of strawberry mousse and gestured with her spoon. "I haven't done anything wrong. Although I've been hearing whispers from your staff, one of your cute security guys to be precise, that the same can't be said for everyone at this table."

Belle looked positively feral and Mitch decided he didn't want to play the game. Unable to keep the hurt and anger from his voice, he leaned across the table and asked quietly, "Why'd you do it, Lena? Why'd you try and sabotage my resort?"

At Belle's loud gasp, the few people that weren't already watching the tableau looked their way. Her hand covered his where it lay on her knee and squeezed. Satisfaction and a spark of hope that she might forgive him sprang to life in Mitch's heart.

"What'd she do, screw you stupid?" Lena shot back.

Belle surged out of her chair so fast, it toppled over. But she wasn't as fast as Mitch or Reece.

Mitch was around the table before Belle's chair hit the floor, grabbing his stepsister by the arm and pulling her to her feet. Reece put his hand on Belle's arm, probably worried she'd resort to the same type of violence Sierra had tried the night before.

"As always, she's a public embarrassment to you, isn't she, Mitch?" Lena mocked.

"Kiss my ass," Belle suggested sweetly. But Mitch could see the pain the comment had caused in Belle's eyes.

"Oh, please," Lena snapped. "I don't know what kind of

game she's playing, but this is ridiculous. She's making a fool of you with your entire family as witnesses. Again. Keep this up and nobody's going to have to wonder if they should doubt your judgment or not. They'll know you've let them all down."

He had to hand it to her, she definitely knew where to twist the knife. Mitch saw a movement out of the corner of his eye and winced when he recognized the straw purse. Grammy Lynn had joined them. Good. He didn't want one single person missing the proof that Belle was innocent.

"You know, the funny thing about computer messages is that even though you can fake an e-mail address, you can't fake an IP address," Mitch said quietly. "And that paparazzi you hired? He's the kind of guy who ignores orders to delete phone records. You—or Diana—covered your asses when you made the calls from the resort. But those text messages you sent him last night? They traced right back to your cell phone, Lena. It was a clever plan. But not clever enough."

His stepsister hissed and wrenched her arm away. With a glare of hatred, she said, "You're just Mr. Golden Boy, aren't you? You think you're so perfect. Everything just falls into your lap. You deserve all these problems. These and more."

"You're such a nasty bitch," Belle accused in a shocked whisper.

"And you're an interfering one. I was this close," she spat, holding her fingers in front of Belle's face, "to winning. You just lucked out, that's all."

Mitch gave Reece a look, and in an instant his cousin had switched places with him. Now Reece had Lena cornered, leaving Mitch free to put his arm around Belle's shoulder.

"No. Even without proof, I knew Belle wasn't behind this."

"How?" Belle asked quietly beside him.

He looked down into her face, her beautiful green eyes glistening with tears and happiness. Mitch's heart shifted, all the worries and fear dropping away as he leaned down to brush a soft kiss over her full lips.

"Because I trust you."

"I WANTED to smack you silly when I first saw you this morning," Belle murmured to Mitch an hour later. After the big show and resulting fallout, she and Sierra had watched gleefully from the sidelines as Lena was hauled off the property by the cops.

Now, an hour later, she and Mitch had escaped to the serenity of the woods for a "picnic" and a talk. She'd rather picnic than talk, but he'd told her to keep her clothes on until he'd said his piece.

Then he'd proceeded to pull her down on the blanket and kiss her silly instead of talking.

"I could tell you were eyeing me like a punching bag," he acknowledged against her hair. His chest shook as he laughed silently. "Don't actually hit me when I tell you this, but it was a total turn-on seeing you that pissed. I wanted to strip you naked and do you on the registration desk."

She pulled back to look at his face and laugh, then she shook her head. "Crazy. You're absolutely crazy."

"I can't help it. It drives me nuts when you get all confrontational."

Belle ducked her head back onto his chest to hide her tears. The one thing she'd always been so afraid of and Mitch loved it. A bubbling kind of joy burst inside her, sending sparks of happiness through her system. Belle wanted to laugh and cry and dance around wildly. She swallowed, not willing to cry all over him again. Apparently she was free to hit him, though.

A beautiful sense of peace washed over her. She had no idea where they were going from here, especially since her contract with the resort would be fulfilled by the end of the month. But she did know she was holding tight to Mitch, and hey, if she wanted to get in his face about any issues that came up, she'd just been green-lighted.

Still giggling at the idea of her aggression being a turn-on, she wondered if the registration area was ever completely private. Belle snuggled deeper into his arms and sighed as she watched the breeze dance through the canopy of leaves overhead.

After a few more idyllic minutes in his arms, though, Belle started squirming. All this cuddling stuff was sweet, but she wanted her picnic.

"I'm still waiting to hear your *piece*," she finally reminded him. "If you'd get on with it, we could move on with this afternoon's entertainment."

Mitch laughed and hugged her even tighter.

"Why'd she do it?" she asked quietly, afraid to ruin the tranquility of the moment but needing to know.

"Money. Apparently she was livid that her father willed his company to me. He'd left her a small fortune, but she thought she should have gotten more. She saw his leaving me anything as a betrayal. She said that's why she refused to sit on the board, to have anything to do with me. She's partnered up with a rival developer and I guess she figured when I tanked here, she'd swoop in and buy the place cheap."

"Crazy," Belle breathed. "She really thought that would work?"

Mitch's shirt rubbed softly against her cheek as he shrugged. "She had the financial backing. Real estate is plummeting and she's got the inside track. Hell, if her plan had worked instead of us…you…catching her, I'd have probably thanked Lena for bailing me out."

"That's like saying if pigs could fly then Manolos would fall from the sky," Belle scoffed. Mitch's brows drew together as he tried to decipher that, but she kept going before he could ask. "Her plan couldn't have worked. At best, it was an annoyance.

A pain in your butt and a crash test in 'what could go wrong' for the resort."

"Sure, now," he agreed. "But you read the list. Hell, you found it. She was saving the big guns for after the resort was actually open to the public."

"What's going to happen to her?" Belle asked quietly.

"We'll press charges. I don't want her jailed or anything, but Reece pointed out that we need to take legal steps just in case she tries something in the future."

She could tell he was beating himself up over it all. Determined not to let Lena leave a nasty aftertaste, Belle pushed the issue.

"You didn't do anything wrong. You're a success for a good reason, Mitch. You bust your ass, you're a brilliant strategist and, like my daddy always said, you have the touch. She couldn't have hurt the resort. Not really."

Belle bit her lip after saying that. While she thought of his hurt as having to do with business, maybe Mitch was suffering emotionally. After all, family was everything to him. "I'm sorry she hurt you, though," Belle added softly.

Mitch's eyes, so hard and irritated a second ago, melted to that soft, sexy cinnamon that she loved so much. He shook his head and grimaced. "She didn't hurt me so much as she slapped at my pride." He took a deep breath that made his chest do yummy things against Belle's breasts and shrugged. "It was bad enough her gunning for me. I mean, yes, her thinking was twisted, but there is some justification in her anger that I took her father's business and not only made it mine but brought my entire family on board and left her out in the cold."

"A cold she chose." Belle repeated what Reece had told her earlier. "You offered her a board position. She's the one who turned her nose up as if it wasn't good enough for her."

As Mitch considered her words, some of the tension left his shoulders. Then he nodded and told her, "She never really connected with my family. Grammy Lynn said it was because she was a snob and we weren't upscale enough. I just figured she felt left out."

Then his expression hardened. "But as much as I might try and understand her reasons for aiming at me, there is no excuse for her trying to incriminate you."

Belle searched herself, but there wasn't any anger left. The sight of Lena's arrogant ass being hauled off in handcuffs had satisfied her need for revenge. Not wanting to waste any more time on Lena or her twisted motives, Belle shifted just a little so her breasts brushed Mitch's chest. Smart man that he was, he slid one hand inside her blouse to cup her, his fingers doing a soft, easy swirl around her hardening nipple.

"No matter, it's done," Belle said, angling her bent leg over Mitch's thighs so she could feel his erection hardening. "She doesn't matter, she's finished. We're not, though."

"And that's what counts," Mitch said with satisfaction.

Their lips met in a kiss that scared the hell out of Belle. Not because of the intensity of it, but because of the sweetness. She could so get addicted to this kind of kissing. It felt like the promise of forever.

"By the way," Mitch said as he curled his fingers through hers and lifted her hand to his lips, "I talked to your father this morning."

Nothing said *cold shower* on an intimate moment louder than the mention of a parent. Belle automatically tugged her blouse into place and shifted just a little so she wasn't pressed against his erection.

"Daddy?" she asked with a confused frown. "Why?"

"I didn't realize until Reece did some digging that your father was in a financial mess, in part because of that property we'd planned to develop. Although he did say that you'd done a fine job of bailing him out of most of his problems."

Belle blushed at the impressed smile he gave her, but didn't say anything. She wanted to know why he'd called her father. More importantly, she wanted to know how the two most important men in her life had gotten along.

"Your dad and I are meeting next week. Apparently we already have a dinner date," he said, giving her a teasing look. "We're going to go ahead with our original plans and develop that property."

Belle had to forcibly refrain from clapping her hands and cheering. She did grin, though, and gave Mitch a tight hug. When she pulled back, she noticed a look in his cinnamon-brown eyes. Dark, intense, direct. It scared the hell out of her. She swallowed. She'd promised herself the days of avoidance were a thing of the past, so instead of distracting him with sex, she asked, "What else? You look like there's something important you want to say."

He gave a snort of laughter and nodded. Then, her hand still in his, he kissed her palm and held their entwined hands against his heart.

"Through everything that's happened, you've believed in me, Belle. I've spent most of my life trying to prove myself, wanting to impress people. But you never needed proof and were impressed despite my mistakes." He looked deep into her eyes and sighed.

"Belle, I love you. I've always loved you, even if I wasn't smart enough to know it. I wanted to marry you six years ago for a million reasons. But love was definitely one of them."

Joy spun through her system so fast she was dizzy with it. Her laughter rang through the trees as she pulled her hand free so she could hug him close. Her body pressed against his, Belle could feel the beat of his heart and gave a giddy thanks, knowing it belonged to her.

"I love you, too," she said softly, pulling back to smile into his eyes. "I love everything about you. Your ambition and drive, your integrity, your devotion to your family. I love your sense of humor and how freaking incredible you are in bed. I just love you, Mitch."

He gave her a huge grin. "Good. Then you'll say yes."

"Sure," she agreed. Then her brows drew together and she shook her head. "Yes to what?"

He carefully rolled aside and reached around to the picnic basket. Pulling a medium-size package out, he handed the festively wrapped box to her and motioned that she should open it.

Lecturing herself for wishing it was a smaller, jewelry-sized box, Belle leaned on one elbow and tugged at the bow. With an excited laugh and a questioning glance, she pulled the lid off the box.

Her jaw dropped as tears filled her eyes.

"Oh, Mitch," she breathed.

Blinking furiously, she pulled out a pair of tennis shoes.

"I want to make sure you have a choice. Six years ago, I wanted to marry you for a million reasons," he repeated. "This time, I only want to marry you for one. The only reason that matters. I love you."

Belle wiped away the tears. She'd be damned if she'd be a weepy mess for the most incredible moment of her life. The man she'd been dreaming of forever, her perfect hero, was being all gushy and she wanted to enjoy every wonderful moment of it.

"Forever?" she asked.

"Forever."

With a cheek-splitting grin, she handed him back the tennis shoes and shook her head. "Then I won't be needing these, will I?"

* * * * *

FROM PLAIN JANE HOUSEKEEPER TO WEALTHY MAN'S WIFE?

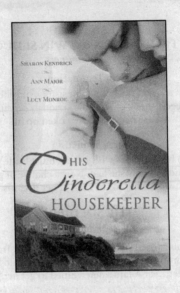

Italian Boss, Housekeeper Bride
by Sharon Kendrick

Shameless
by Ann Major

What the Rancher Wants...
by Lucy Monroe

Available 2nd July 2010

www.millsandboon.co.uk

A RUGGED RANCHER...
A TEMPTING TYCOON...
A COMMANDING COP...

These powerful Australian men are
ready to claim their brides!

Available 18th June 2010

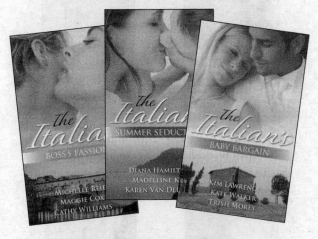

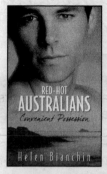

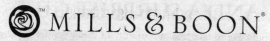

2 FREE BOOKS
AND A SURPRISE GIFT

We would like to take this opportunity to thank you for reading this Mills & Boon® book by offering you the chance to take TWO more specially selected titles from the Blaze® series absolutely FREE! We're also making this offer to introduce you to the benefits of the Mills & Boon® Book Club™—

- **FREE home delivery**
- **FREE gifts and competitions**
- **FREE monthly Newsletter**
- **Exclusive Mills & Boon Book Club offers**
- **Books available before they're in the shops**

Accepting these FREE books and gift places you under no obligation to buy, you may cancel at any time, even after receiving your free books. Simply complete your details below and return the entire page to the address below. You don't even need a stamp!

YES Please send me 2 free Blaze books and a surprise gift. I understand that unless you hear from me, I will receive 3 superb new books every month, including a 2-in-1 book priced at £4.99 and two single books priced at £3.19 each, postage and packing free. I am under no obligation to purchase any books and may cancel my subscription at any time. The free books and gift will be mine to keep in any case.

Ms/Mrs/Miss/Mr_____ Initials _____

_____

Surname _____

Address _____

_____

_____ Postcode _____

E-mail _____

Send this whole page to: Mills & Boon Book Club, Free Book Offer, FREEPOST NAT 10298, Richmond, TW9 1BR